*Good things happen slowly; only the
bad seems to come upon us quickly...
and generally without warning.*

ANCIENT PROVERB

GUN BAY

A Tale of Shipwreck on Grand Cayman

An Edward Ballantyne Novel

William H. White

Gun Bay is a work of historical fiction. Apart from actual or well-known people, English and Caymanian, some of the events, and specific locales that appear in the narrative, all character names, places, and events are the products of the author's imagination or are used fictitiously. Any resemblance to actual events or living persons is entirely coincidental.

Cover Art: *Port Royal Convoy* © Paul Garnett
Author photo: © Visual Xpressions Studio
Graphic design and production: Palazzo Graphic Design
                                        Bradley Beach, NJ
Published by: Sea Fiction Press
                        Red Bank, NJ

For
Ania, Andrew, Graham, Christopher,
James, and Madelaine

ACKNOWLEDGMENTS

Doing what we authors do has been identified as "lonely" toil as well as a "team effort." Both are correct. We do in fact work alone much of the time, but the "lonely" work is often the result of cooperation and assistance from many others. Editors, research helpers, pre-publication readers, proof-readers, layout people, and sometimes, even the general populace all play a role in bringing to light a story in a form that is both entertaining and, hopefully, a bit educational.

Margaret Leshikar-Denton Ph.D – "Peggy" – is at the forefront of those who must be acknowledged, as without her splendid Doctoral Dissertation, available in the Archives of Grand Cayman, this story would not have been possible. She graciously gave of her time and shared, through her dissertation, her experience, in not only researching this story, but also diving the lagoon, the reef, and the surrounds in a systematic, scholarly manner designed to identify, not disturb, anything left to see. Thanks, Peggy; I hope you like the results!

I would not have found Dr. Leshikar-Denton's excellent dissertation without the guidance of Cayman Archivist Trisha Bodden and her intern, Mishka Chisholm. These two ladies, well versed in the collections of the Archives, could not have been more helpful in pointing me to the documents I needed and providing copies of those which were crucial to my story. Thank you ladies!

During my research visit to Jamaica, specifically Port Royal, I was assisted by two young men, Maurice Duncan and Mark Johnson, who each gave up an entire day to drive me around, show me the sights, and wait patiently while I checked some material in the library in Kingston. Without their assistance, it would have been so much more difficult, if not impossible, to accomplish the necessary tasks in a single day.

Several folks gave of their time to read early versions, bringing different perspectives to the experience. Some were old "Cayman hands" who had a good understanding of not only the history, but also of the Island and its people; others came from different viewpoints but were willing to share their "take" on the narrative without any preconceptions of the "real" story.

Rob Holt and Danny Adkins fall into the first category and deserve thanks for their helpful comments and observations. Joe Burns, a longtime pal and former copy writer, gave the manuscript his careful scrutiny for continuity and typos. My son, John White, read the final (more or less) version checking for errors of continuity, character consistency and the like. Thanks, John.

Deirdre O'Regan, tall ship sailor and editor extraordinaire of Sea History magazine, copy edited the book, having performed the same service for the countless full-length articles I have written for that magazine, making her familiar with not only my writing style (such as it is) but with the places where I routinely butcher the language. Thanks Dee!

Gina Palazzo, graphic designer and proprietor of Palazzo Graphic Design in Bradley Beach, NJ, handled the layout, cover design, and forced the content into the format demanded by the publisher. A pre-eminent job, indeed! Thank you, Gina.

George Jepson, editor of Quarterdeck Magazine, very kindly offered not only a cover quote for the book, but a feature story in the magazine and the placement of the cover art on the cover of the magazine. A major thank you to George!

Michael Aye, author of the "Fighting Anthony" series of sea stories, very kindly offered to provide a cover quote for me as well, and read the entire manuscript in less than two days! Thank you, Mike, I truly appreciate the kind words.

Finally, a big thank you to Paul Garnett, superb artist of things maritime, who has created the original artwork for each of my covers from day one! A great image is attention-getting and, while we're not supposed to judge a book by its cover, we all do. So a strong cover is essential and Paul, as always, delivers. For the eighth time, Paul, thank you!

I hope that Kendall Smith and her sister, Hillary Ehlen, enjoy their characters. I had fun writing them and I hope you two ladies have fun reading them! I am sure the real Kendall and Hillary bear little resemblance to the characters of the same names in the story! And thank you to Bowen Smith, their father, for his generous donation to one of our favorite charities!

William H. White
Rumson, NJ

PROLOGUE
18th October 1793

The rhythm of the day had changed. Several hours earlier, dawn had arrived with its usual Caribbean brilliance, but painted with every color of the warm end of the spectrum – reds, oranges, yellows. It did not bode well. As stunning orange and red rays shot into the still-dark heavens, one could not help but be conscious of the majesty of a Higher Power who could devise such splendor. The sea birds swooped and dove into the sea, trying to satisfy their constant need for sustenance, calling to each other, fighting over a succulent treasure captured by a competitor, and skimming the dazzling waters both within the reef and without.

By mid-morning, the sky had paled to a translucent non-color, its usual brilliant blue faded – a bit of dyed cloth left too long in the sun. The birds were nowhere to be seen, their constant calls gone, a strange silence hanging in the air. And the sea itself, normally rolling gently and displaying its varying tones of blue from the shallows inside the reef to the deeps beyond, was flat and reflected the milky gray sky. As the water moved sluggishly outside the reef, little actually rolled over the coral barrier; it seemed as if it just took too much effort to actually get over the barrier and into the quiet lagoon within. There was not a trace of white froth, no curling breakers, no gentle sound of lapping water on the shore. Just a still, dull, milky pool.

The fronds on the palms were still; no soporific rustling sounds, normally a tranquilizing part of the atmosphere, confirmed to even the most casual observer that the breeze had totally died. The trades generally blew a steady northeast here, brushing the eastern end of Grand Caymanas Island with the cooling breath of a gentle lover during the day. When the wind died at sunset, mosquitos emerged in droves, harassing people and animals alike, until after dark when the breeze returned, chasing the stinging pests back to ground. The grasses echoed the silence of the palms and, like the trees, even their colors seemed muted.

A figure stood on a bluff overlooking a scant beach and the sea. Once tall, but now bent from the rigors of seven and eighty years of a hard life, he leaned on his walking stick and turned his face toward the east.

"Feel it in ma bones, I do. This one might gonna be bad." Mordecai Taylor didn't turn his head when he muttered his prophecy; no one was there to hear him. His utterance was more out of habit than of any need to communicate. His wife had passed on ten years back and his children had long since grown and were out on their own; he lived alone and often voiced his thoughts to no one but the palms and animals nearby. All the same, he knew he'd be speaking plenty as soon as the local folks noticed the harbingers of ugly weather. They would be checking with him before they sought shelter on what little high ground there was to be had above the bluff at Gun Bay, moving their few head of cattle and some sheep to what they hoped would provide a safe refuge from the approaching storm.

As he studied the sea to the east, he observed the long swells, oily and eerily calm, as they silently struggled to crest the reef a half-mile off shore. The pale sky displayed a sharp white line toward the horizon, straight as ever could be. He took in the signs he had seen before: the frigate birds and others gone to safety; the lethargy of the water, the dull sands along the lagoon's shore showing none of the usual sparkle, and the stillness of the palms and beach grass all told Mordecai that some really nasty weather was headed his way. It was as clear to him as though he read it on a sign mounted on a post on the beach. Clearer in fact, because like many of his older neighbors, Mordecai Taylor was functionally illiterate.

He shook his head, turned, and leaning on his stick, began the short, but painful, walk back uphill to his modest home nestled into Gun Bluff, the highest point in East End. His stooped frame and the occasional grunt of effort spoke eloquently of his nearly ninety years, some sixty-five of which had been spent in the hard labor of inter-island freight hauling interspersed with infrequent stints fishing for the green sea turtles which gave the island its original name, *Tortuga,* Spanish for turtle. His pale blue eyes, a contradiction to his light coffee skin, took in everything and he was as certain of impending bad weather as he was of the ache in his joints.

East End was a half-day's walk downwind from Northeast Point on Grand Caymanas Island. There was no road, but a few paths had been worn down through the scrub along the bluff.

Walking below the bluff was near impossible on account of the jagged fossilized coral – the locals call it "iron shore" – that made up the coastline for much of the island. The settlement centered along Gun Bay, a protected lagoon inside the reef that surrounds most of the island, save for an area up north where North Sound opens to the Caribbean Sea. And while the area around Gun Bluff and Gun Bay is in the lee and protected from many of the northwest storms which blow through the Caribbean, there are times when the vagaries of nature shift and bring the full fury of the tempest down on the intrepid descendants of the Scots/Irish sailors who had settled here generations before. Some had been pirates, seeking a way out of their previous lives while others were African slaves, either freed from their servitude or escaped from the Jamaican cane fields. Women were mostly Jamaican émigrés who had come with their men or on their own. They all lived their lives harvesting the land and the sea in a somewhat insular fashion with a "live-and-let-live" attitude. Their skin tones, after generations of dilution, ranged from white to dark coffee, and made little difference in their relationships with each other. They rarely went visiting afar, generally confining their overland travels to settlements and villages at Northeast Point or by boat to see friends living by Frank's Sound or Mauger Bay. A full day's trip or more might end up in Bodden Town, the site of what little government existed on the island. Mariners in well-found ships and those with important matters at hand were the only ones who made the trip to Jamaica, some fifty leagues to the southeast.

Taylor stepped up to his porch, leaning heavily on both his walking stick and the well-used railing which he kept in ship-shape repair, like the rest of his home. A cup of tea sweetened with a tot of locally distilled rum would be just the restorative he needed, and he made his way through the entry and sitting room and out the back where the kitchen shack stood. Built into the side of the bluff, the old man's house occupied the only flat land around and his cook shack seemed to teeter precariously on the slope of the hill. But it had stood for more than forty years without falling; Mister Taylor barely noticed that the ground was not level. He had banked the fire after his morning meal and now, with a bit of coaxing, fanning, and some fresh fuel, it burst into a modest flame. The flame stood straight up in the open hearth, varying its direction not a whit in the total absence of the normal breeze which habitually blew through the open shutters.

The copper kettle, one of Mordecai's most prized possessions, eventually gave off a thin puff of steam and, wrapping its handle in a bit of cloth, the old man poured it into his tin cup, which already held a generous measure of black tea leaves. The rum, a local distillation of cane molasses brought from Jamaica and, very rarely, Barbados far to the south and east, would top up the brew. He took his potion to a seat where he had spent countless hours contemplating the sea and nature, remembering his life here in Grand Caymanas and out *there*. His chair was fashioned from the pinrail of a wrecked ship, one not so fortunate as to escape the tricky current that ran around the eastern end of the island and wound up like many others on the protecting reef just to the south of Gun Bay. Some twenty years before, Mordecai and his neighbors had helped the survivors ashore and provided for their sustenance, before turning their attention to scavenging the wreck for whatever material and supplies that could be salvaged. That was the custom here: save the people first and help them in any way possible, then take what you could from the wreck. In fact, much of the wood in his house derived from the hulks of ships that wrecked on the reef at Gun Bay. Those with a keen eye could detect the original nautical use of a good many of the timbers inside the home.

"Mister Mordecai? You there, sir?" The voice floated into his distant thoughts interrupting a most pleasant reverie of turtling offshore. He was still smiling at the happy memory of youth when he turned to the voice and called out.

"Here. I am here. By the side of the house. Who is that?" His voice quavered a bit but was still strong enough to reach the front porch.

"Robert Clarke, sir. Mister Bodden Senior sent me to see you." It appeared that Robert Clarke had run all the way from Old Isaac's Town where he lived. No easy feat considering he was well into his sixties. He strode the remaining few steps to stand before the old man, still gasping a bit as he caught his breath.

"I imagine you ain't here fer your health...nor mine. You likely want to know what I t'ink about the storm yonder." Taylor pointed with his chin toward the distant horizon where the sky was now beginning to darken ominously. The well-defined white line of the horizon he had seen only a short while before was now nearly black.

"Yes sir. That's what Mister Bodden wants to know. And others as well. We – well, that's to say – them others think it might be a bad one." Clarke raised his eyebrows, which being exceptionally bushy and shot with white, produced an amusing picture. All the lines in his weathered face flattened out with the effort and, for a moment, he seemed to have lost twenty years. His dark hide quickly refilled with the ruts and crevices however, once his facial muscles relaxed.

"Aye, Robert. I t'ink 'bad' might be a bit soft. Have a look at the water there. Flat calm it is. Like the waves was gathering strength for a big push. Wind's gonna come outta the east, be right in our face, it is. You can tell Mister Bodden he'll be wantin' to close his shutters up tight as ever he can. And them folks what got they's boats down on the Bay oughtta be figgurin' on gettin' 'em secured good. Aye, I t'ink it's gonna be 'bad.'" Mordecai shifted his gaze back out to the sea and shook his head. "Aye," he muttered, almost to himself, "it gonna be bad."

He noticed a speck at the far reaches of his view and studied it. His pale eyes squinted down in the flat light reflecting from the nearby white sky and white water. Despite the total lack of wind ashore, the speck was indeed moving and soon manifested itself into a two-masted vessel, heading for Gun Bay.

"Must be a breeze out there," the old sailor offered, not realizing he spoke aloud.

"Yes sir. I imagine there must be." Clarke followed Taylor's gaze, squinting as he struggled to make his rheumy eyes focus on the tiny object.

Mordecai, momentarily caught aback at Clarke's comment, shrugged it off and continued to stare, watching as the small schooner hove closer to the cut in the reef. They grew silent; Clarke squatted down next to his old friend as together they studied the scene, each from his own perspective, for an hour and more. They passed the time with idle chat and a fresh cup of tea, made this time by Robert Clarke. Then Mordecai looked down at his visitor.

"That'll be Hoy's boat. Reckon he ain't gonna try for Mauger's.

Might have somethin' to tell us 'bout the storm when he gets ashore. You might jump down to the Bay and see what he seen out there." Mordecai spoke to his neighbor as though he were a youngster, not a man of his advanced years.

Nonetheless, Clarke acknowledged the wisdom of Mordecai's experience and made for the path down the bluff with a solemn "Aye, sir."

By the time the schooner was approaching the cut, the wind she had enjoyed up to then left her, forcing the crew to man the sweeps and row through the break in the reef, riding skillfully in on the back of a small ground swell. At the beach, several of the men leapt overboard from the bow and turned the boat to square it up with the shoreline. The sails dropped and eager hands quickly furled them to the booms as others hauled the boat farther into the shallows. Even from up on the bluff, Mordecai could hear the boat's bottom scrape the sand as the forward motion stopped. He watched Clarke make his way out to the boat and, while the words he exchanged with Cap'n Hoy were unintelligible from the top of the bluff, their import and emotion were clear to the old man watching from above. Aye, this one was 'gonna be bad.'

The old man watched as James Hoy and his crew secured their boat in the shallows and heaved her up onto the sand. Mordecai was proud of the way the younger man had taken to the ways of the sea and boats, taking care of business before climbing the bluff to pay his respects.

Hoy was young – compared to Taylor and Clarke, anyway – only in his mid-forties. His midnight-black skin glistened with sweat and his cotton shirt – he had ripped out the sleeves for ease of working his quarry – was darkened with dampness. Ropy forearms led to enormous hands, rough and calloused from endless hours working his trade.

He had spent most of his forty years on the water like many of his neighbors and, while he sailed his turtling boat out of Mauger Bay, an hour's sail to leeward, he knew all of the residents living from there to Northeast Point. Mordecai had sailed with him early on, teaching him the tricks of catching turtles as well as managing his boat when the weather piped up, and Hoy had an almost worshipful attitude toward his mentor.

"The afternoon's greetings to you, Mister Mordecai. It be

fixin' to blow quicker 'en not. Likely to be right unpleasant out there come dark." James Hoy clambered up the path, only slightly winded from the effort.

"Aye, James. My thought on it as well. Once you get that vessel snugged down good and you're welcome to weather it over right here at the house if you like." Taylor smiled at his young protégé. "How was your success? Find many turtles?"

"That we did early on. Today, nary one to be found. Reckon they all done headed away somewhere to get away from the storm. The beasts can tell when something's gonna happen." Hoy paused and looked back at his crew securing the schooner. "Guess I might's well leave the ones we got right there in the boat. Be as safe as anywhere, there on board." He shook his head in resignation, most likely not totally believing that the turtles or the boat would be completely safe if the storm blew in as they expected.

"Might be able to scare up some palm rope for ya if ya need it, lad. You're gonna want some extra hands to help haul your boat up above the tide line, I reckon. Oughta send one o' yer men to find some folks what can he'p ya." Mordecai smiled, but his tone was all business.

He struggled to his feet, drained his cup, smacked his lips, and walked stiffly to a small out-building, cut into the side of the bluff and not far from his kitchen shack. Clarke followed him while the schooner captain made his way back to his vessel.

"You take this rope down to James and tell him I said use it." Taylor handed a large coil of plaited rope woven from the fronds of the Silver Thatch Palm to his younger associate. This kind of rope was particularly strong and resistant to abrasion. It would be ideal for Hoy to secure his vessel to ride out the storm. If in fact anything would help the schooner – or the people, for that matter – ride out this storm.

By late afternoon, the skies above Grand Caymanas were ominously dark and the rain had begun to fall. It started as a desultory drizzle, only slightly hampering the people's efforts to secure what little property and animals they owned. Word had traveled that "Mister Mordecai t'inks this one be da bad one" and his neighbors had no reason to doubt him. Each family hurried about, closing the shutters on their homes, catching the smaller livestock – chickens, a few goats, some ducks and geese – and penning them into whatever shelter they could find, often consolidating their animals with those of their neighbors. Larger beasts, cows and a few horses, were driven to the top of the bluff and tied to stakes driven deep into the sun baked soil, both to keep the animal from wandering off or from being swept away should the unthinkable happen. Prized possessions that could be carried were also moved to what higher ground there was on a rather flat island whose highest point was a mere sixty feet above the sea. The still air had become oppressive; even drawing a breath became somewhat of an effort.

Steady rain now pocked the surface of the lagoon and ticked noisily as it struck the fronds of the palm trees. Wary eyes watched the water for further signs that the storm was still a distance off. The wind had yet to pick up. Maybe Mister Mordecai was wrong this time; maybe this wouldn't be so bad…just some rain and a bit of a breeze. Might all this preparation be a wasted effort? Would they be recovering their animals and possessions in the morning, opening their shutters to the morning sun just like always, no harm done? Of course, they all understood that being prepared is the better course to follow even if the storm goes elsewhere.

By nightfall, the wind began to rise. It started with a gentle rustling of the palms and grasses, a noise so ordinary that most of the citizens barely noticed. The animals seemed to sense something though, and were restless, unable to stand in one place and uttering low sounds as if to reassure their fellow beasts. Most turned their backsides to the wet breeze, lowered their heads, and swished their tails listlessly.

As the wind grew stronger, the quiet rustling of the palms gave way to a thrashing noise as the trees swayed and bowed before it. The many Silver Thatch Palms sounded like untended sails flogging mightily in the gale. The rain came harder, slanting through the trees with force and stinging the face and exposed skin. And when the wind started a low keening sound, akin to the moaning of some poor soul lost in desperation, people commented to one another that the storm would most likely be on them in the middle watch. They had little idea of just how bad it would be. Some still thought Mister Mordecai might have exaggerated a bit, but they made their preparations nonetheless. The older folks could recall the storm of 1751, which temporarily split their island in two, from Little Pedro Point west of Boddentown all the way to the North Sound. Many lost their lives in that one, and those who could remember took the signs seriously.

As the darkness fell, hastened by the heavy, low clouds scudding across the slightly lighter sky, people on the bluff could see the water beyond the lagoon roiling with white-capped rollers, crashing over the reef with a steady cadence, many of the waves continuing undiminished across the lagoon to thunder onto the shore, pushing resolutely toward the base of the bluff. When they could no longer see the effect of the tempest in their bay, those who stood on the bluff at Mordecai Taylor's property could clearly hear, over the wind and rain, the seas booming as the waves crashed ashore. Many had made their way up to Mordecai's house, ostensibly to check on and help the old man, but pressed, they might admit to looking out for their own safety at one of the few bits of higher ground on the island.

As the hours passed, the storm rose in fury and the roar of the wind overpowered all but the thundering surf, which now, according to a few hardy souls who ventured out to look, was crashing ashore into the base of the bluff and sending salt spray nearly over the top of it. Prayers offered by hopeful souls seemed to have little effect in moderating the disaster facing them all, but as the night wore on, more and more of the residents of East End abandoned any hope of sleep and joined their voices to those of the prayerful. Mister Mordecai, not a particularly religious man and one who had seen enough of what Mother Nature could do at will, sat alone in his front parlor listening to the storm, smoking a cheroot, and drinking cold tea liberally laced with his own form of sweetener. Occasionally, when the wind sucked open a blind, he rose and, braving the soaking rain pounding into his home, pulled it closed, trying to reinforce the latch as best as he could. His neighbors who had come to "help" him remained rooted to whatever spot they had picked – mostly in the back part of the house – and simply watched as the old man struggled alone to keep his house, and them, secure.

James Hoy, soaked to the skin, burst into the front room with a deluge of wind-driven rain. The flickering yellow lamplight could not disguise his ashen look as he sought his mentor.

"That's the Almighty wrestling with Satan out there. Right in the lagoon. Might as well not even be a reef. Waves gotta be masthead high right into Gun Bay. Never seen nothing like that. Schooner's just gone. Too dark to see much, but she's as gone as if she wasn't never there." His voice quavered a bit and with good cause; the waves were near breaking on the top of Gun Bluff.

A few men moved to the door, and squeezed themselves out, trying not to flood the house with the rain now being driven horizontally. They could see little in the blackness of the storm, but relied on their senses to develop a picture of what was happening outside the house. Salty spray, spume, and pelting rain assailed their faces, making it difficult to breathe without turning away. They staggered off the porch and found themselves in mid-calf deep water *almost at the top of the bluff.* Soaked and shaken, they made their way back to the door, pounding on it for assistance from within to open it against the force of the gale. They could taste the metallic tang of fear as they regained the relative safety of the house and reported to their friends and neighbors what they had seen outside. As if to punctuate their words, the house shook with every gust, and the water swirled beneath it.

CHAPTER ONE
Mid-October 1793
HMS *Europa* off the Bay of Biscay

It might have been the change in the ship's motion that awakened me. Or a lurking sense of pending trouble, perhaps from a dream. I remained with my eyes shut, listening for some telltale sound from the deck – the slap of bare feet running to carry out a change of sail, the shout of orders, the rumble of a gun carriage – that would provide me more information than whatever it might have been that woke me. Nothing.

Well, presumably it's not a Frenchy, then. There's no drum beating, no shouts of "Quarters" or call of the pipe. Mayhaps the wind has veered a bit. About time!

I had little idea of the time. I recalled that our surgeon had shared out a carafe of fine claret with me; I enjoyed several hands of whist and retired. Standing no watches as a supernumerary in His Britannic Majesty's sixty-four-gun ship *Europa,* was a delight heretofore unknown to me in my naval career and one that I savored. Once I reported as second lieutenant in His Majesty's frigate *Penelope,* it would all end and I would be standing my watches, running a division, and managing all manner of chores under the direction of the first lieutenant. On patrol as a member of Commodore Ford's Jamaica Fleet, I could expect my full ration of heat, disease, malingering sailors (and possibly officers as well), and fleet or individual actions with our perennial enemy, the French.

Likely better than my last cruise, I thought, still abed and waiting for the other shoe to drop topside. *Two years at sea, collecting the* Bounty *mutineers from their lives of promiscuous leisure with their Tahitian women, and shipwrecked on the other side of the world! At least here I'll have the opportunity to shoot something beyond water spouts! And most likely not be shipwrecked!*

Without warning, the ship heeled sharply, not quite rolling me out of my cot, but ending my reverie and bringing me fully awake and standing on the deck groping around for a candle. Definitely the wind had veered and, it seemed, increased in strength. Good! Now that I was fully awake, I dressed and took myself up the ladder from the gunroom to the spardeck. Not a proper uniform, but simply some nankeen trousers, a homespun shirt, and, because it had been cold, my great coat.

"Well, Mister Ballantyne. I trust the recent boisterousness in the weather did not disturb your slumber!" The scratchy, nasal, whine of the first lieutenant, Jeremy Winthrop, greeted my arrival.

We had sparred quietly since leaving Portsmouth two weeks prior, in early October. He seemed filled with animosity toward me, perplexing to me because until boarding the ship, we had never met. When I questioned some of the other officers about it, they merely smiled and nodded. Apparently, our first lieutenant was less than loved by his shipmates! But it appeared, and I think rightly so, that everything I did or said caused him to offer some caustic remark designed to provoke me. So far, he had failed, though it was quite tiring to restrain myself continuously from responding in kind. He was, after all, senior to me, an important consideration in the Royal Navy. I chewed my cheek and, turning to face him, once again held in check a suitable response.

"Not a bit, sir. Delighted, indeed, to see it. 'Bout time, I'd say. Been too long wallowing and slogging along in the light airs we have enjoyed since Portsmouth." *And this pig of a ship that sails like a sodding haystack needs a bloody gale to make it move!*

I was standing just off the quarterdeck, while Winthrop occupied that hallowed bit of the spardeck, separated from me by a railing and some three feet of height. Without permission, I dared not encroach on his domain, and an invitation was not likely to be forthcoming!

In the glow from the binnacle, I watched his eyes narrow as his brain whirled, struggling to find something objectionable in my comment. His pinched face, scarred by a bout of the pox during his youth, a prominent nose and chin, and eyes set too close together, along with his nasal, whiney voice, gave rise to all manner of nicknames that I had heard from his petty officers and warrants. Even some of his wardroom officers, out of his hearing of course, referred to their first lieutenant as the "Dull Hatchet," a sobriquet arising from not only his physical appearance, but from his lackluster personality and possibly, his less than rapier-like brain. Was he a good officer? I had not been aboard long enough to determine that, but I was given to believe that he had some interest in the Admiralty which, according to some, accounted for his present post; first lieutenant in a sixty-four was a plum assignment and frequently led to a command position, perhaps of a fifth- or sixth-rate frigate.

During the time Lieutenant Winthrop dwelled on his response, the topmen had reefed the foretops'l, eased off on the braces, and, under the shouted direction of the master, set up the ship's sails to take advantage of the change in the wind. As the sails were trimmed and *Europa* responded – sluggishly, I thought – we began charging through the seas, gouts of seawater splashing aboard forward. For *Europa,* we were flying. I pictured my old ship, *Pandora,* sailing alongside, romping through the growing seas like a thoroughbred and leaving the larger ship in her wake in short order. That is, had not *Pandora* been lying on the seafloor off New Holland where she had wrecked on an uncharted reef some two-and-a-half years back.

"I'd reckon that sixth rate you came from would be hard pressed to keep up *this* pace, eh, Lieutenant?" The whiny voice interrupted my thoughts, even as it echoed – at least – the *subject* of them.

"Oh, I'm sure we'd have managed somehow, Mister Winthrop. A right weatherly ship, she was. And with a well-seasoned collection of petty officers, her crew handled her remarkably well. We enjoyed breezes like this for much of our voyage across the Pacific." I said this last mainly to drive it home that he had not doubled the Horn, and that according to our messmates, he had spent the entirety of his naval career in either English or French waters. Nor had he seen much action in our on-going conflict with the French. Hence, he had had little opportunity to prove his mettle and use it as a stepping stone to greater responsibility; only interest at the Admiralty could supplant merit for performance.

"Where she remains, even as we speak. A bit of a run-in with some rocks, I understand. Off New Holland, wasn't it?"

He knew damn full and well the entire story. Having spent the first week and more of our voyage together, he had questioned me closely about it to augment what he had read in pamphlets and newspaper accounts arising from the courts-martial and subsequent hangings of three of the mutineers which followed our return to England. And the successful completion of our commission, even though Captain Edwards failed to bring home *all* the mutineers or their ship. Some had succumbed when we were wrecked and so it might be said that they got their just desserts in any case!

"Aye, sir. New Holland it was. The Endeavor Straits, actually." I tried my utmost to keep my voice level and not rise to his provocation.

The wind had strengthened, even since my arrival on deck, and with its keening in the rigging, conversation became difficult. Having had enough of the first lieutenant's supercilious sarcasm, I cupped my hand behind my ear when next he spoke and shrugged my shoulders, then stepped farther away, toward the grating over the midships gundeck. The spray flew from *Europa's* bluff bow, wetting the deck almost to the mainmast and, since I had planned on returning to my cot forthwith, remained far enough aft to avoid getting wet my own self.

I considered rousing Black, my servant who accompanied me on my new assignment, to find a bit of hot food or drink, but considering the lateness of the hour, decided against it. It appeared that all was under control on deck and no one would be needing my wisdom or counsel at this point. I made my way to the scuttle and down to the gundeck toward the gunroom, as the officers' mess was known. The purser's glim at the foot of the ladder guttered and flickered, throwing out a dim yellow light which, after the dark topside, seemed remarkably bright to my unaccustomed eyes.

"Something I might get you, sir?" The familiar voice startled me.

"Black! What are you doing up? Figured you to be lost in some erotic dream, swinging in your hammock." Good man, Black; uncanny in his ability to anticipate my every need.

We had developed a fine relationship during the *Pandora's* cruise. I had rescued the former gentleman's houseman from the ranks of my second division; somehow, I thought he might be better suited to being my personal servant than to serving our long guns. I was right. Jonas Black was loyal to a fault. I declined his offer, told him off to bed, and retired to my own where the events of the past year drifted lethargically through my mind, ultimately returning me to the arms of Morpheus.

Nearly a year previously – late October of 1792 – when the trial of the *Bounty* mutineers had ended and three of the miscreants had been hanged, I found myself with no ship, no orders, and no immediate prospect of either. So I made the obligatory leg at the Admiralty in Portsmouth, requested permission to take leave, and departed that city where it all had begun almost exactly three years before. I had no idea whether my parents had received any of the letters I had sent – most likely, they had not – and so unless they had read the newspaper accounts of the trial, they would have no idea that my immediate obligations were over. I gave Black his freedom, requiring only that he let the Admiralty know where I might find him when I returned.

I managed to secure passage on a stage coach (ironically it was a post chaise so I might be arriving at my father's farm along with my letters!) and settled in for the lengthy, bumpy, cold ride to Exeter, in Devon, from whence I would endeavor to find transport to Whatley. I recalled with a frown that the last time I had returned to the farm, I had been furloughed from the Navy following that ugly business with the American colonists and was less than happy to be ashore. That time, I spent three miserable years working alongside my siblings and parents on their small plot where they raised vegetables, and tended a handful of sheep, pigs, and some scrawny cattle, all the time pining for a ship, any ship, and writing letters of supplication to the Admiralty. I was a *naval officer,* not a farmer, slogging about in the countryside in muddy gumboots! This time, in contrast, I rejoiced in what hopefully would be a short respite from the rigors of sailing 'round the world, fighting with natives, privation, and shipwreck – all in the name of service to my King.

The coach bumped along over the cobbles heading out of Portsmouth and found the Post Road in good time, the weather being cold but moderate. We kept the side curtains on the coach mostly closed and managed to keep much of the brisk autumn air outside. With precious little mud and obstacles to contend with, the driver kept up a fair clip, jouncing and rolling the four of us within.

I studied my fellow passengers as we bounced along the ruts; two men, one of whom appeared to be a drummer of spirits. The other could have been anything to judge from his outward appearance. I made the leap to my supposition of the first's employment based on his bulbous red nose and the fact that he seemed to have a small bottle secreted within his cloak from which he took the occasional wee taste. The third passenger was a lady, a quite attractive lady. At least, she appeared attractive from what little of her I could see what with all the coat, hood, and muffler she clasped tight to her person against the cool air making its way into the coach around the side curtains and loosely fitted doors.

She sat directly across from me and our knees seemed to meet with each roll of the coach. The first few times it happened she glowered at me. Perhaps she thought I was doing it intentionally, with some devious motive. I smiled back and apologized, shifting my knees to the side. As the coach rolled around a particularly sharp curve, her legs followed and, once again, we were knee to knee. This time she looked at me and smiled, albeit ruefully, and shifted her legs, more slowly than I might have, I thought. She had a lovely smile and what I took to be blonde hair of some length, which she had tucked up under some contrivance on her head and further concealed with the hood of her cloak. Gloves covered her hands, obscuring the existence – or not – of a wedding band, and her skirt reached all the way to her feet. It would have been impossible for me to see them in any case, without leaning forward and staring down. Rather too obvious, but I was interested.

"I am Edward Ballantyne." It seemed only proper to introduce myself to the lady if we were going to be rubbing our limbs together for the entire journey to Exeter!

"How nice for you." Her voice was soft and seemed to come from deep within the recesses of her throat. She neither smiled nor frowned at me; in fact her expression changed not a whit. She simply stared at me with clear pale eyes which might have been green or possibly blue.

I retired to within myself, collecting my wits for another clever sally, which seemed reluctant to appear. I closed my eyes.

In a state of half sleep and half wakefulness I thought I heard that soft, husky voice again…"Mister Ballantyne?" No, I'm simply dreaming it. She wouldn't …"Mister Ballantyne?"

My eyes popped open and there was her face, close aboard

to my own. I blinked. Then blinked again and responded. "Yes, Miss...uh?"

"I am sorry I was rude before. I do not take kindly to strangers – especially naval officers. I am sure you meant no harm, only wishing to pass the time on the ride. I am Kendall, Kendall Smith. Are you bound to Exeter as I am?"

"I am, yes, Miss, uh, Smith." I stopped. I considered my next words, not wanting to provoke another silence. "Kendall...an unusual name as a given name. I have known it as a surname, but have not before heard it as a Christian name." I noticed her countenance darken slightly at my words and hastily added, "It has a nice ring to it. I'd say a pretty name for a pretty face." The storm clouds in her face cleared, and I breathed a silent sigh of relief.

"And why, may I ask, are you heading to Exeter? Not where I'd expect to find a naval officer. It's hardly a port city!" She smiled at her cleverness. Then, as an afterthought, added, "You're not going to the dreadful prison hulks on the Dart, are you? I know they're not terribly far from Exeter. Perfectly horrible they are, I have been given to believe." The smile had vanished and her eyes grew large in what I took to be consternation.

I paused, any number of clever answers ripping through my mind. I settled on the simple response.

"Yes and no, Miss Smith. I am indeed headed to Exeter, where I hope to find conveyance to my parents' home in Whatley. And no, I am certainly not going to the prison hulks!" I smiled my most disarming grin, fairly dripping with charm, I thought.

"There's a relief, now, isn't it! I could hardly engage in such intimate conversation with a felon!"

Intimate? So far we exchanged names and destinations. Hardly what I'd think of as *intimate*. And why on earth, were I indeed a felon en route to prison, would I be going except in chains and under guard? But I had hope now at least! Encouraged, I pressed on.

"Have you kin in Exeter, Miss Smith? Or are you, as I, simply bound there as a way stop to elsewhere?"

"I do have kin there; in fact I have three children there, presently under the care of my sister. I could not take them to London with me and it seemed better for them to remain at home. My sister finds them pleasant and has often mentioned taking care of mine is no more troublesome than minding her own three."

Hmmm. Three children in Exeter. Wonder where Mister Smith might have got himself off to? Perhaps he's dead?

"And your husband, if I may be so bold as to enquire? Is he not there – in Exeter – as well?" Seemed a harmless enough question, and one that might be construed as logical, given her previous remark.

Her eyes grew hard, and she studied me for a moment before she answered. "He is dead, Lieutenant Ballantyne. Killed some two years back fighting the Spaniards from the deck of HMS *Endymion* in the Bay of Biscay. Dreadful action it was, I was given to believe, with many casualties. He was buried at sea, as you might expect."

Well, that explains her fondness for naval officers.

"I am sorry to hear that, Missus Smith." I corrected my earlier form of address based on this new information of her status. Then, when perhaps I should have maintained my own counsel, asked, "Was he an officer?"

"He was, Lieutenant. His passing was the purpose of my visit to London and then Portsmouth. I've experienced a bit of difficulty in securing my widow's benefits, paltry as they might be. But with three children...well, you know, I'm sure." Tears began to well up in her eyes.

"I trust you were successful, then...with your, uh, errand?"

Again, she looked at me carefully, obviously debating how much she would expose by telling me more of her personal life.

"Time will tell, but I cling to the hope that the Admiralty will correct the oversight."

"Indeed." There seemed little else to say.

I leaned my head back to the hard wood of the coach's rear wall until the bouncing became unbearable. Whereupon, I simply let my head fall forward and dozed off wondering about the widow's animosity toward naval officers, when her husband had been one and died in service to his King. I came to no conclusions before I drifted off.

A long night of interrupted, fitful sleep and a change of coaches later, in early afternoon we arrived in Exeter; I recalled that there had been no change of conveyance during the last time I made this trip, albeit in the opposite direction. Nonetheless,

I was here in Exeter, and now I had to find some way of getting to the farm in Whatley.

I bid farewell to the lovely Mrs. Smith, offering my hand to help her out of the coach. She might have left her own in my grip for a moment or two longer than I thought necessary, but I enjoyed the contact and her smile of thanks. We waited together while the driver and his assistant dragged our dunnage from the roof, handing the valises and trunks down to eager hands. Mrs. Smith's trunk slipped from his grip, fell, and landed in the cobbled street quite unceremoniously, the latch springing open as it hit. Having already collected my own, I set it down and, after closing and latching hers, picked it up while she bawled out the "clumsy driver and his worthless assistant" in language that would have made a bosun envious. Both men blanched and recoiled at her invective.

Hmmm. There's a side of the lady I had not experienced in our short acquaintance. Likely a good thing we're going our separate ways – wouldn't want to have that tirade directed at me!

Not sure of where either of us was going, I hailed a young man with a cart and put her rather heavy trunk into it, instructing the young man to wait for the lady's direction. Mine I left on the side of the road while I scanned the area for a place suitable for a light meal and a pint and where I might hope to find a traveler or conveyance heading on to Whatley.

"Missus Smith," I began, as she turned away from the "worthless" driver to face me, "I have put your trunk into this young man's cart. I am sure he will be careful with it, and take it wherever you direct him.

"It has been a pleasure sharing the ride with you and, should our paths cross again, perhaps you might permit me to buy you dinner."

"That would be lovely, I'm sure, Lieutenant. My home is just a short distance from here and I would welcome a visit from you. And perhaps, I will serve *you* a meal!" She smiled, quite genuinely, I thought, and stepped to the boy waiting patiently with the cart and her trunk.

Was there more to that invitation than it appeared?

"Follow me, young man, and keep up. We haven't far to go." And she stepped off as smartly as ever could be, without even a glance back at me.

Perhaps not!

I lugged my chest into a nearby public house that was just beginning to bustle with a midday gathering of early drinkers and diners. It was not so dark within as to hide the less-than-tidy quality of the place and the grime, which graced not only the windows but the walls as well. A collection of tables – some empty, for which I was grateful – and mismatched chairs crowded into the center of the room, and a long counter stood against the far wall. The publican, a brawny chap with muscular arms revealed by the rolled-up sleeves of his striped shirt, leaned against the counter, a towel draped casually over his shoulder. A door behind him led to another room – maybe a kitchen or scullery.

He met my glance and nodded once in greeting as I made my way toward what might be a suitable table at which I might take my ease.

Wonderful odors emanated from somewhere, suggesting that there might be a cook who knew his business in spite of the somewhat seedy nature of the place. The smells made my mouth water and I realized that I was rather sharp-set after the privation of the long coach ride. I thought a taste of bitters might go down well also. I set down my chest and sat myself down as well, being careful not to rest my arms on the table top which surely would soil my clean, if none too crisp, uniform.

"What's yer pleasure, Admiral?" I turned to find a pleasant-looking young woman standing just off my larboard quarter. Endowed with an impressive top-hamper and long blonde locks, she smiled prettily at me and pursed her lips as she waited for my order.

A multitude of clever answers flitted through my tired brain, but discretion won out and none chose to make an appearance. "A pint of your best bitters, if you please, and some melted cheese and toast will answer nicely for now. And it's just lieutenant; admiral is a long way over the horizon, should it be even there!" I smiled to show my appreciation for her attention. As an afterthought, I added, "What's your name, miss?"

"Hillary, it is, sor. Hillary Ehlen. I ha'en't seen you about these parts afore. Just passin' through, are ye?" Her smile was quite fetching.

She leaned over, ostensibly to wipe some grime off the table and, in the process, gave me a glimpse of her prodigious charms, an opportunity I could scarce resist, gentleman or not!

My goodness! I had to catch my breath for a moment before I could respond. Hoping to appear sophisticated and unaffected by her display, I smiled bravely.

"No, Hillary Ehlen. It's true I have been absent for some time, but I grew up just over to Whatley and my family still farms there. I am headed that way, in fact, today. Just down from Portsmouth, I am." She obviously noticed the uniform, so that I was in from the seat of naval power in England oughtn't to be too much of a surprise.

"Aye, and how do you plan on gettin' to Whatley? A bit far to walk in that fancy suit yer sportin', I'd think. Might want to spend a night or two 'ere in Exeter whilst you locate suitable transport." Now she smiled. "Might be I could recommend a suitable place for you lay up for a bit..."

Oh my! Careful Edward. "I haven't got that far in my plan as yet. Thought I'd have a bit of dinner while I figure it out. And a pint." I raised my eyebrows questioningly at her, reminding her that she had my order, now go fetch it!

She left with a sour look and I took the opportunity to inspect my fellow diners. A mixed lot, they were, ranging from what appeared to be a drayman in a soiled plaid shirt and canvas trousers to a gentleman in proper frockcoat, shirt, and stock. Most were seated alone or leaning on the bar by themselves. A paltry number, there could not have been more than a dozen in the place. Perhaps it was just early in the dinner hour and more would be coming in as time passed. Other than the barmaid who took my order, Hillary Ehlen, there were no women in the place that I could see. Not a surprise, as most pubs attracted only a certain type of woman and even they would be unlikely to appear so early in the afternoon!

As I continued to survey the room, a bright flash drew my attention to the entryway. Silhouetted in the open door stood what appeared to be a female form, well swaddled in cloak and hood. She stood for a moment, perhaps allowing her eyes to adjust to the darkness within, then headed straight away for the exact spot where I was sitting. As she approached, she threw back the hood that had concealed her face and shook out long auburn (not blonde as I had thought) tresses. She wore an expression of concern, but smiled slightly as she drew near.

"Lieutenant Ballantyne: I must be addled from my trip. I was rude on the coach and wish to make amends. You have no conveyance to Whatley and are obviously desirous of sustenance. I suggest that you allow me to remedy both those issues at once.

"Please join me at my home where I will see to a proper meal and then arrange for you to travel on to your family's home. It is but a short walk from here, far cleaner, and I am a fair hand in the galley. It would be my distinct delight to carry you and your dunnage to your family's home in my cart following our meal." She smiled as she extended the invitation.

The "fair hand in the galley" had to have come from her association with a seafaring man, most likely her late husband. As would "dunnage." Remembering my manners, I stood quickly, while contemplating my response. And knocked over my chair in the process, which naturally drew every eye toward me and the lady to whom I now spoke.

"While this is hardly the place where I would, by choice, take a lady to dine, we are both here and I have ordered a pint and a bit of food. I would be most pleased to have you join me and allow *me* to buy *you* some dinner." I, too, offered what I hoped was an engaging smile.

Edward you are an idiot! The lady was offering you a proper meal and who knows what else. Must you always be the perfect gentleman?

The barmaid, Hillary, chose that moment to reappear with the tankard of bitters I had ordered. She set it down on the table and made no pretense of subtlety as she looked over Mrs. Smith, top to bottom.

"Hmph! Will there be another for dinner, sor? Or is the lady not plannin' to stay?" The tone of her question made it abundantly clear which answer she preferred. And her stare at Mrs. Smith seemed venomous at best.

I looked from one lady to the other, whilst they looked at each other, glaring and obviously deciding something between them. At that moment, to them, I did not exist!

"Well, Lieutenant Ballantyne? My offer stands. I am sure the meal you would enjoy at my home will be more pleasant than what you might find in this...establishment." Mrs. Smith continued to stare at Hillary. Now she served up her own venom.

What to do? Clearly, the widow Smith's offer was a good one and most assuredly a better choice from a culinary standpoint than dining here. I wasn't even sure of the name of this place, not having noticed as I entered. And there might even be other benefits such as a pleasant ride to Whatley. Or whatever.

On the other hand, the barmaid seemed anxious to please and would be put off were I to leave abruptly, having ordered both food and drink. And it was as plain as the nose on your face she didn't want Mrs. Smith to join me here, an observation I attributed to jealousy or natural predatory competition. I did want to get to my family's home soon and remaining here in the pub offered little chance of that, other potential benefits notwithstanding.

"Missus Smith: your offer is most kind and if you will allow me a moment to settle up here, I shall be delighted to accept. But in fairness to this young lady, I feel I should pay for what I have ordered." I could feel the daggers emanating from Hillary's eyes as I spoke – daggers not aimed at me, however.

"That would be splendid, sir. I shall await you without. I should likely be keeping an eye on the young chap minding my belongings." She smiled at the barmaid – a smile of victory, perhaps? Regardless, it was clearly insincere, and she turned, walking briskly to the door without a further word or look back. She pulled up her hood as she made the door.

Hillary glared at me, saying nothing, while I counted out the proper amount for my fare, handed it to her, and offered my most winning smile.

"You'll likely get a better meal, Admiral, but it's the rest you'll be missin' I suspect. Dried up old prune, she is, and not likely to be much in the sack, I'd warrant. But I'll be 'ere should you change yer mind." She strode away, dropping the coins I rendered into a pocket in her apron.

Speechless, I watched her disappear through the doorway in the back; the publican continued to lean on the counter with a quite neutral expression. Either he was unaware of the transaction that had just occurred, or he didn't care. I struggled to quantify what I had just heard, but could reach no conclusion. In any case, I thought it prudent not to linger and, with a shake of my head to clear it, shouldered my trunk and made my way to the door. My prospective hostess was waiting outside as promised with her shanghaied porter, and I added my chest to his load. At that moment, the heavens opened, pouring down a cold, hard rain, instantly soaking us, cloaks or no cloaks.

She laughed gaily, as though nothing more than a sudden summer sprinkle had hit us. "We must step right along, Edward. It's not far!" I did notice her first use of my Christian name. Perhaps her victory gave her license.

Not far indeed! Soaked we were, both of us, when she called a halt to our forced march in front of a modest home separated from the street by an archway covered in flowerless vines over the gate. In an attempt to distract myself from what I hoped was in my immediate future, I wondered what kind of flowers they might produce in the warmth of summer.

"Come along, young man. Just through here." She spoke over her shoulder as she pushed open the gate and hurried up a short path to the front door of a stone dwelling, much like its neighbors on either side.

Both the porter and I followed and while he struggled with the cart over the uneven flagstones of the path, I had no impediment and stepped upon the raised step just as Mrs. Smith pushed open the door.

With our baggage inside and the porter paid by yours truly, Mrs. Smith offered a welcoming smile as she shrugged out of her sodden cloak and draped it casually over a hat rack just inside the door. I cast a glance into the darkness past the front hall and could make out a parlor facing the street and, beyond, a door leading to who-knew-where. I hung my soaked – and dripping – cloak and hat on the hook next to my hostess's wrap, turned to her, and smiled expectantly. I had anticipated that she would call out when we came in, announcing her return to her sister, children, or someone, but it quickly became obvious that the house was empty save for us and she remained silently smiling at me.

"Let me light some lamps and a fire to warm us. My! It surely is damp in here! Let me find some dry clothes and make a quick visit to the greengrocer, and I'll fix us something to eat. If you would prefer to take off your jacket, I suspect you'll be more comfortable and it will dry more quickly.

"Would you like something to drink? I am not sure what is at hand, but there must be something!"

I followed her into the parlor, hung my jacket over the back of the ladder-back chair she indicated and offered to lay a fire in the hearth. Which she accepted, happily.

The meal, prepared from the spoils of her "quick visit to the greengrocer" was delightful, proving without a doubt that her promise of a better meal than what I might find at the pub was not mere braggadocio. The fire warmed us and, courtesy of it and a bottle of whiskey, the room seemed to become quite warm. A bottle of fine port appeared following the conclusion of the meal, adding to my slightly addled state. Idle chitchat, some gentle banter and laughter, likely augmented by the spirits we both consumed, made the time pass quickly. And the rain continued unabated, ticking on the windows in counterpoint to the crackling of the fire. Quite without warning, my hostess grew serious and turned the heretofore frothy conversation to a more thoughtful subject.

"I hope you enjoyed the meal, Edward. And that you might think it better than the fare you would have enjoyed in the Bear and Owl" (I had not even noticed the name of the place, but she had and it soon became apparent why). "I also hope the company and surrounds are more appealing. While my sister is constructed somewhat differently than I and likely offers more...*physical charms* than I, she is rather coarse and crude, and properly suited to her employment I suppose."

I was shocked. "Your *sister?*" I thought you mentioned in the coach your sister was minding your children. Surely not..."

"Oh my goodness, not *her!* I would not trust that...*wench* to mind my pet dog! I have another sister – there are three of us – but *that* one, oh my! She is an embarrassment. My sister Miriam and I barely acknowledge her, and, as you may have observed, she holds little affection for me – or Miriam, for that matter. Hillary has never married. She prefers – how shall I put it? – to keep her options open. That Miriam is married to a somewhat dreary clerk in the city offices adds little to the affection that Hillary might otherwise feel for her."

It took me a moment to absorb this new information, offered as casually by Kendall as though she had been mentioning that the weather had cleared. Hillary Ehlen spoke in a manner quite different from the refined speech that Kendall used, comported herself in a quite opposite direction, and was as unlike my hostess as anyone might imagine. My head was reeling! Was it the whiskey? To think I had very nearly…Oh my!

As it turned out, we did not set out for Whatley until the following morning. The rain had not let up – indeed, it had actually increased – precluding an hour-plus ride in an open carriage. Having been soaked through once today, neither of us was keen to go through it again. We passed the remainder of the afternoon chatting amiably. Kendall shared with me some family history and explained that Hillary seemed disinterested in improving herself and her manner as had the other two girls, much to the chagrin of their family. Perhaps, she opined, her preference for her common speech and deportment made her more appealing to the clientele she served in the pub.

Periodically Kendall would step to the window and watch the rain, shake her head and offer a "tsk tsk" under her breath.

"Clearly, you will have to spend the night here, Edward. While it is not luxurious, the spare room is quite comfortable and a fire in the grate will warm you adequately. We shall enjoy another meal and then retire so as to make an early start in the morning. I hope you won't be discomfited by the delay." She smiled and fetched another bottle of whiskey, surprising me at her apparent capacity for ardent spirits.

The evening meal of consisted of toasted cheese – more than likely better than I would have received at midday! – and some hearty burgundy wine. I suspected that with the combination of liquors I had consumed, I would have slept well lying on a rock, let alone on a soft bed in a comfortable room with a fire! Kendall showed me to the spare room after the meal was complete and left me to my own devices. I hardly recall disrobing! Did I – or she – light a fire? I collapsed into the soft bed and fell quickly into an untroubled sleep, aided no doubt by the quantity and variety of strong drink I had consumed, the thrumming rain, and the warmth from the crackling fire in the grate.

It was some considerable time later that I awakened to a soft knocking on the door. I listened, thinking I had been dreaming it, but there it was again. I lifted my head from the pillow.

"Come in, Kendall," I spoke loudly enough to be heard.

"Who's Kendall, sir? The captain would like you to attend him in his cabin." Black's presence had wiped out any chance I had of revisiting my visit with the lovely Mrs. Smith.

CHAPTER TWO
Mid-October 1793
HMS *Europa* in the Bay of Biscay

I arrived at the door to the cabin, which was guarded by a perfectly turned-out Marine, who snapped to attention as I approached.

"Lieutenant Ballantyne to see the captain." I growled, still agitated that my wonderful dream had been interrupted.

He knocked on the door, received what I took as an affirmative grunt from within, opened the door, and repeated my name. Another affirmative grunt, a bit louder this time. And the delicious aroma of coffee, bacon, and toast wafted out.

"You may go in, sir." The Marine offered unnecessarily as he opened the door wide and stepped out of the way.

"A good morning to you, Mister Ballantyne. Please sit and join me while I break the fast. Perhaps you would care to partake?" He raised his eyebrows expectantly.

Captain Fitzgerald's cheery greeting, augmented by a pleasant smile was the direct antithesis of his first lieutenant's behavior. I had met Fitzgerald when I first came aboard, but had yet to be invited to the cabin for a meal. Of course, I really didn't expect to be, being only a lieutenant. Had I been a post captain or master commandant, perhaps I would have seen the inside of the cabin sooner. Nonetheless, I was pleased that he had finally got around to extending the invitation. It made me wonder what I might expect. I was not in the best of humor, having had my dream of the first (and possibly the most exciting) of several trysts with the lovely Kendall Smith interrupted by my servant. But, I consoled myself, it wasn't Black's fault. Fitzgerald's pleasant demeanor and the prospect of coffee and a proper breakfast helped improve my disposition; I was long past being nervous at an invitation to the captain's table.

"Thank you, sir." I smiled and took the proffered seat at his table. It dawned on me as I sat that I was some sharp-set and my mouth watered in anticipation of the captain's generosity. An array of toast, pork, and some fruit preserves was distributed around the table. It occurred to me that he must have planned this meeting in advance as there was more there than one person could eat. The wonderful aromas I had enjoyed while awaiting entry had come to life and were distributed before me at the captain's board.

He's got something on his mind beyond a pleasant visit with his charming passenger. I smiled inwardly at my well-concealed *bonhomie!*

A carafe of coffee sat in a gimbaled rack on his sideboard, held securely in place against the rock and heel of the ship in the now increasingly boisterous weather.

As his steward decorated a plate with several slices of toast and some strips of pork and placed it before me, I looked at the captain inquiringly. It was considered poor form for a junior to speak first. So I ate. And immediately my mouth was full, Fitzgerald began.

"I presume you are enjoying your passage in *Europa,* Lieutenant? She is not a particularly weatherly ship, nor is she fleet of foot, but she is solid and can take a beating if she has to." He smiled again. "Likely a poor substitute for your last ship, though *Europa* is still swimming!"

Another reference to the poor Pandora, *left on the bottom in some uncharted spot in the South Seas. But sunk or no, she accomplished her mission!*

I chewed quickly and swallowed. "Yes, sir. It's a rare pleasure to be a passenger, as it were. And yes, indeed, *Europa* does certainly swim!" *Like a bloody haystack.* I kept *that* bit to myself, choosing not to comment on the sailing qualities of his command; even agreeing with his own assessment might knock me down a bit in his estimation. "Your officers seem quite competent, and I have been enjoying the company of the doctor. A fine fellow with many stories!"

"Splendid! Are you bored yet? I know a man of your experience would likely prefer to be...*involved,* as it were. Surely this must be considered a trifle *tame* by the standards of your last cruise."

Uh oh. Yet another reference to my past. Where was this going? Had he heard of the friction between his first lieutenant and me, especially as related to my previous cruise? Better to leave it alone – at least for now!

"Well, sir. I must say it is unusual for me not to be standing watches and running a division, but I expect that will happen soon enough once we have made our southing and land in Jamaica. I have been given to understand that the frigate *Penelope* is a fine vessel with a competent crew and captain. As you may recall, she is where I am assigned. But, at the moment, I am enjoying the respite but not the lack of wind! It is a source of dismay to me, as I am sure it is to you, that we are still no farther than Biscay after some two weeks out. As you might surmise, I am eager to get to my new ship!" I knew he would not be happy with our sluggish pace either.

His face clouded briefly as I spoke, but quickly returned to the cheery countenance I had seen when first I entered the cabin.

"Since you have been spending time with the good doctor, I suspect you may have heard that Lieutenant Williams is ailing with God-knows-what. At least that is what the surgeon tells me. He has taken to his cot and is refusing sustenance. Not able to perform his duties. I am proposing that you, Lieutenant, become acting third lieutenant in his stead for either the duration of the cruise or until such time as Mister Williams is pronounced fit. What say you to that?"

Do I have a choice? I am a commissioned officer in the Royal Navy and a Royal Navy captain is requesting me to stand to my duty. "No" is not an acceptable answer. Perhaps it will be good for me to get my hand back into the job before I have to report to my own duty station.

"That would be most welcome, Captain. I will likely enjoy being a part, even temporarily, of your ship's company." *Except for that buffoon first lieutenant of yours!*

"I assume Lieutenant Winthrop will not be surprised at this assignment?" *I could only hope!*

"Mister Ballantyne: it is high time you learned something about me. I don't give a tinker's damn about what Mister Winthrop – or anyone else, for that matter – chooses to think of my actions and decisions. Except, of course, for the Admiralty!" He had begun quite sternly, but finished with a smile. "Now, since you have accepted my offer and are, as of this moment, officially third lieutenant in His Majesty's Ship *Europa,* I suggest you finish your breakfast and get to work!" He smiled again, lifting the, perhaps inadvertent, sharpness from his words.

I held no delusions about my new found position and responsibilities; I would be reporting to Winthrop and I hardly expected him to change his tune just because the captain had appointed me to his wardroom – albeit temporarily. And, as *Europa*'s officers had constantly reminded me, their ship was a significant change from the old *Pandora:* bigger, larger numbers of sailors and Marines, more guns, and more officers. Unlike *Pandora,* which sailed in singular splendor, we were overseeing a collection of some two dozen merchants with a couple of brigs helping to herd the lumbering civilian traders southwards. No, this employment would be greatly different from my last, but, mercifully, of much shorter duration.

Before two days had passed, I was in it up to my armpits! Lieutenant Williams had apparently done little save what was absolutely necessary to organize his division and hence his petty officers and a couple of warrants had taken charge. Needless to say, an officer – even one they scarcely knew – coming in after some two weeks at sea and reorganizing their routines was a bit of a shock. It was also apparent that Mister Williams was not high on the first lieutenant's list of favorites; Winthrop made it abundantly clear that he thought I might be marginally better than my immediate predecessor, though it obviously pained him to admit it. He hovered about the quarterdeck when I had the watch, clearly determining for himself that I knew the difference between a brace and a sheet. It was awkward at best and grated on my nerves. Within a day or two, it all changed.

The morning of 22 October dawned grey and sultry; I knew, as I had the morning watch when the sun struggled to put in its daily appearance. A long rolling ground swell had replaced the rough seas of the days previous, and the wind had abated considerably, causing us to order our convoy to make all sail. Now the lack of wind had spread our merchant charges over a wide area of the ocean as they drifted at different rates and the other escorts seemed no more able to keep them together than were we. Their futile efforts put me in mind of trying to herd cats!

Either the first lieutenant valued his sleep more than keeping an eye on his new third lieutenant, or he had determined that I did indeed know how to manage a ship. I shared the watch with only a junior midshipman named Charles Shipley, a youthful but enthusiastic lad from Devon, actually not too far from my birthplace of Whatley.

"Deck there. Flashes and gunfire off the larboard bow. Over the horizon. No ships 'at I can see." The lookout called down from the maintop where had just resumed his post aloft at daybreak. I grabbed up my glass and scanned the area ahead and to larboard where he indicated. I saw nothing – no ships, no flashes. And in the heavy morning air, I heard nothing.

"Mister Shipley, take a glass and have a look, if you please. Scuttle along up to the maintop and see if you might see whatever it was caught the lookout's attention."

I had hardly finished speaking when the youngster sprinted forward, leaped onto the bulwark, and was in the ratlines, a long glass slung over his shoulder. I watched as he climbed, agile as a monkey, quickly ascending to the fighting top. He barely paused to catch his breath and had the glass to his eye making a proper sweep of the horizon. Ah, youth!

He called down from his lofty perch. "Nothing, sir. I don't see a bloody...hold on! There! Just a point off the bow to larboard. Flashes. Almost looks like lightning. Seems a bit closer...might be heading toward us." Young Shipley continued to stare forward as he provided a running commentary on what he saw through his glass.

"Very well, Mister Shipley. You may return to the deck, if you please," I shouted up. Apparently there was a squall lurking over the horizon.

Once he made the deck, the midshipman hurried aft, saluted stiffly, and reported what he had seen again.

"And it appears to be dark, sir, to the sou'east, where I would think it should be getting lighter." He added, almost to corroborate his report.

"Mister Shipley, nip below and have a look at the glass, if you please. We might be in for a spot of nasty weather."

The youngster ran off to do my bidding while I pondered my choices.

Hmmm. We're sailing toward some weather, likely a squall or worse. Without a breeze, there's not much I can do to get out of the way. Likely shortening down before it arrives would be prudent. Cap'n can't fault me for that! Even Winthrop couldn't find a problem with exercising some caution.

"Yes sir, dropping it is. Quite quickly too, I perceive." Shipley was back quick as ever you please, eagerly reporting his findings.

"Mister Shipley. My compliments to the captain, if you please. Advise him I intend to shorten sail in anticipation of what I perceive to be a storm coming this way, should he have no objection. You might add that we should probably notify the merchantmen as well."

As the youngster retraced his steps below to do my bidding, I ordered the quartermaster to prepare a hoist indicating "shorten sail" and sent the messenger to roust the gunner and the sailing master. We would fire a half-charge of powder to weather and hope that the other escorting ships would hear it. The cannon shot would draw their attention to the signal aloft which they would then relay to the rest of the convoy.

I had just received the word from the gunner that the shot had been extracted from the number one gun forward and the powder charge replaced with a half charge, when the captain appeared on deck, followed closely by my midshipman. The topmen were standing by at the shrouds, awaiting the order from the sailing master to lay aloft to reef the courses and tops'ls.

"What have we here, Mister Ballantyne? You're planning on *reducing* sail when we have barely a breath of breeze? I think a bit of a blow might be welcome and we should take full advantage of it."

"Aye, Cap'n. It appears to be more than a 'bit of a blow' I think. I have seen these storms in the Pacific and they can be quite ferocious and sudden. But perhaps I am a bit premature, sir. I shall belay the order."

"Very well, then. Carry on. Wait a bit to see what develops. We are behind schedule so I am loath to shorten down before we truly need to. And keep me informed. I appreciate an officer who is thinking ahead and not waiting until his ship is in extremis before he acts." Captain Fitzgerald smiled in the half-light of dawn and walked casually to the hatch that would take him back to his cabin.

I called to the sailing master. "Stand your men down, Mister Gibson. We'll not be reducing sail just yet."

To the gunner, who stood just off the quarterdeck awaiting

my order, I spoke more quietly. "Your crew can stand down also, Mister Simpson. Leave number one charged as it is. I will inform you when to recall your crew. As you were."

We continued to roll in languid seas, sails slatting, yards banging in their chains, the helmsman unable to hold a course. I was relieved at eight bells by the fourth lieutenant, who cast an eye aloft and around the ship.

"Likely to be a quiet morning, I'd warrant. Would you not agree, Lieutenant Ballantyne?" He clearly thought little of my warning about the squall.

I went below with Midshipman Shipley to enjoy some breakfast, me in the gunroom, he in the cockpit with his mates.

The gunroom was quiet, only a few officers, struggling to bring themselves alert, stewards, including my man Black, patiently serving out toast, pork, preserves, and coffee. Not much conversation save when I stepped in, a few greetings and a nod from Black.

"What's going on topside, Edward? Sounds like we've lost the breeze yet again." Second Lieutenant Jason Carden looked up from his food, his voice quiet.

"Not a bloody breath, Jason. But I think we'll be finding some wind rather sooner than later. Looks like a storm to the sou'east – appears to be fast moving, as well. Could hear the thunder. Might not be anything, but then again..." I shrugged.

"Hmmm. Cap'n know? He don't like surprises like that, we've found." Carden stated, focusing his stare directly at me as I took my seat. "I imagine the Dull Hatchet has yet to appear, but watch out for him. If he discovers the cap'n ain't been told about something, he'll do it and then ride your arse unmercifully. There'll be the devil to pay, then; that's for certain."

I considered this warning as Black poured coffee into my cup and I helped myself to a few strips of pork from the platter on the table.

"Aye, I was ready to shorten down and informed Cap'n Fitzgerald, but he wanted me to wait a bit. Then I was relieved by O'Hara and he didn't see anything particularly threatening, despite my calling his attention to the stillness, the milky white seas, and flat-topped clouds to the sou'east. When we saw portents like that in the Pacific, I can tell you we took notice. Mayhaps it's different here in the Atlantic. Could be nothing, or we might be in for a nasty surprise. It's been my experience that those squalls can pounce on the unsuspecting quite without warning."

"Hmm. Well...I would imagine we'll know one way or the other soon if you're right."

"Right about what?" Lieutenant Winthrop, his voice as whiney as ever, stepped into the gunroom, made his way around the table and took his usual seat at the head.

"Nothing much, Mister Winthrop. Edward and I were just having a bit of a go on the weather...or lack of it" Carden did not acknowledge his superior's arrival any further.

"Not much weather to discuss, from the feel of the ship, I'd say. Pretty quiet out there, it appears. Haven't been topside yet myself, but doesn't feel like we're making much progress. Weren't you just on watch, Ballantyne? What's going on up there?"

"Jason is right, sir. Not a great deal. Very quiet at the moment. But I did see some weather well to the sou'east that might be coming our way."

"You informed the captain, I presume?" The close-set eyes drilled into me as I responded.

"I did indeed, sir. Not an hour before I was relieved. He told me to carry on as we were."

"Who's got the watch now?" The man's voice seemed to become ever more nasal and discordant.

"O'Hara, sir. And the master's mate...I can't recall his name. Kirkpatrick? Kilpatrick?"

"Very well. I am sure between them and no wind to worry about, they can't get into much trouble." Winthrop laughed, a sound akin to a cat being tortured.

Quiet returned as the first lieutenant tucked enthusiastically into his breakfast; Carden and I shared a look, a shrug, and resumed eating in silent contemplation of our private thoughts.

It was only a few hours later – I had been doing some paperwork and meeting with Mister Simpson, the gunner, about some issues he had – when I heard above me the patter of rain hitting the deck. It didn't surprise me; the day had dawned with the promise of dismal weather. The ship had been slatting and rolling in the easy ground swell unabated all morning; the sails hung limply, sheets and lines slapping with the roll of the vessel, blocks thumping against the spars and squeaking as lines moved within them. The rain simply added another unpleasant aspect to the already disagreeable conditions. I was glad it was O'Hara with the watch, rather than me!

Shortly before the watch would change at noon and a new "day" would begin on board, I went to see Lieutenant Williams, still ailing, about a few issues Gunner Simpson had brought to light. First Lieutenant Winthrop was coming the other way down the passage when the ship lurched and took a heel, throwing us both off balance, and him into me. I caught myself on the bulkhead, and cushioned his fall with my own body as he staggered into me, both of us surprised at the sudden change in the behavior of *Europa*.

"What the bloody hell is going on? Get out of my way, Ballantyne, you oaf. That damn fool O'Hara has obviously..." For the record, Winthrop was leaning on me, not the other way 'round. Obviously, he did not appreciate the service I provided in softening his contact with the bulkhead! His expletive was cut off by another heavy roll that frustrated his regaining his footing immediately, but he sorted himself out and, with one hand on the bulkhead, stepped quickly aft toward the ladder. I followed. Neither of us took the time to collect boat cloaks or tarpaulins, as the need to get topside quickly supplanted any need for personal comfort.

We emerged on deck to a scene quite different from that which I had left some four hours previously: driving rain, men running hither and thither, grabbing halyards and sheets, braces and clewlines. Officers and petty officers shouted into the wind, issuing orders to heavers and haulers, topmen, and idlers. The storm, apparently with little warning, had caught us clearly over-canvassed and in danger of losing a topmast, the bowsprit, or worse. Sails, their sheets cast off in a reactionary response to the sudden fury, flogged with earsplitting thunder, creating an incredibly dangerous situation for the topmen aloft trying to gain control of them. We could see more sailors making their way up the ratlines to assist in the effort, and the bosun and sailing master, both red in the face, bawled orders aloft from the deck, barely heard over the pounding of the rain and the flogging sails, banging blocks, and ropes slamming into the masts. This cacophony was set over the screaming wind, ranging from a low moaning to a high-pitched keening that could set one's teeth on edge. I thought briefly of our charges and the three smaller ships escorting them; I could only imagine how the gale might be beating them up, and what they might be doing to manage. Perhaps they had reduced sail when I first thought of it before breakfast! I no longer held the watch, making their plight someone else's problem!

Winthrop had ascended to the quarterdeck and was berating the fourth lieutenant in his easily recognizable high-pitched voice that rivaled that of the bosun in volume, waving his arms and gesticulating wildly as the watch officer was attempting to issue orders in a measured way that would return the ship to safety. Clearly, the first lieutenant's bellowing was not helping. Watching the animated tableau, I struggled to suppress a grin, in spite of our somewhat dire circumstances. Winthrop made a comical figure, the rain pouring off his hat and down his neck, his britches soaked through, the water flailing about him as his ever-increasing animation distracted the overwhelmed young man trying his best to maintain some control of himself and regain control of the ship.

The captain chose that moment to step onto the deck, quickly taking in the situation and the roles of the various players in it. I noticed that he wore an oiled canvas jacket, a tarpaulin hat secured to his head with a scarf of some sort, and sea boots. Smart man! The rest of us were soaked through and through!

The rain steadily increased, and, with the wind gaining strength as well, the conditions on deck were decidedly perilous. The wind was blowing the tops off waves that seemed to grow as each passed, some lifting *Europa* upwards and at the same time, heeling her over. Others simply slammed into the wooden impediment to their continued progress, sending spray and spume, and sometimes green water, onto the deck. As each wave met the side, its top spilled over onto the deck, sending white water raging down the spardeck to cascade like a waterfall through the gratings into the gun deck below. Not all the salty offerings went below; an ample supply remained on the spardeck, sloshing toward the stern. The lee scuppers were awash, sometimes only ankle-deep, at other times, knee-deep. It was a frothy, churning maelstrom capable of knocking a man off his feet. Moving about topside, even with the hastily rigged safely lines fore and aft, was risky business. I grabbed a sailor as he passed, and instructed him to rig more safety lines rigged on the spar deck. He simply looked stupidly at me, uncomprehending, until a wave, washing down the deck, swept his feet out from under him and carried him to the break of the quarterdeck. I let him go.

Captain Fitzgerald took his first lieutenant by the arm – I watched the scene as I stood in the sometimes-knee-deep water that swirled about me while I clung to the mizzen pin rail – and led him to the bulwark and away from the watch officer who, with his warrants and petty officers, seemed to be handling the issues before him quickly and efficiently.

I could not hear the words Fitzgerald spoke, but I could see Winthrop's body sag – he was only a few feet from me – as his stern-faced captain sorted him out. The first lieutenant turned and stalked off the quarterdeck and down the ladder, pushing past any in his way, myself included, and disappeared down a hatch. It occurred to me that I should be checking my divisional guns below, ensuring they were properly secured against the gyrations of our ship. One of those three-thousand pound behemoths coming loose would be devastating to any caught in its path and surely, with sufficient momentum, could punch through the side of the ship. I followed the angry first lieutenant down the ladder.

When I stepped off the ladder on the gun deck, I was taken aback by the relative quiet; the wind's scream was decidedly lessened, enough that I could actually hear men shouting to one another. Straining through the gloom of the half-light, I could see a handful of sailors moving down the line of cannon checking that each was properly secured to the bulwark and that the gunports were closed and lashed. A couple of petty officers shouted orders under the watchful eye of the warrant gunner. I made my way to him and stood for a moment beside him, saying nothing. Suddenly, he sensed my presence.

"Oh, my Lord, Mister Ballantyne! I didn't see you there, so intent I was watching these mother's sons o' lubbers to be sure they…"

I cut him off and offered my own apology. "Sorry to startle you, Gunner. Just making sure we weren't likely to have any of these get loose on us. You have a crew below as well?" *Europa* had two decks of guns, being a sixty-four, and the damage from a loose gun carriage on the deck below us would be instantly disastrous, especially in these seas, should one break loose there.

"Aye, sir. Petrie and the second are down there checkin' 'em." He paused, taking in my soaking clothes and bedraggled appearance. "Was you checkin' the topside carronades, sir?"

Damn! I didn't even think to look at them, so intent I was on watching the first lieutenant get his comeuppance!

"Came down to borrow a few men to have a look, Gunner. When they're done here, send 'em topside, if you please." I scrambled. Only a few days in charge and I had forgot something even a midshipman would know!

The warrant looked at me hard for a moment, then knuckled his forehead and said, "Aye, sir. We'll be done here quick as you please. Them topside guns should be fine, but I'll have a look."

"Thank you." I continued to stand in the ankle-deep water covering the deck as I silently watched his men – I had yet to earn the right to call them *my* men – go about the task of checking the breachings on each gun carriage, pushed snugly against the closed and secured gunports to ensure they were, in fact, tightly closed.

The motion of the ship had eased little and I knew without going back on deck, that the wind and seas still reigned supreme. I could only hope this squall would blow through as quickly as it had arrived and cause no damage worth mentioning. I moved cautiously aft, from cannon to cannon, steadying myself from the herky-jerky motion of the ship, found Black, and changed into some dry clothes – nankeen trousers and a homespun shirt again – and fetched my oiled tarpaulin coat. I was certain to need *that* once I returned topside! With little to do below, I made my way to the ladder to again face the maelstrom, getting an early taste of the soaking I would endure as I tried in vain to dodge the cascade of seawater pouring through the scuttle that some fool had thoughtlessly left open.

While I had been below, the topmen had successfully reduced sail, gaining control of the flogging tops'ls and courses. Looking aloft at the masts and yards carving stomach-churning circles in the dark sky, I could only imagine how difficult it must have been! With the ship gyrating in every direction, rain pelting down, footing tenuous at best, and communications impossible, it was a wonder that those intrepid seamen could manage it at all! I closed the scuttle, breathing a silent prayer that my job was on the spar deck and gun deck; I did not have to be aloft with them.

With sail reduced to a couple of headsails, a double-reefed foretops'l, and a bare scrap of a mizzen, the terrible shaking from aloft was gone and the ship rode the seas more easily. I was relieved to see that the topside carronades and long guns had their muzzles and carriages securely lashed to the bulwarks and no longer presented a potential for going adrift. While the yawing and pitching seemed to have eased a trifle, we were still being blown onto a constant heel of thirty and more degrees, which I knew caused *Europa* to present a good portion of her underbelly to the huge seas, a rich target to a particularly large wave determined to roll the ship onto her beam ends. I wondered how long it might be before someone, likely the captain, determined we would be better off running down before the tempest.

Looking down to leeward and even squinting through the driving rain to weather, I could see nary a sign of another ship, only monstrous waves. I assumed a perilous perch aloft would offer the same view of an empty storm-tossed ocean as well. Trying to maintain any communication or control over our merchant charges was quite impossible at this point; I knew that any rational merchant captain would be running off before the wind, riding down the waves rather than slamming into their breaking crests – convoy order be damned. As far as I reckoned, we had ample sea room and the general rule in situations like this in the navy was every ship looks after herself and regroups when the storm passes. And we had, in the sailing orders, established rendezvous points en route for just such an eventuality or in case we got ourselves attacked by a few Frenchies. Trying to maintain a course in these conditions was risking disaster, and I assumed Captain Fitzgerald would be ordering a course change post haste. We would not be the first ship to simply disappear at sea, never to be heard from again. I shuddered at the thought!

The wind seemed a living thing. Howling like a demented

and tortured soul one minute then going completely quiet the next, as though waiting for a reaction from the audience before starting to moan again, ultimately working itself up once again to a full-throated, penetrating scream. Mercifully, I thought the rain might have eased a trifle. Hard to tell though, with all the spume and spray flying through the air. The seas, however, had increased. They loomed over the ship, huge rollers cresting at what looked like main-yard-height, only to have the tops blown off in a constant cloud of froth. I was transfixed watching them, great horses racing across a rolling grey expanse, white manes billowing around them, unrestrained and wild with foam flecking their edges and scud filling the air and streaking the sea. The sky was grey and forbidding with low squally clouds, ragged and torn and even darker than the sky above them, whipping across it, leaving wisps of themselves trailing in their wakes. They looked at once as solid as the earth, but with a soft, constantly changing dimension I found mesmerizing to watch. Thunder rolled and cracked, shooting brilliant shafts of lightning toward the sea and from one cloud to another. A tingly sensation seemed to inspire every soaked hair on my head to stand tall, as if daring the wind to knock them down again. The air had a salty tang to it, sea spray mixed with driving rain in nearly equal proportions. Driven by the wind, the wetness worked its way into every opening in my clothing. Once again, I was wet through. Nothing for that, I told myself – press on!

I grasped the mizzen mast pinrail, bracing my body against the motion, ducking the seas that came crashing over over the windward bulwark, sending gouts of seawater down the deck and below, through the grating to the gundeck. My watch mate, a white-faced Charles Shipley, had appeared, a wraith through the rain, staggering aft along the grating as he clutched the safety lines rigged fore and aft. He joined me and, as soon as he had grabbed ahold of the pinrail, he shouted, almost in my ear, "Mister Ballantyne, sir: are we going to sink? I have never seen such a storm!"

"I think not, Mister Shipley. *Europa* is a sound ship and able. She will see us through this bit of nastiness with nary a scratch!" I wished I believed it with the same conviction I tried to instill in my midshipman! I added a smile to try and further allay his fears, though his gaze was so fixed on the world beyond the ship, I doubt it signified to him.

The poor lad was without an oilskin or protection of any stripe; he had lost his hat – I suspect it had long since been blown overboard – and in addition to being quite thoroughly soaked, he was clearly terrified. His hands clutched the pinrail in a death grip, his legs spread wide to maintain his balance, and water, likely both rain and sea, poured down his face, dripping off his nose and chin. His eyelashes blinked away the water from his deep-set eyes; he would not abandon his death grip on the pin rail to wipe them with his hand. A more miserable young man would be difficult to imagine! My encouraging answer, obviously designed to calm his concerns, might have eased his mind a bit, but the terror in his eyes told me he was still a long way from convinced! I smiled again through the rain, hopeful that my own unconcerned attitude might bolster his self-confidence.

Just as I was about to offer further confidence-building words of wisdom, a deafening crack of thunder, so close to us that it seemed onboard of the ship, interrupted me. Sharper than a cannon's roar but quite as loud, it was followed almost at once by the unmistakable crack of overtaxed wood giving way – the sound a breaking tree would make ashore. It could be heard clearly above the shouts of men on deck, the angry seething of the seas, and the roar of the wind. Shipley heard it also and swiveled his head around seeking the source. Squinting through the downpour and spray, I could see men scurrying aft from the foredeck. I quickly discovered their motivation; the foretopmast, apparently struck by the lightning bolt we had heard bare moments before, had shattered and was crashing down to the deck. Catching in the rigging, it hung for a moment, then fell farther down. The reefed tops'l billowed out, unrestrained now by sheet or brace, fouling in the rigging and the splintered stump of the topmast that remained above the foretop. Suspended over the deck, the lethal spar held for a moment, a pendulum alternately threatening to crash to the deck or fall harmlessly into the sea to leeward. The end of the tops'l yard, tenuously attached to the broken mast by its lifts and chains, fouled in the shrouds, and banged ferociously into the mast with every roll of the ship. The sail, ripping itself to shreds, snarled around every obstacle in range. For some reason,

I started forward toward the midship boat racks, and, perhaps not wanting to be left to his own devices, Shipley staggered after me, shifting his hands to the safety lines as he struggled to keep his feet. The motion of the ship, now affected by the swaying spars, skein of lines, and shredded canvas, changed to a jerking, drunken stagger, unpredictable and treacherous to anyone trying to move around the deck.

Topmen and deck sailors now swarmed around the foremast. The topmen climbed carefully into the weather ratlines, while the deck sailors, under the direction of the bosun, gathered dangling lines, trying to control the broken piece of topmast and the tops'l yard without getting skewered in the process.

Quite without warning, the whole mess plummeted into the sea, slamming into the hull as it dragged alongside by the still attached halyards, braces, and shrouds. Eager hands leaped onto the lines, knives working feverishly to sever the link to the ship. Saws and hatchets appeared, wielded by desperate sailors unnecessarily encouraged by their shouting petty officers, as they hacked through the heavily tarred shrouds. The rigging was dragging the ship perilously to leeward, and; we could not regain control until the mess over the side was cleared. Her bow swung off the wind, pulled by the wreckage, until *Europa* laid almost broadside to the seas. Her roll, already dangerous, increased as the unrelenting seas smacked into her exposed windward side. Horrified, I watched as the leeward tip of the main yard touched the water with almost every roll and wondered if my earlier, and somewhat cavalier, comment to Shipley might have been a bit premature. Everything was happening very quickly, but each moment seemed to stretch into long minutes as if time were standing still.

Yelling, cursing, and orders permeated the air along with the crash of the seas and the roar of the wind. Sailing Master Gibson, the bosun, and his mates, were all shouting orders and instructions intended to ease our situation, but they merely added to the confusion. Lieutenant Winthrop, having returned to the deck and obviously desirous of being helpful, was grabbing sailors and pushing them willy-nilly into the tangle of lines, halyards, sheets, and braces, screaming at them in his easily distinguishable, piercing voice to cut anything they could grab. With his voice raised above the others, it was naturally the one the sailors heard – I could hear it from upwind! But he seemed unclear as to what he desired the men to accomplish. Gibson attempted to redirect them until Winthrop turned his ire on him; then he simply stepped back and let the first lieutenant direct the operation.

Water poured over the bulwark with almost every roll, threatening to wash any man on the leeward side into the scuppers. And most of them were already there anyway, working feverishly to carry out the conflicting orders yelled by warrant, petty officer, and officer alike. Through the driving rain, I spied Captain Fitzgerald on the quarterdeck, watching the scene before him. His posture appeared calm, but the clenching of his jaws and the grip he maintained on the rail offered testimony to the concern he had to feel for the immediate future of his ship. From time to time, he turned his head, apparently shouting direction to the four quartermasters struggling with the big double wheel.

"Ballantyne! Don't just stand there gaping! Bear a hand here. Round up some men who can help us get this mess over the side! Look lively, man." Winthrop's high-pitched whine cut through the wind and storm noise like a knife.

I snapped my head around to where he stood, knee-deep in swirling water, clutching at a safety line with one hand while, with the other, he yanked a sailor nearly off his already unsteady feet and pushed him into the snarl of lines clogging the deck between mast and bulwark. How he even noticed me standing there was a mystery that would have to wait for a solution until calmer times!

"Aye, sir. I'll see who I might find!" I shouted and began to make my unsteady way aft. Shipley remained rooted where he stood.

"You. Sailor! Get yourself forward there and bear a hand with the rig. Lively now!" I shouted and pointed at each man I saw not otherwise occupied. Some merely stared at me; others threw a half-hearted salute and started moving cautiously toward the snarl of men and rigging between the main and foremasts.

"Mister Ballantyne! A moment, if you please." The captain's voice floated forward to me, muted and distorted by the gale, crashing waves, and screeches of distressed rigging and groaning planks in the ship. I waved in response and continued aft to the quarterdeck.

"Sir?"

"What progress are they making up there? I need to get this ship headed downwind sooner than later. Is Winthrop accomplishing anything, or...?" He stopped, not wanting to demean his first lieutenant to a subordinate.

I hesitated. Bad form it is to slander one's superiors, but in this case, I thought the captain likely was well aware of his first lieutenant's shortcomings. And the way he phrased the question...

"Hard to tell, sir." I shouted through the storm. "There are quite a number of men working to cut free the tangle and get those spars clear. Not sure if Mister Winthrop is helping or not. He *is* making an effort." I did not say 'an effort' at what, however!

"Hmmm." I had to assume that was Fitzgerald's utterance; I could hear little below the volume of a shout.

"Helm, try to bring her off another point, if you please." The four lads at the wheel put their backs into forcing the double wheel around with seemingly little to show for their efforts and grunting.

Suddenly, the bow sheared farther off the wind. We heard a roar – human rather than wind – rise up from forward, and watched as half the foretopmast, most of the tops'l yard, and the torn, ragged scraps of the sail rise on a wave and drift down the length of the hull, banging on the side as it passed. A few tentacles of line, tenacious in their desire to maintain contact with their host, dragged irresolutely behind the tangle, and briefly delayed its passage down the side of the ship. Ultimately, the strain from their weight and the trapped water combined to part them and one or two sprung up to the bulwark, snapping like a mule-skinner's whip, as the tension was released.

At once, the danger of capsizing had passed. With her bow more or less downwind, *Europa* still rode wildly, but now, without the length of her side and underbelly exposed to the towering waves, she had regained a more vertical attitude. Her motion was now more erratic, both yawing and pitching. She acted more like a corkscrew than a sixty-four gun ship of the Royal Navy!

First the bowsprit would bury itself in the back of a wave as the stern lifted, and immediately she would roll down and dip her mainyard into the foam under her lee. Then she'd roll back, the bowsprit lifting toward the racing gray clouds, describing dizzying circles in the downpour, while the mainyard flew to the windward side, not quite touching the frothy crests. The captain seemed unaffected and remained calmly rooted to the deck next to his helmsmen, one hand resting lightly on the binnacle, the other held behind his back, his feet splayed in a comfortable posture.

"Meet her, lads; hold her there." Captain Fitzgerald glanced into the binnacle and read the heading. "That'll do nicely. Just keep her running down." He raised his head and I could see him searching for something – or someone – forward.

"MISTER WINTHROP! The quarterdeck, if you please!" Fitzerald did not need the bosun to "pass the word." There was little doubt in my mind that the first lieutenant heard the captain, especially as the wind carried his voice forward to where Winthrop still basked in the limited glow of his perceived success. I thought it prudent to make my escape and not be witness to what I suspected might be the first lieutenant's dressing down...again.

CHAPTER THREE
Late November 1793
Aboard HMS *Penelope* off Hispaniola

"Ship! Broad on the leeward bow. Four leagues and headed nor'west." The lookout's cry caused a momentary pause in the action on deck. Hands stopped what they were doing to cast their eyes horizon to leeward, knowing they could not see from the deck what the lookout had spotted from the maintop. But look they did, some even moving toward the bulwark hoping for a closer view. Fruitless.

"Get your selves back on it, lads. Nothing to see out there and the officers'll take care of whatever it is. You just get on with yer scrubbing and floggin'." The junior bosun's mate in His Majesty's fifth rate frigate of thirty-two guns, *Penelope*, was not a bad sort, given only rarely to harsh outbursts and never to cursing. For the most part, his men liked – or at least tolerated – him.

A bit of grumbling, low, under their breath, but his deck gang returned to their dawn ritual of scrubbing the weather deck and flogging it dry with rags and swabs. The ship, in company with another thirty-two gun frigate in Commodore Ford's Jamaica Squadron, HMS *Iphigenia*, was sailing north off the French held island of Saint Domingue in the bight of Léogâne, cruising for French traffic – warship or merchant. For a crew actively seeking a contest with their French enemies, every contact spotted became a potential prize, offering spoils and shares of hard currency to each Jack Tar involved in the capture.

"Mister Goodwin: your glass to the mizzentop, if you please, and smartly now." The fourth lieutenant, the junior watch officer, slung his long glass about his neck and scrambled for the ratlines that would take him to the directed station.

"And mind you get it right. That vessel could as easily be English or Spanish as anything." The added admonition from Captain Bartholomew Rowley was the result of a mishap, when a misidentified ship almost came to grief after the said Lieutenant Goodwin called her French. Granted, she was sloppily managed and not showing her colors, and only a last-moment signal caused Rowley to abort firing a broadside. It would have been awkward at best and career-ending at worst. Goodwin likely never heard the words, already three steps above the bulwark, his glass banging heavily on the tarred rope ladder.

The captain continued to ruminate to his second lieutenant, Jack Farnsworth, who was standing at his side. "I would not be a bit surprised were she one of the supply ships due in several weeks ago, allowing for a bit of unpleasant weather or a run-in with the bloody Frogs. *Europa,* a sixty-four gunner, is bringing a good-sized convoy from England. Admiral likely doesn't want us shooting at them! Seem to recall they were due around the early part of the month. 'Course, it's still the season for those damn *hurricanos* as our Spanish friends call them, so who knows where they might be." Rowley was particularly expansive this morning, sharing his thoughts with Farnsworth, a fine officer, who had the watch.

The second lieutenant, for his part, barely heard the captain, focused instead on his junior officer, who was now perched at the mizzentop, struggling to free the glass which had slipped around behind him. The young man was not having much success, but Farnsworth noted with a slight grin, he stayed with the task and eventually was peering through the telescope in the wrong direction.

"To the leeward, Mister Goodwin, to leeward!" Farnsworth shouted aloft, received a wave, and noted the young lieutenant shift his focus to the right.

"Quartermaster: signal *Iphigenia* if you please. 'Investigating vessel to north of my position.' With your permission, of course, Captain." Farnsworth was nothing if not proper. Normally, he would have simply issued the order to the quartermaster, but with Rowley on the quarterdeck, courtesy dictated obtaining his approval for almost everything.

"Of course, Mister Farnsworth. By all means. And you might want to bear off a trifle in the event Mister Goodwin determines her to be worth our 'investigation.'" Rowley smiled, fully aware as he spoke that Farnsworth would be issuing that exact order with his next breath.

"Sailing Master: stand by to ease your sheets, trim your braces. We'll be bearing off directly." The second lieutenant shouted forward to the man responsible for managing the work of actually sailing the ship, leaning on the bulwark, enjoying a morning cheroot.

Without responding directly to the officer, the warrant quickly set the evolution in motion, issuing orders to deck sailors and topmen alike to man stations for sail handling. Like a well-rehearsed ballet, the men moved into the right positions from where they would be able to leap to lines, into the rigging, and elsewhere when the sailing master blew his whistle. Farnsworth smiled, enjoying the knowledge that these well-trained men were *his* men and that he had had a hand in training them.

"Sir...on the quarterdeck! French, she appears. Flush deck, showing tops'ls and jibs, not in any apparent hurry." The cry from young Goodwin brought the officers' attention back to the mizzentop where the fourth lieutenant still held the glass to is eye, braced on a shroud against the easy roll of the ship beneath him.

"Mister Goodwin. If you are certain of your identification, you may return to the deck. We are bearing off directly to have a look."

The second lieutenant waved his arm at the sailing master who had most certainly heard the exchange. Immediately the whistle sounded and the topmen sprang into the rigging as the haulers on deck jumped to the pinrails to clap onto the sheets and braces.

"Bring her down a point, if you please, helm. Make your course northwest a half north." Farnsworth spoke quietly, believing that shouted orders often led to confusion and un-necessary haste, thence to mistakes.

Rowley and his second lieutenant watched in silence as the ship bore off, sails were eased to best catch the wind on her new course, and men secured the lines to their pins. All in relative silence save for the whistles used by the bosun and the sailing master to direct the tasks. Even the sails and lines were quiet; only the forecourse announced to all that it had been eased a trifle more than was necessary. The slap of canvas on lines and spars died away as the shiver and shake of the sail was quickly brought under control.

Penelope, her new heading more favorable to her sailing capabilities, dug her shoulder into the swell, heeled a few degrees further, and fairly leaped ahead. The officers watched as

Iphigenia followed suit, easing her own sheets, bearing off, and tried in vain to catch up.

"Hmm. A puzzle, sir, as to why our consort might be following. My recollection was that I told them merely that *we* would investigate. Not sure we need us both for a single vessel. And if it turns out that Goodwin was in error, we have both left station for no reason. Do you think I should signal them to remain, or let them follow along?" Farnsworth spoke quietly to the captain; Goodwin, now returned to the deck, had resumed his position and overheard the exchange. He bristled, but checked himself, and made a concerted effort to speak calmly, albeit to his superior's back.

"Mister Farnsworth. I know I am inexperienced for which I am sorry. I also realize that I was in error several months back in identifying an English trader as the enemy. I am quite certain that the ship ahead of us is indeed French, a warship, and most likely attempting to run even as we speak. Before I returned to the deck, I observed her making more sail, so it would appear she has seen us, as we have seen her. Sir." When he had finished speaking, Goodwin realized that he had held his teeth clenched throughout, perhaps giving a touch more anger to his carefully considered words than he had intended.

"Very well, Mister Goodwin. Your sentiment is noted. I will refrain from making a judgment as to the identity of the vessel until such time as I might glass her myself from the deck. You may see to casting the chip log and entering your findings on the slate, if you please." Farnsworth did not even turn to face his young charge.

Damn interest! How do these youngsters get through the examination for lieutenant and know so little! Must have an uncle or cousin in the Admiralty or Whitehall. Farnsworth gritted his teeth, but said nothing aloud. It would make him appear less than professional to his captain.

The two ships raced after the unidentified vessel, *Penelope* well in front and gaining with every minute. Neither Farnsworth nor the captain had a clue as to why *Iphigenia* had elected to join them rather than remain on station in the Bay, watching for French warships or traders trying to gain the open water. The captain glassed his consort, half a league astern.

"Should that ship turn out to be a Frog as Mister Goodwin has prognosticated, I am sure that Captain Sinclair will want to be a part of it when we bring her to action. His crew is as frustrated with the lack of excitement as ours, and, whilst they would, of course, share in the prize money as long as they were within sight of us, it is more to his liking – and my own – to lay her alongside, pikes and cutlasses in hand, and board her in the smoke. Makes his men feel as if they actually earned their pay. Would you not agree?" Rowley, through watching Iphigenia, now swept the far horizon as he spoke, unconcerned with whether or not Farnsworth agreed. Nor did he care a whit about the sentiment of his second lieutenant.

As the hours passed *Penelope* seemed to gain little on the strange ship; her crew became more agitated as the watch changed, the midday meal was parceled out and the afternoon eased into evening. Rowley ordered more sail crowded on, which as quickly as the quarterdeck aboard *Iphigenia* noticed, was imitated there in a futile effort to catch up. Nervous chatter passed down the weather deck, the gun deck below, and around the galley camboose, as the sailors discussed in animated terms what they would do with their prize money. Many sailors lingered near their quarters stations, ready to take up the call the instant the drum began to beat the ship to battle stations. The overwhelming sentiment seemed to discount a joint action; there was more glory – much more glory – in a single ship contest in which the English would triumph...as always they have over the French. *Iphigenia,* as the men imagined it, would be relegated to standing by in the unlikely event the Penelopes needed help. After all, one had mentioned, it was just possible the ship ahead, while indeed French, could be carrying a heavier weight of metal and thus, the assistance of their consort would not only be welcome, but necessary.

"That bloody ship is French, sir. I'd bet a month's pay on it. Else why would they be running?" Farnsworth had returned to the quarterdeck ready to assume the watch once again. He used his night glass to study the distant ship, which, while now visible from deck level, would not be brought to action for some time to come. Captain Rowley simply grunted in reply. He had long since come to the same conclusion.

"I expect he'll try to lose us in the dark, Mister Farnsworth. We'll not let that happen, now will we!" It was not a question.

"Aye, sir. I have no intention of losing him." Farnsworth bristled a bit at the admonition, thought himself way too skilled to let some sodding Frenchman get away with any ruse that might break the chase.

"Call me when you're within a league of him, Lieutenant. It might be that we can bring him to action in the middle watch." With that, Rowley stepped off the quarterdeck and disappeared down the scuttle to his cabin.

"Mister Goodwin. Take a turn about the deck and ensure that all is secure, if you please. We will be keeping a lookout in the foretop through the watch. See to it, and have him changed at each turn of the glass rather than on the hour. I want to know the minute something changes with that ship. He is to use a night glass. Step lively, now."

Goodwin hesitated. "Sir. Are we now under the impression the ship is French?" He waited, then added, "As I suggested this morning?"

Farnsworth turned, lowered his telescope, and glared at the impudent young man. *How dare he?*

"Yes, Mister Goodwin. That is why we are chasing him across half the bloody Caribbean. Humph!" The impatient growl from Farnsworth gave the young fourth lieutenant cause to smile in the dark as he turned to carry out his instructions. But that changed quickly.

Not so much as an apology, damn his eyes! I knew that ship was French when I glassed her from the mizzentop this morning. One bloody little error and tarred I am with it forevermore. Goodwin's smile had turned into a thin white line across his face as he made his way forward.

Brazen little bastard! What does he think? I am going to apologize to him for doubting his identification? Not on his life! Rather should see to getting him transferred quick as we're back in Port Royal! Ahhh! The impudence of these young people! Farnsworth realized he was squeezing the night glass he held to the point of it hurting his hand.

The watch progressed, albeit slowly to those who continued to wait for the call to arms. Quarterdeck to fo'c'sle, foretop to orlop, the men chafed to fight. At midnight, the watch changed again, men appearing on deck to relieve haulers and topmen, quartermasters to relieve the helm, signalmen standing by, and petty officers and warrants passing on instructions to their respective reliefs. The men talked quietly among themselves as the sweet aroma of tobacco drifted aft on the breeze, the occasional arc of a glowing ember, little more than a firefly, danced from the bulwark only to be snuffed out as it landed in the black sea. Conjecture ran rampant, each cluster of men offering a definite opinion as to when it would start, how quickly it would be over and, of course, the obvious outcome.

"Heard it from the first lieutenant, myself, I done;"… "Overheard Captain Rowley and Mister Farnsworth barely a moment ago"…and of course, the least credible, "Mister Goodwin told me his own self…"

As the starbowlines, relieved now and heading below, made for the hatch, the new lookout in the foretop cried out.

"Deck there! On deck! Ship well in sight, maybe a league distant. Showin' a light aloft, she is."

The men on the ladder, stopped, reversed their direction and rejoined their mates on deck. Others, who had already gained the gundeck, continued to their respective quarters stations near the cannons lining both sides of the ship. Certainly, none among them had any interest in stringing his hammock and crawling into it, even for a short while!

Stephen Ware, first lieutenant of *Penelope* and second in command, raised his night glass and peered through the gloom ahead. He could make out the light reported by the lookout and see the chase, a darker smudge against the dark sea dappled with the reflections of the stars. He could even see the rig and sails alternately blot out and then reveal the stars in the heavens as she rolled in the seaway.

"Mister Allen, my compliments to the captain: the chase is within a league, if you please. And lively, now."

The midshipman tossed off a casual salute in the dark and scampered toward the hatch to fetch the captain. Ware turned his glass astern, looking for a sign of *Iphigenia,* still struggling to remain in sight, gaining not a jot.

Without her guns, this could go against us. Rowley has not a clue as to how the chase is armed or pierced. But he ain't likely to stand off and wait for Sinclair to join up. Where's the glory in that! We'll be engaged within the hour, be my guess. Obviously, the first lieutenant did not share his captain's opinion, offered freely and often during the course of the day-long chase, that this would be a quick and easy victory, with or without their consort. In fact, Ware recalled, Rowley had opined that Sinclair would likely be in the way should he, through some miracle, catch up in time to join in.

"What have we now, Mister Ware? Our prize closes, it appears. Young Mister...uh..." having forgot the name of the midshipman Ware had sent, Rowley simply pointed at the young-ster who was standing quietly by the helmsmen. He went on in spite of his lapse. "The midshipman mentioned we had closed to within a league. If this breeze holds, we shall engage within the hour. You may have the Marine beat *Heart of Oak* and we shall see what we shall see."

As an afterthought, he added, "What of *Iphigenia?* Is she still back there?" He picked up a long glass – not a night glass – and peered through it.

"Aye sir, but not in a position of be of any help. Were you thinking of waiting for her to join up?" Ware, noticing that the captain had grabbed up the wrong telescope and would be un-likely to see Sinclair's ship, offered hopefully, his tone suggestive.

"Not on your life, Ware! We'll handle this easily." Rowley's confidence, possibly misplaced due to his lack of information as to what ship he was chasing, bubbled to the surface quite convincingly.

"Aye, sir. Sailing Master: hands to sail handling positions, if you please. Drummer, we'll have *Heart of Oak,* now." Now facing forward, the first lieutenant raised his voice only slightly.

At once, gruff shouts floated aft as the sailing master moved his sailors to their positions to shorten sail and the drummer began the tattoo called *Heart of Oak* that would send the men to their battle stations. Few of them had to move, having been waiting for this moment now for several hours. Almost at once, the rumble of heavy gun carriages moving into battery broke the quiet as the gundeck came to life, the sailors all ready to fight.

The ship's wake was aglow with bioluminescence, from the

microscopic creatures near the surface winking and lighting their displeasure at having been disturbed by the ship's passage. The creamy bow wave, unnoticed by the crew on deck, pushed out to the sides, equally alight with the tiny creatures which, upon safely reaching the undisturbed water farther from the ship, blinked out.

"Mister Johnson!" Ware called out to the sailing master. "Have your men ready, if you please, but refrain from shortening until I give you the word. We still have a bit of ocean to cover before we'll engage."

Unseen, Johnson waved his acknowledgment through the dark.

"Damn! Can't see a bloody thing with this glass. Must be something wrong with it! Give me yours, Mister Ware." Rowley had finally discovered the error of the telescope and snatched the night glass from under the first lieutenant's arm without so much as a "by your leave."

"There's Sinclair. Must be well over a league astern. He'll not be joining in *this* one, I think. We'll have to manage it ourselves." The captain muttered, as if to himself.

"Perhaps it might be prudent to give *Iphigenia* a chance to catch up, sir. We don't know what that ship is. I doubt she's a fifty gunner, but she could outweigh us in broadside. With both ships, there would be little doubt as to the outcome. Sir." Ware couldn't help himself; he thought the captain to be over-eager, reckless even. And he was right. No one knew what or whom they were chasing.

"Nonsense, Ware. You're not worried about the outcome of this, are you? Good God above! I would wager she's French of equal or less weight of metal than we are and apparently, not as swift a swimmer or she would have outdistanced us long since. Delay? Not on your life, sir! I shall position us close alongside, offer her a broadside or two, and accept her surrender. And we shall have a plum prize for our trouble! You'll see."

"Aye, sir. Shall I order us reduced to battle sail now?" Ware began to raise his hand to signal the sailing master.

"Not yet, Mister Ware. We shall wait until the last possible moment. I want us alongside as quick as ever possible. No point in giving those Frogs any more time to prepare than necessary."

Whatever are you talking about? We've been chasing them since dawn. If they aren't prepared by now... Of course, the first lieutenant would not dream of vocalizing *that* sentiment!

"Sir, second division guns are manned, tompions out, ports open and pieces in battery." Fourth Lieutenant Goodwin raised his hat in salute to the first lieutenant as he reported his status.

Almost at once, two midshipmen appeared from the darkness, doffed their hats respectfully, and reported the other guns ready below, as well as the bow chasers – carronades – forward on the fo'c'slehead. And still *Penelope* forged ahead, heeled to the steady breeze on her quarter and gaining on the chase with every cable's length they traveled.

The chase, showing several lights aloft, was by now clearly visible from the quarterdeck without the benefit of a long glass.

"Mister Ware: it would appear that she has run out her battery. You see that? Looks like she's figured out we might not have peaceful intents! And those lights she's showing aloft – you think they could be some Frog signal?" The captain studied his quarry intently, not even turning to address his first lieutenant.

"That would be my guess, Cap'n. And she has surely run out her guns. I would assume you're planning on taking the windward gauge?" Ware raised his glass to study the French ship. "We could send up some random lights forward, if you like, sir. Might confuse her while we gain a few more fathoms on her."

"Capital idea, Mister Ware. See to it. And have the bow chasers ready to fire as quick as ever they get the range."

A hurried conference with the bosun resulted in a pair of lanterns run up into the foretop, one red, one white. There was no immediate reaction from the chase. Then, quite without warning, the lights she showed in her mizzen rigging winked out.

"Hmm. Don't think we fooled 'em much, Cap'n. Reckon the bow chasers will have to do our talking for us!"

"Mister Farnsworth! See to the bow chasers, if you please. You may direct their fire as you see fit." Captain Rowley shouted forward to the second lieutenant, who was roaming the weather deck, pacing back and forth with eager anticipation.

"Aye, sir. Shouldn't be long, from the looks of her!" Farnsworth called out, waving his hat, either in salute or in joy of the anticipated action.

Penelope charged on. For now it was clear as she closed on the French warship. For it was now readily apparent that not only was the target a warship, but she was clearly prepared and ready to fight off the English frigate. From *Penelope*'s bow, the second lieutenant could make out the name emblazoned on her transom: *L'Inconstante.* He sent a seaman aft to report his discovery to the quarterdeck.

"I don't care a bloody fig what her bloody name is! It will be changed quick as ever you please once she is our prize and purchased into the navy!" Rowley growled at the messenger. "Tell Mister Farnsworth to stand by to fire at *L'Inconstante,* and her name be damned!"

The seaman ran off to relay the message, though probably not exactly as uttered by the captain!

BOOM! BOOM!

"Sir! She has fired her stern chasers at us!" Ware seemed surprised that their quarry would actually get off the first shots. He waved frantically toward the fo'c'sle and raised his voice. "Mister Farnsworth: lay one into her, damn all! What in heaven are you waiting for?"

The captain saw the twin splashes well ahead and to leeward, smiled in the dark, a bit more sanguine. "Short, they are. Don't have the range yet. You saw the splashes forward, Mister Ware? Aside from offering a response, I would doubt that Mister Farnsworth will have any better success."

"Aye sir. Shall I order him to…"

BOOM!

One of the two 18-pounder long guns in *Penelope*'s bow spoke, a gout of flame shocking the darkness. *BOOM!* The other immediately added its voice to the concussion still ringing in everyone's ears from the first.

"Mister Farnsworth! Hold your fire, if you please. No sense in wasting our shot and powder!" Rowley's voice seemed muffled after the shock of the cannon roar, but a faint "aye" floated aft from the fo'c'sle.

The ranging shots offered by each contestant were just that: tests to see if they could reach their target. No more were fired; the Frenchman determining to wait until he was sure, and Rowley directing his ship more to windward so as to offer his full broadside when the time came. And *Iphigenia,* her guns silent and well beyond their range, plowed on in an effort to be in position to participate before the fight was decided.

An hour and more into the middle watch, Rowley's efforts at positioning *Penelope* paid off and, with a deafening roar, the English broadside fired in ripple fire, each gun sounding off so close to its predecessor that it sounded like one continuous roll of thunder. And *L'Inconstante* answered her, shot for shot. The two were separated by less than a musket shot and little of either ship's iron missed a target. The French aimed to hit *Penelope's* hull, while, thinking more of the prize he could gain if he did not have to destroy the enemy, Rowley ordered his lieutenants to take down the Frenchman's rig and kill or wound her crew and officers.

English canister, bar, and chain shot flew across the water, cutting shrouds, running rigging, and sails with the ease of a hot knife through butter. The Frenchman's mizzen topmast came down with a crash, its shrouds cut clean through by the English rigging cutters. *L'Inconstante's* deck was a flurry of activity as her crew worked feverishly to cut away the wreckage and, as quickly as they could, push the whole mess overboard. Though her ability to maneuver was severely compromised, the ship continued to fight fiercely.

Penelope's gun captains, as ordered by the quarterdeck, shifted to grapeshot, scything through the French crew as they struggled with their fallen topmast, leaving men and officers dead or wounded, and chasing the uninjured to seek cover of some kind, any kind. When the English fire shifted, to concentrate on the mizzen-mast, the farthest aft in the ship, much of the English shot ripped into the quarterdeck, wreaking havoc on the ship's helm and on the men and officers stationed there. But the Frenchman's guns, mostly below the weather deck and protected from the English shot, maintained a steady rate of fire.

French shot crashed into the English hull, bulwarks, and decks, throwing long-leaf pine and oak splinters aplenty into the air, felling any unfortunate enough to be in their way. The larger of the splinters could skewer a man like a pig on a spit, and even the smaller ones could take off an arm or create a wound sufficiently onerous that the surgeon would ultimately have to remove the damaged limb. Suddenly, the larboard hammock net-ting caught fire, incinerating fifty and more hammocks stowed there as protection from musket balls and grapeshot. Whether the French had fired hot shots or the fire was the result of some-thing else would never be known, but Rowley promptly ordered his ship about, to buy enough time to extinguish the flames. Splintered bulwarks were left ragged, large chunks of the wood missing, but what was left, offered some added protection.

"Cap'n? Beggin yer pardon, sir." The raspy voice of the car-penter drew Rowley's attention from the fire fighters.

"Yes, Jackson. What is it?"

"Aye, sir. The aft hold is sounding three feet and forward we've got almost five feet of water. I have men on the pumps and we're keepin' even for now. But forward is what I'm concerned about. Looks like we took a ball or two right at the waterline. Stuffed it with hammocks and wood, but she's still comin' in right hard. Might have to fother it and set it up proper-like." More words than the usually taciturn carpenter had uttered at one time in anyone's memory. It spoke eloquently of his genuine concern.

"Very well, Jackson. Do the best you can now and keep the pumps going. We'll be finished soon with this and be heaving to. You can fother the hole and any others then. And keep an eye aft. Have someone sound that hold every fifteen minutes. Let me know if the water gets ahead of the pumps. Dismissed" Rowley was curt, but it was understandable; he knew the damage his ship had sustained was not yet life-threatening and he wanted to get back to the fight before his adversary had time to recover.

"Mister Ware. Let us get back to it. She's still showing her colors. Another broadside or two and we might convince them that surrender is the proper course! Bring us about, if you please, and we'll fight the starboard side this time." The half-moon pro-vided ample light for each of the antagonists to see their targets, their own injuries, and the set of their sails.

"Aye, sir. And it would appear *Iphigenia* has come within range. Indeed, I think she..." Ware's words were cut off by the joint thunder of *Iphigenia*'s and *L'Inconstante*'s simultaneous cannonades.

The English ship had given the enemy a raking fire from

astern as she drew within range and bore off, leaving the way clear for Rowley to bring *Penelope* back into the fray. *Iphigenia* slipped away, a wraith, albeit a deadly one, in the ghostly moonlight, her wake streaming white behind her. Clearly, Captain Sinclair knew his business and Rowley found it gratifying that he was willing to work in partnership with *Penelope* to finish off their enemy rather than wait at a safe distance until *Penelope* was unable to continue, then dash in and finish off the enemy, taking the credit and glory for the win.

The French captain, frustrated that this new Englishman had attacked and then managed to gain a position safe from return fire, aimed his wrath once again at *Penelope,* the only target he had, with renewed vigor. Ware raised his arm, ready to signal the midshipman stationed at the gundeck hatch to pass the order below to "fire as they bear."

"Hold your fire, Mister Ware. I want every shot to count now. We must finish this before we have lost our prize!"

The first lieutenant lowered his arm, his enthusiasm held in check. While delaying their penultimate broadside was clearly a proper decision, it allowed the French gunners, unhindered by the whining English rigging cutters and grapeshot that had been flying over their heads, the opportunity to reload and offer their own broadside, now consisting primarily of grapeshot. The effect was devastating, particularly to Midshipman John Allen who, standing as he was amidships by the grating over the gundeck, had the misfortune to be in the way of a cluster of deadly grapeshot. The balls that missed his torso flew high, neatly decapitating the young man, killing him instantly, his mutilated head rolling away to leeward. Another several shots from the French battery wreaked havoc on part of a gun crew on the fo'c'sle, wounding several and dismounting the gun. The inboard end of the bowsprit splintered as well, greatly weakening that spar to which all of the forward leading stays for the foremast were attached. If those stays parted, or should the bowsprit give way, the foremast would come crashing down, a severe and possibly devastating event.

"Alright, Mister Ware. Let us finish this before those Frogs can do any more damage. Bring the ship around to open our starboard broadside. Let us show them again what good English iron can do!"

Penelope eased off, exposing most of her broadside to the enemy just as the messenger from the quarterdeck, who had replaced the unfortunate Midshipman Allen, arrived below with the shouted message to "fire as they bear." The syncopated thunder rolled aft as each gun spoke in turn, drilling into the French hull as well as sending deadly grape and canister across her deck. *Iphigenia* ranged up, fired her bow chasers into the Frenchman's larboard quarter at almost the same moment.

With three ships firing, the night air, usually pure and sweet smelling at sea, stank of burnt sulfur, an acrid fog hanging over the battle scene despite the best efforts of the breeze to clear it away. The atmosphere was bitter – tasted sour. The lanterns about the deck gave off a weak, yellow glow, barely visible through the thick smoke. Those men on the gun decks of each ship choked and wheezed in the foul miasma, eyes watering, and noses running as they struggled to do their jobs and ignore their labored breathing. Some had tied their neck cloths over their noses and mouths; it did little good, beyond giving them the appearance of highwaymen and bandits.

"*Monsieur!* Quarter! We ask quarter! I 'ave strike my *drapeau!*" The heavily accented French voice floated unseen across the water.

"Well done, Mister Ware. It appears we have taken a prize. Let us prepare a boat to pay the Frogs a visit and see what is what. I think Mister Farnsworth should go…and perhaps, Mister Goodwin might enjoy the experience. After all, it was the fourth who properly identified the ship!" Rowley sounded as if he might be about to gloat over his victory, a victory not entirely his own, and one that might have ended differently had not *Iphigenia* showed up when she did.

CHAPTER FOUR
Late November
HMS *Penelope,* southeast of Cuba

Lieutenants Farnsworth and Goodwin had launched the blue cutter as quickly as the action had ended to row the short distance to their prize and accept the French surrender. They were accompanied by a clutch of sailors and a half dozen well-armed Royal Marines. The surgeon would make his way there later to offer his assistance to the French surgeon who likely had more injured than did the English. And it was possible there was no surgeon aboard at all, simply a surgeon's mate who would have to cope with some horrifying injuries. But waiting until the ship was safely in English hands and the unwounded ones among the crew confined in a secure space was simply, in his mind, common sense. In the meantime, he and his mates had more pressing concerns taking care of their own wounded in *Penelope.*

"What have we here, Mister Goodwin? Seems as though we will have some assistance in securing our prize." Farnsworth observed another boat, obviously from *Iphigenia,* already secured alongside.

The armed Penelopes quickly followed their officers up the battens to the Frenchman's deck and took positions around the break in the bulwark to ensure their safety. Each carried a musket and a cutlass, while the officers wore their swords and each had stuffed a pistol into his sword-belt.

"Well, here's a threatening lot! A rum collection of cut-throats, it would appear! Welcome aboard His Majesty's Ship *L'Inconstante,* gentlemen. Whom do I have the pleasure of addressing?" A haughty lieutenant in the uniform of the Royal Navy sneered at Farnsworth and Goodwin.

"I am Lieutenant Jack Farnsworth and this chap is Lieutenant Goodwin, fourth lieutenant in *Penelope.* On behalf of our captain, Bartholomew Rowley, I want to thank you for your help in our capture of the prize; had you not appeared when you did, it might have proved more difficult." Farnsworth smiled benignly at his inquisitor.

"Help you? *Your* capture? Oh my goodness. You lot were making a complete hash of it, and, had we not showed up to finish the job, the Frogs might be standing on your deck waiting for your Captain Rowley to turn over *his* sword instead of the other way round!"

"And who do I have the distinct *dis*pleasure of addressing, sir? I am assuming you would be from *Iphigenia* since there is no other about. And for the record, *Penelope* had mostly sealed the fate of *L'Inconstante,* while you were still attempting to catch up!"

"I am first lieutenant in His Britannic Majesty's frigate *Iphigenia,* Jonathon Jones, at your service, sir." He turned about and started to walk away, off-handedly introducing a midshipman who had stood behind him as he did so. "And this is Midshipman Jason Simmons, also of *Iphigenia.*"

"Well, that sets the fox among the chickens, eh, Mister Goodwin. Nasty fellow, that. Let us see what's about and perhaps we'll come across the captain before he does." Farnsworth glanced about the shadowed deck, noting dark stains in a number of places and a few seamen prone, clearly alive, but apparently grievously wounded. A few dark shapes were lying about, indistinct in the gloom, which the two officers took to be bits of flesh – an arm here, a hand there. "I imagine their surgeon, should there be one aboard, will welcome some help when Mister McMahon decides it is safe enough for him to venture forth."

Goodwin struggled to swallow the gorge rising in his throat. He had not before witnessed the brutal aftermath of a naval battle, and while he could scarcely tear his eyes away, the scene was almost more than he could bear. He managed to avoid embarrassing himself in front of his superior or the suddenly arrived French officer who seemed to appear as if from the trick of a conjurer.

"*Monsieur? Zee capitan,* 'e is gravely...em...how you say? Wounded? *Oui* zat ees it, wounded. 'E ees below. I am *sous lieutenan'* Jacques Beleau, at your service. Zee *premiere,* 'e ees *mort.*"

"How's your French, Mister Goodwin? Mine is less than useful it appears. I gather this chap is an officer from his uniform, though which I have no idea. He said something about the captain, so I would hazard a guess that he is not the man we need. The captain is wounded, I collect? That's about all I can manage, so unless you can handle the lingo, we'll need someone who can." Farnsworth doffed his hat, returning the salute offered by the French officer as he spoke.

Goodwin rattled off a few sentences of excellent French, causing Lieutenants Beleau and Farnsworth to smile. Beleau responded more quickly to Goodwin in his native tongue.

Goodwin turned to Farnsworth.

"Yes sir. This is the second lieutenant. You were quite correct; their captain is wounded and their first lieutenant has been killed." He turned back to the Frenchman and spoke more rapid-fire French.

"What did you tell him?" Farnsworth was clearly frustrated that he was forced to depend on this youngster's superior linguistic skill. Certainly not the way it was supposed to be!

"Sir. I thought it prudent, given our competition, to secure the surrender from the captain first. Might help put the Iphigenias in the right frame of mind. I asked Lieutenant Beleau if he might take us to the captain. That is, if he's not too dreadfully hurt."

"Well done, Goodwin. Let us step along, then." *Maybe this young man will work out after all!* Farnsworth smiled at his subordinate and the Frenchman.

They followed the Lieutenant Beleau to a scuttle and thence below. In the dim light of the gundeck, the British officers were horrified at the carnage. Guns were dismounted, blood had splattered about the bulkheads and decks, and loose shot rolled to and fro as the ship wallowed in the easy seas. Farnsworth said nothing – kept his eyes focused ahead. Goodwin, not yet inured to the sight, stared open-mouthed at the carnage and again swallowed as the bile rose in his throat. Neither of them paused as they followed their guide, gingerly picking his way aft to the captain's cabin. When they came to a bulkhead with a closed door, the Lieutenant Beleau rapped sharply on it.

"Oui" The voice filtered through the closed door – apparently the French did not disassemble the cabins as a first step in going to quarters as did the British men o' war – and was answered promptly by Beleau.

"I assume he stated our arrival and purpose?" Farnsworth whispered to his junior officer.

"Indeed, sir. And that there were officers from two British ships aboard."

"We needn't concern ourselves about that for now, Goodwin. We will accept the surrender and make arrangements for a prize crew and for the surgeon to come aboard. I shall be depending on you to translate what I tell the captain, exactly as I dictate."

"Of course, sir." Goodwin nodded as Beleau pushed open the door revealing the tableau within of the captain lying on his dining table as the surgeon bent over him.

The cabin was in shambles, the gallery windows blown in, furniture overturned, and the air thick with the smell of expended gun powder. The two British officers could see that *Iphigenia's* raking shot had told brilliantly. A few iron shot rolled about near where one of the stern-facing guns stood a bit askew, but in battery with its snout poking out the gunport. Blood, likely from the surgeon's ministrations, pooled on the deck under the table, but the one element that took young Goodwin's breath away was the task being performed on the French captain. The doctor had just completed removing the captain's left arm midway between the elbow and shoulder. The man's detached forearm, wrist, and hand lay grotesquely in a pan on the deck, its fingers curled almost into a fist through some strange post-mortem contraction. A tourniquet, fashioned from a leather strap, had been tightened on the remaining part of the arm, just below the captain's shoulder, while a cauterizing iron heated over a brazier near at hand. Once hot enough, the surgeon would use it to stanch the bleeding. Through all of this the captain was not only conscious, but apparently cogent.

"My God!" Farnsworth gasped; this time, it was he who had to swallow the bile rising into his throat so as not to embarrass himself. "Sir, I had no idea you were so badly wounded. We shall wait outside until the doctor has finished his ministrations. Translate that, Mister Goodwin." A coppery taste and thickened tongue encouraged a hasty departure.

"*Non.* Eez not necessary. Do'tor is nearly complete. Remain." The captain spoke through clenched teeth to the British officers, then rattled off something in French to his subordinate.

Goodwin translated. "He told Beleau to present you his sword, sir. And then offer his congratulations on a well-fought battle. Your tenacity in the chase," he said, "was implacable... uhhh...unrelenting."

Beleau had located the captain's sword and was offering it, hilt first, to Farnsworth with a sad smile and a flood of French. Goodwin struggled to keep up and finally stopped trying.

"He said basically the same thing the captain did, sir. Also that he had six and more sailors killed along with their first lieutenant. Some twenty men were wounded, including, obviously, their captain. He asked that our doctor assist their own with the more seriously wounded if that might be arranged."

"Tell him we will see to it at once. And that I shall pass his compliment along with the captain's sword on to Captain Rowley. And tell him we thank him for his courtesy and will take our leave, so the doctor might continue his ministrations."

Once Goodwin had translated his superior's words, Farnsworth steered him out of the cabin onto the gundeck and thence up to the spardeck. The officers from *Iphigenia,* led by a young officer or possibly a midshipman, were about to head down as the Penelopes stepped onto the weather deck.

"Their captain is severely wounded and being treated by their surgeon. I would suggest that decency might prevail and you would give the man a few moments of peace before you badger him for his surrender. Which would be quite superfluous as I have already received it on behalf of Captain Rowley and *Penelope.*" Farnsworth lifted the French sword he carried, testament to his successful visit to the captain's cabin. He tried, unsuccessfully, not to sound like he was gloating, having trumped Jones's ace quite handily!

For his part, the *Iphigenia* officer offered an angry "harrumph" and pushed passed the others as he led his midshipman below.

Their waiting boat ferried them back to *Penelope* and returned quickly with the surgeon, one of his loblolly boys, and another dozen Marines. A prize crew would wait until sunup; until then, the crews of the victors and vanquished would try to get some order restored to their ships, ease the suffering of the wounded, and, should time permit, get some sleep before another very long day would begin.

It seemed that dawn rushed into the darkness sooner than ever it might have – at least that's how it seemed to the officers in *Penelope's* gunroom who had been up throughout the night organizing the prize crew, repair parties, and receiving reports as to what elements of their ship and their prize would have to be replaced or jury-rigged before sailing for Port Royal. Daylight found the three ships rolling in the gentle swell, each hove to, with English boats plying the clear turquoise waters between them. The wind had dropped to barely a breath and only the ripples in the sea kept the image of the ships floating above their reflections from appearing as if they were part of a painting. The sun rising in the eastern sky and casting its glow on the still sea signaled only another day of hard labor on top of the long night and previous day's toil; the beauty of the sunrise was lost on the stalwart men of both navies. The English sailors pulling the oars in the small boats were bone-weary and their stroke showed their exhausted state. Sloppy movements, blades skipping on the wave crests, and the men themselves slumping over their oars at any opportunity. And the officers were no less tired.

The dawn tinted the water from east to west, turning it briefly orange; then the fiery ball rose into the clear tropical sky. The men working on deck snuffed their lanterns and candles, observing without really noticing that yet another day had begun. It would be filled with the backbreaking chores of setting their ships to rights, rowing the cutters to and fro, and working aloft in the heat of the day repairing the shot-up rigging. The rush of battle and the joy of potential prize shares all dissipated in the reality of the new day; now it was time for the drudge work to begin in earnest. There seemed little excitement about the decks now!

Penelope had a bowsprit to rebuild, as well as bulwarks to repair, hammock netting to replace (not to mention the hammocks that burned), and a prodigious amount of knotting and splicing to do in the rig. *L'Inconstante* would take several days to put to rights before she could be sailed to Jamaica for condemnation. From all appearances, *Iphigenia* seemed relatively unscathed by the action, but then, she came late to the party. Nonetheless, Captain Sinclair had positioned his ship close aboard on the opposite side of the prize, sent men aboard to assist with repairs, and Marines to help herd the French crew into the hold. His surgeon was still aboard the prize assisting the French doctor and *Penelope*'s surgeon with amputations, stitching up splinter wounds, and bandaging the less serious injuries.

Captain Rowley prowled his decks, saying little to his crew already sweating in the early morning sun as they labored to make the necessary repairs under the direction of their petty officers. From time to time he would offer a word to a warrant officer, suggest a better way to do the task at hand, or dole out a rare compliment. His particular attention was reserved for the foredeck, where bosun and the carpenter were rigging a spare t'gallant sail to fother the hole at the waterline on the larboard bow.

A gang of deck sailors and a handful of idlers had spread out the sail on the fo'c'slehead; it covered most of the foredeck even with a bight folded in the middle. Rowley watched as the bosun oversaw a couple of his mates attach stout hempen lines to each corner through the cringles that would normally be used to attach the sail to the yard. Other men, crawling on the sail itself, worked tar and oakum into the fiber of the canvas, smearing it on thickly. The mixture was smelled powerfully strong, and the odor caused a fair amount of sneezing, hacking, and coughing amongst the men covered in it. But this gooey coating would hopefully create a seal when the sail was hauled over the hole in the ship's bottom. Their work was accompanied by the clanking of the chain pump as men worked in shifts to try to keep ahead of the water threatening to flood their ship. Like their shipmates working at other tasks, the pumpers looked tired, but self-preservation and fear of the bosun's cat o' nine tails motivated their unending slog around the pump.

When Bosun O'Malley was satisfied with the work done to prepare the sail, he had the lines from the two starboard corners led under the bowsprit and back to the deck, where two gangs of sailors grabbed ahold and took a light strain. The remainder of the seamen picked up the sail and fed it over the side, glad to have the odor going overboard with the canvas. Others clapped onto the lines attached to the larboard corners. Once the sail was in the water and began to sink, the men, larboard and starboard, holding the after most lines began walking toward the stern, effectively dragging the slack sail under the ship.

Now the carpenter, Mister Jackson, directed the operation, keeping a careful eye on how far aft the sail was pulled. When he was satisfied that it would cover the twin holes in the ship's hull, he halted the men from dragging it any farther and signaled to O'Malley to secure it. Then he disappeared below. Captain Rowley stepped to the bulwark and peered over the side, determining for himself that the sail was properly positioned to stop the influx of seawater. Still the pump clanked along, sending a steady stream of water, thick as a man's leg, into the scuppers and over the side.

When Jackson arrived on the orlop deck, his men had readied all manner of stuffing material including timber balks, the remnants of the burned hammocks, some blankets from the purser's stores, and more tarred oakum. The carpenter had the men force the material into the hole from the inboard side and against the sail, itself pressed into the void by the water pressure from without. When he was satisfied, they nailed the timber balks across the hole and spread oakum and tar liberally around the edges. While it would not prevent *all* the water from coming in, the emergency repair had reduced the torrent to a mere trickle, easily managed by the pumps.

"That oughta hold it. Least we won't be sinkin' any time soon!" Jackson said to his men. "Good job, lads." He smiled briefly and returned to the deck.

"Well?" Rowley confronted him at once he appeared through the hatchway.

"Aye, sir. She's gonna hold, I'm thinkin'. The lads done a right fine job, indeed. Likely another half a glass on the pump and the hold should be pretty well dry. There's always gonna be a bit of a trickle and some water, but ten minutes a watch oughta take care of that easily." Jackson knuckled his forelock as he made his report.

"Very well, then, Mister Jackson. I imagine you'll want to see to the repair of the bowsprit now we're not likely to be sinking any time soon! I am anxious to get the ship underway again." Rowley did not wait for an answer – he knew what it would be – just turned about and made his way aft.

Two days more saw *Penelope* put to rights, a new bowsprit, fashioned from a spare yard, repaired bulwarks, and a minimal level of water in the bilges. The running and standing rigging aloft had been knotted and spliced; two shrouds which had suffered from French shot were now replaced with properly tarred rope. Aside from the fothered shot holes in her hull and a few rents in her sails, *Penelope* was now sea-worthy, ready for anything short of a full gale that she might encounter en route to Jamaica. *L'Inconstante* was a somewhat different story.

The mizzen topmast had been replaced with a mainyard, cut and reshaped by the French sailors under the supervision of English topmen. It was hoisted aloft and dropped into position mostly by the English sailors as only a handful of French seamen were willing to help their former adversaries.

Those less than compliant had been locked below and were carefully guarded by Royal Marines. To further ensure French cooperation, a swivel gun had been mounted at the hatch, loaded with grapeshot, and aimed below. Another Royal Marine manned the gun.

Much of the *L'Inconstatnte*'s rigging had been cut up and shot to pieces by the English rigging cutter shot fired from *Penelope*. Bosun mates and topmen from both of the British ships now worked together aloft in *L'Inconstante* to knot, splice, and replace running and standing rigging, as well as several sails holed in too many places to be useful. Several yards had to be replaced as well. The French Navy, apparently, did not supply a sufficient quantity of replacement spars to effect a major replacement, so many of the yards had to be dragged by boat from the British frigates.

The biggest problem the victors faced was not in the rig or even the mizzen topmast, but the damage suffered by the foremast. It had taken two major hits, one of which took a large chunk out of the mast some eight feet above the deck. The second came from what appeared to be from a six-pounder swivel shot that had drilled into the upper section of the lower mast. The ball remained embedded in the wood. Without question, the foremast would have to be replaced or splinted to keep it from falling once the sails were set. Since there was no suitable replacement available until the group reached Port Royal, the carpenters would have to jury rig some type of splint to render the mast useable.

Both parts of the damaged mast saw the same type of repair: balks of timber were affixed to the mast, over the wounded areas, and, the carpenter said, were sufficient to "get us back to

Jamaica, long as we ain't got to deal with much bad weather."

Spikes driven into the mast and frapping turns made by wrapping thick line around and around secured the timbers and added sufficient stiffness to the damaged spar. Were there storms or even strong winds, it might be a different story. There were spars in the navy yard at Port Royal to replace it – and the mizzen topmast – but first they had to get there.

Two days after *Penelope's* repairs were completed, *L'Inconstante* was declared sea-worthy enough. Rowley, as senior commander, ordered the little fleet underway – destination Port Royal, Jamaica.

CHAPTER FIVE
December 1793
Aboard HMS *Europa* in Port Royal, Jamaica

My dear Kendall:
I do hope this missive finds you well and in good health.
I trust the weather there has not been too awfully dreadful, but I
know how it can be in November and December. I am sure you
are cozy in your tidy house, enjoying your warm hearth and an
occasional taste of sherry. Oh! How I savor the memory of the
times we shared your comfortable parlor! Those memories have
lived most vividly in my dreams. The time we spent together was
truly the one bright constant that kept me sane during the year
I languished in Whatley awaiting the pleasure of the Admiralty.

Other than the hurricane we encountered two weeks out of
Portsmouth, our weather has been quite delightful: favorable
winds, relatively calm seas, and only a few rain squalls accom-
panied by the attendant strong breezes. Europa *has managed to*
take all of it right in stride, slogging along at her slow, stately
pace. We arrived in Port Royal only a few weeks later than
anticipated, but that, of course, was from the complete lack of
a breeze initially and then the aforementioned hurricane which
cost us dearly in time. First to repair the damage to Europa, *then*
to find and regroup our charges.

We never did discover the merchant brig Helen G, *which dis-*
appeared without a trace or any notice during the storm; none
of the merchants nor any of the escorting Royal Navy ships could
offer a clue as to what happened. My guess – and it's only a
guess – is that she foundered in the storm and is lost with all
hands. A real tragedy, but sadly, one of the hazards of our
profession, both military and civilian. So sadly, we brought
in our charges short one. Only five of them remained here in
Port Royal, the others headed off with a new shepherd to other
islands where England has interests and need for supplies.

I had been given to understand that this vessel, Europa,
would be returning to England with the next convoy leaving
Jamaica, but now it appears that the commodore will keep her
here as his flag ship. I can sympathize with the officers aboard
as they will unlikely spend much time at sea whilst carrying the

commodore. The sailors, on the other hand, will undoubtedly enjoy the time in port, as it means a good deal less work for them! Of course, she must go into the Dockyards first to replace the jury-rigged foretopmast we – I should say the bosun and carpenter and their men – fit at sea using a spare main yard. The other damage we suffered from the storm will have to be repaired before the commodore, Adm. Ford, hoists his pennant aboard. I am given to believe that that will occur sooner than later.

As you may recall, I have been ordered to report into HMS Penelope *as 2nd lt. upon arrival here in Port Royal, but sadly, she is out on patrol and as yet, I have discovered no intelligence concerning when she might return. I suspect it will depend upon her assignment and her luck in encountering French shipping, both of a commercial character as well as naval. Hopefully, it will be soon, as I would like to move into my new responsibilities as quickly as ever I might. While I am quite comfortable here in this floating cathedral, I pine for the speed and excitement of a frigate, especially if there is a chance at finding some of those French devils and taking a prize or two. That is what we must do to bring an end to the conflict between our two nations! (And the prize shares will not be unwelcome either!)*

I am being called on deck now for some reason, so will lay this aside and conclude it when possible. I am hopeful of getting it into the next ship leaving for England, so that it will not be six months before you receive it. So for now, my sweet, au revoir.

Well, here I am again! I was called topside, yesterday, to witness a most pleasant sight: three ships entering the roads and coming to anchor off the naval dockyard here. One of them was my future home, Penelope! *(which was why my mates had called me up to witness their arrival.) She looked some cut up but that was explained when we espied the ship following her was showing the Union Jack above* the *French* tri-colour! Penelope *and her consort had taken a prize, a fine, sleek frigate, which should provide a nice purse in prize shares for all hands. Of course, not for yours truly as I was not on board, sadly. The prize had a bit of a battered look about her and I gleaned from my observation that the conflict must have been hotly contested! The other English frigate,* Iphigenia, *brought up the rear of the little parade and looked reasonably unscathed. I am sure there is a story there, which I will discover, I suspect, once I have reported to my new commander. I wonder how long it will take for the dockyard here to put* Penelope *to rights. I pray not overly long as I am not interested in remaining in this pest hole of disease, lewd behavior, and drunkenness any longer than is necessary!*

And speaking of drunkenness etc., last evening several of us, including Lieutenant Williams went ashore in search of some diversion – innocent diversion, I hasten to add! You may recall my mention of Lieutenant Williams in my previous letter; it was he whose responsibilities Captain Fitzgerald had requested that I assume while he suffered from a mysterious malady en route. He now seems restored to perfect health. Either through the ministrations of the good surgeon and his potions or simply with the passage of time, the man seems to have made a remarkable recovery. Captain Fitzgerald was somewhat skeptical of his sudden return to robust health, just a day out of Jamaica, but there was little he could do about it. I gave him back his division (quite happily, I might add) and returned to my previous "duties" of supernumerary. A pleasant respite from duty if only for a day or two! Now where was I? Oh yes, our excursion ashore.

Several of us found a pleasant – or so we thought – tap room where we might enjoy a pint or two, followed by a meal of anything other than salt beef, dried peas, and biscuit. (That meal was our norm most days for the past week and more as the fresh provisions were either spoilt or consumed and the barnyard of chickens, goats and several hogs had failed to survive the hurricane.) The first part went well: we were served by a pleasant mulatto lady who smiled and spoke in an island dialect we struggled to comprehend. Quite unlike your sister Hillary in every way! As we enjoyed tankards of the local rum – very tasty, I might add – the establishment began to fill up with officers from other ships, and a handful of sailors and some civilians, which I collect were from the dockyard. Needless to say, the atmosphere changed quickly and quite drastically, going from the quiet almost empty public house to a packed, noisy, and somewhat rowdy room. And then the ladies – or, I should say, women of seemingly easy virtue appeared.

Loud, garishly painted, and in every tone of the race, from nearly white to dark as night, they strolled in accompanied by the hooting and whistles of the throng of men. Except of course, our little group who, for the most part, was, to a man, horrified and remained mute. But as we were seated at a table, several of the newly arrived women espied us quick as ever you please and made their way directly to us. Apparently our status as officers and our quiet demeanor identified us as newcomers and, dare I suggest, 'easy-pickings' for them! Two of them dragged up chairs and, uninvited, joined us, suggesting we should buy them tankards of the fine rum we had been enjoying. Two others stood, edging their bodies close aboard, and offering suggestive comments that, in their minds, might lead to further "companionship" and the likelihood of a few coins for them!

Well, my dear Kendall, I can tell you even your sister, Hillary, would have been shocked at this unseemly behavior. Our second lieutenant, Jason Carden, labeled them at once the "poxie-doxies" assuming as did we all, that our visitors most likely carried all manner of disease, the type of disease that would be treated by a naval surgeon in a most painful manner employing mercury and large syringes. I shudder at the thought! Three of us were for leaving immediately, but young Jack O'Hara, our fourth lieutenant, inexperienced in the wiles and ways of fallen women, insisted on remaining, if only for a short while, "just to see what may happen," as he so naïvely put it. We assumed that he had little interest in participating in the festivities, that his curiosity related only to observing the antics of the men in the room as the spirits (both liquid and human!) flowed in excess. In hindsight, it appears we quite misjudged the young man.

It did not take long to satisfy his curiosity – at least in part. Men full of ardent spirits and too few women to handle their needs – imagined or otherwise – seem to offer a host of opportunity for all manner of trouble and within less than the turn of one glass, there was a shouted curse followed by a bottle flying through the air. Which, almost before it crashed into the wall, was followed by several others. Shouts, names, and curses in both deep voices and higher pitched ones raised a devil of a ruckus. We were quickly surrounded by drunken men, fighting each other for the privilege of squiring one of the poxie doxies, many of whom, including the ones who had unceremoniously joined us, were swinging bottles, chairs, and fists as freely as *the men! One of the women suddenly sprawled across our table, knocked temporarily insensible by a bottle to the head, and lay in some* dishabille *to the delight of young O'Hara. Watching his expression change provoked a gale of laughter from the rest of us: his eyes grew large as saucers and his mouth hung agape as he tried, unsuccessfully, to tear his eyes from the young woman's immodest display. That all of our tankards suffered from her unseemly and ill-timed arrival caused us some considerable consternation and Carden and I decided it would be an appropriate time to take our departure. Young O'Hara resisted our urgings to leave until one of the women, apparently under the assumption that he was responsible for the condition of her cohort, still lying in decadent splendor on our table, knocked him soundly on the head with a pewter tankard, fortunately empty. While it did not render him senseless, it did inspire him to take flight and he quickly joined the rest of us in leaving! We laughed for some time the remainder of the evening about his youthful behavior, and, after a while, even he saw the humor in it.*

A second establishment provided that which we had sought in the first, namely some fine spirits and decent food. We managed to provide our own entertainment with quiet and, I might say, civil conversation, part of which centered on young O'Hara's naiveté, all good for further laughs. After an hour or so, two lieutenants strolled in and sat near at hand, carrying on a conversation that we could not help but overhear.

They were discussing the value of the French frigate their ship had recently taken and what the prize shares might amount to when the court condemned her and, presumably, she would be purchased into the Royal Navy. I could not help but lean back to better hear their conversation since it seemed apparent these chaps were stationed in my future ship.

I had to ask. "Excuse me, gents. Would you happen to be from Penelope?"

Well, my dear, they both looked up and inquired as to why I would think that and who was I to ask in any case. I explained away their concerns and they at once confessed that yes, they were indeed from Penelope, *and yes, they had taken the French frigate whose arrival into Port Royal I had witnessed. Then they joined us in a spirit of bonhomie and, I think, the hope we might be persuaded to buy their drinks. That did not happen, (in fact, in consideration of their promised new-found solvency, they actually bought us some drinks!) but we passed a quite pleasant evening with them, heard all about the capture, and learned why the other British ship seemed mostly unscathed in the action. (She had arrived late to the action, only firing a few shots and apparently receiving even fewer! All to the delighted gloating of the Penelopes.)*

We made our stumbling way back to Europa only slightly worse for wear and encountered the surgeon in the gun room, with whom we enjoyed one final taste before retiring for the night.

Which is what I must do now my sweet. In the morning, I will try to find an outbound vessel that might carry this to you with my love.

Edward

CHAPTER SIX
Mid-December 1793
Port Royal, Jamaica

Since I had made the acquaintance of some officers in *Penelope,* I decided to visit the ship to see for myself how badly she might be cut up and make a leg to the commander. Since I still remained a supernumerary in *Europa,* I had no obligation to seek permission, only to beg a ride ashore in one of the cutters that plied the waters to and from the Dockyard with dispatches, official correspondences, and officers seeking a respite from the day's duties. I suspect Lieutenant Winthrop was only too glad to have me begin the process of moving bag and baggage elsewhere and he promptly approved my seat in the next shore-bound boat.

Once ashore at the boat landing, I glanced about at the ships alongside and the veritable beehive of activity all around. Carts and sledges hauled all manner of lumber, spars, cordage, and supplies from an unseen site inland to the piers. The carts were drawn mostly by horse or mule, while many of the sledges were hauled by human strength alone in the form of colored men, muscled to a fault and sweating profusely in the tropical sun. They sang, much as our sailors do to find a rhythm when walking about the capstan, in words that were unintelligible to me but with a melody at once repetitive and unforgettable. I watched and listened to the busy noise and singing, the creak of wheels, shouts of muleteers to their charges, and steady pounding of someone driving tre'nails or spikes into the side of a ship near at hand. The smell of freshly tarred cordage, new canvas, and paint filled the air. I smiled to myself as the aroma harkened me back to when I last had smelt it, and I recalled the pleasant memories of my last visit in England. I am sure Kendall and Hillary would be less than delighted to know that the aroma of Stockholm tar and canvas called to my mind images of the two of them!

"Mind yer back, there sor. Don't want to run you down, now do we," an English voice, belonging to a civilian worker, shouted as he guided some Negroes dragging a well-laden sledge through the unpaved street behind me.

I stepped out of the way, marveling, as I watched them go by, at the strength of these colored men and the apparent ease with which they moved what was obviously a heavy load. They had ropes over their shoulders which were protected by a folded bit of cloth and they leaned forward into the task. Their work song and the aromas that filled the air, mingled with that of honest sweat, became stronger as their load passed. I wrinkled my nose and took a step backward, ostensibly to ensure I was out of their way, but hoping to put a bit more breathable air between us. I found the dockyard smells pleasant; the emanations from the haulers less so!

Once they passed, I crossed the boulevard (if a path barely wide enough for two carts to pass could be called such) and tried to determine which of the vessels alongside might be my new home. I spotted the French prize quickly – the English flag still showing above the French one caught my eye immediately – and I figured the British frigate would be nearby.

It took me not a moment to discover the whereabouts of *Penelope*, recognizable from her jury-rigged headrig and abundance of men aloft. I walked carefully down the quay, minding my step and staying out of the way of the workers and sailors hurrying to and fro. A ladder offered access aboard, and I stepped onto the deck, struggling to recall the name of at least one of the officers I had met the preceding evening. No sooner had I passed through the bulwark onto the deck, than an officer, vaguely familiar, greeted me. We exchanged salutes, and, to my surprise, he called me by name.

"Ah! Good morning, Mister Ballantyne. A pleasant evening it were last night, what? I took the liberty of mentioning to Mister Ware, our first lieutenant, this morning that Goodwin and I had encountered you last night. I hope you don't mind! I thought, as you were assuming my position, it should not present a problem."

Then it came to me: Jack Farnsworth, *Penelope's* current second lieutenant and the man I would replace. "Not a bit, Jack. I collect he was not dismayed to be losing such a fine officer?"

I had no idea if he was "a fine officer" but thought a bit of varnish might be in order.

"I suspect he'll be glad to be shed of me," he smiled broadly at my obviously transparent effort. "We have not always got on so well."

Hmm. Am I going from the pot into the fire? I have been living under a disagreeable first lieutenant for some six weeks, but at least I knew that was temporary. Now, I am to be permanently assigned under one? Have to try and find out a bit more about this chap!

"Oh?" I offered, hoping my surprised expression and imprecise response might elicit more than the vague commentary already shared.

Farnsworth lowered his voice and cast a look about us before he spoke. We were along for the moment.

"Well, a bit of a stickler now, isn't he. As I mentioned last night, he's a bit eager as well. Always trying to be a jump ahead of everyone, even Cap'n Rowley. And not always well thought out. Often just blurts out his thoughts without which he might have allowed us not to think him the fool, if you take my meaning. You will recall, I am sure, that I told you last evening, it was he who advocated waiting until *Iphigenia* caught up before we engaged the Frog. Thank goodness the cap'n scotched that idea. They'd have only been a bother and in the way. Rowley – now there's a fine fellow and able. A right fair cap'n on top of it."

I had a dim recollection of his mention last night of the decision not to wait for *Iphigenia* to come up, but the details seemed lost in the haze of the great quantities of drink we all had consumed. I wondered briefly how Farnsworth had recalled it so easily.

He's been living it the past two or three years, you dolt! He didn't have to recall what was said last night.

"Hmm. Well, that's a bit of a sticky one, isn't it. Any suggestions as to how to deal with him?"

"Not a one, Edward, not a one. Been managing to keep my distance over the past year and more. We all keep hoping his relative at Whitehall – I am told it's his wife's sister's husband – will find him a nice brig to command and let another gunroom deal with him!" Farnsworth smiled sadly knowing I would have to live with this buffoon for the foreseeable future. "Come below. I'll introduce you to whomever might be around. One bit of good news: the first lieutenant is ashore on some errand or other. It must be of a pleasant nature or he would have sent Goodwin or a midshipman!"

And so, off we went, Farnsworth in the lead, to a hatch and down to the gun deck. Eighteen-pounders, sixteen to the side, crouched in silent menace to any who dared offer offense to the Royal Navy or King George – as the officers and men in *L'Inconstante* so recently discovered! One carriage had been badly damaged and its gun was lying on the deck beside it, with two sailors hunched over it.

"That's one for the scrap yard, I fear. Took a French ball right through the gunport. Killed two of the crew, wounded another unfortunate soul. We'll have a replacement aboard, quick as ever, along with one to replace one of the bow chasers that suffered injury." Farnsworth offered when he noticed me looking at the wreckage.

"One of the mids caught one dead on, he did. Took his head clean off!" He added almost as an afterthought, then continued to describe the injuries suffered by *Penelope*. He continued to walk, talking over his shoulder.

"Bowsprit took one, same as the bow chaser done; jib boom got a bit splintered but the carpenter got that fixed up Bristol right quick. Bowsprit's another matter and'll have to be replaced. Took a couple into the hull right at the waterline. Fothered it pretty well, but she'll have to be careened rather soon to repair that damage. I imagine we'll be hauled over to the careenage in the next day or two – or as soon as the work aloft is done. And we'll need half a dozen and more seamen to replace the ones wounded too bad to work and of course, the few what got killed."

Hmmm. Looks as though I will have an ample supply of headaches to occupy my time once I report in. Unlikely Jack and his lads will have this put to rights all that quickly.

As we moved aft toward the gunroom, he pressed on, describing the devastation suffered by the defeated French frigate. He spoke as though he were ticking items off a shopping list and quite without a shred of emotion. "Mizzen topmast shot to pieces, rig cut up right nicely, mainyard in several pieces, two or three carriage guns destroyed, foremast holed below the partners, and twenty and more of her sailors and officers badly wounded or killed outright. Including the captain – lost an arm, he done. Surgeon just lopped it off right there in the cabin. Saw it my own self, and let me tell you, Edward, almost caused me some embarrassment when I saw that arm and hand lying there in a pan on deck fresh cut off! Damn! A sight it was!" He produced a small white handkerchief from his sleeve and wiped at his mouth, as though simply the thought of it could again 'cause him some embarrassment.'

He caught his breath and went on. "Blood and bits of flesh lying about the deck surely upset the young fourth lieutenant I had in tow – Goodwin, you met him last evening. A grisly sight it was indeed. But the captain's wound...most distressing!"

"Good morning. Mister Farnsworth. Who might this fellow be?" An officer, lieutenant by rank, headed us off just as we were entering the passageway past the officers' quarters which would take us to the gunroom.

I looked carefully at the man in the gloom of the half-light reflected from the gundeck and from a few pursers' glims stationed about. To say his was not the most handsome countenance I had ever beheld would be beyond kind! His chin appeared to have dribbled down his face and fetched up just below his mouth. There seemed to be no form or substance to it – just a lump of flesh hanging there, an afterthought. His nose was a misshapen bit of clay stuck randomly below his eyes, molded without expertise, and seemed to be barely more than an extension of his cheeks. He likely had seen some brawling, I suspect, in his younger days judging by the form taken by his oddly shaped nose! But his eyes – oh my! Deeply set into his face, they were dark in color and surrounded by darkened patches of skin (had he been burned at some point?); his eyes seemed to never be still, but at the same time, bore into whatever he studied – which just then, was me. Bushy eyebrows on an overhanging brow topped off the nightmare that was his face. At least his hat would not fall down over his eyes! I am sure the poor light did little to improve his appearance!

"Good morning, Mister Ware. I had been given to believe that you had gone ashore on an errand. May I present my friend, Edward Ballantyne. He is the officer who will be replacing me. Lieutenant Ballantyne, our first lieutenant, Stephen Ware."

I straightened up and doffed my hat in a proper salute, which was summarily returned. Ware grunted a terse greeting, but seemed little interested in furthering his acquaintance with me. Likely knew it would happen soon enough when I reported into the ship. For now, his focus lay on Jack.

"Oh yes, Farnsworth. I recall the captain mentioning you were expecting a transfer. Have you your orders?"

"I would imagine they will appear when our mail catches up to us here in Port Royal, sir. Hopefully, before Christmas!" Jack shrugged his shoulders.

"Naturally, you'll be expected to remain aboard and do your duty until such time as they arrive.

"Lieutenant Ballantyne, perhaps you can stay wherever it is you are currently employed until we send for you. Wouldn't do to have extra officers aboard. Just get in each other's way, now, wouldn't it? Nice to have met you. I would imagine we'll be seeing more of you shortly." Ware nodded once and marched off in pursuit of whatever errand had been his earlier intention.

Farnsworth looked after him, turned to me, and smiled. He kept his voice low. "Well! I am sure that was a distinct pleasure for you! Gives you a bit of a look at what's over the horizon, what?"

I had nothing to offer in reply. We continued on our earlier mission and quickly entered the gunroom, currently occupied by two others, deep in conversation.

"Gentlemen: may I present Lieutenant Edward Ballantyne, recently arrived in our tropical paradise in *Europa.* He will be assuming my duties as quick as ever my orders turn up." He stopped, looked at me, and winked. "Can't have too many officers stumbling about getting in each other's way. Just wouldn't do, now would it."

"That bit had to have come from Ware! He's not above shooting his mouth off that way." A weary looking chap, thin to the point of being gaunt, a couple of days of stubble gracing his cheeks, and with glasses perched on the end of a longish nose, glanced up at us, smiled, and stood. "Nice to meet you, Lieutenant. I am sure you'll be enormously happy in His Britannic Majesty's frigate *Penelope,* scourge of the Caribbean, tormentor of the French, and invincible in every way! Henry McMahon, at your service." He stuck out a delicate hand, which I took in my own and gave him a firm shake.

The sleeves of his none-too-clean shirt were rolled to his elbows exposing corded but thin forearms; the shirt was open at the neck and his stock hung loosely, untied. A few tufts of white fur showed at his throat adding credence to his obviously advanced age. Thinning white hair and a lined face capped off the old fellow's look. His eyes, light blue, they were, fairly twinkled with good humor, and I smiled at the sight.

Old body, young eager eyes! The man is not as old as he looks. Must have seen some "interesting" service.

His somewhat unkempt appearance broadened my smile which I immediately tried to suppress, thinking it better to remain somewhat professional at this point. Nonetheless, I could not totally hide my joy at the casual atmosphere these men enjoyed in *Penelope.* Yes, I thought, I might be happy here, Lieutenant Ware notwithstanding!

"Henry is our surgeon. Rarely does he do much beyond sit here in the gunroom, offering to any who will lend him an ear, the wisdom of his many years. On the rare occasion when his services are called upon, he is quick with his knife and saw, usually out of laudanum, and unsympathetic to the screaming that accompanies his ministrations." Jack's description drew a nod and smile from the doctor.

"You forgot to add, Jack, that he's always generous in sharing his spirits with those suffering from an overdeveloped thirst and a paucity of supply," Henry shot back. Farnsworth grinned, ignoring the jibe, obviously directed at himself.

Definitely good men! I confirmed my earlier surmise that I would like these chaps! *Seems to be a camaraderie here that I will enjoy.* I now gave in and smiled broadly at the repartee.

"And this young lad you may recall from last night, Edward." Jack turned to the young man sitting across the table. "William, I reckon you'll remember Edward. He was the fellow who caught you just before you hit the deck in the Broadside Public House last night."

"Oh yes. Of course I remember Mister Ballantyne...and I stumbled, or rather tripped. I was not as drunk as you think I might have been," the fourth lieutenant blurted out, but a crimson face offered testimony contrary to his words! So much for not embarrassing him!

"And I remember you, Mister Goodwin. I am sure you were not a bit more than muzzy - as were we all! An entertaining evening it was indeed! I trust we will have the opportunity to revisit it in the future!" I extended my hand in greeting, smiled, and tried my best to put the young man at ease.

I visited with them for a while, then the good doctor suggested, as it was now well past time midday, that we find a convenient establishment ashore and enjoy our meal there. The third lieutenant would be overseeing the civilian workers and holding the watch, so he would remain aboard. I did not have the opportunity to accomplish my original mission – meeting Captain Rowley – as he was ashore, paying a visit to Admiral Ford. Time enough for that later…tomorrow, or perhaps, the next day.

The next week and more passed slowly; work progressed on *Penelope* at a snail's pace. She was dragged to the careenage, hauled down, and work begun on her wounded hull. Their French prize, *L'Inconstante,* was refit faster, as most of her damage mostly was confined to her topsides and rig. A replacement foremast had delayed the proceedings a bit, but one was now in place and fairly swarmed over by riggers, fitting it out with new shrouds and stays. I later discovered the need for haste, but at the time, was unaware that Admiral Ford had plans for her.

After being adjudicated a fair prize by the Admiralty Court, the ship was installed as a vessel of the Royal Navy in the usual piecemeal fashion, to wit: the ship itself – the hull and rig – was purchased for the Admiralty by the Naval Storekeeper, while the ordinance, stores, powder, and shot were purchased by the Office of Ordinance. The comestibles – water, wine, beef, and other foodstuffs – were purchased by local Jamaican merchants for varying prices as the market suggested, ultimately to be sold back to the navy at a decent profit. The whole process was accomplished in fewer than two weeks, and she was read into the service under her French name. She was listed, as one might expect, as a "12-pounder, thirty-six gun frigate."

L'Inconstante's twelve-pounder guns presented a small problem for the Port Royal armorer. Royal Navy frigates generally carried eighteen-pounders and the Dockyards in Jamaica did not stock twelve-pound iron shot. What shot was found in the magazine aboard the ship would answer for a while, but obviously more would be required at some point.

The yard workers completed her repairs, spruced up her paint, and rove new running rigging as necessary – mostly replacing that which had been hastily knotted and spliced at sea following the battle. As Christmastime approached, the ship was pronounced ready for sea, save for a crew.

Commodore Ford appointed Post Captain John Lawford, to command her. Joseph Bogue, an Irishman, but capable nonetheless, was named first lieutenant. My friend from *Penelope*, Jack Farnsworth, would be her second lieutenant, ordered there by none other than Commodore Ford, his recently arrived orders from the Admiralty in Portsmouth be damned! William Earnshaw would sail as third lieutenant.

I assumed my new position in *Penelope*, replacing Jack as originally planned, and found the ship in fine shape, especially following the recent repairs. Much of her rigging had been replaced, gunports refit, bulwarks and bowsprit rebuilt, and several guns and carriages hoisted aboard and manhandled into position forward and on the gundeck where the previous ones had been wrecked by enemy fire. The hull forward was now tight and strong with new futtocks and planks where French shot had wounded the hull at the waterline.

Jack and I met often to discuss our ships, enjoy a taste of the local rum, and share stories and tales heard about the waterfront. I found him a veritable fount of information about my new ship and, especially, my new shipmates – intelligence I hoped would be helpful in not only doing my job, but in dealing with the foibles of the men I would become associated with.

One evening, as we supped in a quiet public house, he had shed his usual cheerful countenance and clearly wished to discuss his own problems. We drank sparingly, ate less, and talked most. He had little interest in gossip from Penelope, instead, turning the topic to that which preoccupied his mind.

"We need a crew, Edward. We can't sail the bloody ship with four officers, a couple of midshipmen, some servants, and an invalided cook. It was one thing for Ford to gather a few officers from other ships in port, but finding two hundred twenty sailors – especially some that actually know a mainyard from a spanker boom – is turning into a problem. We can't dither on this…we already have a mission! No time to wait for men to be ordered here from England. Leaving, we are, in January, to escort a large convoy to Europe." Jack was becoming overwrought. "I may be stopping by *Penelope* and any other vessels in the harbor to 'borrow' a few hands. I hope you won't object too strenuously!" He had the good grace to smile as he warned me he might be stripping my crew right out from under my nose!

Then he smiled more broadly at my reaction. Once again solemn, he continued. "Seriously, Edward, I know Commodore Ford has requested the Jamaica Council – that's their Executive Council, you know – to authorize him to impress men for his needs – our needs. I am given to understand they have agreed as long as we don't take landsmen or too many men from any one ship. We can't interrupt trade here; that's sacrosanct. And we're limited to two hundred fifty souls. I'll be damned if we can collect that many, but should we, you might find a few in *Penelope* as replacements for the ones what got killed in the recent engagement. Lawford has already said he will only need two hundred twenty. God alone knows how we're going to press that many without affecting the traders hereabouts. Or taking landsmen."

As if he had suddenly run out of complaints about the ship and crew – or lack thereof – Jack changed the subject abruptly. Maybe he was trying to distract me from dwelling on his forthcoming raid on my crew!

"The commodore renamed her, you know, Edward. She's HMS *Convert* now. Seems there was already an *Inconstant* in the Royal Navy – though why anyone would actually name a ship that quite escapes me. But *Convert* she is and will be for all time – or at least until she winds up in the knacker's yard, or God forbid, on the bottom! I certainly hope the ship and we might convert some Frenchies to a gloomy English prison hulk and soon. The run I've had on the Jamaica Station has sapped my purse; some prize shares would be right helpful to my potential pecuniary embarrassment, notwithstanding the benefit I – and the other Penelopes – derived from our capture last month. Those funds settled the debt I had already incurred but left precious little for future expenses." He smiled at his plight, a predicament most navy men have all experienced at one time or another.

"Little did I expect to be serving in our prize. But here I am. And a fine vessel she is. Those Frenchies may not be much on fighting – though these particular lads gave it a real go – but they surely can build a fine, sweet sailing ship! I just wish she had some decent guns. Those little twelve-pounders aren't much against the eighteens our frigates carry. I reckon the fact that she has thirty-six of 'em somewhat makes up for the light shot she throws.

"Course, gettin' sailors aboard to man the guns is my biggest problem right now."

Hmm. He's back on the crew plight again. Maybe I should just invite him over to select whomever he fancies. Or, better, perhaps I'll just round up a clutch of them and march them right over to L'Incon...Convert! *That'll be the day! Right likely, that!*

"Say, Jack. In the spirit of friendship and cooperation, why don't I just muster my lads aboard *Penelope* and you can come and select those you would like." I smiled. I think he actually thought I was serious at first – right up until I began to laugh at his expression.

"Damn you, Ballantyne. You had my little heart just tripping over itself in glee! That was surely a mean-spirited thing. You're going to have to buy the next round to make amends for such dastardly behavior."

"Me? Buy the next round? Surely you are jesting, Farnsworth. I am not the one who just reaped the benefit of a fine prize and the fattening of my purse. But never for a moment think I shan't appreciate your generosity!" We both laughed at our own cleverness and ordered the young barmaid to supply us with additional pewters, to the detriment of our individual sobriety.

The next morning, our first lieutenant, Mister Ware, announced at breakfast that the denizens of the gunroom – us officers in *Penelope* – had been invited to a Christmas gathering at the home of a local planter, a Mister Ebenezer Malloy. Mister Malloy, it seemed, in the weeks immediately preceding Christmas, traditionally fêted naval officers at his home with a lavish feast and celebration. The affair would take place in two days' time, carriages would be sent for us, dress uniforms with swords and medals (for those who could boast of such) required.

I inquired if the party included only our officers or if others would be in attendance as well.

"Did I not say, Mister Ballantyne, that Mister Malloy wished to entertain *English naval officers?* Or did I say just the officers of *Penelope?* Apparently I did not make myself clear: *all* the naval officers from *all* the English ships in Port Royal are invited and most will likely be in attendance."

Actually you did not say that the first time.

"Thank you, sir. I understand." I smiled benignly.

One of the other officers – might have been the surgeon, if I recall – inquired about the likelihood of nubile English lasses being in attendance. He received a silent scowl, followed by a barely suppressed chuckle from several of us at the table.

Hmmm...the oldest amongst us is asking about...My my my!

The day's chores were carried out without incident. Working parties loaded provisions and stores for our forthcoming deployment, while shot and powder were brought out by a lighter dispatched from the Ordinance Office. Ashore, a gang was busy filling water casks and floating them out to the ship behind the blue cutter. Once alongside, the casks were hoisted aboard and sent directly below, where, under the watchful eye of the purser, they were stacked and lashed down so they would not shift in a seaway.

That evening, I took young Goodwin ashore with me to have a visit with his former boss. The fourth lieutenant was agog at the thought of the party at planter Malloy's home and the prospect of finding – and actually *talking* to – a few young ladies of proper society. He did mention to me that in all his visits ashore, so far, he had only trafficked with ladies of "less than noble birth," not to put too fine a point on it.

"I would imagine, Jack, you are planning to attend the soiree at Malloy's tomorrow evening?" I asked once we had found the chosen tavern, our friend, and a table. We ordered our usual tankards of rum. Food would wait a bit tonight.

"Wouldn't miss it, Edward. Went last year; it's a delightful evening: superb food, ample spirits – he makes his own from his own sugarcane, you know. Vastly superior to this barely adequate swill we take here! Young ladies are always invited and, with the prospect of an abundance of handsome and worldly officers of the Royal Navy – like us, always seem to be in excellent supply!"

Young Goodwin perked up at this, put down his tankard, swallowed, and studied his superior officer, no doubt assessing the risk of further questioning on the subject.

"Mister Farnsworth: are these 'young' ladies really young?

Or are they all the matronly wives of other local citizens?"

"William. First of all, you no longer work for me. When we're ashore in a social situation, you might call me Jack should you wish to. Secondly, the young ladies of whom I spoke are indeed young, some are the daughters of other planters, while some are, in fact, wives. But from my experience, it would seem that most are of the opinion that any opportunity for change should be embraced when found...if you catch my drift."

Goodwin, the beginnings of a smile crossing his face as his brain digested the words he had just heard, broke into a lascivious grin as the full impact of Jack's utterance bored into his consciousness. He didn't say anything – he didn't need to; we both saw his delight at the prospect of his 'prospects' the next evening! As he did not have a servant attending to his needs in *Penelope,* I made a mental note to lend him the services of my man Black to ensure he was turned out properly.

"But, young man, you must remember you are an officer of the King and comport yourself with dignity and aplomb...and discretion!" Jack smiled as he offered the sobering reminder. I don't think Goodwin even heard him, so intent was he on the thought of what the next night might bring.

The evening passed as usual – mostly quiet, but sometimes more boisterous with both the conversation and food amply seasoned with the flavorful spices of the Caribbean and, naturally, more than sufficient quantities of local rum to wash it all down. Goodwin and I staggered to the quay to find a boat that might take us out to *Penelope,* now anchored a musket shot from the wharf, while Jack wandered about the dockyard seeking his apparently missing ship, HMS *Convert.*

CHAPTER SEVEN
A week before Christmas, 1793
Port Royal, Jamaica

Overcast skies and sporadic showers did nothing to dampen the spirits of the nearly score of officers waiting on the quay for the promised carriages. Banter and gaiety was the order of the day and I took careful note of young Goodwin whose temperament ran the gamut from dour silence to barely contained joy and anticipation. And posturing. Mostly posturing...

He engaged other ships' officers in animated conversation with one hand resting confidently on the pommel of his sword and the other plucking nervously at the buttons – well-shined courtesy of Black – on his blouse. I tried not to eavesdrop, merely remaining aware of his position and attitude, but I could not help but overhear some of his more excited emanations.

"Quite a bash, this party. At least it was last year!" He exclaimed to a pair of midshipmen from another ship. Of course, they couldn't possibly know that he had not been here last year!

A bit later, to another lieutenant: "Bloody servant did a terrible job on my boots. Had to have him go over them again and again! Couldn't show up with dull leather, now could I? So difficult to find a good one, these days." His boots were done by Black, done once and done perfectly!

"Lieutenant, would you mind awfully stepping over here for a moment. I have something of the utmost urgency on which I need your advice." I took hold of his elbow, giving him no opportunity to resist.

"Oh, Lieutenant Ballantyne! How might I be of assistance?" He stepped cheerfully along until I judged we were out of earshot of our colleagues.

"Goodwin. Your prancing about like a damn popinjay will gain you nothing but trouble down the road. And trust me, you're not about to impress any of the lieutenants here. Perhaps the mids will be, but once they find out you have been filling their sails with bluster, you'll find yourself a laughing-stock." My voice was barely more than a whisper, but the tone and words conveyed clearly my sentiment. And were he to miss the import of the word, he could not miss the glare with which I fixed him.

"Remember that you are a *junior* officer and conduct your-self accordingly." I stopped, and took in his dismayed look. He looked about to cry! Had I been too harsh? I didn't think so.

Out of the corner of my eye, I noticed two of the carriages starting toward us. I raised my voice slightly. "Well, thank you Mister Goodwin, for that sage counsel; it will prove most helpful, I am sure. Oh! Here comes our transport. Let us see to getting aboard." I smiled as we walked casually to where the first carriage would be halting to accept passengers. I am sure Goodwin was at once stunned at my sudden course change and grateful that I had not embarrassed him in front of the others. And he did not cry. He did, however, make sure he rode in a different carriage than I!

The wet weather continued, with a drizzling rain, little more than a mist, settling over us, adding to the prodigious puddles already waiting to trap the unwary pedestrian, and putting a sheen on the backs of the two fine horses hitched to the carriage. It had little effect on the spirits of the officers assembled save to evoke a sentiment from some that the evening's festivities might be more entertaining were they under a roof of some stripe and the occasional curse from those who attempted in vain to maintain a fire on the stub of their cheroots.

I had not caught a glimpse of Jack Farnsworth, but I knew he would be attending. Perhaps a different carriage, one closer to where *Convert* was moored, would carry him and his fellows. I knew we would cross tacks once we arrived at Mister Malloy's plantation.

The ride, uncomfortably damp – there were no tops on our carriages – ran along the edge of the sea, following the lengthy causeway from the dockyards to the main part of the island. I had not realized, in my meanderings around the town, that Port Royal was so distant from the rest of the island. The carriage took us down a narrow spit of land with the sea barely a biscuit toss away on either side. It was perfectly flat, of course, puddled here and there with pools of indeterminate depth, which I was pleased to see the driver take pains to avoid. From time to time the pleasant colored chap at the reins would turn and point out some particular point in which seafaring men such as ourselves might have an interest.

"I sure you gen'men know we ridin' on what called the

Palisadoes. They tell me dat's Spanish. Means 'fort' or the like. Used to be one out here. Hung ol' Calico Jack Rackham right there, they done. Bad pirate he were, indeed. And them women – Ann Bonny and Mary Read, they was called – pirates as well! Musta been sixty, seventy years back, dat was." He pointed at a crumbling tower just to the waterside of the docks as he continued to muse to himself about the rarity of women pirates.

"Used to be a big town here. Aye, big. Always full of hustle and excitement. Pirates, booty, ships, women, taverns...aye, it was all here. Then 'bout a hunert years ago, de earthquake took it all. Dropped the whole town right into the harbor, it done. Wasn't much left, dey tell me after that, but what they was, got took by the big wave right after. Musta been sometin' ta see, I'd t'ink!" He continued. I can't speak for the others, but I was enthralled with his "tour" and kept shushing the revelers with whom I had the misfortune to share the coach.

He went on. "Built it back up, they done, but a *hurricano* come in and blow it all down, easy as kiss my hand. 'At was back in '74 or so. I recollect it good. Just got here my own self to work de cane when dat happen. Bad, she was. And scared outta my wits, I been. Never seen such a storm. But dem white folk, dey build 'er up again. Kept the dockyards for you navy folk, but den the fire come...place got de voodoo on 'er, you ask me. Reckon dem navy ships gonna be headin over to Kingston quicker 'an ever like ever'tin else round here. Want to get away from de spell." He stopped talking, shaking his head at the memories he had stirred up; then, after muttering some barely audible incantation – perhaps trying to cast off the demons and spells of Port Royal – he remained quiet, focused on his team. With skilled hands on the reins, he guided them off the causeway onto the track toward Kingston and the mountains beyond it.

Now on more solid ground, our worthy helmsman set his course to the northwest and, immediately, the road began to rise up, gaining the hills above Port Royal. We caught glimpses of Kingston, but as we climbed we quickly lost sight of the sea in the mists. Quite without warning, a crumbling tower loomed out of the clouds, close aboard to larboard.

"That's what folks call Fort Nugent it is. Tol' it been built by some white man to protect his property from de slave uprising.

Long time back, it were." He laughed. "Ain't nothing like that gonna protect him, we want to get to him! More o' us than dem, dat's for sure!" He turned around and looked at us, an almost-evil grin breaking out across his face. One of my fellow passengers laughed a nervous sort of laugh.

As he turned his attention back to his horses, the grin faded and he continued. "Sides, it's all mostly gone now, it is, like ol' Nugent, and that tower there is all that's left. But we still here. Hmmph!"

We continued up the hill, following the course of a stream that tumbled down the hill on our starboard hand. I doubt my traveling companions, even the somewhat nervous chap, noticed much of anything, so enthralled they were with their own cleverness. Our driver stayed focused on his team and offered no further illuminating commentary on the countryside; truth be told, there wasn't much beyond thick jungle-like vegetation to be seen. In spite of the excited anticipation about the forthcoming evening, I found myself dozing off. It was the gentle swaying of the carriage and the rhythmic, muted *plop* of the horses' hooves in the muddy roadway, or perhaps the droning conversation of my companions – or maybe all of these things – that caused me to drift off, wrapped in the warm damps of the tropical clime.

I dreamt. The carriage approached the entrance to the place we would be – it seemed some strange, what with overhanging boughs of indeterminate trees, noisy birds of bright plumage, and servants in multihued livery lining the path. The path itself was composed of sparkling stones and shells, twinkling in the pale light of a half-moon. Just inside the entrance my eye caught a glimpse of Kendall Smith, dressed in her traveling rig and flanked by her sisters, Hillary and Miriam.

Hillary was costumed in fine attire, ready for a fancy-dress ball or a royal audience. That she was not in her barmaid attire caused me to look twice at her. I had to look twice at Miriam to ascertain if it was truly her, as I had met her only once. She seemed to be wearing nightclothes, or something similar, of a dusky neutral color. They were laughing and gesticulating in obvious joy at some shared amusement. It seemed perfectly unsurprising to me that they should be in attendance.

"Good evening, ladies," I uttered as I approached them. "How nice to see you all together and enjoying this fine occasion."

The three studied me for a moment, serious expressions replacing the hilarity that had, only seconds before, brightened their faces.

"Good evening to you, as well, sir. You will find the other guests just there, through that entry." Hilary pointed somewhat vaguely to starboard where the dark passage gave way to a bright opening. I could see indistinct forms moving about within – whatever the space was beyond.

I ignored the barmaid, and her out-of-character cultured speech, and addressed her sister. "Kendall? It is I, Edward. You don't recognize me? How is it you are here in Jamaica? Why did you not tell me you would be here? And your sisters as well? What are..."

"Just pass through there, sir. Just there. Join the others, if you please." Again she pointed down the passageway. And Kendall remained mute. She neither smiled nor frowned, her expression gave nothing away.

I was dismayed that, after our relationship had grown so pleasantly in England during the year I awaited orders, she ignored me so perfectly. Her barmaid sister did so as well. I tried another tack.

"Hillary? Do you not recall me – Edward? The 'admiral', as you were wont to call me. Can you not remember the several afternoons in the taproom and the evenings that followed? They are indelibly imprinted on my memory. Remember? Your sister had returned to Portsmouth on her perpetual errand with the Admiralty, and you were kind enough to take me in so I would not have to make the trip back to Whatley. Surely you remember..." I stammered, *sotto voce,* one eye on Hillary, the other fixed firmly on Kendall. Again, no reaction from either.

"Just pass right on through there, Lieutenant. The others await your arrival." Hillary's voice, though with an educated tone, was exactly as I remembered it, soft and syrupy, coming from the back of her throat. But her stare was vague – unfocused, as though she were looking at something well beyond me.

Dismayed, I did as instructed; I stumbled through the passage into a brightly lit room, which seemed at once both indoors and, at the same time, outdoors. My thoughts swirled about, perplexed by the reaction – or rather, the lack of reaction – from Kendall and her sisters. It took me a moment to take in the confusing scene before me. Several sparkling chandeliers were suspended over a collection of tables and chairs, and what I took to be a huge carpet, with dozens of people milling about. I could not make out to what the heavy lamps were attached as when I peered upwards, I saw only sky – stars, moon, and clouds – above. Branches swayed gently, whispering in the night air, and brightly plumed birds flitted from one to another. I was speechless at the spectacle, and still quite befuddled at seeing Kendall and her sisters here in Jamaica.

A liveried servant approached me. It was my own faithful man, Black, presenting a tray of tall tankards for my consideration.

"Black! What are you doing here?" I thought I spoke the words, but heard nothing and neither, apparently, did Black.

He moved along, his tray held aloft, offering a tankard to each of the guests. I was aware of a chap standing near at hand and spoke to him.

"Mmmph uonmop, htuerhnhgg?" My mind heard the actual words quite distinctly, but what came out was some different!

The fellow spoke not a word, nor did he linger to hear more of my gibberish, but wandered off, listlessly toward the center of the room. I saw Jack Farnsworth and young William Goodwin talking with Captain Rowley and an officer with but one arm and wearing a French naval uniform. I set my course for them.

As I drew closer, I could see that the front of Jack's shirt and blouse were red with blood – fresh, by the look of it – with some still tracking down his front. He appeared oblivious to his condition. I, however, was horrified!

"Jack...Jack! What has happened to you? Why are you covered in blood?" I hastened my step in his direction.

My friend barely acknowledged my presence, glancing my way before turning back to his friends and continuing his conversation. His companions seemed equally ignorant of his condition.

They were conversing in French. I speak some French (really, what educated Englishman these days cannot speak at least *some* French!), so, trying a different tack, I bid them all a pleasant evening in plausible, if not perfect, French. They all looked at me much the same as did the fellow I had just left – as though I were speaking some unintelligible heathen tongue. I repeated myself, speaking more slowly and distinctly.

Nothing. No change in their expressions. And then they turned away from me and continued their conversation as though I did not exist! I was stunned...

"Lieutenant! We are here! Let us alight and see what is afoot!" A voice from my larboard called out.

At last! Someone who recognizes me as a proper English officer!

Overjoyed, I turned to see just whom I might thank. I was quite surprised to discover I was still in the carriage! Two of my fellow riders were attempting to crowd around me to disembark, while the chap next to me nudged me in the side and spoke from close aboard.

"Oh my, yes! Indeed. Let us alight!" He would never know how delighted I was to stumble out of the carriage and groggily follow the others into broad entranceway, filled with fragrant tropical flowers and people who laughed and spoke to me! And, while I did indeed look, I found no sign of Kendall, her sisters, or a blood-soaked Jack Farnsworth!

At least two dozen officers filled the room, speaking and chewing on bits of meats and sweetbreads being passed throughout. And not by Black! Our host stood by the door as we entered, shaking our hands and wishing us the joy of the season.

"A pleasure to meet you, Mister...uh, Malloy. A true delight to be included in your generous celebration! I am Edward Ballantyne, 2nd in His Majesty's frigate *Penelope*." I doffed my hat to him; he bowed and offered his hand, which I shook.

"Ah, *Penelope*. Recently took a plum prize off Santo Domingo, I collect. Must have been a rousing good time!" He chortled – a sound that seemed to emanate from the bottom of a rain barrel.

A large and imposing man, Mister Malloy was impeccably turned out in an off-white suit. His waistcoat, adorned with a gold chain, seemed to strain at its buttons around his mid-section. His face was quite flushed; perhaps from the heat or maybe from the excitement of the moment, but I did notice that moisture dribbled quite liberally down his cheeks, over the folds of flesh, and onto his collar. A pince-nez perched on the end of his bulbous nose caused him to lift his head up in order to examine the face of the person to whom he spoke. His several chins disappeared whenever he did so, but there remained considerable excess flesh overflowing his collar. When I looked into his eyes through the wrong side of his spectacles, they became overlarge and somewhat comic in appearance. I smiled at his welcoming gesture.

"So am I told, sir. I did not have the good fortune to be in the ship at the time. I am only just reported to this employment – arrived a few weeks ago from England in *Europa,* William Fitzgerald commanding. I am given to understand that the French prize has been read into our service as HMS *Convert.*"

"Yes, yes, quite so. Lawford's got her, I believe. Fine man, he is, and will do well with the command." Malloy smiled again, peered through his spectacles at my face as he did so, seeming to commit it to his memory. Without a further word, he dismissed me simply by turning his gaze to the next in line behind me. I moved along with the others.

We made our way through a large open room filled with tables of food, tankards of what I took to be rum or a fruit punch (none were being passed by Black or anyone else, for that matter!), and ladies and gentlemen nicely turned out. The men were both civilians – friends and neighbors of our host, I assumed – and naval officers. Beyond them, I could see the garden behind the house dotted in the bright colors of blooming flowers, all vying for attention. The burnished pewter sky seemed only to brighten the display, detracting not a whit from the joy and brilliance offered without. I grabbed a tankard from the table as I passed and headed out of doors; it seemed a trifle less confining. And to my joy, the rain had quit – at least for now!

We were well up the side of a mountain, the land terraced to hold Malloy's crop of cane, his gardens, and, of course, his splendid house. The mist hung below us, obscuring the view of the harbor – were we even facing in that direction? – and whatever else lay below us, giving one the feeling of being quite cut off from the rest of the world, high up in the clouds. I suspected that on a clear day, the view must be wonderful. Nonetheless, I was rapt in my contemplation of the beauty near at hand that surrounded me.

Very gently, something else attracted my attention; I was drawn from my reverie by a brilliant aroma – roasting meat and the attendant spices already made familiar to my senses by the few weeks I had spent in this tropical delight. I followed the scent along a path and discovered a firepit with an entire pig of some prodigious size suspended above it by an iron rod poked through and through. A Negro man, shoeless and shirtless – no doubt due to the heat of the fire – wearing canvas pantaloons that stopped mid-calf, stood to one side and slowly turned a crank that rotated the pig's carcass over the low fire. His shoulders flexed with the effort, rippling his shiny coffee-colored skin in rhythmic waves. Already the flesh of the animal was crinkly and dripping fat into the fire which aroused the flame to greater effort wherever the drops fell. The man noticed my approach and nodded in acknowledgment.

"That is wonderful! Smells perfectly splendid," I offered.

"Yassuh. Got a ways to go yet." The man smiled at my compliment and continued to turn the handle.

The fat sizzled and sputtered in the fire, little flames jumping up in a vain attempt to reach the roasting pig. The smell was mouth-wateringly delicious and I could not draw myself away.

Presently another man, also a Negro, also dressed in the same tattered canvas trousers and wearing a non-descript shirt with the sleeves ripped out, arrived carrying a basket. He spoke to his comrade working the spit in a dialect I had no hope of understanding and began to ladle a powdery substance from the basket onto the glistening pig. He distributed the mixture of aromatic spices across the whole carcass while the other chap continued to turn it round and round. The smell of spices and flowers became overpowering, but, at the same time, captivating. Some of the powder fell off and into the fire as the pig turned, causing little volcanoes of flame to shoot up, but the chap just ladled more on as fast as it fell off.

"Mister Ballantyne! There you are! Didn't see you topside and wondered where you might have got to. But then I smelled this delicious aroma and had to investigate. I should have known I'd find you here!" The first lieutenant of HMS *Penelope* was headed down the path under full sail. I had nowhere to escape to.

"Ah, yes, Mister Ware. The smell quite captivated me also.

Been watching these chaps here work their magic on what I assume to be our supper!"

"Aye, likely right. Have you tried this rum? I collect our host distills it here from his own cane. Very much superior to the swill we find in Port Royal, it is!"

In truth, while I had carried the tankard procured earlier in the house, I had been so enthralled with everything around me that I had yet to taste it. So I did.

"Yes indeed. It is a fine brew, to be sure. I hope some of the younger lads exercise some restraint with it. I suspect they might consume more than a day's ration!" I smiled, hoping that, with his all-consuming need to control everything, he would trot off to ensure none of the younger gentlemen became overly intoxicated. He did!

I continued to watch the two men season and turn the roasting pig as the dreary day gave up its struggle and succumbed to dreary night. The fire glowed and, in the different light, the pig carcass seemed to give off its own light as it reflected the fire's glow on its flanks. My mouth continued to water, and I pulled heartily on the tankard, finding the flavorful rum a pleasant addition to the other sensory delights.

Gradually, I became aware of the presence of more people in the garden just up the hill, and, taking a final draught of my pewter, made my way up to join them. They seemed to be enjoying themselves as snippets of laughter and female voices drifted down to me.

Several groups of officers, some midshipmen, and a gaggle of beautifully turned out ladies stood in clusters, each group in a pool of light cast by the seemingly unlimited oil lanterns resting on tables, hanging in trees, and suspended from tall poles stuck into the ground for that purpose. Each of the men, I observed, held a pewter tankard, while the ladies did not. Those members of the fairer sex who took spirits did so from a stemmed glass vessels. On a more careful perusal, however, I noticed that some of the younger ladies were, in fact, as handy with the pewters as were their male counterparts. Was it a coincidence that they drew a larger number of officers into their midst than did those ladies with the more dainty stemmed glasses? I think not!

Making my way across the lawn, I discovered my friend

Jack Farnsworth (and nary a trace of blood was visible!) in animated conversation with another officer – another lieutenant – while a pair of raven-haired ladies looked on. As I approached, I could see in the limited light that the ladies both wore horrified expressions; they fanned themselves vigorously, one with a handkerchief, the other with a proper fan. Ample décolletage invited the eye to stare, but the expressions they wore dragged one's eye right back to their pretty, but dismayed faces. The men's voices had grown loud and edgy, and each stood close to the other and pointed accusing fingers at each other's faces, perhaps accounting for the ladies' disquiet. There was obviously a serious confrontation underway, driven, I surmised, either by a surfeit of spirits or a conflict over who would squire the ladies for the evening – perhaps both. I worked my way through a couple of other groups and drifted into the backwater of Farnsworth's little cluster, straining to overhear their words. It was not necessary to strain my ears for long; their voices rose with their animus.

"...and you, sir, are simply an arrogant and, might I offer, an obnoxiously insufferable person. I could not be more glad that I do not have to share a gunroom table with you. In fact, it is hard to imagine why some contrived but fatal accident has not yet befallen you at sea!" Farnsworth was concluding what was obviously a lengthy bombast, standing close aboard and speaking his rant into the very face of his conversational opponent.

"I knew you would take an aggressive stance when first I encountered you. Your ship could no more have taken that Frog frigate alone than you could have taken flight. Though I truly wish you might have!" This remark drew muted giggles from the ladies.

He continued, unfazed by their reaction. "When you turned up aboard and tried to claim our victory as your prize, I actually mentioned to the young chap with me that you and your kind were trouble. Should you not retract your ill-conceived insult, you shall have to answer to the consequences. And I have several witnesses to your abuse.

"Ladies, I assume you will stand by my assertion that Lieutenant Farnsworth has viciously insulted me?" The officer looked from one lady to the other, his eyebrows raised, his lip curled in ill-concealed contempt.

"Well, sir, we did hear him offer an opinion which seems to differ somewhat from your own," one the ladies offered. "But I would surely be reluctant to suggest he 'viciously insulted' you." The one with the fan paused her fanning and spoke up. From the look of her companion, I gathered that they were in agreement.

"You – lieutenant – you must have heard this sorry excuse for a King's officer insult me?" The offended lieutenant was looking right at me, over Jack's shoulder. "You have been lurking there behind us for the past several minutes. Surely, it was long enough to have heard him disparage my character."

I stepped forward as Jack turned, having been heretofore unaware of my presence. "Well, sir. I did hear raised voices and what was obviously an argument about something, but I would be less than truthful were I to offer an opinion as to the character of Mister Farnsworth's comments."

"And you are?" The lieutenant, surprised that I knew his antagonist's name, stepped closer to me, placing himself abeam of Jack.

"I am Lieutenant Edward Ballantyne, sir. Second in His Majesty's frigate *Penelope*. Recently joined, in point of fact."

"Ah! The plot thickens! *Penelope,* eh? My assailant here is recently detached from *Penelope*. Perhaps you two are acquainted?"

"Indeed. And friends, as well." I smiled and nodded to Jack.

He drew himself up to his full height, about half a foot below my own, and in what I took to be a most haughty tone, offered, "I am Lieutenant Jonathon Jones, First in *Iphigenia*. I collect you were not in *Penelope* during the late action we are discussing, so I shall illuminate you. I am sure whatever you might have heard from any in *Penelope* is a quite distorted and inaccurate version that would favor their position.

"It was my ship's timely arrival at the scene that made it possible for us English to take the French frigate, *L'Inconstante*, as a prize. It was our highly accurate fire that ultimately disabled the Frenchman and most likely wounded their captain, provoking the surrender.

"Rowley's lot would have surrendered their own ship within an hour had we not arrived when we did. Consider, sir, that *Penelope* had received several shot below the waterline and was taking water furiously. Also that her rig and bowsprit were shot to pieces rendering her quite unable to maneuver. But this refugee from Bedlam expects me to believe that they might have accomplished a victory alone, and in fact, accused me on more than one occasion of 'getting in the way' and further, of trying to claim a prize to which we were not entitled. And, as recently as bare moments ago, he repeated the preposterous and insulting claim, impugning my ship, my crew, and myself with his slanderous remarks."

"You are a pompous ass, sir, and disagreeable on top of it. I think you have offended these ladies with your outrageous and rude remarks. I choose not to associate further with you." Farnsworth spat out his words, spun about, nodded to the ladies, and started to step off, leaving the sputtering Jones in his wake.

"Hold, sir. I cannot give you a pass on your rude insults. I am calling you out, Lieutenant Farnsworth, here and now, in front of these witnesses. I demand satisfaction." Jones had again raised his voice but was barely coherent, spittle flying from his mouth as he challenged my friend to a duel.

For my part, I was stunned...speechless. I had never witnessed such a display, even in the company of mutineers or survivors of shipwreck! Some standing near at hand had taken notice of the verbal brawl and were watching, smiling as though they anticipated fisticuffs; others stood motionless with mouths agape, clearly horrified at the display. But they all had one element in common: not a one uttered a word. Whether stunned speechless or eagerly anticipating further conflict I knew not; they held their collective breath, as did I.

"Accepted, sir. As the challenged party, it is my prerogative to select weapons, time, and place for satisfaction. My second will advise you of my choices in the morning. Good evening." Farnsworth nodded curtly, turned and, grabbing my arm, walked away.

"Jack! What the bloody hell have you done? This fool Jones has challenged you to a duel. You know nothing of his skills at pistols, swords, or anything else. What will you do?"

"Edward. I first took him to be drunk, but we have not been here long enough for him to get so intoxicated. I did meet him when we boarded the Frenchman last month; he was there before Goodwin and I arrived, in fact. Tried to claim the ship as *Iphigenia*'s prize the moment we stepped on the deck. This whole thing started then, and, while *I* had pretty much forgot it, apparently it has been festering in his bosom ever since. It is irrelevant who claims the prize from the standpoint of shares – each ship will receive the same and would have even had *Iphigenia* never fired a shot, as you no doubt know. But I never dreamed it would come to a duel.

"Nonetheless, he has challenged; so I must either apologize or accept. He is an arrogant ass and most likely would not accept my apology even were I to offer one. You heard my response to him; we will fight. I would be honored if you would agree to act as my second."

"Would it not act to your credit…What? You want me to *second you* in a duel? I know nothing of the art of dueling! How can I possibly perform such a task? Would it not, as I started to say a moment ago, be of benefit to you – and the Service – if you were to apologize? Say you understand there was a surfeit of ardent spirits involved and that it is likely you both acted rashly? Show yourself to be the bigger man. I can carry your response to him in the morning to save you the possible embarrassment, if you wish."

"No, Edward. That will not answer; I will fight, and I would still like to name you as my second. You have only to perform those duties as necessary, which is to say, act in my stead for communications and see to the weapons I select. It is not difficult."

In spite of my protestations, I did know something about dueling, but never from first-hand experience. I had been witness to a duel in my first ship, as a lowly midshipman. And I was more or less aware of the duties of the second.

On some level – it was not a subject to which I had devoted a significant amount of thought – I understood the second's job was to organize the duel, ensure, with the other second, that the weapons were of equal measure and, perhaps most distressing, should my principal fail to perform, I would be expected to take his place. I had never dreamed I would have to act in that capacity, and did not relish the idea of doing so now.

I tried again.

"Jack, I can see to your requirements as you wish. But I can as easily give him your apology as I can your choice of weapons,"

I offered hopefully.

Jack shook his head, his mind clearly firm in its resolve. "No, Edward. I will not apologize to that bloody, arrogant fool. As I said before, I doubt he would be likely to accept it. I am sure, in his self-inflated opinion of his prowess, he will best any who goes against him with any choice of weapons. I think we should get it done more quickly than not and so I am thinking that tomorrow evening on the strand in Port Royal would answer perfectly. Don't you agree?"

"If you wish, Jack. So be it. I will make the arrangements in the morning, as soon as you decide on your weapons." What could I say? The man was my friend and had asked me to second him in his foolishness.

"Splendid, Edward! And thank you. Now let us partake of some this brilliant food they are offering and perhaps another tankard of the fine rum Mister Malloy makes right here on his plantation. What happened to those two ladies I was entertaining before I was so rudely interrupted?"

Jack looked around, did not see his consorts of mere moments ago – *how could they have escaped so quickly?* Dismissing them out of hand, he made his way toward the sideboard, quite casually, I thought, for a man about to engage in what would likely turn out to be a fatal duel...for someone. I followed him and we both carried on to a table groaning under the weight of wonderful, colorful culinary delights. The exotic aromas alone – the identification of them was well beyond the capabilities of my palate – were almost sufficient to ease my concerns. But still they lurked, hiding in the fog of additional spirits, making the occasional lurch into the forefront of my conscious and allowing me to think there was still a hope of distracting my friend from the course he had selected. I resolved to continue my efforts during the remainder of the evening, as long as we both remained somewhat lucid.

The festivities continued in spite of the desultory drizzle; Negro slaves with various talents appeared dressed in interesting costumes to sing their songs and dance while accompanying themselves on locally constructed drums, guitars, and some type of whistle. Others demonstrated some island crafts such as making hats from palm fronds, a favorite with the ladies who each tried their hand at it.

Plantains fried in coconut oil and served with rice and peas, as well as in other equally delicious ways, were served with various fowls each prepared in a different fashion. My recollection of the best was a spicy version called "jerk" which was both hot and sweet at the same time. I recall eating a quantity sufficient to cause minor discomfort in my lower regions a short time later. Fish of every imaginable description, delicious and brilliantly displayed, followed the exquisite roasted pork, whose preparation I had earlier witnessed, and the whole meal was capped off by a superb figgy dowdy pudding liberally laced with the plantation owner's rum. It must have been close to midnight when the last of us tripped down the path to a waiting coach for the ride back to the dockyards.

I was vaguely aware of laughter and a bottle being passed around by someone who had managed to secure it on his person when leaving the party and of course, I partook. As did we all.

In spite of our gaiety and high spirits, I could not help but think about the events that would transpire on the morrow, and the dream I had experienced in the coach from Port Royal flashed briefly through my addled brain. Was it a harbinger of what was to take place?

CHAPTER EIGHT
The Next Day
Port Royal, Jamaica

The rain that had early plagued the party was gone, blown out into the Caribbean with a late night squall that passed us after our return to the Dockyards. The day dawned stunningly clear, with brilliant skies, and a landscape awash in every conceivable color, each made brighter by the clear air and pure light of a new day. Even sounds seemed crisper, sharper. I barely noticed.

For me, it felt as though the pall of unpleasant weather had infused my very bones, right to the core, with dread and an overwhelming sense of duty. I had slept in fits, perhaps a result of my consumption of copious quantities of Mister Malloy's fine spirits and spicy food. The delightfully exotic food had spent the night chasing through my poor stomach like a children's game of blind man's bluff held in a sea of ardent spirits, all to the beat of the native drums which had earlier entertained us. Or perhaps it was that my head was reeling in contemplation of the duties I was bound to perform, not the least of which would occur by the end of the day. Likely a combination of the two maladies. And now, my head still swam with the burden of my tasks, helped not a whit by the residual effects of rum! It seemed as if my whole body fairly thrummed with the pain of my nocturnal indiscretions.

I first had to seek out Jack, determine his choice of weapons, actual time and proper place where one or the other would get himself killed by the day's end, then communicate it to the arrogant Lieutenant Jones, or his second, in *Iphigenia*. Then I would have to turn up two evenly matched pistols – if that was indeed to be the choice he made.

Cutlasses would be a bloody sight easier! Perhaps swords or épées? What would give my sponsor the advantage he needed?

I ruminated on this and the myriad other issues chasing through my still-addled brain whilst sitting in the wardroom, picking at the breakfast Black had put before me. I was deep in thought when Mister McMahon strolled in, sat down opposite me, and, in barely a glance, took in my troubled look.

"A bit more rum than you might have needed last night, Edward? You look a trifle peaky, if you don't mind a medical opinion."

"Aye, Henry. Peaky I am. You are most perceptive. Must be your many years of experience in the medical profession. But, alas, I cannot blame it entirely on the rum. I expect I shall be needing your services – your *professional* services – before the day is out."

"Oh?" Henry was not given to unnecessary speech.

"Aye. Have you not heard of the foolishness that your former shipmate, Jack Farnsworth, has got himself involved in? No…of course, you could not possibly have heard yet. But it will be all over the Dockyard before the sun is much higher, I suspect."

The good surgeon looked at me, a neutral expression offset by a slightly raised eyebrow. He nodded, encouraging me to continue.

"He has been called out by of *Iphigenia*'s first lieutenant, one Jonathon Jones, and of course, has accepted the challenge. And worse, he has named me his second!"

For a moment he said nothing; his expression remained inscrutable and he continued to study my face as though he might determine at any moment now that I was having sport with him, or had quite lost my sanity.

"You are serious, aren't you. This is a terrible turn of events. I recall meeting Mister Jones on the deck of the French frigate we took a month back; as arrogant a soul as I ever hope to meet. I would wager that he precipitated the conflict, eh?" Without waiting for a response, he plunged straight ahead.

"And while Jack is a fine officer and a good man, I am given to understand he is quite unskilled in the art of weaponry. What has he chosen as the weapons they will use? It is his choice, of course, as you no doubt are aware."

"Aye, your surmise is spot on; Jones engaged Jack in an argument and, when Jack's temper rose, called him out. I happened to be standing at hand during the latter part of the dispute. I tried to talk our friend out of the challenge, suggesting he apologize, but he would have none of it.

"And yes, I am quite aware, Henry, that he is to choose the weapons, location and time. He has set the time for this evening on the strand just outside the dockyards. At least that was his choice when we parted last night. I am, as yet, unaware of his choice of weapon, but I assume it will be pistols. I am planning to visit *Convert* directly to determine his desire in that regard."

I stopped, thought for a moment, and added, "Would you care to accompany me? Jack has a high regard for your opinion and with two of us, the cold light of day, and the effect of the rum from last night gone, we might be able to dissuade him from this foolishness."

"Aye, Edward, I think that's a fine idea. I will check on a couple of patients in the sick bay and meet you topside directly." Henry stood, swallowed the remains of his coffee, and departed.

I stumbled up the ladder and recoiled in the brightness that assaulted me immediately I gained the weather deck. Knives shoved into my eye sockets would likely not have been as painful. I squinted my eyes nearly shut and looked about for someone to organize a boat for us. A midshipman – I could not recall his name - stood on the quarter deck keeping an eye on the ship. As I approached, he stood tall and doffed his hat in salute.

Which I returned in kind. "Please have the cutter manned. The surgeon and I will be going ashore directly."

He scurried off to do my bidding as I stood about, waiting for McMahon to turn up.

The short boat ride ashore, followed by an even shorter walk to the pier where HMS *Convert* was alongside, saw little conversation between us; we were both consumed with the enormity of the potential disaster looming before us. We stepped aboard Jack's new ship, the Navy's newest acquisition, HMS *Convert,* and asked the watch, another youthful midshipman, to fetch Lieutenant Farnsworth, if he would be so kind. I took the opportunity to look around.

The ship was flush decked with carronades mounted fore and aft, as well as on the quarterdeck amidships. They were not as large as those our ships typically carried, but there were more of them. Through the grating beneath our feet, I could make out any number of long guns on the gundeck, but with the deep shadow, I was unable to determine the size or the number. I did recall Jack telling me they were twelve-pounders. Most notable in the ship were the sailors, or rather, the absence of any about the deck; Jack's press had yet to be effective, I guessed.

"Well, here's an interesting pair. Come for an early tea social, I assume?" Jack's voice held none of the misery I was feeling.

When I turned to face him, his ebullient smile positively

radiated good cheer. His eyes were clear; he was freshly shaved and, I noted, without a nick. He seemed positively jolly. Hardly seemed right that one facing the possibility of dying before night-fall should be so cheerful. Could he have forgot the events of the previous evening. I could only hope ….

"Jack…" I began. He cut me off in an instant.

"Yes, Edward. I am jesting, of course. You are here to determine if I have come to my senses yet. Correct?" He smiled at me.

"Well, Jack, I reckon you…"

Again, he stopped me. "I am quite in control of my faculties, Edward. And I fully expect you to carry out your duties as my second for a duel with that contemptible ass, Jones. Who, I might add, is scarcely worth drowning, though I would happily expend a bullet in his behalf should you conclude that we are to meet with pistols.

"And while I always welcome the company of the noted surgeon in HMS *Penelope,* I sincerely hope he is not here as an advocate of your idea of rational thought. I am quite sane!"

I could only shake my head in despair. Sane, indeed!

"Gentlemen, let us take ourselves to the wardroom for a wee dram, or a cup of coffee. Edward, from the look of your eyes, you might be well served by the former!" Jack laughed at his own humor and stepped quickly to a hatch, down which we followed.

"Gentlemen, may I present Lieutenant Edward Ballantyne, second in *Penelope,* and Henry McMahon, surgeon in the same vessel." Jack introduced us to the three men sitting over coffee around the table and then asked them to "give us a few minutes, if you would be so kind."

The three left, nodding to Jack and then to Henry and myself. We took seats and a steward poured out coffee into cups, placing them before each of us. It was a quite passable brew.

"Jack," began the doctor. "Edward has told me of the madness in which you have embroiled yourself. This childish behavior is a recipe for disaster – and I fear the disaster may be for you. I am well aware, even if you are not, of your complete inability in the use of firearms; I would imagine that your antagonist, Lieutenant Jones, is likely more skilled and, should this silly duel actually take place, will most probably kill you dead." A ringing silence filled the room after Henry's speech.

"Harumph!" Jack looked at me and then at the surgeon. "I cannot possibly back away from this now, Henry. I must proceed to whatever conclusion the fates have ordained. Besides, I would sweetly give up my life in defense of my principles. My lack of proficiency with a pistol is not a suitable reason to back away. Furthermore, Jones might be equally unskilled and thus the contest could be more even. We don't know. So I would offer that you two gentlemen should attempt to plan a duel that stacks the cards in my favor, if that is possible."

"How are you with an épée?" I asked. Jack simply stared at me. I tried another tack. "How about a cutlass?"

Though not a very gentlemanly weapon, I offered that it might answer in this instance.

"I think it must be pistols, Edward. I don't fancy being run through with a blade. And a cutlass is not exactly suitable for a duel, now is it." His remark about cutlasses was not a question; it echoed my own sentiment, which I had kept to myself rather than embarrass my friend.

"Oh! Then you'd rather have a ball snuff your life? A ball through the heart or your thick head?" Henry was clearly annoyed with Jack's lack of wisdom – or his unwillingness to accept our pleas that he abandon this madness.

"At least with a pistol, he has a chance of missing – there's only one shot each, right?"

"Aye, Jack. One shot each and possible you'll both miss in which case, as I understand the rules, we will reload the bloody weapons and try again. Unless one of you apologizes and then it's bloody-well over." I was angry and unable to hide it.

"Then, clearly, that is the way we will proceed. I happen to know of a lovely brace of pistols – matched, I believe – right here in *Convert*. One of our midshipmen is the proud owner, though why a young gentleman – he's all of fourteen, I think – would have need of such is quite beyond me. I shall inquire if we might have use of them." Jack rose from the table, apparently on the hunt for the matched pair of pistols.

Henry looked at me, speechless. I was not. All the surgeon had to do was show up at the appointed time and place and either administer medical aid to one or the other, or pronounce one of them dead. It fell to me to arrange the duel, contact the charming

Lieutenant Jones and his second, and see that the whole affair went smoothly and according to the rather strict rules laid down for such foolishness.

"Henry! Think hard, man. How do we stop this? I fear the worst and would be bereft should our friend succumb to his pride...and principles!"

"I can think of nothing short of acting in an ungentlemanly way – fixing one of the pistols to misfire or adjusting the sight to be misaligned. Short of that, I think we must rely on the hope that Jones is as inept with a pistol as is Jack." Henry's expression could not hide his pessimistic view of the likely outcome.

We sat for a few minutes in silence, digesting the implications of what Jack had set in motion.

"Got them! Midshipman Sherwin was only too happy to lend us the pistols. Lovely they are as well! Have a look!" Jack blew into the room like a summer squall, brandishing a flat box of highly polished dark wood fitted with brass fixtures.

"Lovely, I'm sure." Henry's obvious disapproval and his lack of interest in the weapons, despite his earlier suggestion of "fixing" them, brought him to his feet. "Come, Edward. I must return to the ship and you have errands to run."

We left Jack to reflect on his foolishness and admire his newly borrowed pistols. Perhaps he would also reflect on the words both Henry and I had nearly shouted into his face and come to his senses. No, I didn't really think he would do that!

The surgeon and I parted company immediately we had left *Convert;* I headed for the boat dock where I might expect to find transport to *Iphigenia,* and he to where we had landed in the jolly boat from *Penelope.* I trusted it would return for me when my own errand was completed.

"Lieutenant Jones, if you please." I spoke to the midshipman guarding the break in the bulwark, identifying myself and my needs, as I climbed up to the deck of HMS *Iphigenia* from a filthy local bumboat rowed by a local man of color.

My mood had deteriorated further since leaving Jack's wardroom and was not helped a bit by the surly boatman who seemed convinced he was doing me a favor by accepting my money for rowing me less than a pistol shot into the harbor. In spite of my relatively short time here, it was my observation that, when unsupervised, many of the local populace held a small opinion of us, which was frequently characterized by sullen accession and grudging execution of our requests.

During the short and silent ride from quay to frigate, I had gone over in my mind what I would say to Jones and grew increasingly annoyed with Jack for getting me into this mess and with myself for agreeing to act as his second. And with Lieutenant Bloody Jones for instigating the whole mess from the outset! I stood at the midship break bearing the weight of the world, generally feeling a bit sorry for myself, and growing more agitated with each passing moment. Of which there were many!

"Please, sir. If you would, come this way; Lieutenant Jones is tied up at the moment and asked that you wait in the gunroom until he is available." The young gentleman had finally returned and would, it appeared, be bearing the brunt of my increasingly foul mood.

"Did you tell Mister Jones who it was wanted to see him? I believe I offered my name when I came aboard." I remained stationary. Let bloody Jones come to me, damn all!

"I am quite certain, sir, that I mentioned that 'a Lieutenant Ballantyne wished his attendance.'" And then he repeated Jones' instructions about waiting in the gunroom.

"I will be quite happy to await his presence right here. I have no desire to await his pleasure below." I snapped, causing the youngster to physically recoil and take a step back. "You may convey *that* to Mister Almighty Bloody Jones."

He could barely escape quickly enough and hurried off, I am sure, to suggest to his first lieutenant that the gentleman awaiting topside was none too pleasant, not so much a gentleman, and perhaps a trifle riled.

In due course – it would have been an accession to me had he appeared quickly – I heard his nasal voice behind me. "Ah, Lieutenant Ballantyne. How lovely to see you this fine day. How may I be of service?"

Indeed! Withdraw your bloody challenge and stay away from us, damn your eyes!

"I am here in my capacity as second to Lieutenant Jack Farnsworth, Second in HMS *Convert,* to answer your challenge of last evening." Without giving him a chance to interrupt, I pressed straight on. "Lieutenant Farnsworth has selected pistols as his weapon of choice and the beach to windward of the dockyards for the site. Shortly prior to sundown. Two bells in the first dog watch, he requested."

"Humph! I had thought he would be appearing in person to apologize for his rude behavior rather than sending a second to arrange a duel. But, if that's his choice, so be it. I shall be there with my own second, Lieutenant Peter Sedgewick. You will, I presume, provide the weapons?"

"Aye, we will provide the weapons...and a surgeon to pronounce you at the scene after my sponsor shoots you dead. I shall look forward to seeing you there." I turned, stepped to the bulwark.

And then I realized I had no boat waiting for me. There was nothing below me but the sparkling blue water of Port Royal Harbor. A bit awkward, what? Jones took in my predicament in a glance and, whilst almost suppressing a smirk, offered me the services of his jolly boat. Which, in due humility and probably with less grace than might have been appropriate, I accepted.

Once aboard *Penelope* again, I found the surgeon and told him of my adventure...or rather, my *mis*adventure...aboard *Iphigenia.* He did not have the grace to suppress his outright laugh at my departure from the ship, and before long we were both laughing and giggling like a couple of schoolgirls with a secret.

"Enough of this foolishness, Edward. We must make the arrangements for the duel. There is much to do: get the pistols from Jack, see to the proper place, and arrange for a wagon or at least a coach.

"You get over to the beach – you know the place Jack has selected and I do not – and whilst you're about it, organize a wagon or something that can transport any who might require it to the hospital – or the mortuary. I am going back to *Convert* and have one more go at ending this foolishness. But as I suspect I shall be unsuccessful, I will secure the pistols and bring them back here. We should fire both before the event to ensure they work properly." Henry paused, scratched the stubble on his cheek thoughtfully, and gazed off into the distance.

"Is there anything else we need prepare for? What about the rules? Do you happen to have a copy of the handbook detailing the rules for organizing a duel?" His words were clever, but his tone and demeanor suggested otherwise.

"Is there such a thing?" I had no clue as to what might be involved, but hoped that showing up with loaded pistols and a surgeon at the proper place and time would answer satisfactorily. I had no interest in having our adversary, Lieutenant Jones, offering criticism or his own special wisdom about our preparations and execution.

"It occurs to me, Henry, that with our man being a miserable shot, we need to tip the scales a bit in our favor. I am thinking a close range might help – say three or four paces rather than the customary ten or more." While close range would be favorable to both of them, the longer distance would most definitely prove disastrous for Jack. "What do you think about that?" I had thought of little else once I realized we were going forward with this for better or for worse and shortening the distance between the duelists was my only solution, short of altering one of the pistols to misfire.

"And tell Jack to stand sideways rather than full on. That way, there's less of a target for Jones to hit. From a medical standpoint, there is less of a chance that the bullet will hit something vital. I have no idea of Jones's competency with a pistol, but it seems foolish to provide him with a broad target which, at the close range you wisely suggest, would be almost impossible to miss." Henry's idea was an improvement.

We had the jolly boat take us ashore once again. The day was wearing on, and I wanted time to put everything in place without undue haste.

Damn your eyes anyway, Jack Farnsworth. Why'd you have to do this to us? And take the chance of getting your own self killed in the process?

The location Jack had specified, outside the walls of the dockyard and near to the sea would be satisfactory. There was nary a soul to be seen and ample space could be had for our meeting. The sand was soft and white, the gentle sea lapped contentedly on the shore, and the seabirds soared and dove overhead, as they had since time began. At the verge, between the sand and the scrub and weeds, grew a profusion of brilliantly colored flowers – reds, yellows, oranges, and purples all competing for attention. I could not help but think what a lovely place this would be to enjoy a pleasant evening with a loved one when Kendall popped unbidden into my mind. A glass of spirits, a nice meal, the fragrance of tropical flowers and later, the stars overhead reflecting on the placid sea would provide a perfect backdrop for a secret tryst. It seemed incongruous that such a felicitious spot would shortly become host to the imminent and gloomy proceedings about to take place here. And it mattered not a whit which of the antagonists would succumb; obviously I preferred that my friend might prevail, but the loss of either of them would be a waste of a life – even the obnoxious and arrogant Lieutenant Jones. It depressed me to even contemplate it.

The beautiful, bright flowers forgotten, I wandered back to the confines of the dockyard, entering through its large wooden gates, quite lost in thought. As I dodged a heavily laden wagon, I recalled that Henry had instructed me to procure a conveyance of some stripe. Where could I secure a wagon? Perhaps the quartermaster's stores might be helpful.

They were only too happy to arrange for a wagon and two-horse team with a native teamster and promised it all would be available at the gates at the appointed hour. They seemed not a bit surprised that I should be needing their services; perhaps my earlier prognostication about the news of a duel spreading quickly was not far off the mark. So that was done. Now we had only to wait for the appointed hour to arrive.

Henry was back aboard *Penelope* when I returned, sitting in the wardroom, a full glass at his elbow and the richly carved box open in front of him.

"What ho, Edward? I assume from your gloomy countenance you have discovered the dueling grounds to be satisfactory?" McMahon greeted me with scarcely a glance, so intent was he on the pistols before him.

His use of the proper term for the sanctioned area for dueling – which clearly our beach setting was not – did not escape me. I threw myself into a chair, weighted down by my responsibilities, first to nip this silliness in the bud and then see to the successful conclusion of it should I have failed at the first. My head sagged into my cupped hands.

"Aye, Henry. I have. And arranged for a wagon, team, and driver to haul off the corpse when it is done." My tone gave away my fear that it might not be Jones riding in the wagon. I lifted my head to look at the surgeon.

"How did you find our friend? Was he still filled with the confidence of the uninformed? The presence of those pistols would suggest he has not changed his mind."

Now the doctor tore his gaze from the pistols and looked at me. "On the contrary, Edward. He is quite ready – eager, in fact – to proceed with the event. Even mentioned that he had instructed his steward to brush his best uniform and hat. I could see straight away that any effort at dissuading him from this foolishness would be fruitless and so kept my own counsel. We have but to wait and see the outcome. You, of course, will have a few additional responsibilities to fulfill before that outcome. And as you suggested, we should put these fine weapons to the test."

"Yes, I do have a few 'additional responsibilities' as you so cleverly expressed it. And one of them would be firing the pistols. Let us take them topside. I shall find the gunner to see to them." I stood, reached across the table, and took the box from in front of him. I left the wardroom with it tucked safely under my arm.

The three of us, the surgeon, the ship's gunner (Mister Bowen, and a more seasoned hand would be hard to imagine), and I stood at the bulwark amidships. The fancy box sat on the pinrail before us, empty. Bowen held one pistol and, after a thorough examination, loaded it. I held the other, awaiting his ministrations.

"Mister Ballantyne, you may take this one. Hand me the other, if you please." Bowen was serious, handling the pieces with care and respect, aware of their ultimate purpose. He also knew well Jack Farnsworth.

"Now, gentlemen, let us determine if these weapons will shoot as pretty as they look!" Bowen raised the pistol he held in front of him, aimed at a seagull taking its ease on the water some fifty yards distant and fired.

The hammer fell, raised a spark, ignited the powder in the pan, and sent a flame into the breach of the gun. It fired. A small flame shot out the end of the muzzle on the heels of the ball and was accompanied by a sharp crack as the lead projectile flew toward the unsuspecting gull. The ball hit the water immediately astern of the bird, shooting a small geyser into the air and startling it into flight.

"Well, that one works nicely, I'd offer. I was not aiming at the bird, as you saw." Bowen smiled as though he actually expected us to believe his fable. We both knew with certainty that he was aiming at the gull.

"What's going on here? Why are you shooting? Mister Ballantyne, Mister McMahon, what do you think you're doing?" The nasal whine of Lieutenant Ware cut through our momentary deafness.

I couldn't tell him we were preparing weapons for a duel; that would not answer. I thought quickly as I turned to face him and put a hand on the surgeon's arm to still his reactionary response.

"I was gifted this lovely pair of pistols, Mister Ware, and Gunner Bowen was kind enough to offer to have a look at them for me. It would never do to need one and have it not function properly, now would it?" I spoke quickly, improvising a tale I thought would answer.

"Very well, then. In the future, you might let the watch know – or me, should I be available – that you intend firing, so as to not create a disturbance, you know. Can't have such careless behavior aboard my ship, now can we." It was not a question. I simply nodded.

No sooner had Ware taken his leave than Bowen put out his hand for the second pistol, handing me the first as he did so. With little fanfare, he raised it to his fore, sighted down the barrel at the water – there was no bird within range this time – and pulled the trigger. As might be expected, it performed admirably and sent a ball to roughly the same spot on the water as the first. He handed it back to me.

"Very nice pistols, Mister Ballantyne. They both seem well balanced, smooth acting, and accurate. I trust they will answer well for your needs."

I noticed as I took the pistols from the gunner that Ware had stopped, turned, and was about to step toward us again when he saw that we were finished. He simply shook his head and continued on whatever errand he had originally set out upon. McMahon and I followed him as far as the gundeck. All was now in readiness for the duel, and, while we both would have further roles to play before the day was out, we had done all that was necessary now.

As eight bells rang out from the belfry in the bow, signifying the hour of 4:00 in the afternoon, I collected our surgeon and together we made our way to the break in the bulwark where the boat I had previously organized floated over its reflection in the clear, still waters of Port Royal Harbor.

"Are you ready for this?" I inquired unnecessarily of McMahon as we took our seats in the sternsheets of the cutter.

"I am, yes. But more importantly, are you? Remember, Edward, it is you who must stand in for Jack should he come to his senses and not show up."

I had avoided thinking about that facet of the contest since early morning. Now Henry had dragged it out and laid it squarely before me. The answer was, obviously, no, I am not ready to stand in for Jack. While I despaired over my friend getting himself killed, I had no intention of putting myself in his place to get killed! I had hopes of returning to England one day and rekindling my relationship with the lovely Kendall Smith, not standing in front of a fellow naval officer while he fired a loaded pistol at me!

"All but that, Henry. All but that. It strikes me, however, that Jack would not miss this for the world! You saw him this morning; he was actually excited – almost giddy – about facing Jones. It far exceeds my comprehension as to why, but that is our friend."

We strode purposefully toward the open gates of the Royal Dockyards, Jamaica. I could see the wagon I had requested as we rounded a storage building. Two grey mules stood at the bow, disinterested in all but when they might get a bag of oats tied under their muzzles. They swished their tails in a half-hearted effort to chase away the bothersome flies that circled and buzzed above them. Occasionally one or the other would paw at the ground giving the illusion that he – or she? – was eager to get moving. But given that they were mules, I doubted that motivation! Clearly they could not care a whit about the role they would shortly play in the drama about to unfold.

"We may as well ride, Henry. I would reckon that would be our wagon there by the gates. No sense in walking in the heat when we don't need to."

I introduced myself to the driver, a sullen native who did not offer a name but nodded when I gave him my own, and we climbed aboard. The man wore what I recognized as the accepted costume for the native employees of the Crown: a tattered shirt of an indeterminate plaid, canvas trousers cut off and frayed below the knee, and a broad brimmed straw hat. I took a seat on the side of the wagon behind him and gave him direction to the site on the beach I had selected previously. He whistled at the mules, snapped his whip over their rumps, encouraging them to step forward...which they did. He gave no indication of having heard me, but followed my instructions as I uttered them and steered the wagon through the gates.

Though it was not yet 5:00, the appointed time for the antagonists to face one another, there was already a sizeable group of men and a few women who had gathered to witness the duel.

Nothing like a little bloodshed to draw a crowd! I thought, shaking my head.

How they had got word of this I had little idea, but as I had earlier noted to Henry, rumors travel quickly in a naval yard! Some of the spectators were carrying baskets of food that they shared with their neighbors. and more than a few were passing bottles from hand to hand. I noted that the local folks seemed keep their distance from the navy people, both civilian and those in uniform. And I further took note that more than one of the naval employees had already partaken of drink, obviously to help them get in the festive spirit of the occasion. Oh my!

The low buzz of conversation stilled as the surgeon and I disembarked from the wagon and made our way to the sandy field of honor. I imagined that the spectators inquiring amongst themselves if one of us was a duelist. Some pointed, whispering to each other. They watched as we stepped out across the verge and made our way onto the soft white sand, which soon would be tinted with the blood of one of our fellows.

I carried under my arm the box containing the brace of pistols, one of which would offer the fatal shot. I prayed it would be fired by my friend and not the haughty Lieutenant Jones. At the moment, neither was loaded; that would come when both parties were present to witness the act. The crowd began to stir, a further rumble of conversation growing like a wave about to break on the beach. I broke out of my reverie to espy Jack and several others marching purposefully down the hard-packed path toward where Henry McMahon and I stood. Jack appeared calm, though I was certain that under his unruffled exterior he was – he had to be – as anxious as I was. And I was not the one about to face a man with a loaded pistol who was trying to kill me!

Lieutenant Farnsworth was impeccably turned out; his blue coat well brushed, golden epaulet glinting in the late sun, boots well blackened, and his shirt and stock as white as the sun-bleached sand on which we stood. His hat was square upon his head; a cockade, perched jauntily on the larboard side, bobbed as he walked. He wore no sword, but was, I noticed, wearing spotless white gloves. His eyes shifted to the wagon and the two mules pawing the ground impatiently. I could not hear him, but I noticed that he said something – perhaps clever, were I to judge by the reaction – to one of his mates. He did not break stride and was quickly in company with the doctor and me.

"Gentlemen: I see my unworthy opponent has yet to put in an appearance. Perhaps he will decide I am not worthy of his time and talent and miss our meeting. You did tell him, Edward, where we would meet, did you not?" Jack spoke a bit louder than was necessary; whether for the benefit of our growing audience or from a spate of nerves I could not fathom.

"Aye, Jack. I gave him rather complete instructions. I would expect him – ."

Henry cut me off mid-word. "I would venture that he has arrived! See there...the carriage? Appears he brought along his own entourage as well."

We looked where the surgeon had pointed with his chin at the new arrivals. I could easily distinguish the lofty Lieutenant Jones, center among a cadre of some five or six officers. They approached and while Jones said nothing, a young man showing the single epaulette of a lieutenant, stepped forward and doffed his hat to Henry McMahon.

"Sir: I am Charles Easley, representative of and second to Lieutenant Jonathon Jones. I collect you are the representative of Mister Farnsworth?"

"No young man, I am most assuredly not. The man you seek is here, Lieutenant Edward Ballantyne, second in His Britannic Majesty's frigate *Penelope*." Henry stepped aside after directing Lieutenant Easley to me.

My, aren't we formal! The thought flashed unbidden through my consciousness. *Likely best to be proper!*

Then added, "I am here in my capacity as a naval surgeon to provide medical assistance should your primary and ours not succeed in killing each other. And to see to the disposal of which-ever unfortunate succumbs." I noticed Henry did not smile.

Easley looked at me; studied me, actually. "Very well, then. Mister Ballantyne, have you prepared the weapons? I shall, of course, have to see to them before I can let my principal risk using an improper pistol." He stuck out his hand, obviously expecting me to offer the brace of pistols.

I waited a beat or two, not taking my glare from his eyes, before answering. "Yes, Mister Easley. I have them right here. But I am a bit puzzled. I distinctly recall Lieutenant Jones mentioning only this morning that a Peter Sedgewick would be seconding him. How is it that you are here and not Lieutenant Sedgewick?"

"Lieutenant Sedgewick has declined the opportunity to par-ticipate, Mister Ballantyne. I have taken over his role in this unfortunate affair. You need not concern yourself with the reasons for his decision. Suffice it to say that I am here in his stead and would appreciate the opportunity to examine the weapons." Again, he stuck out his hand, waiting for me to offer him the box.

Are all *the officers in* Iphigenia *cut from the same bolt of cloth? I have rarely seen so much arrogance in one place! They must all think themselves superior to any and all!*

I again hesitated in handing over the box. It was admittedly a childish tactic designed solely to annoy and show him that I was not in the slightest cowed by his misplaced superiority. When a sufficiency of time had passed – likely only a few moments – instead of handing him the box, I simply opened it before him and showed him the contents.

As he examined the pistols, I said, "When you are satis-fied, and as the rules provide, I will see to loading them in your and your principal's presence." I had no idea what the "rules" provided; I had not seen any, but I thought a bit of perceived expertise would not hurt! And since Jones had picked for a second a similarly minded chap, I found no issue with treating them both to a bit of the same medicine!

After little more than a cursory look at each, Easley replaced the two pistols and closed the box, apparently indicating his satisfaction. He said nothing.

Jack, during all of this, had also remained mute, standing to the side of the group, eyeing his opponent and smiling slightly. Perhaps he was trying to look confident; I thought he looked the idiot. I nudged him.

"Mister Farnsworth: are you ready for me to load the pistols now? And then we shall go over the rules for this duel."

"Aye, Edward. Let us proceed. I am anxious to get on with my evening."

Jack. You're playing the fool! This is serious business. Jones could kill you! I kept the thought to myself, but scowled at my friend, hopefully to communicate the message.

"Very well, then. Mister McMahon, would be kind enough to hold the box whilst I see to the pistols." I tried to keep my voice steady, swallowing the quaver that threatened to destroy the confident air I hoped to convey.

Henry took the proffered box, holding it in front of him on the flat so that I might open it. I retrieved one of the pistols, carefully loaded it, and handed it to Easley for his examination. When he handed it back with an agreeable grunt, I repeated the process with the other.

"Mister Jones, would you step over here, if you please. I would like to offer the rules for this engagement."

Jones did as I instructed, watching Jack all the time, for what I have no idea. Perhaps expecting him to bolt like a startled horse.

"The two of you will stand back to back, just here with the pistols pointed skyward. On my order, you will each advance three steps..."

"*THREE* steps? Are you mad, man! That is suicide. Duels are properly fought at ten paces – or more." Jones's outburst brought a murmur from the spectators, most of whom had edged closer so they might hear our words.

"Three, Mister Jones. Three steps is what I said. Do recall, if you will, that the challenged party establishes the weapons, place, and procedures. You may end the matter right now, should you wish to withdraw your challenge." I would not be cowed by the arrogance of our opponent and stared him down.

"Very well, then, three it shall be. Then what? Do we hurl rocks at one another?"

"No, Lieutenant. And your sarcastic wit is wasted here. Save it for your gunroom! After you have each taken the requisite three paces, you will turn on my order, then fire. Should you both miss, we will begin again, unless one of you concedes the contest. The shot need not be fatal; a wound will constitute satisfaction."

There was nearly complete silence. Even the spectators barely breathed. The gentle lapping of the waves on the sand offered the only sounds. Jack and Lieutenant Jones glared at one another; I knew there would be no recanting now. This duel was on a course to disaster for one or the other of these two – perhaps both.

"Are there any questions? The light is fading, so I would suggest we get on with it." I would arrange the two so that when they were to fire, Jack's back was to the low sun, putting the bright light in Jones's eyes.it wasn't much of an advantage, but it was the best I could do. Henry moved close to Jack, telling him, I am sure, that he was to stand sideways as we had earlier agreed. And then he stepped back. Jack nodded his understanding, and I noticed the smile was gone from his face; he looked properly serious.

"Very well, please take your places."

Both Jack and Lieutenant Jones carefully removed their jackets and hat. Jack took off his gloves. Each handed their garments to one of the attendants; Henry held Jack's, as I was then holding the two pistols. Jones's shirt and stock were as fresh as Jack's and I was a bit surprised to see he was not as solidly built as I had earlier surmised. A smaller target for my man, I lamented.

Jack stood, facing the water and the sun, as I directed. I handed each a pistol; the selection was random as they were identical. I think Jones might have, for a moment anyway, taken pleasure in the fact that his adversary would be looking into the sun – until he realized they would both be turning and then...

They held their pistols in front of them, each pointed aloft as I had instructed. Jack looked at me and winked his eye, a signal, I assumed, that he was ready, whatever the outcome.

"You will step out on my count. One." Each man took a step forward; Jack toward the water and setting sun, while Jones went inland. They stopped and awaited the next command.

"Two." Again, they moved, their boots crunched in the sand. They stopped, awaiting what would likely be the order that would prove fatal to one of them. There was no noise now, no murmuring in the crowd, no banter from the witnesses, just the timeless lapping of the water on the shore. Even the wind seemed to await the outcome.

I looked at Henry, at the others in Jones's contingent. All seemed to be holding their breath, as I was.

"Three!" It came out louder than I expected.

Each man took the requisite step, then instantly turned to face his opponent. Jack, remembering his instructions, turned only part way to the fore, his right arm and pistol outstretched in front of him, his body sideways to his opponent. Jones swung all the way around, fully facing Farnsworth, and extended his arm.

Crack! Crack! The two shots were so close together they sounded as one. Both men stood in place, not moving. Without a breeze sufficient to move it away, the smoke from their discharged pistols floated easily over each man. The smell of burned powder briefly overcame the gentle smells of the sea, sand, and wild flowers.

Bloody hell! They both missed. Perhaps I can talk them out of a repeat...

"Jack!" Henry's shout interrupted my thoughts.

I looked at my friend. A spreading bloom of crimson had appeared on the right side of his previously snowy shirt, his arm had dropped to his side and, at Henry's shout, he turned his head to look at us, surprised and questioning. Then he looked down at his front. And his knees gave way.

In an instant, the vision that I had seen in my dream of Jack in a blood-soaked shirt flashed into my mind, turning into the reality of what I saw before me. I shouted – unintelligible even to me – but, unable to move, I remained rooted to the spot I had chosen to witness the duel. I watched, helpless, as the pistol dropped from Jack's limp hand, landing silently in the sand at his side. His expression was one of surprise, shock even, as though this finish was the farthest thing from his mind.

Before he could fully collapse to the sand, Henry was beside him, easing his fall. The surgeon ripped open Jack's shirt and peered at the wound in Jack's chest. He looked at me and shook his head, barely perceptibly. I found my sensibilities and, moving quickly to his side, dropped to the sand beside my friend.

"Sorry about that, Edward! Reckon my luck has run its course. I hope 'Old Nick' is ready for me! Likely to be seein' him rather sooner than later, I'm afraid." Blood bubbled from his lips as he spoke.

"Jack! Don't worry about it, my friend. Henry here will fix you up good as new. You'll see. 'Old Nick' will just have to wait on you! Right, Henry?" I knew it was more hope than reality; the blood coming from Jack's mouth was a plain indication his lung had been punctured.

"You just rest easy, Jack. I will see to getting you back to rights quick as ever possible." Henry's positive words fooled no one, but Jack offered a faint smile, as though he believed the surgeon.

"Did I at least hit him?" Jack whispered, amid more bloody emanations.

"I don't know, Jack. I was concerned about your well-being, not Jones'. Didn't look, now, did I." Henry had placed a folded bit of cloth from his medical box over the hole in Jack's chest and he was pressing it into the wound.

I tore my eyes away from my friend and sought out his antagonist. All I could see was the cluster of his associates standing in a group where I had last seen Lieutenant Jones. One of them called out.

"Doctor! Could you step over here, if you please! It appears as though Mister Jones needs your attention."

Henry looked up at the group. "I am afraid Mister Jones will have to wait for a moment; I am occupied right here, now. Is he hurt?"

"Aye, sir. Cruel hurt, he seems. Took the bullet in his arm, he done. Bleedin' like a stuck pig." Another voice, the inflection Irish, answered Henry's query.

"It's unlikely it will prove fatal, then. Clap a cloth on it and sit him down. I will see to him presently."

"Looks like you scored at least one point, Jack. Sounds like Jones took one also." I tried to be uplifting.

"Aye...I heard. Got him in the arm. Well, I 'spose that's better than a complete miss, what?" Jack's voice was increasingly strained and growing quieter with each passing moment.

"Just be still, now, my friend. Let Henry do his work. We'll get you in the wagon quick as ever you please and over to the hospital where he can give you some proper care." I stood as I spoke, casting about for the wagon, still parked on the verge.

"You there. Lieutenant! Could you ask your surgeon to see to my friend, please. He's bleeding copious amounts." Another of Jones' entourage called out, seeing me when I stood.

"Sorry lads. Surgeon's a bit tied up at the moment. You're welcome to get Mister Jones into the wagon. We'll be taking it to the hospital straight away. But get on with it; we cannot wait on you." I responded, distracted.

I waved to the driver of our wagon, motioning him over. Slowly, he whistled up his mules and guided them toward where Jack lay on the sand. I noticed that Jones's men were trying to get their man on his feet to walk to the wagon.

He was only shot in the arm! Why the bloody hell can't he walk on his own? I wondered briefly, not particularly caring.

I squatted down next to Jack again. His eyelids fluttered as he sensed my presence, opened his eyes and with great effort whispered to me. I had to bend close to hear him.

"Should have listened to you, Edward. This has ended badly. I'm terribly..." He gasped, Henry wiped more blood from his mouth.

The surgeon put a finger on Jack's neck, then bent down and laid his ear to Jack's chest. When he looked up, his expression was grim. He shook his head, a barely perceptible movement; his pronouncement driven home when he laid Jack's coat over his upper body and face. Then Henry stood up.

"Here, now. Could you give us a hand here. Lieutenant Jones is failing quickly. Needs the surgeon and the hospital right quick." Jones's associate called as soon as Henry stood.

"Well, get him into the wagon. We'll drop you at the hospital on our way to the mortuary." Hearing McMahon say it – even though I knew well Jack was dead – produced a profound sense of melancholy in me, kept me rooted to my place beside him.

I looked up as his friends half carried Jones to the wagon; his face had lost its sunburned healthy color. He was deathly pale and his sleeve was soaked in crimson. I could see a steady stream of blood emanating from the wound even through the bit of rag his subaltern held against it.

"He's likely to bleed out, we don't get him to where I can work on him. Looks like Jack's ball hit an artery." Henry spoke to me *sotto voce* and stepped forward to assist loading the wounded lieutenant into the back of the wagon.

Leave the bloody bastard. Let him walk if he's able, was my less-than-Christian response, though I uttered not a word.

CHAPTER NINE
30 December 1793
Port Royal, Jamaica

"I wonder just how much effort you might have put into dissuading your friend, my former second lieutenant, from pursuing a potentially fatal confrontation, Mister Ballantyne. Most who knew him were well aware of his complete incompetence with firearms. It appears you are the beneficiary of his demise." Captain Bartholomew Rowley, commander of HMS *Penelope* growled at me as I stood to attention in his cabin.

"Sir," I spoke. "I tried right up until they faced each other to convince Lieutenant Farnsworth that he was on the wrong course. I even offered to carry his apology to Lieutenant Jones. He would have none of it. Mister McMahon also made repeated efforts to appeal to Jack's – I mean, Lieutenant Farnsworth's more rational side. When our efforts failed, we had no choice but to carry on and try to give our man the best possible chance of survival. And yes, the surgeon and I established the rules in an effort to offset his lack of skill with a pistol." I resented the captain's accusation.

"Well, be that as it may, we'll never know, now, will we? In the event, you are being ordered into *Convert* in Farnsworth's stead. You will report to Captain Lawford before the new year on the orders of Commodore Ford." Rowley seemed to be addressing the creased sheet of paper on his desk, rather than me.

"Were it up to me," he continued without looking up, "I'd have sent you to *Iphigenia* to take second behind whomever they moved into Jones's job. Let you deal with his mates and friends over there. You should congratulate yourself, Ballantyne; you managed to cheat the navy out of the services of two capable officers in one fell swoop! McMahon's amputation of Jones's arm has likely ended a promising career. I doubt Jones will be fit for duty anytime soon and will most probably never go back to sea... should he survive the surgeon's attentions." Rowley now raised his none-to-pleasant gaze to glower at me.

I drew myself up straight and met his stare straight on. His ill-informed allegations made my blood boil and I struggled to maintain my composure. I would not, could not, allow him to lay this whole episode at my doorstep. And my being responsible for Henry amputating Jones's arm was beyond preposterous! I was not even aware that he had carried out the operation until well after it was a *fait accompli.*

"Captain Rowley. We don't know each other yet as I have only recently reported into your ship...and, it would appear, will not be remaining under your command. Were we to have the time for you to know me, you would know that I abhor killing in anyway save in the course of battle, where it is generally unavoidable. Further, Jack Farnsworth was my friend, and the last thing I would want is for me to profit from his loss. Especially this way. And further still, I would surely submit that my shifting to *Convert* is in no way an improvement in my station; I was second here in *Penelope* and, as I am taking Farnsworth's position, I will be second in *Convert.* I resent your imputation and will not accept the blame or responsibility for Lieutenant Farnsworth's actions. Or for the surgeon's.

"According to Mister McMahon, Jones was hit in the upper arm which destroyed a piece of the brachial artery and shattered the humerus bone; he had little choice but amputation...to save the man's life. I am hardly responsible for that, sir."

I paused for an instant...could feel the heat and color rising in my face. I took a breath and added, "If that is all, sir, I shall see to shifting my chest to *Convert.*"

"You are an outspoken young man, Lieutenant. Perhaps it is for the better that you will not be sailing with me. It would likely prove difficult, I am sure. You are dismissed." Rowley continued to glare at me, daring me to respond further. He face was deeply colored, and the beads of sweat coursed down his cheeks. As I turned leave the cabin, he returned his gaze to the papers on his desk.

Before the end of the day, I had presented myself and my servant, Black, on board His Majesty's Ship *Convert,* still conveniently moored to the quay wall. I was pleased to see that the press had enjoyed at least some success and, while I know Jack had not sent anyone to pick a "few hands" from *Penelope,* I would certainly do so and enjoy it! Captain Lawford, on deck as he oversaw some adjustment to the new foreshrouds, noticed me come aboard and welcomed me into his ship. Together we lamented the loss of my predecessor and friend. And mercifully in this ship, there was no mention of my being to blame for Jack's somewhat reckless behavior.

"Once you have a look about and settle your baggage, I shall look for you to come to my cabin, Ballantyne. I can tell you now that we will be escorting a large convoy – perhaps fifty ships – to North America and onwards to Europe. I expect we will be sailing toward the middle of January. But for now, get yourself situated and we can then go over some of the details, as I know them to be as of this moment." Lawford took a quick look about the deck, up at the rig, and retreated to his cabin. I did the same.

Black, my faithful servant who had followed me through the far reaches of the Pacific, shipwreck, Atlantic hurricane, and several different ships, had already prepared my cabin as he had been trained to do. My chest was unpacked, stowed beneath the hanging cot, and my clothes properly hung up.

"Those Frenchies build a nice ship, Mister Ballantyne. Bit of a different arrangement from one of ours, but nicely done. I have yet to meet many of the men, but I collect I will in due course." Black greeted me as I surveyed his handiwork.

"You haven't met many of the men yet, Black, because there aren't many aboard. Mister Farnsworth had organized a press, but, so far, it would appear it has enjoyed only limited success. I expect I shall be expected to fill out our complement as quick as ever I might!"

Satisfied with Black's efforts, I stepped across the passage-way into the wardroom, there to find Lieutenant Bogue, the ship's first lieutenant, and Lieutenant William Earnshaw, third. They sat opposite each other and looked up at the same moment when I stepped into the room. A steward stood behind Lieutenant Bogue.

"Gentlemen, may I introduce myself. I am Edward Ballantyne, late of HMS *Penelope,* and Jack Farnsworth's replacement. It is a pleasure to be here; I only wish Jack were with us as well."

They introduced themselves in a friendly manner and without any trace of rancor, actually agreeing with my sentiment about Jack. The steward turned out to also be named Bogue, a confusing state of affairs I thought until *Lieutenant* Bogue explained the young man was his nephew, getting in some sea time in hopes of one day gaining a midshipman's warrant.

We then fell to discussing the condition of the ship, the

paucity of crew, and the pros and cons of the few midshipmen already aboard. Mister Bogue – as first lieutenant he was second in command of *Convert* – described to me what the press had so far accomplished – we were about half our crew short – and then went on to discuss the lack of warrants and petty officers. And Marines.

"I expect a small contingent of Royal Marines to turn up at any moment," Bogue stated. "Their captain is already aboard. You will meet him presently. A decent enough chap – for a Marine!" He smiled broadly at the jibe. There was a long-standing rivalry between the Royal Navy and the Marines.

"Something on the order of forty of our men have come with Cap'n Lawford from his previous command, *Hound,* a sloop of but twelve guns. Good men, all, and eager to put to sea on a frigate. Several petty officers and capable they are, but alas, few warrants came over."

I offered that I knew of some warrant officers who might be happy to join the ship if I could obtain authorization for them and was immediately gratified with the smiles my announcement produced.

"By all means, Ballantyne. We need a good bosun, a gunner, and a surgeon. A few more petty officers as well would be helpful, you know. You don't happen to have a pot full of them lying about, now do you?"

Bogue was enthusiastic to say the least. He brought me up to date on the repairs to the ship, so that I could at least pretend to be well-informed when I spoke to Captain Lawford.

He laughed. "Aye, lad. Always good to seem to know what you are about! You likely should step along to see the old man; he does not appreciate being kept waiting."

I hurried to the cabin, thinking about what I might say to induce Henry McMahon to come aboard as our surgeon. After all, one cannot press a warrant, and he might feel some sense of loyalty to Captain Rowley. When I stepped to the door, I was surprised to see it unattended – then I remembered we had no Marines aboard yet. I knocked.

"Yes?" Came quietly from within the room.

"Lieutenant Ballantyne to see the captain, sir." I did my best Marine guard impression.

"By all means, Ballantyne. Come in."

The cabin was similar to most of the frigate captains' cabins I had seen: to starboard, there was a small alcove for sleeping with a curtained area in the gallery hiding his "seat of ease." Athwartship in the center of the room was a table with seating for six with a sideboard along the larboard bulkhead. A wash stand was fixed to the sole near the sleeping alcove while the captain's desk and chair occupied a cramped space in a forward corner. Opposite was a somewhat unusual piece of furniture, for a small frigate, a rocking chair, which at this moment contained the person of Captain John Lawford.

A pair of square-lens spectacles perched on the end of his smallish nose, causing him to drop his head to peer over them at me. He was not a large man which made his cabin appear more spacious than in fact it was. His thin, graying hair was neatly tied back in a queue; it gave evidence of having recently been powdered. I had already noticed a formal white wig resting on a stand near his sleeping chamber. He was in shirt-sleeves, his stock loosened, and his coat hung from a peg near his desk. On his feet, he wore black slippers.

"Take a seat, if you please, Lieutenant. And, officially, welcome aboard HMS *Convert*. Rowley's loss is my gain. In point of fact, our mutual friend, the late Jack Farnsworth, had suggested that, should we be able to make some changes, you would be an excellent addition to our complement. And now, here you are... under somewhat different circumstances than either Farnsworth or I – or you, I daresay – had imagined.

"So tell me about yourself. Commodore Ford mentioned only that you had recently been out with Edward Edwards in his quest for the scoundrels from *Bounty*, but little more." He removed the spectacles, carefully folding them before resting them in his lap. His eyes were sharp and even a glance could be described as piercing.

"I knew Edwards some years ago; not a pleasant chap, as I recall. Unless he has changed in the past ten years, I would imagine that your commission with him must have been... *interesting*...what?"

"Aye, sir," I began, taking the proffered chair. "Quite correct in that. I was indeed out with Captain Edwards in *Pandora* and found it to be a most interesting adventure. Shipwreck can be a broadening experience, not to put too fine a point on it!" I stopped, as Captain Lawford was beginning to laugh out loud. "That it can be, Edward. I have not had the pleasure – and hope not to – broadening or otherwise. Tends to besmirch one's record, doesn't it. But I am interrupting you; do carry on."

I described the high points of the *Pandora* commission and pointed out that, with the unpleasantness with France as yet unbegun when we returned to Portsmouth, I was set ashore on half pay. I languished for about a year and then received my orders to *Penelope*. I did not mention, of course, Kendall or how I had occupied my time ashore.

"So with the *Europa* convoy leaving Portsmouth, I managed to arrange a ride – or perhaps, more accurately, the Admiralty arranged a ride – to Jamaica. And here I am. At your service, sir." I did not think adding the details of the voyage in Europa would add anything to the report.

During my monologue, Lawford had said nothing save an occasional grunt or "aye" but did not interrupt me again. When I stopped, he stood, extended his hand and again welcomed me aboard. He shifted across the cabin to his desk where he again sat down. I turned in my seat so as to face him.

"I mentioned, I believe, what our commission would be when first you stepped aboard. To expand on that theme, I will tell you in more detail so as to put you 'in the picture,' as it were. I have always felt it productive to ensure that the entire choir is singing from the same hymnal.

"Commodore Ford has assigned us to escort the convoy that Europa was originally taking back to *Europe.* I am sure you learned that our good commodore has determined that *Europa* would make a splendid flagship – surely a sixty-four would be a significant improvement from the sixth rate from which he has been flying his flag.

"But I was describing our assignment; at the present, I am told we will be escorting as many as fifty ships, most sailing to Europe, but some to North America. Of course, as we are now back into the unpleasantness with the French, we should expect to encounter some privateers here in the Caribbean and then, quite probably, some warships once we approach the continent.

Fifty ships would make a plum prize and would be a mighty temptation for any antagonist, even a harbor-loving Frenchman! Bearing the responsibility for their safe arrival will surely keep us busy should we encounter any of them. We will be practicing our crew on a daily basis in sail handling and gunnery until they are proficient to my satisfaction. You and Mister Earnshaw will be overseeing the training on the great guns. Our gunner, when we secure one, will manage training on the swivels and small arms. Mister Bogue and Mister Popplewell, our sailing master, will deal with the sail handling effort.

"I am hoping for an uneventful commission, assuming we are able to fill our complement of hands and avoid any unpleasant weather – and the French! A rather tall order, I suspect!" He smiled, perhaps a bit ruefully.

Then he said, "And speaking of filling our complement, your predecessor was in the process of procuring hands from the press and from among the landsmen here in Port Royal and Kingston. The men who came from *Hound* with me are fine men but would be hard put to manage by themselves. Mister Farnsworth had made some inroads with the press, but we remain far from complete. Continuing his efforts in that direction will be your first assignment. Commodore Ford has authorized a press of some two hundred fifty souls. We have fewer than half our complement aboard at the moment and while I surely will not need – nor could I berth – two hundred fifty, we'll will need at least two hundred. Two hundred twenty would make me very happy indeed."

Lawford paused as he looked off into the near distance, perhaps at the distorted image of the harbor beyond his quarter gallery. Then he continued. "It has occurred to me, Ballantyne, that with Commodore Ford's duties requiring his presence here in Port Royal, *Europa* will not be sailing any time soon and so we might avail ourselves of some prime hands in that vessel, should there be any. You, of course, having only recently sailed in her, would be a better judge of them than I, so I will leave to you the delicate task of pressing the commodore's crew!" He smiled, likely thinking he had presented me with a Gordian knot to unravel!

"Aye, sir. I will see to it." I paused, thinking. Now it was my turn to stare out the gallery windows. He noticed.

"Yes, Lieutenant? Is there something else on your mind, hmm?"

A thought had occurred to me and I had only to decide how best to express it to the captain. "Actually, Cap'n, there is. Mister Bogue mentioned that he needed a few warrants – a gunner, a bosun, and perhaps a surgeon. I might be able to find one or two of them...in *Penelope*. And while I suspect it would make Cap'n Rowley none too happy, our needs could be said to be greater, especially with *Convert* under orders, as it were. Obviously, as warrants, we can't press 'em, but perhaps a quiet word to the commodore..." *And if Cap'n Rowley were to be unhappy, who better to make him so than yours truly!*

"Capital, Ballantyne, capital! I shall drop in on the commodore straight away! A 'quiet word' with him should answer nicely, assuming, of course, that you can convince them to join us. He is quite keen that we fill our complement and sail on time. Pressures from the merchants with goods to transport, I imagine."

He dismissed me, suggesting I have a look about and meet some of the men and the midshipmen. I stood, thanked him for his time, and took my leave as he began to shuffle the papers on his desk.

When I got back to the wardroom, Bogue and Earnshaw were deep in conversation which promptly stopped when I entered. Both looked up. *Were they surprised at my return?*

"Please carry on with your conversation, gentlemen; I am sorry to have interrupted you. I shall see if I might round up a mid or two and have a look about the ship. Should you need me for anything, send a steward to find me."

"Oh no, Edward. You mustn't leave. We were simply discussing where we might find the remainder of our complement. Since we're scheduled to sail in perhaps only a fortnight, I should like to have as much of a full crew as we can muster. Sit, and let us discuss our...and now your – problem." Bogue smiled broadly as he spoke, easing my concerns over what they might have been discussing. I was uneasy about being labeled a pariah – as Captain Rowley had done – by my fellow officers.

"Cap'n Lawford has suggested that *Europa* might be able to provide us with more than a handful of sailors, as she's unlikely to be sailing anytime soon. It occurs to me that we might send a mid and a small party out to her to select some prime hands. And, Joe, he might be able to help with some warrants." I did not offer to the first lieutenant any insight as to who or where they might be found.

"Very well done, indeed, Edward. Aboard less than two hours and already you have put yourself in our debt! I think young Sherwin might be able to manage a press gang, don't you, William?" Bogue's broad smile and quick decision to send Midshipman Thomas Sherwin to carry out my suggestion aboard Europa put a smile on my face as well. And Earnshaw quickly agreed with the choice.

"Aye, too bad we haven't a few Marines to send with him; might add a bit of a punch to his status. But there's the rub, I reckon. He'll have to manage it on his own. Might show some metal!" Earnshaw rose, presumably to find Midshipman Sherwin.

The days passed quickly, filled with time-consuming, frustrating, but unquestionably necessary events; pressing crew, taking on stores, water, and finding spare yards, cordage, and lumber with which we might repair damage – either from a storm or an encounter with the enemy. The commodore, good to his word, had responded to Captain Lawford's "suggestion" about the warrants with alacrity. And Midshipman Sherwin did indeed 'show some metal' and, within a week's time, had marched a score of sailors down the quay where they filed aboard, signed articles, and joined our crew. I discovered that about half of those who had come from Europa and were quite pleased to be in a frigate, especially one heading back to England.

I ran into my friend Henry McMahon in a shore side public house shortly after the year changed. Initially I had worried if anything had been said about him transferring and how he might react. I needn't have.

McMahon greeted me effusively and seemed barely able to contain his joy over his new orders. "I am given to understand, Edward, that we shall again be shipmates. I can tell you I look forward to a return to 'Old Blighty' in *Convert*. Been too long since I took my leave from her cold shores. This unhealthy atmosphere here in the tropics provides all too frequently an opportunity to test my limited medical skills. Entirely too much sickness is inspired by the tropical air; breeds depression as well as untold maladies.

"Should you have had anything to do with the commodore's

action, I thank you. I expect to be transferring my dunnage and medical equipment within the week. I know Rowley is anything but pleased, but as I understand it, *Convert*'s need is greater than *Penelope*'s, what with your orders and such."

I failed completely in suppressing a broad smile. "You haven't heard anything about the bosun or gunner from *Penelope* by any chance, have you, Henry?"

"Edward, you scheming bastard! Don't tell me you are playing puppet master, pulling the wires behind the curtain? I say! How have you managed to confound Rowley so completely? And more to the point, how have you convinced the commodore to... never mind that. I don't want to know."

McMahon was smiling, laughing actually, so I knew I was on safe ground with him. "Well, Henry, I would not be so bold as to say my intent was to 'confound' Cap'n Rowley, but I can honestly say I am not sorry to hear of his condition!"

And then I told him of my confrontation with our former commander immediately prior to my reporting into *Convert*. I refrained from any remark regarding my suggestion to Captain Lawford about visiting the commodore.

"Ahh! That explains much! And I can't say I am sorry to be out of that ship. Especially out from under Stephen Ware. In fact, I think he might have been more put out by the loss of the three of us than was the captain!"

We toasted our good fortune and continued to revel in the anticipated joy of returning to England, each for our own reasons. Other officers, some from *Europa* and young Goodwin from *Penelope,* joined us and we all became quite boisterous. The first lieutenant in *Convert,* Joseph Bogue, appeared, joined us at my invitation, and shook hands all around. He quickly entered into our gaiety and stood us all to a new round of drink. We, all of us, appeared well on course to gilding our livers and would suffer the next day's hot copper, but undoubtedly in good company!

I am given to believe that many of the other patrons thought simply that we were reprising a celebration of the new year. The only pall on the evening came when several officers from *Iphigenia* arrived, took a table across the room, and silently glared at us – or at least at Henry and me – for several minutes. For our part, after taking note of their arrival and a glance in their direction, we quite ignored them. But one of them in particular seemed unable to shift his gaze from us and ultimately rose from his seat to make his wavering way to our table, a menacing scowl across his face.

He marched – as best as a somewhat drunken man might – straight toward Henry, who sat adjacent to me, glaring at him with ill-concealed contempt. Finally the surgeon stood and when fully erect, was some half a foot taller than his silent assailant. Our visitor's eyes followed Henry's face as it rose above his own.

"Is there something you wanted, Lieutenant? To join us, per chance?" Henry's expression was quite neutral, his tone likewise.

"I would not be caught dead joining you, sir. You are a disgrace to the Service." Our visitor growled, though his words sounded a bit muddled: "You are a *dishgrace* to the *Shervish.*"

"And yet, here you are, hovering over us like a hungry sea bird waiting for a scrap of carrion to fall at your feet. Are you not fearful that your mates will see you with us? I repeat, sir, what is it you wish from us?"

"You destroyed a fine officer with your butchery, sir. Lieutenant Jones, who is my...indeed, our...friend, will never be the same again and will likely have to leave the service. A one-armed lieutenant is not about to rise to command." A contemptuous curl of his lip accompanied our visitor's words.

"Well, Mister Friend-of-Lieutenant-Jones, I would offer that a dead lieutenant is even less likely to rise to command. And that is precisely what Jones would have been had I not relieved him of his arm. Would that have been your preference? I somehow doubt it was his."

"Hmmmph!" Was the only response before our assailant turned none too steadily on his heel and made his somewhat circuitous way back to his mates.

"Ah! The courage instilled by ardent spirits! While it would have been most ungentlemanly, I was quite prepared to defend myself should it have come to it." Henry spoke with a rueful smile as he took his seat and lifted his pewter in silent salute to our departed visitor.

Days were accomplished, stores were aboard and stowed, and we attained most all of the two hundred crew that Captain Lawford had set as his minimum. Two hundred twenty did not seem likely. Many of the pressed men, mostly the landsmen, had become 'volunteers' when word was passed of the 5£ bounty each would be paid to volunteer, no matter they actually were pressed. Before we finally raised our sails and put to sea, our crew – officers and men – had grown to two hundred seventeen twenty-nine Marines, and twenty-eight supernumeraries who were aboard simply to get back to England for one reason or another. Another midshipman, a pleasant young Scottish chap of some fifteen years, named Colin Campbell, turned up, courtesy of Commodore Ford, to join our masters mate, James Hutchins, and Midshipman Sherwin, who had already distinguished himself by successfully running the press gang.

We also would carry one prisoner, shackled below and allowed on deck for but one hour each day. I also discovered, when going through the muster book to establish quarters stations and a watch bill, that two of our crew were fictitious, a not uncommon practice to sweeten someone's pocket. I did not bother to track down the culprit – or culprits, but neither did I assign the non-existent men to posts or watches! And we found a gunner who, while not from *Penelope*, answered our needs quite nicely. Some of the merchant vessels began to appear at Port Royal by mid-month, and Captain Lawford announced we would soon sail, and advised us to put our affairs in order, settle any open bills ashore, and stand by. We would sail in company with the merchantmen to Bluefields Bay, where we would rendezvous with the remainder of our charges.

CHAPTER TEN
Late January 1794
Port Royal, Jamaica

"Mister Ballantyne, you will take Midshipman Sherwin with you and visit the ships on this list. Deliver the sailing instructions to each captain, explain the standing night orders, signals, and convoy route. Make sure they know the rendezvous points along the way should they become separated from the main body. You might also mention the potential for trouble as we near Europe, in case they have not heard of our renewed troubles with France." Lawford handed me a piece of foolscap, his neat and precise hand easy to decipher, indicating the vessels I was to visit. There were fifteen.

Captain Lawford had summoned the officers, warrants, and midshipmen to attend him in his diminutive cabin. Once we were all jammed in, shoulder to shoulder, he explained his plan to sail within the week and detailed for us the information we were to pass along to our charges. He had split, more or less, the nearly thirty ships that had been arriving over the past week and were now spread out off Port Royal, in the bight and nearly to Kingston, assigning about half to me and the remainder to Earnshaw and Campbell.

"Cap'n, would it not be more easily managed to ask the captains or first officers to simply come to us and meet all together at, say, Fort Charles, to receive the information just once, rather than having to go through it with each?" Joe Bogue, First Lieutenant, spoke quietly, torn between the obvious efficacy of his suggestion and the wishes of his captain.

Lawford's eyes narrowed slightly, his mouth a thin line. "Well, Mister Bogue, that might indeed be an improvement had we more time to collect all those rascals and put them in one place. I think we might best accomplish this as I suggested, utilizing the services of Lieutenants Ballantyne and Earnshaw. I suspect that were we to simply hoist a signal in Convert to convene as you suggest, without first giving them the signal book, we might find ourselves quite ignored. That would never do!" Lawford smiled at his first, taking the sting out of the gentle rebuke.

"Aye, sir. Merely a suggestion. And it will be a good rehearsal

for when we have to instruct the next lot…in Bluefields, that is."
Bogue backed off at once.

The weather had been a trifle unsettled. Thunder storms had been rumbling through Port Royal, rattling shutters and soaking the landscape with their downpours. Work on the ship continued apace without regard to the weather; crews striking below stores, spares, and provisions getting repeatedly soaked, but with the steamy temperatures, almost enjoying the brief respites from the heat. Since Earnshaw and I had most likely a full day and more of ship visits ahead of us, we left directly after being dismissed, making a quick stop in our respective cabins to collect our boat cloaks and, in, my case, my tarpaulin jacket and hat. Our assigned seconds had collected the necessary sets of paper for each ship including the signal books, printed sailing instructions, and standing orders for each vessel and had deposited an oiled cloth bag of them at the break in the bulwark ready to go into the boats.

Earnshaw, accompanied by Masters Mate James Hutchins, set off in the blue cutter smartly managed by a well-practiced crew. Sherwin and I followed them in the yawl, not nearly as smartly managed due to a crew of mostly landsmen. I suspected that by the time we had completed our assigned visits, they would be a great deal more skilled!

The first name on my list was *Britannia,* a ship-rigged vessel anchored about a musket shot directly off Port Royal. According to my list, she mounted eight carriage guns, each of twelve pounds, and eight small swivels that could be moved to various points about the ship, including to her tops. Her crew consisted entirely of civilians, of course, causing me to doubt their capability with the guns should there be trouble! Most merchant captains would not expend the powder and shot necessary to properly train a crew in the use of the armament, and hence, when there was trouble, the crew at the guns often proved to be more of a liability than a help.

I studied the ship as we approached. Her sides were streaked with grime, salt, and rust, signaling that she had been long at sea with little attention to maintenance. To my eye, most of her standing rigging looked slack, or at least not set up the way I would wish, and I noticed that some of her hempen shrouds were quite devoid of any slush or tar. The sails furled to her yards betrayed the work of sloppy topmen: bags between stops, corners hanging, and, to my mind, too few stops holding the sails in place. Surely not a tidy job aloft! The whole picture suggested the guns would be scarcely more than ballast.

All in all, a sad excuse for a proper vessel I thought. *Glad I am not sailing in her!*

As we pulled alongside and the men tossed their oars almost in unison, the watch, a sloppily turned out seaman, leaned over the bulwark and shouted down to us, inquiring as to our intentions; we responded, and our bowhook quickly secured the boat to the main chain wale, just forward of the break in their bulwark. Manropes appeared and Sherwin, carrying the bag of instructions, and I scrambled up the battens to the deck.

"Lieutenant Ballantyne and Midshipman Sherwin for Captain Martin, if you please, sir." I answered somewhat brusquely the question posed by the watch, but we had little time to linger given the lengthy list of ships we would visit. The man tossed me a somewhat mocking salute, instructed us to "wait right 'ere, if you please," and slouched off toward the stern, presumably to find the captain. I was little impressed with his off-hand manner until I reminded myself, yet again that this was the merchant service, not the Royal Navy!

After standing about for some lengthy period, during which we enjoyed a brief downpour making me glad I had thought to bring my oiled jacket and hat, a different sailor – this one was a bit neater in his dress - appeared and directed us to follow him aft where, presumably, we would be granted an audience with the captain. We trundled down one ladder and followed our guide down a short passage, which ended at a closed door. He knocked.

"Enter!"

We stepped into the cabin where a short man, bewhiskered, and only partially dressed – he wore trousers, slippers, and an open blouse which was none to clean – stood peering out the quarter gallery windows. Our guide remained without.

"Captain Martin?"

"Aye, lad. That's who I am. What is it you need?" A gruff voice, Irish accent, and, unlike his countrymen, little warmth in evidence.

"It's not what *we* need, Captain, but rather what *you* will need from us.

"I am Lieutenant Edward Ballantyne, second lieutenant in HMS *Convert,* and this is Midshipman Sherwin. We have been instructed by our commander, Captain John Lawford, to provide you with the sailing directions, signals, and other pertinent information necessary to sail with our convoy."

He turned toward us. A frown appeared on his grizzled face though why I could not fathom. Were we disturbing his reverie as he studied the filthy waters of Port Royal? What I offered was important – and very necessary – information.

"Aye, lad. You can just leave it there on the desk and move yourselves along to the others. This ain't my first convoy with you navy sods and I am well aware of the drill. Only thing I need to know is when do you plan on gettin' underway? We been rottin' here in this unholy den of iniquity now comin' on to a fortnight. My sailors're spendin' more time ashore in the taverns and whorehouses than in the ship. Lost two men already – one simply vanished and one killed in a fight, stabbed to death by some crimp, I'm given to understand – and I can ill-afford to lose any more. Had another man pressed last month down at Saint Christopher. Ships belong at sea and sailors in 'em, not rottin' in some hell-hole full of diseased strumpets and liquor guzzling pirates!"

I was stunned! While true that I have not had much experience in dealing with civilian shipmasters, I surely did not expect this reception! I stared at Captain Martin for a moment, digesting his vitriol, and then took a breath. Perhaps his anger toward the navy stemmed from the loss of a man to the press, but it seemed a bit much for the loss of one man.

"Captain Martin. Regardless of your attitude regarding participating in a convoy which, I might offer, is designed to protect your ship, cargo, and crew from the likelihood of attack from England's enemies, I am tasked with providing you with the information you will need so that we might maintain order in what will be a quite large group of ships. Should one or more of the vessels act contrary to the sailing orders, not follow signals when given, or become separated from the convoy for whatever reason, they put the rest of the ships in peril. *Convert* will be the only escort on the first leg and the cooperation of each captain is crucial to the successful completion of the voyage. I would appreciate your sending for your mate, so that I might run through Cap'n Lawford's instructions with *both* of you and explain the signals we will be using to maintain the convoy. I will be as quick as ever I might, but I must insist on performing this duty." I put some iron in my voice and posture but did so without raising my voice.

Martin's head jerked up at me, studied me for a moment with a scowl, nodded, and bellowed through an open scuttle above his head.

"On deck there. Pass the word for the mate to lay below. Now!"

An uneasy silence enveloped the three of us as we waited on the arrival of his first mate. He neither sat nor invited us to do so, and so we stood, a bit awkwardly, as we stared at each other and out the gallery windows.

"Mister Sherwin, perhaps you might bring out the material we will need to go over once the mate appears.

"Cap'n, do you mind if he uses your dining table?"

"You do whatever you like, Lieutenant. You likely will in any case. Damn navy sods. Always playing the regulations and rules!"

"Aye, Cap'n. We do. That's why we have the task of shepherding you lot across the ocean." I was growing weary of his attitude and could scarcely wait for the mate to arrive so we might get on with it and leave. A welcome knock on the door came after only a few more minutes and the first mate stepped into the cabin in response to a terse "enter."

"Mister Mate, these navy sods need to explain the rules and regulations for the convoy to us. Think we're on our first ride. And they need for *both* of us to hear it. Bloody stupid, you ask me!"

"Good morning. I am Lieutenant..."

"Get on with it, Lieutenant. The mate don't give a fig for who you are. Just say your piece and go pester some other poor soul."

"Very well, then Cap'n." I seethed. Picking up the signal book, I opened it and flipped through a few pages, then handed it to the mate.

"These are the signals we will be using to communicate with the merchant vessels in company. You will note that each consists of a day signal of flags as well as a night signal of lanterns hoisted aloft. In some cases, we may fire a weather gun to call attention to the signal, but not always. It is your responsibility to maintain a lookout specifically for any signals." I watched the mate to see if he had taken a different attitude about all this than his captain.

Looking up from the book I had handed him, he noticed me looking at him and nodded; a good sign, I thought, and carried on.

"I have marked on this chart the rendezvous locations should you become separated from the main body of the convoy. Do not wait at any one for more than a week before carrying on."

A 'harrumph" from Captain Martin greeted that instruction which did not surprise me given the impatience he had earlier demonstrated over his enforced wait in Port Royal.

I went through the remainder of the instructions, saving for last what I thought might be the most important. "It is most crucial, gentlemen, that *no* ship get ahead of *Convert*. While I expect the ships to be some spread out – there will be fifty and possibly more of you – I cannot emphasize enough that each and every one must remain astern of us at all times, but especially at night. We will be your only escort until we reach Cuba where I am given to understand a navy brig will be joining. They will take station in the rear for the crossing, but until then, it will be only *Convert* and we must keep station to the fore. You will be responsible, of course, for your own navigation." I looked at Captain Martin as I said this, half expecting an argument or retort of some stripe. I was not disappointed.

Another "harrumph" issued forth from him. "Bloody orders. Your job is to protect us from pirates and privateers. We dinna need all your damn orders. Gammon, that's what it is. Just get us across to England; that's your job, lad. Not handin' out bloody orders like we was in your bloody navy."

"One last item, Cap'n: has your crew been trained to any degree on the carriage guns you carry...or the swivels? Our records indicate your owners show eight of each aboard."

"Aye, eight there are. And the bloody owners ain't got the sense of a jellyfish. They see to loadin' me down with the sodding guns, but don't give me but a bit o' powder and enough shot to fire each of 'em but a few times. So are the men trained? Not on your life, Lieutenant. We'll be relyin' on the Navy should there be a problem. So you stiff-collared coves better be able to do your job and protect us! That's why you're there, ain't it?"

Just as I thought and so typical of many merchant ships. I had heard of captains who provided powder and shot out of their own purses so as to train their men, but the amiable Captain Martin was clearly not in that group. I chose to ignore the challenge.

"Thank you for your time, Cap'n. Mister Mate. We expect to weigh within the week for Bluefields Bay to join up with the rest of the convoy. I wish you a pleasant voyage." While I resisted the urge to get caught up in another harangue from this irritating man, I did, I think, manage to inject a suitable level of insincerity into my good wishes.

"Well! That went well!" Midshipman Sherwin mumbled to me as we gained the weather deck. "What a delight he must be to sail under!"

I laughed. This young chap might actually have a future. He surely had a sense of irony. He was droll beyond what I had expected. "Aye, indeed. But we needn't worry about that. Pity the poor sods who do sail with him."

We clambered over the side and down to the boat, where I directed our coxswain to the next vessel on the list, hoping the master might be of a different stripe than Captain Martin.

A long row to the eastern end of the bight took us to the brig *Betsey,* a properly turned-out vessel with freshly painted sides, a taut rig, and her sails furled on her yards tight and neat. We answered the watch's hail as we had before and drifted alongside with our oars tossed, almost smartly. A line dropped down to the bowhook who secured it within the boat, and Sherwin and I clambered up the boarding battens, clutching the heavy manrope that had been smartly decorated with fancywork.

"Sirs? How may I assist you?" A pleasant chap in seaman garb greeted us as we made the deck. Taking in our uniforms, he added, "I would collect you are likely from the navy ship going with the convoy?"

"Aye. Quite right you are and it's your captain we seek...as well as the first mate." I answered him with a smile, noting as I did so a figure dressed in a frock coat, black trousers, and tall hat hurrying forward from the stern.

"Well, there he comes now. That would be him just there." The sailor pointed his chin at the man I had just spotted.

"Gentlemen! Welcome aboard *Betsey*. How may I help you? I am Richard Kent, master." He stuck out a huge paw, which I took in my own hand to shake, noting as I did that his hand quite nearly enveloped mine.

To say that Kent was a large man would be gross understatement. He was some advanced in years – maybe in his late-forties – with coarse features, a formidable set of dark whiskers, shot with grey, which almost concealed a livid scar running from the corner of his left eye down where it disappeared into his whiskers. Grey hair pulled back into a proper queue and tied with a length of tarred hempen twine showed below the brim of his black high-crowned hat. Dark eyes set under a pair of bushy brows were alive and animated as his thin lips curled into a warm smile. He showed a paucity of teeth. And the few remaining that I could see were stained and chipped. I shortly found out why when he pulled a well-used pipe from his pocket and clamped it firmly in what teeth he possessed. His skin had long ago weathered to a rich mahogany color – the result, I surmised, of a lifetime at sea.

"Lieutenant Ballantyne and Midshipman Sherwin. His Majesty's frigate *Convert*, late of the French navy. We will be escorting you and some fifty or so others to North America and Europe. We would like to acquaint you and your mate with the procedures and signals we will be using for the convoy."

"Excellent, excellent! Come with me. We shall repair to my cabin straight away and get out of this beastly sun!" The man was fairly dancing with enthusiasm; whether to get out of the 'beastly sun' or at the prospect of actually starting the voyage was unclear. "Johnson, find Mister North and invite him to attend me in the cabin, if you please."

The sailor who greeted us, Johnson, turned at once to fetch the first mate, and Captain Kent hurried aft to the scuttle below. We hastened after him.

While his cabin was indeed "out of the sun," it was very nearly as warm within as it was topside. It was modest – actually "tiny" would be more descriptive – equipped with a table in the center that served double duty as both desk and dining table. Six chairs were crammed into the space around it. A curtain to one side almost concealed his cot and a peg for his clothes, while a similar curtain on the other side hid his seat of ease. The quarter gallery windows, remarkably clean, gave us a distorted and wavy view of the harbor and of several ships anchored near by. Several windows were open, allowing a bit of a breeze to rustle the papers on his table.

Kent shed his frock coat, draped it onto a peg by the door, tossed his hat into the table and threw himself into the chair at the far end, waving us to chairs on either side. "Sit, sit. Bloody hot here, even out of the sun. Take off your jackets if you wish."

Then, raising his gravelly voice, "Burke! Burke, I say. Bring us some lemonade, you scurvy rascal!" He shouted through the open door to presumably his steward or servant.

"Save for a tot of rum and lime juice from time to time, I do not allow ardent spirits in my ship; too easy by half to wind up with proper and good sailors who conceal it and then turn up drunk. My people are mostly happy, even without it. They don't abstain ashore, of course, and more than likely make up for the paucity of spirits aboard! Of course, a few do bring their doxies from ashore aboard, but the mate makes sure they're gone when we sail." He smiled with genuine mirth.

Now this is a happy ship. At least the captain is happy, which is to say he would not be so were his crew miserable. And of course, the women aboard is not unusual. Even in the Navy I knew of men who had, from time to time, brought their whores aboard, even though the regulations allowed "wives" only.

A sharp rap on the doorjamb announced a new arrival. The man at the door carried a large pitcher and a tray of glasses, and I cleverly deduced that he was Burke, the captain's steward, and not the mate. And a glass of sharp lemonade was a welcome respite from the heat and tension of our previous visit.

Not a moment after we had each taken a large draught of the tangy tonic, another knock announced the arrival of the mate.

"Mister Cowen, meet Lieutenant...uh, I'm sorry Lieutenant. Your name seems to have slipped its moorings." He actually looked abashed at his lapse.

"Ballantyne, Cap'n. Mister Cowen, a pleasure. And this is

Midshipman Sherwin. We are sent by Cap'n Lawford of His Majesty's Frigate *Convert,* to provide you with the signals and procedures for the convoy." I glanced at my list. "I see you will be dropping once we are well-past Cuba, when the convoy turns east, to make your way to America. nonetheless, we will expect you to obey our signals and instructions until you depart.

"Let me take you quickly through the signal book and the charts you will need." Sherwin took his cue and produced the necessary documents, spreading them out on the table.

"Yes, of course, Lieutenant. We would be silly buggers, indeed, to go off on our own. It will be hazardous enough to make Boston without seeing some bloody French privateer; I have heard they are lurking off the coast north of the Floridas. So you may rest assured we will adhere to your signals promptly. And depending on any reports we might receive at sea, we might stay with the convoy a bit longer to enjoy the safety of numbers, as it were." He smiled around his cold pipe, then withdrew it to sip from his lemonade.

The briefing went smoothly, few questions from the captain or mate, and Sherwin and I took our leave, wishing both gentlemen a sincere *bon voyage.*

The remainder of our visits, while time consuming, were carried off without undue problems; the captains and first mates, where available, were, for the most part, glad to have the navy escorting them and paid heed to our instructions, asking intelligent and relevant questions and making notes as needed. We were invited to dinner aboard one ship, *Lion,* commanded by a most charming individual, a Captain Thomas King, who was most generous in his compliments of the navy and set a memorable table. *Lion* was ship rigged, clean, and loaded with molasses and sugar for England. We lingered longer than we should have and finished the last of our assigned vessels as the sun fell behind the mountains to the west, plunging the harbor into sudden darkness. A tired boat crew rowed a tired lieutenant and midshipman back to *Convert.*

"You won't believe what you missed, Mister Ballantyne!" Midshipman Colin Campbell greeted me at the entry port, practically breathless in anticipation of telling his story.

"Hmmm. The convoy is cancelled and we're going to remain

indefinitely here in Port Royal." I smiled and answered with the first thing that popped into my head, knowing full well that would not be what he had in mind.

"No, no, no! Of course not. One of the sailors, Dryden, I think his name is, is accused of murdering a woman, a doxie, right on the gundeck. In front of two of his messmates! Can you imagine! Happened just after you and Thomas...er, I mean, Midshipman Sherwin, left this morning."

Actually, I could imagine...easily. I happened to recall Dryden, rated able, who shipped as a volunteer from Port Royal, collecting the 5£ bounty. He seemed a bit sketchy, though he did manage to produce a paper giving his rating, but we could determine little beyond that he had been ashore for a while in the port. I suspected he might have an issue ashore, but with the paucity of skilled sailors aboard, he passed muster. And our surgeon pronounced him healthy after a cursory examination. But he did have an air of violence about him, bubbling just below the surface. In fact, Henry mentioned the man made him nervous just examining him.

"Well, isn't that something! What will happen? Will he being tried aboard or sent to the brig ashore for trial? We can hardly delay our departure on his account." I really didn't care a fig for what happened to the man, was simply making conversation with the enthusiastic youngster. "What is the captain doing about it?"

"Don't know about Cap'n Lawford, but Mister Bogue tells me they will court martial him right here aboard – he said something about the commodore sending over a sufficient number of senior officers to sit on the board – and it will be in the next few days. Meantime, the bugger's in irons...chained up down in the orlop deck.

"Can you imagine! He actually cut her throat right in front of his messmates! Shouldn't be much of a court martial, I would think. Got him dead to rights!" The young man's enthusiasm advanced with each of his exclamations.

I thanked the youngster for his animated delivery of the news and took my leave, looking forward to a bite in the gunroom and settling into my cot for a night's sleep. Some of my mates, including both Earnshaw (why wasn't he as tired as I?) and Bogue invited me to accompany them ashore to quaff a few cool drinks, but I simply wasn't keen for it and begged off.

Whilst I partook of a bit of toasted cheese that Black had prepared for me, Henry McMahon wandered in and took a seat, pouring himself a glass of claret.

"I reckon you have heard of all the excitement today, Edward. I, for one, will be glad to be shed of the bugger once he gets shipped ashore for a court martial. Cap'n Lawford doesn't want to wait for the commodore to convene a trial here on board. It means we'll lose a few men who witnessed the heinous crime, but Lawford's itching to get to sea. Can't say as I blame him. I certainly have had enough of this pest hole."

I smiled at the surgeon's exclamation, agreeing with it, and somewhat surprised that the man who had spent more time in the local public houses and watering holes than in the ship would have reached such a conclusion. Perhaps he had extended his credit beyond that which even the prize shares from his time in *Penelope* would cover.

"I was given to understand from young Campbell that he would be court martialed aboard. Something about the commodore sending up sufficient senior officers to provide a proper board. So, he's being put ashore, is he?"

"Aye, ashore he is. Lawford's looking to weigh anchor in the next day or so." McMahon's information seemed more credible than the midshipman's.

"Be that as it may, Henry. If you will excuse me, I am fatigued from my day and plan on retiring. I will see you in the morning. I bid you a pleasant good night!" And I stood, took my leave, and quite missed Henry's puzzled look.

The morning dawned bright, the sun climbing above the horizon into a cloudless sky; the day promised to be a hot one. The decks were holystoned, washed down, and flogged dry; hammocks were rolled tightly and stowed in the netting along the weather deck, and the men fed their breakfast of burgoo and fresh fruit.

It seemed to most of us in the wardroom that the ship was ready in all respects to sail and the conversation centered on when Captain Lawford would determine to leave. January was racing toward February, and we were already well past our previously announced departure date. The crew was beginning to become a trifle testy, daily undergoing all manner of sail drills, dumb show with the great guns, and inspections. The heat added little to their moods, and I thought we were all ready to get back to sea. *Iphigenia* and *Penelope* had sailed ten days earlier, heading back out on patrol, no doubt hoping for another plumb prize like the ship currently under my feet! I was more than a little jealous and had shared my thoughts with Henry McMahon who echoed them, whether in sympathy or reality I was uncertain, but it was nice to have a comrade who shared my own feelings.

"I am given to understand that we are to receive half a dozen or more French prisoners this morning, most likely crew from this very ship! Cap'n told me they're bein' sent off to England for holdin, or tradin', or who-knows-what. Oughta be interesting for 'em to be in the ship's company and then prisoners in the same ship!" Marine Captain Jeremy Dolan laughed as he shared this bit of news with us – only our first lieutenant, Joe Bogue, was aware of it – speaking around a sizeable mouthful of fruit. A dollop of the juice ran down his chin, escaping from within as he spoke, but he seemed not to notice. Maybe that was what we had been awaiting.

"What're you going to do with them, Jeremy? Can't very well put the buggers in the orlop for the whole voyage." Earnshaw seemed concerned about the welfare of our guests.

"Who gives a bloody shyte, lad. They're Frogs. They can ride in the rope locker for all I care. My sergeant is taking care of their accommodations, and I am sure he'll be mindful of their comfort!" Our Irish-born Marine captain sneered.

A sharp rap on the doorframe interrupted the conversation before Dolan could become any more riled. One of his Marines stood at attention outside the entry, awaiting permission to speak.

"Yes, Parsons? What is it?" Dolan seemed annoyed at the interruption; we were relieved we would not have to listen to further diatribe from our Marine colleague.

"Cap'n asks the officers to attend him in the cabin, sir. Quick as ever they might."

"Very well, you may return to your duties." Dolan barely looked at the man, returning his gaze to his audience and visibly trying to recall the thread of his earlier pronouncements.

Breakfast remained unfinished, a small sacrifice to avoid the obnoxious Marine, and we all stood and made ready to leave the room. Dolan, when he saw he had lost his audience, followed us, and we were soon all crowded into Captain Lawford's cramped cabin.

CHAPTER ELEVEN
Tuesday, 28 January 1794
Port Royal to Bluefields Bay

"Gentlemen I offer good news: at last, we are ordered underway by Commodore Ford. We are to leave on the first tide with a fair breeze for Bluefields Bay where we will collect the remainder of our merchantmen. I anticipate weighing tomorrow when the morning ebb starts, assuming this breeze holds.

"As much as I would prefer to sail today, I think we need to give our flock a bit of warning. To that end, Mister Ballantyne, please arrange to have the Blue Peter at the dip on the foremast, fire a gun, and let our civilian friends know their time has come!"

"Aye, sir. I respectfully suggest we should fire a gun several times, as not all of them are as vigilant as we might wish for." I was thinking particularly of *Britannia* and her rude captain, Daniel Martin.

"As you wish, Ballantyne. Make it so." Lawford nodded his agreement, clearly not caring a fig whether the navy fired one, two, three, or a dozen warning shots.

I had seen any number of sailing cards throughout the port, announcing the imminent departure of the flotilla and inviting any who had cargo or a wish to sail to England to enquire at several of the various ships. One announcement – it was in the post office – offered passage and mail delivery to HMS *Convert,* to be sailing within the week. An encouraging bit of news, I recall thinking at the time, ever hopeful. It had been about a fortnight ago that I had seen it.

"Mister Bogue, you will ensure that all hands are aboard, shore-side accounts settled, and the ship is ready for sea in all respects."

"Aye, Cap'n. She's been ready for sea over a week now, she has. As to the people, I would be reluctant to give them time ashore regardless of their accounts; too easy it is, to pull a ruse and do a runner. Already had a couple runners and I wouldn't want to have any more."

"Perhaps, should you feel there might be a valid account to be settled, you might have one or two accompanied by one of our young gentlemen; I doubt they'd run!" Lawford smiled, again, clearly not overly concerned with the details. He just wanted his ship and the convoy at sea.

It was surprising to me, what with our sailing having been "imminent" for a week and more, that the ship, aloft and alow, at once upon the meeting's conclusion, became a hive of frenetic activity. Tops'ls and courses were loosed from their harbor furls, to be held to the yards by its gear only, others simply clewed up, ready to be dropped or hoisted quickly once the order was given. Overseen by the bosun and his mates, running rigging was checked, coils were removed from the pins and re-coiled to ensure each sheet, halyard, brace, or buntline would run freely when needed. Standing rigging was checked for the little problems that could lead to bigger ones which could take down a mast if not sorted out. The carpenter and the purser checked stowage of provisions and supplies in the bowels of the ship, ensuring they would be secure for the duration of the voyage and stowed so as to be accessible in the proper order.

Sailors, when not being "started" by the bosun's cane, sneaked wistful glances ashore, dreaming up excuses to offer as to why they should be allowed to go ashore. Lieutenant Bogue remained unmoved by any – real or illusory – and as a result, we suffered no runners on what appeared to be our final day in Port Royal.

By the time the day ended, a day which had been punctuated by the repeated firing of half charges from the bow chaser calling attention to the blue and white signal fluttering midway up the foretopmast, all hands were quite used up. A few of the seamen settled on the fo'c'sle, swapping stories, dancing half-heartedly to a poorly played fiddle, swatting mosquitoes, and smoking pipes and cheroots. The officers settled in the wardroom, enjoying the relative quiet, some pleasant wine, and the cool air wafting in through the open scuttles. Conversation centered on expectations for the commission, which merchant vessels we might expect to be problems – of course, I mentioned *Britannia* more than once – and what news any might have on the course of the war with our perennial foe, France.

The 28th of January, 1794, began inauspiciously; a grey day with a sultry north-north-westerly breeze threatening rain at any moment. In these latitudes, when the generally easterly trade winds backed toward the west, unpleasant weather frequently followed. But a westerly, should the wind make it that far around the compass, would be a fair breeze for the short sail up the coast. The crew on watch at dawn holystoning the deck, washing and flogging it dry, putting up their hammocks, and eating their breakfast. Bogue and I went over the watch, quarters, and stations bill to ensure all positions were properly manned with "real" people, while Earnshaw and the mids supervised on deck preparations for getting underway. A boat from the shore made its approach and came alongside. The cox'n requested a sling be lowered and, when it was, sent up several large sacks of mail, official and otherwise, which we were to carry to England. In the same boat were two additional supernumeraries, invalids from the Port Royal hospital, who were likewise to be carried to England; they would be required to pay for their meals. My personal observation made me a bit suspicious, as they did not appear to be terribly incapacitated by whatever maladies they might have suffered!

I was still standing on the quarterdeck when the semaphore at the dockyards, just like the one at the Royal Dockyards in Portsmouth, but shorter in height, began its mechanical gyrations which our quartermaster quickly interpreted. "Commodore sends: permission to weigh, God speed and good luck."

"Mister Campbell, compliments to Cap'n Lawford. His presence on deck would be appreciated, if you please. Quartermaster, you may two-block the Blue Peter now, and tell the duty gunner's mate to fire a gun." I continued to watch the tower for any additional signals, even as I spoke.

Lawford issued orders as he appeared from the hatch. "Stations for getting underway, if you please, Ballantyne. Let us execute smartly. I am sure the commodore is watching. Also a gun to signal to our charges."

I offered a crisp "aye, aye, sir," and cast a glance at the foretop mast where the blue and white flag now fluttered from the truck. Lawford looked aloft, saw that I was ahead of him, and smiled in acknowledgment.

A flurry of orders rang throughout the ship and, as though punctuating those orders, the forward 12-pounder fired a half charge on Mister Earnshaw's order. With the Blue Peter two-blocked and the roar of the gun startling every sea bird and most of the inhabitants ashore, our civilian charges should be well aware of our intentions.

The deck became a hive of activity, probably appearing as confusion personified to some of the members of the 10th Regiment of the British Army and their commander, Colonel Amherst, who had taken passage aboard, but was, in reality, carefully choreographed and designed to be efficient. The soldiers, curious to watch, scrambled to get out of the way and generally failed to do so, but the sailors managed to perform their well-rehearsed dance anyway. Everyone had a job; those so assigned grabbed the long wooden bars, shot them home into the top of the capstan and, to the order of the bosun, began the 'stomp and go' march around the device to haul the anchor up, at long last, from the depths of Port Royal Harbor. Other hands scurried to positions on deck, clapping on to halyards, sheets, and braces, while the topmen scurried up the ratlines and laid out on the tops'l yards. Their feet balanced precariously on the footropes, whilst their bodies leaned out over the yards, releasing the few remaining ties that would allow the sails to drop free. In perfect concert with the call from the bow, "anchor's in sight," the heavers on deck put their backs into the halyards, hoisting the tops'l yards, and allowing the sails to billow and flog gently in the light wind. Other men pulled on the braces to bring the yards around to catch the wind, and once the sails began to fill, more hands sheeted them home and the ship gathered way, jibs backed to force the bow to fall off to larboard.

And so, with a minimum of fanfare, His Britannic Majesty's frigate *Convert* rode the easy, damp breeze from the dockyard anchorage, bore off around the point of Port Royal, and headed barely south of west into the broad reaches of the Caribbean. Thirty merchant vessels followed slowly, straggling out as each master or mate won his own anchor. Dull thuds sounded astern and echoed off the hills, as Fort Charles fired a salute, followed by the crack of one of our stern chasers as we answered it.

Under the guise of watching the merchant ships round the point, I studied the structure through my glass and noted the large stretch of sand and scraggly vegetation between the outer wall and the sea. The wall had been built originally at the edge of the water, but the 1692 earthquake, I had been told, had raised a portion of the sea bottom, causing the large separation. The outboard side of the point gained land in the disaster even as the area on the harbor side had dropped precipitously into the water, taking buildings, carts, and draft animals, and people with it, just as our carriage driver to Mister Malloy's party had explained.

"You may tack the ship around and make your course north-a-half-east once we have cleared those islands there, Mister Ballantyne. I want...four leagues...between us and the coast. Should this breeze hold as it now stands, we'll need to keep at least that much water between us and the lee shore. Should it strengthen or shift significantly, call me. Bosun, set the starboard watch. Quartermaster, signal our flock to remain astern of us... and leave it flying until they are all around the point.

"Sailing Master, you may set her courses and stays'ls, if you please. We shall wait on the t'gallants until we see how our friends keep up." Lawford's orders started a flurry of activity, as they were bawled out fore and aft by the appropriate mate or warrant. To those on the quarterdeck, he made the formal announcement, "Lieutenant Ballantyne has the deck."

I watched as he strolled forward, touring the weather deck, talking to a few men as he passed them. I was quite certain that nothing escaped his observation and could see him pointing out details he wanted corrected to the various petty officers he encountered. Each man knuckled his forehead in silent acknowledgment of whatever order the captain gave him.

The breeze remained north of west and I was able to bring our course a bit more westerly than southerly, trimming sheets as we gained sea room. *Convert* shouldered her way into the easy swell, swimming sweetly with a decent turn of speed. I knew the ship would sail faster once we came around to a reach, taking the breeze on our beam – and heading generally northeast toward Bluefields Bay, a short sail along the southern coast of the island.

"The damn Frogs do know how to build a ship, would you not agree, Edward? Pity they are such damnable people! Permission to come onto the quarterdeck, sir." Our surgeon, hatless with his wispy hair blowing in the wind, smiled as he continued up the three steps to the raised quarterdeck, not waiting for the formality of my permission.

"Of course, Mister McMahon. And welcome. I assume all is

well with sick bay and you and your mates are well prepared to deal with the usual maladies that so often spring up on a long voyage?" I reckoned that formality was to be the order of the day, at least for now.

"Ha ha. Yes indeedy. We are ready. Do try to avoid the French, if you please, though. I suspect they would like nothing better than to take possession of their fine ship once again! Seriously, though, Edward. I honestly doubt some of the maladies claimed by our passengers! They appeared quite hale to my eye. Of course, I was not permitted to examine any as they were not signing on as crew, but they seemed relatively healthy – or at least as healthy as one could be in that pestilence filled island!"

"I don't imagine that that's our problem, Henry. They will likely not give you any trouble if they're not really sick. However, I am sure there will be the usual quantity of malingerers to drive you to distraction."

"Aye, there likely will! But I am sure my vast collection of potions will satisfy their needs, quick as ever you please!"

I glanced at the compass, steady in the binnacle, cast an eye back to our charges astern, and said, "Excuse me, Henry." Then I shouted to the sailing master, who was standing by the main-mast obviously awaiting an order.

"Mister Popplewell – stand by to trim your sheets; we will be hauling our wind directly."

To the quartermasters at the wheel, "Bring her up a point, if you please. Make you course due west." The wind seemed to be veering now to a more northerly direction.

Convert responded to her helm quickly, in fact, quicker than Popplewell's men could trim their sheets, and the main course and forecourse both flogged for a moment, provoking shouted curses from both the bosun and the sailing master.

"Lay into those sheets, you bloody lubbers. This ain't a pleasure cruise for your sorry arses to take yer time over. Get them sheets hauled home, damn all!"

The sails filled properly, the sheets secured under the watch-ful eye of Popplewell and the bosun, and the ship gained a knot as she responded with a will to proper management! We would be tacking over to the northeast soon and I gave the sailing master the word to keep his people available. Of course, I was hoping the wind would, in its current unpredictable state, back once again more to the west and allow me to tack sooner, and make Bluefields earlier than expected. Fat chance! And it was starting to rain.

Convert continued to push through the confused seas, the rain spat down in fits and starts, and ahead of us, I could see heavier – much heavier – rain slanting down, obscuring the horizon. I looked astern, glassing the ships of the convoy, now a bit spread out, but all on the same course as were we. Some were bunched close together, as if seeking comfort in the company of the others, while several others seemed to fan out from the pack, preferring the room around them, should they need to maneuver for any reason. One appeared to be pulling into the van of the group, set to the royals, and, even in the relatively easy breeze, had a bone in her teeth and was showing more of her bottom than I would have expected. I studied her for a moment through my glass and then it dawned, clear as day; it was Martin in *Britannia,* pushing ahead of the others on a course that would put his ship ahead of *Convert.*

"Quartermaster, look up the signal for 'remain astern of me' and hoist it with *Britannia*'s number, if you please. Bloody Martin's testing me, I reckon." The last bit was directed at Henry; the quartermaster was already paging through the signal book.

"He's the bloke was so hospitable to you and young Sherwin a few days back, was he not? Apparently your instructions failed to impress." Henry smiled, enjoying the opportunity to have sport at my expense.

For the moment, I ignored him, calling to the messenger instead. "Pass the word for a gunner's mate."

"Well, Mister McMahon. We'll see whether or not I might impress him now!" I glassed the merchant again.

She is a handsome vessel and well managed. I can under-
stand how a master might be tempted to give her her head, but
Martin ought to know better.

As I swept along her deck, enjoying the graceful line, pleasant shear, and now taut rig, I caught a reflection from something near the stern and angled my long glass to see what might have caused it. It was another glass, aimed back at me; that bloody Martin was seeing how we would handle his behavior! Damn all!

"Quartermaster! Is that bloody hoist ready? And where is the gunner's mate I sent for?"

"Here, sir." A sailor whose name I could not recall knuckled his forelock as he waited for my order. He had been standing just off the quarterdeck while I had been caught up in my perturbation with *Britannia* and her rude master.

"A half charge in number 2 bow chaser, if you please, on my command."

He touched his forehead again, being without a hat to doff, and stepped smartly forward to see to pulling the shot and charge from the long 12 on our larboard bow.

"You want the hoist up now, Mister Ballantyne?" The quartermaster and his mate held the halyard with the flags bunched up under his arm.

"Yes, by all means. That...or rather, the master on *Britannia* is watching us even now, so by all means, make the signal. Perhaps we won't need the gun."

I glassed the ship again, now abeam of *Convert,* and saw now two glasses watching us, obviously aware of the flags standing out from the mizzen gaff. In spite of the signal, the ship showed no sign of slowing; no figures were making their way aloft, no scurrying about on deck, and little movement on the quarterdeck. Just as I would have expected from Captain Martin.

I saw the gunner's mate standing just forward of the foremast pin rail; he faced me, obviously awaiting my signal. I waved my hat and shouted, "Fire as you will."

CRACK! The gun spoke almost immediately with the sharp sound that a half charge will produce rather than the deepthroated roar of a full powder load. I took up my glass again and directed it at *Britannia.*

"Ha! That got the bugger's attention. He saw the bloody signal – just wanted me to fire the gun to make it official. Bastard! He's sending his people aloft even now!" I growled, more to myself than to anyone in particular, but the good surgeon heard and commented.

"You're going to have trouble with him again, I suspect, Edward. It is my notion that he's enjoying testing you. And while I am sure he is unaware that you currently have the deck, he is most assuredly aware that you will be paying attention to his antics."

"Aye, I would collect you are quite right, Doctor. But here's Cap'n Lawford. Come up to see what I am shooting at, I imagine."

"Have you a problem, Mister Ballantyne?" Lawford cast his eyes about the ship and then at our flock, most all of which were scattered in clusters astern. Except for the full-rigged ship that was just past our beam and taking in her royals.

"Just calling attention to our signal to remain astern, Cap'n. Cap'n Martin there seems to be testing our resolve to remain in the van and he's apparently got the ship to do it! You may recall I was ill-treated by him and his mate some days ago."

"Is this personal, Lieutenant? I can't imagine he would be able to see your figure on the deck, here, from that distance. Even the Navy hasn't a glass *that* good!"

"I am sure he does not know I have the watch, sir. I suspect he is simply acting in his own interests, perhaps for his own entertainment. But he does seem to want the protection offered by the convoy, else he would have sailed a fortnight ago on his own. He's an obnoxious and rude chap with an able and weatherly ship. I would wager that we'll not see him take his place and follow along like the others."

"Very well, then. Keep me informed should you find difficulty in keeping them at order, if you please. This is only the first day out and we are not even out of Jamaican waters." Lawford nodded, muttered something about "damn civilians," and returned to the scuttle that would take him below.

The watch changed shortly thereafter, Earnshaw relieving me of the forenoon watch. I hastened below to find some dry clothes which, to my delight, my man Black had already laid out for me. Henry was already at table in the wardroom when I stepped in, deep in discussion with Bogue on something that had them both smiling broadly.

"Oh, Ballantyne! The good surgeon was just regaling me with the difficulty you seem to be having with one of our charges. Perhaps we should simply let the man sail off on his own and take his chances. He likely has a fast enough ship to outrun most pursuers, should he encounter any and then he won't be causing us a concern." Joe Bogue was only partially joking I thought.

"Can you imagine the issues that would cause the cap'n? I suspect he would be less than enthusiastic about such a notion, Joe.

Perhaps were I to remain off the quarterdeck, Cap'n Martin would find it less entertaining to test me. Maybe Mister Popplewell could take my watches!" I laughed at the absurdity of the thought.

"You'll not escape the duty *that* easily, Edward! I am sure that Cap'n Martin will tire of his game quickly and find some other way to annoy us." All of us laughed at Bogue's remark.

The day proceeded without further incident, the rain let up after washing us thoroughly in the downpour I had seen earlier, and, as the wind backed again to the west, we tacked over to head toward Bluefields Bay. We dropped our best bower just about dark, as five bells rang out, marking the time as half past six. Our charges filed in dutifully, each finding sufficient room and depth among those ships that had gathered here to await our arrival. Even *Britannia* kept her place in line, though I was sure that Martin and his chief mate glassed us carefully as he guided his ship to the far corner of the anchorage.

Captain Lawford gathered us once again in his cabin, explaining that he would call the newly joined captains aboard tomorrow to handle the chore that Earnshaw and I had managed in Port Royal in one fell swoop. There were but nine ships swinging to their anchors awaiting our arrival so it would not be a chore to have them meet and get their sailing instructions in *Convert*.

As there was little in the way of habitation on shore, and likely even less in the way of entertainment, we all, officers and sailors alike, remained aboard for the evening, finding amusements in, for the seamen, dancing, yarning, or simply enjoying a smoke. The officers managed to enjoy some decent claret, a few hands of whist, some backgammon, and listening to Henry McMahon's tall tales of previous service. Captain Lawford had invited the two midshipmen, Campbell and Sherwin, along with our lone master's mate, James Hutchins, to join him in the cabin for the evening meal, thus ensuring that all hands were suitably amused.

The morning of 29 January dawned, if not bright, at least dry, and following the routine chores of stowing hammocks, holystoning and washing down the decks, and breakfast for all, Captain Lawford ordered the signal for the newly joined captains to repair aboard *Convert*. To call attention to it, he also ordered one of the swivel guns fired, of course without a ball.

Presently, we could see boats in the water, making their way toward us, some well managed, others less so, but nonetheless, covering the half league from the farthest without undue difficulty. Not a breath disturbed the surface of the Bay and the boats, cutting through the flat calms, left interesting patterns in their wakes. Once each had discharged its passenger (in some cases, both the master and his mate appeared), the boat either returned to its ship or simply drifted alongside, the crew resting on their oars.

Our visitors were invited to assemble on the quarterdeck where Popplewell had rigged an awning and set out some chairs. Lemonade, tea, and water were available to those desiring any refreshment. A few bits of bunting and some colorful flags and it would have appeared that the captain was hosting a soiree of some stripe!

"Gentlemen, welcome officially to the convoy. We will be sailing forthwith for Great Britain and North America. The purpose of this meeting is to provide you the necessary information regarding your responsibilities as members of this convoy, what you might expect from us in *Convert*, and procedures to take in any of several different situations." Lawford stood by the binnacle, resting one hand on the wheel and held the other behind his back as though he had secreted a surprise for a child.

He introduced each of us, midshipman and officer, by rank and assignment in the ship and then himself, saying, "I am John Lawford, Captain, and commander of His Majesty's Frigate *Convert*. I have been directed by Commodore John Ford, Jamaica Squadron, Royal Navy, to see you safely to home waters. We will sail through the Gulf of Florida and thence make our landfall at Cape Clear in Ireland. I know there is one or two of you who will be making for ports in America and you will be released as appropriate.

"I am ordered to be attentive to the ships and vessels under my care and to keep them together by every means in my power and to provide you with such orders and directions as I might judge appropriate to the occasion." Lawford shot a glance in my direction as he uttered those words. I smiled in acknowledgment.

"Obviously, our progress will be determined by the slowest among you and I would request your patience to set your own pace to comply with that fact. I am instructed to let none of you part company with the convoy until such time as we have reached our destination.

"Midshipman Campbell will pass among you, providing you with the written directions, signals you might expect to see, and procedures to follow in the event of an attack by the French, either in force or by individual private vessels. Naturally, each of you will act according to the exigency of the moment should that eventuality come to pass."

Each of the captains and, where they were present, their mates, examined the booklets given out by Campbell. Lawford waited, drumming his fingertips on a spoke of the wheel as he stood by. The sun had broken through the clouds and, in spite of Popplewell's awning, it was becoming beastly hot, and no breeze to provide any respite. Lawford, dressed in full uniform, fore and aft bicorn hat, was sweating profusely. I am sure he would have liked nothing more than to retire to his cabin and strip off the heavy wool garments, protocol be damned!

"One item, gentlemen, of utmost importance. It is mentioned in the booklet you have, but I would be remiss were I not to bring it to your attention personally. Your ships must remain behind *Convert* at all times. It is possible that another vessel of the Royal Navy will join us before we make our crossing, but for now, I must insist that you adhere strictly to this order.

"Are there any questions?"

"Sir. I am aware personally of at least another five or six vessels, including two schooners bound for the Carolinas in America, that have yet to appear. I would respectfully request that we await their arrival." A somewhat rough looking chap wearing a none-too-clean white shirt, open at the neck, a low-crowned hat, and black trousers had stood to speak. His dark hair was long and tied in a queue which was unsuccessful in hiding the white shot through it. Whiskers grew down each side of his face and deep-set eyes gave him a menacing look, but his tone was anything but. A soft Irish lilt made his words sound more like an invitation to a dinner than a request to delay the sailing of fifty some ships.

"And you know of these ships, how, Cap'n...?"

"O'Leary, sir. Of the brig *Countess of Galway*. Two of the

masters are – ya might say – close acquaintances and the others are in company. Expected the buggers several days ago from Longwoods on the north coast, but these bloody light westerlies must have delayed their sailing. Good men all, they are, and fine seamen. I could not imagine anything untoward happening to them."

"You are fortunate, Cap'n O'Leary. I suspect we will be stuck here for a few days until these damnable winds turn favorable. As long as they remain from a western quarter, I am forced to delay. With luck, your strays will attend us in short order."

As it turned out, not only was he quite correct in his assessment of the winds, but Captain Lawford was also right about the delayed ships joining up. Well, almost right.

Three days after the meeting in *Convert* with the masters of the Bluefields ships, the watch called our attention to a lone horseman riding along the shoreline and firing a pistol into the air.

"What the devil do you supposed that's all about?" Bogue enquired of Earnshaw and me as we stood at the bulwark, sweating, trying to find a bit of a zephyr to cool us, and discussing when we might actually sail.

"Not a clue, Joe. Might be someone trying to attract the attention of someone in the fleet. Look there, a boat's pulling toward shore. Where's he comin' from, do you think?" Earnshaw pointed at a small ship's boat with only two oarsmen making for the little strip of sand where the horseman paced.

"I'd wager he's off that Irisher's brig, the one whose master was acquainted with the ships not yet here. What was it, *Galway something or other*, right?" I offered, trying to recall the master's name.

"Aye, *Duchess of Galway,* it was, I think. O'Leary the master." Earnshaw seemed to have used most of his energy pointing out the boat, but managed to mumble a further contribution to our collective memory..

"*Countess,* it was, *Countess of Galway* not *duchess,* you dolt. It was only a few days back he told us. But you got the master's name right I think." Bogue laughed, pointing his jibe at both me and Earnshaw.

By the time we had finished discussing the brig and its master, the boat had scuffed ashore on the sandy spit and the rider was dismounted from his horse. I had purloined a long glass from the quarterdeck – they would not be needing it for a spell, I thought – and focused it on the scene playing out before us. The horseman and the officer from the boat were engaged in an animated conversation of which naturally, we could hear not a word. After a few minutes, the two shook hands and returned to their respective conveyances. The boat's crew pushed their craft off the sand, jumped in, and began to stroke back the way they had come. The horseman, for his part, rode down the beach a short distance, then followed a path up a hill and into the jungle growth, disappearing from our sight.

We watched at the boat made the side of the Irish brig, proving our earlier assessment correct, and then shortly a signal broke from the main yard of the same ship.

"Midshipman Sherwin, can you make out that hoist yonder?" Bogue called out to the youngster currently assigned as the watch officer.

"Aye, sir. Already got it. It requests permission to send a boat to us."

"Very well, you may answer in the affirmative, if you please." Bogue responded, then walked to the hatch, presumably to find Captain Lawford.

I wondered if the new information would cause him to decide we should sail.

CHAPTER TWELVE
6 February 1794
Northwest of Jamaica

My unasked question was answered within a few days; the weather cleared and the wind veered back to where it belonged, blowing a steady breeze from the northeast. Within another day, it strengthened to a half gale and, with an early morning gun calling attention to our signal, the fleet made sail, straggling out of Bluefields Bay as they followed *Convert* to sea. They would never be mistaken for vessels of the Royal Navy!

We gained some sea room and hove to, awaiting the slower or less alert among our flock to catch up. Already hove to and waiting for us were four vessels, a ship, a brig, and two schooners which had finally found a fair wind to make it 'round the end of Jamaica from the north coast. These, then, were the ones O'Leary had hoped we would wait for. He got his wish, though not by our own choice!

Lawford sent Master's Mate Hutchins in the jolly boat to each of the new arrivals with the sailing directions, signals, and the admonition to keep up but remain behind *Convert* – the same rules we had provided all the others. We were now fifty-eight vessels strong of varying sailing abilities and speeds. It would be a challenge to keep them together and protected! But those were our orders and so we would somehow manage to carry them out.

"Make your course west north west, if you please, Mister Earnshaw. Mister Popplewell, we'll have tops'ls and jibs set. And the driver with a single reef should not cause any undue issues. You may see to it."

The captain had paced the deck anxiously while Hutchins was off on his errand and issued his orders immediately the master's mate stepped on the deck. The boat was still being hoisted. He was obviously anxious to move this lumbering and unwieldy collection of vessels forward and his not being able to take advantage of *Convert*'s brilliant sailing abilities made him chafe at the bit in frustration.

"Be certain your lookouts keep a sharp eye out for stragglers and be sure the watch discourages any of our charges from leaping into the fore!"

"Aye, sir. We have the signal to remain astern of the escort rigged and ready to go. I have also kept one of the swivels loaded with a powder charge in the event we should need to get someone's attention." Earnshaw shot a glance at me and then smiled broadly at his junior watch officer, the recently returned Master's Mate Hutchins.

"I suspect that our friend, Cap'n Martin, was suitably chastised by Mister Ballantyne and will be unlikely to try the same foolishness again, Mister Earnshaw. But there may be one or two others who feel the need to test us!" Lawford smiled thinly at me, turned and left the quarterdeck for his usual daily tour of the ship.

The clear weather, a pleasant breeze from the right quarter, and seas that, while not exactly calm, were certainly not boisterous, made for a most delightful morning and I feel sure that all hands reveled the fact that *finally* we were underway for England. By the time the noon meal was finished and I took the watch again, the wind had dropped to a whisper and, with the captain's blessing, we set the courses and stays'ls, noting that many of our flock had done the same.

With a certain sense of foreboding, I did seek out and then glass *Britannia* and was relieved to find Captain Martin behaving himself about a dozen ships back and to leeward of our course. I shared my sentiments with Sherwin who had the good manners to smile at my obvious relief. And for now, at any rate, the calm winds and seas most likely would preclude any of our flock from further testing our resolve to remain in the vanguard of the flotilla.

The remainder of the day passed quietly and uneventfully; I began to think (hope?), perhaps a trifle prematurely, that the commission might actually go smoothly, save of course, for a possible run-in with a Frenchman bent on doing us harm. Night fell with its customary suddenness. It always seemed – and in spite of having been in the Caribbean for more than a month now, I was still unaccustomed to it – to go from daylight to dark in the blink of an eye.

The evening passed uneventfully – watches changed, the wind remained light and fair, and the vessels for which we were responsible kept their positions within the flotilla. In spite of the light breezes, Captain Lawford ordered us to reduce sail to allow the sluggards in the group to catch up. We slatted most of the night, but, as I heard the morning watch take the deck, I felt the motion of the ship change, and assumed that the fickle breeze had reestablished itself and that *Convert* had once again made sail. Following a pleasant meal properly served by Black and Bogue's man, his nephew Richard Bogue, the first lieutenant and I made our way topside to find the ship once again sailing nicely. But in the wrong direction!

Earnshaw had the quarterdeck.

"Bill," Bogue began as we stopped by the rail to the quarterdeck.

"Don't bloody ask, Joe. One of the bloody schooners has signaled that they're sinking and the cap'n has ordered us back to help them. Damned Irish! They keep us waiting three bloody days and now this!" Earnshaw colored quickly as he realized his gaffe. Bogue was an Irishman.

"Sorry, sir. I meant nothing by the remark. Just a bit vexed at yet another delay. Nothing to do with the fact that the schooner is Irish, of course. Just a leaky hull, is all. I am sure we'll have it sorted out quick as ever you please!" Earnshaw was talking fast, trying to cover his blunder with an excess of words.

Bogue, for his part, took no umbrage at Earnshaw's remark and simply smiled. Once we arrived at the stricken schooner, Captain Lawford ordered a boat over and sent Midshipman Campbell, a carpenter, bosun's mate, and several hands in addition to the boat crew to sort out the problem. As it happened, their pump had failed and it took our carpenter barely thirty minutes to have it fixed and working properly. The boat returned, was hoisted aboard, and once again we retraced our course through the hove-to fleet to retake our position in the van.

We made the signal, punctuated it with a shot from a swivel gun, and the flotilla again made sail, setting its course to the west north-west. I assumed the watch on the quarterdeck, relieving Earnshaw at the meridian. We took advantage of the fine breeze and quickly drew well ahead of the convoy.

"Was that cannon fire?" I asked Sherwin, who cocked his head, listening like a pet dog waiting for its master to open the door.

"Didn't hear it, myself, sir. Where did it come from?"

"Couldn't be certain, but from astern be my guess."

"Compliments to the captain, Sherwin, and would he please join me on the quarterdeck." I spoke without lowering my glass, hoping to catch a glimpse of smoke from the fleet before the wind blew it away.

"Well, Mister Ballantyne, what have we now? Someone else sinking or perhaps some fleet-footed vessel wanting to take the lead?"

Lawford's appearance startled me, so intent was I on peering through my long glass. "Haven't a clue, sir. But I did hear, quite distinctly in fact, two guns not a moment ago, and I am fairly certain they came from astern."

"Well, of course. They would, wouldn't they. That's where the fleet is. The question is – who fired them and why."

The captain picked up a glass – one kept separate for his use – and studied the ships astern for some time. Finally, he lowered his telescope, sighed resignedly, and gave me the order neither of us wanted.

"Turn out the hands and bring her about, Lieutenant. I suppose we must go and have a look. Damnable luck, it is. I had hoped to sight the Caymanas before dark today. Not bloody likely now, I reckon." As if to punctuate his remark, the ship's bell forward sounded five clangs, signaling a half after two in the afternoon.

We made our way – again – through the fleet, inquiring of several we passed who might have fired the two guns. Each ship answered the same way: pointing to their sterns, the direction in which we were sailing.

Lawford remained on the quarterdeck, pacing up and down, side to side. Sometimes he would walk forward, watching his ship and the others we passed, hoping to see which of his charges needed our help *this* time!

Finally, we were at the back of the fleet; only a schooner and a brig remained ahead of us. Through the glass, I could make out a figure on the bow of the schooner waving his hat, the same one we had rescued just this morning.

"Appears to be that schooner, again, Cap'n. Same one. Shall I round up alongside?"

"Aye, best you do that and back the fores'l. No telling what their problem is this time."

Once we were abeam of the vessel, about a pistol shot distant, Lawford jumped up on the bulwark at the mizzen shrouds. Holding his speaking trumpet to his lips, he shouted across the water.

"What seems to be the problem, Captain? You're not sinking again, are you?" I am sure he tried to keep the irritation from his voice, but even with the speaking trumpet distorting it some-what, any among us could hear it clearly.

"We thought we would be left behind, we did. Off you sailed on your merry way and left us to keep up as best we could. These waters are fairly alive with French privateers." The voice that came from the schooner carried none of the sweet mellifluous tones of an Irishman; this was whiney and petulant.

"We are still in sodding Jamaican waters, you dolt. Make all sail and get that bloody vessel moving. You're costing me too much time. Lagging behind is a sure way to attract a Frenchman and if you are so far astern, I cannot help you." Lawford made no effort to hide his rancor this time.

"Get her moving, Mister Ballantyne. Tops'ls, forecourse, stays'ls, and driver, if you please." Lawford jumped off the bulwark and stomped to the hatch below.

And once again, we sailed through the fleet, the signal to make all sail flying from the mizzen gaff, and took our position at the van. During the second dogwatch, the captain ordered our nighttime sail configuration of double-reefed tops'ls, jibs and driver, and a course change to the west. This was, of course, relayed to the fleet, many of whom had seen *Convert* execute and followed suit, even before the signal was made. Darkness fell with its customary suddenness and the clouds above precluded most of the starlight from reaching the sea. The ships all showed the proper lights and, we hoped, the night would remain quiet with none of our flock sinking or being left behind.

I assumed the watch at eight o'clock in the evening with my midshipman, Tom Sherwin. Mister Popplewell was hanging about, his sextant in hand, hoping for a glimpse of a heaven-ly body or two for long enough to determine our position. We had shot the sun at noon, but since then had changed course so many times, running back and forth through the fleet, that the sailing master was not entirely certain of our exact whereabouts. But there was plenty of sea around us and the bottom was a long way down. I told him as much.

"I am sure that by dawn, Mister Popplewell, the sun will shine once more, and you'll be able to find our position easily. We have only to wait 'til then." I tried to calm the man's concerns, but he simply looked at me, unconvinced that his fears were unfounded.

"Sir...Mister Ballantyne? Is not that one of our vessels there off the larboard beam? Appears to be gettin' ahead of us."

Sherwin was holding a night glass to his eye. He did not remove it when he spoke, preferring to remain focused on whatever ship it was he saw. I picked up my own glass, focused on the ship, a brig, actually, and cursed under my breath.

"Sod all. Bloody hell. Someone's not paying attention.

"Quartermaster, the light signal for 'remain astern' if you please, and, once it's up, offer them a shot from the larboard swivel. Damn civilians – why can they not follow simple orders!"

CRACK! The swivel let out its sharp report and a two-foot streamer of fire. I watched the brig to see if anything would come of it. Through the night glass, I could see a figure on the quarterdeck glassing us, then other figures moving about the deck, some into the rigging. Apparently, my signal was clear enough, and as I watched, the tops'l was shortened down with a single reef and a stays'l struck and furled. The vessel fell back, merging into the fleet to our stern.

The remainder of the watch passed with no untoward events; Popplewell eventually gave up hope of a star sight and retired, and at midnight, Bill Earnshaw assumed the watch with young Colin Campbell.

For my part, I sent Sherwin off to bed and made my way to my cabin. As I passed the wardroom, our surgeon called my name.

"Mister Ballantyne. A glass with you, sir, if you've time."

I was tired; it had been a long day, but I felt a wee dram of Henry's fine claret would go down well and perhaps help me sleep. I detoured into the wardroom where McMahon sat with the first lieutenant, a carafe of wine on the table between them. Bogue's servant, Little Bogue, as we had come to call him, stood by the sideboard. I could almost hear him groan inwardly as I took a seat and waited as he stepped forward to pour me a glass.

"Why thank you, gentlemen. Always a pleasure to share a glass with you both."

"And how are we getting along up there, Edward?" Bogue aimed his chin toward the ceiling.

"All seems quiet at the moment, Joe. Had one eager chap in a brig – not sure which it was – who thought he should be in the van, but dropped back quick as ever you please when I advised him of his error. You likely heard my announcement! Popplewell was frustrated as usual with the clouds; seems he was again unable to get a proper sight and you know how he hates to rely on dead reckoning. Says 'dead reckoning can reckon you dead quicker than ever!' He finally gave up trying and retired shortly before Earnshaw showed up."

We enjoyed a bit of banter and good-natured complaints about some of the dreadful masters in our flotilla for a while, and then I excused myself to drag my tired body to the cabin I shared with Earnshaw, who of course, had the watch on deck. I quickly stripped off my shirt and trousers and fell into my cot, likely asleep as quick as my head touched the pillow.

It couldn't have been five minutes, or so it seemed – in hindsight, it was well over an hour – before I was rudely awakened by shouting, bare feet slapping the deck over my head, sails luffing, shouting, and a general flurry of activity topside.

Bloody hell! Now what? Some dolt has got himself ahead of us again. My groggy mind calculated, trying to determine which of our eager...or inattentive flock it might be.

But then the cacophony over my head continued and I recognized Captain Lawford's voice raised along with Popplewell's, both issuing orders which, while I could not distinguish the exact words, held enough urgency to suggest something was seriously wrong. I fairly leapt from my cot, threw on some trousers and a shirt, and hastened for the ladder to the weather deck, quite ill-prepared for the scene that greeted me.

I first thought I was still asleep and dreaming, but the reality hit me, quite literally, when a sailor slammed into me on his way to the ratlines, nearly knocking me on my arse. A muttered apology and he was gone, headed aloft without a look astern. The tops'ls were loosed and flapping as heavers on deck struggled to raise the yards, both fore and main. There was a great deal of shouting from forward, and, in the distortion caused by the blackness of the night, it appeared that at least one ship, possibly two, were close aboard our bow – obviously the cause of the alarm. Their forms were barely discernible, just darker shapes – and very large ones – in the already profound darkness.

Orders flew from the quarterdeck. Both Bogue and the captain were issuing instructions, Lawford from the quarterdeck and the first lieutenant from amidships. Sailors struggled with braces, attempting to haul the main tops'l yard around to back the sail and stop the ship. Bogue's purview. The captain was trying to bring the ship around by wearing, but she would have none of it. Then I heard two guns fired from ahead of us; too far to be the ships close aboard so there must be someone else who had got themselves ahead of us.

With a resounding CRUNCH, the ship on our starboard bow ran on board of us, driving athwart our hawse and clipping off our jibboom as clean as if it had been sawn. I was nearly knocked to the deck by the crash, but managed to catch myself by grabbing at the mainmast fife-rail. More shouting, more running – this time the general confusion included yours truly as I pulled myself together, shouted aft something that likely made no sense, then scrambled to the bow.

Bogue, having got there before me, was assisting the bosun in directing the effort to untangle the bow of our ship from the other. Sailors with hatchets and knives hacked at anything they could find, some imperiling themselves in the effort. On the merchant ship a similar scene was playing out but with seemingly more noise and greater confusion. Someone had brought forward a pair of lanterns, unshuttered to provide as much light as possible to the scene, and in their glow I could see the damage to *Convert* as well as the merchant. We had lost our jibboom, but they had lost theirs and half the bowsprit, along with their sprits'l boom. Their headstays hung from the dangling spars, providing no support for the foremast. The mast could come crashing down on both of us at any moment!

We finally separated ourselves, got the tops'ls braced aback, and bore clear by falling off to the westward. At which time a voice – it might not have even been from *Convert* – shouted "breakers ahead, and close!" For a moment, everything stopped. All anyone could hear on either ship was the rush of the seas alongside and the keening of the wind in our rigging. And the muted thunder of the sea breaking on either rocks or the shore not a pistol shot away.

"Stand by to sheet home the tops'ls. Mister Popplewell, get her moving." Lawford's voice rang out in the silence, a signal for the general mayhem to begin again. More quietly to the quarter-masters on the wheel, he ordered, "Bring her head up; make your course north."

The sails filled with a *thump* and *Convert* began to move again, her bow swinging to starboard. Yards were secured, sheets coiled, and order resumed. But only for five minutes.

With a crash, the same ship fell on board of us again, almost in the same spot; only this time, the impact forced our head around making us pay off before the wind. The cry rang out again, louder this time and apparently from right over our heads, so it must have been from one of our topmen in the foremast. And this time, caught unawares and with nothing to grab at, I *did* fall backwards, landing unceremoniously on my arse.

"Breakers. Breakers ahead and close!"

Popplewell ran forward, gathering sailors to again try to clear the tangle of wood and cordage and, this time, our starboard anchor which was firmly fouled in our adversary's tangled head-rig. I had picked myself up, grasping a ready hand from a sailor – who it was I could not tell in the dark – and hastened into the mess on the fo'c'sle-head. The sailing master was already there, directing men wielding hatchets and axes in hacking at the shrouds from the merchant vessel's bowsprit – likely the fastest way to separate our two ships. We could all hear the breakers now, quite clearly, even over the general confusion aboard both ships.

And then we struck.

CHAPTER THIRTEEN
8 February 1794
East End Reef, Grand Cayman

This time, it was not just me who sat down suddenly; everyone on the bow did and with no more grace than I had displayed earlier. There was a great rending, the sound of wood crushing, rigging parting, and, on the merchant ship now irrevocably attached to us, the frightening sound of the foremast toppling. It was only happenstance that it fell into the water forward and to her starboard and not on us!

"Release all sheets and braces! Topmen aloft! Lay up and out! Clew up all sails." Lawford bawled from the quarterdeck.

Popplewell, from amidships, directed his voice aloft where the topmen were struggling to get some stops on the sails. "Get that canvas secured! Step lively you men if you value you hide."

I ran back to the quarterdeck, right astern of the first lieutenant. Captain Lawford, his gaze fixed on the tops of the masts, held his night glass tucked under his arm. His expression was grim.

"Your orders, Cap'n?" Bogue asked quietly.

Before Lawford could answer, the carpenter stepped onto the quarterdeck and announced, "Sir. We're making water forward at quite an alarming rate. Not sure if the pumps will be able to keep up."

"You needn't worry about us sinking, Chips. We're on the hard and not likely to be moving anytime soon." I thought Lawford's droll comment was a worthy one, given our circumstances. "No matter the seas breaking, I doubt they'll carry us clear."

As the training of our men took over, quiet, save for the orders being shouted aloft, returned, at least in *Convert*. But I knew from the noise, shouting, wood breaking, and general chaos around us that we were not alone on the reef. In addition to ourselves and the damned merchant which forced us to take the hard, I could distinguish voices and lights from at least another four or five vessels at varying distances from us. These must have been the ones firing their guns, the ones we had heard shortly before disaster struck. How could they have got themselves so far ahead of us, especially when they all understood the standing orders to remain astern of the escort? Did they wait to fire their warning shots until they were already on the reef?

Within ten minutes, the carpenter was back. "Sir. The water is up the orlop deck and she's bilged. We may not be able to save her, Cap'n."

The captain nodded in the dark, clenched his jaws tighter, and looked around as though he just noticed Bogue and me and the carpenter standing there, awaiting orders. "Mister Bogue, be so kind as to cause a gun, a long gun rather than a swivel, to be fired at intervals for the next fifteen or so minutes. Perhaps we might prevent further mishaps."

'Mishap!' Hardly a bloody mishap. We're on the bloody reef, for God's sake. The ship is bilged and we're sinking, damn all! And you call it a 'mishap?'

"Quartermaster, hoist the light signal for 'steer due west and heave to' if you please.

"Pass the word for the surgeon, messenger." Lawford spoke again. His voice was still controlled and unhurried.

Moments later, Henry appeared out of the darkness. "Cap'n. You sent for me?" A quarterdeck gun, a twelve-pounder, fired at that moment, causing Henry as well as the rest of us, to start.

"I did, Mister McMahon. Have we any casualties, either from the collision or the grounding? I am given to understand the orlop is flooded so should you need a sickbay, you may use my cabin."

"Thank you, sir. I am told we have some who succumbed – five in all, I collect – but the injuries I have seen are all minor. It appears most of the lads were lucky – except, of course, for the ones who were not." Sometimes Henry could just not help himself.

"Very well. At least that's something. Who were the ones who have died?" Another long gun spoke its warning.

Henry listed the names of the five sailors, all heavers who got hit by falling blocks and bits of the rig when we hit the reef. "Most of the unlucky sods suffered from crushed skulls, hit as they were by some of the blocks aloft, and one poor soul was skewered like a pig on a spit by some iron strap or the like. Caught him in the shoulder and ran right through his body."

The captain nodded grimly in the dark, offering no comment. Hearing nothing more from Lawford, the surgeon turned and left the quarterdeck.

"Bosun; hoist out the boats if you please. Make sure they're well secured as we will remain aboard until dawn. No point in tearing off into the dark without knowing what the shore is here." The captain was astonishingly calm.

For my part, a single thought took over my brain, consuming my consciousness. *"Another shipwreck. Two ships, two wrecks! Must be some kind of a bloody record. Maybe it's me! Am I an albatross, a jinx? Two shipwrecks in two ships in just over two years? Of course, Black was with me in* Pandora...*so maybe it's him!"*

Crashes, shouts, splashing, confusion flying through the darkness, the unmistakable sound of ships taking the hard, interrupted my own self-pity and, for a moment, any talk in our ship. Two more had joined us on the reef, obviously having paid no attention to our signals or the guns. This would be a long night. I wished for a moon, but it was not to be; the darkness was intense and complete. The ship moved with a jerk, responding to the still moderate seas that were running. The accompanying screech of rending wood was more terrifying than the movement. We were being pushed farther onto the reef along with the others that shared our plight.

"Make as much secure as possible on deck and set a watch, Mister Bogue. We will assess our situation once it's daylight. I shall be in my cabin, unless the surgeon wishes to make use of it." Lawford spoke very quietly, stepped off the quarterdeck, made a turn around the spardeck speaking to a few sailors and warrants that he encountered, and went below. His demeanor was subdued, exhibiting a quiet melancholy, almost a sadness. And how could he not?

"Joe? Do you think we'll get off the reef? When *Pandora* hit off New Holland, she got off after several hours and lightening her. But then, of course, she soon sank. You think that will be our fate as well?"

"Edward, you're the expert on shipwrecks, my friend. I have not had the pleasure before tonight. According to the carpenter we're taking water faster than the pumps can handle it and the ship is bilged. That does not sound promising to me." Bogue was instructing the bosun and sailing master about setting a watch – we would not need a full watch, certainly, but also more than a shore watch – and really paid little more than lip-service to my question, tossing off a sarcastic and, I thought, caustic riposte.

Since I had no further responsibilities at the moment, I retired below, perhaps to find Henry and share a glass of commiseration. Earnshaw had already left the deck, his underway watch more or less ending once we were no longer underway. The two of them were settled in chairs in the wardroom, both on the same side of the table to accommodate the list our ship has assumed. Earnshaw was busily scribbling with the stub of a pencil on what appeared to be several sheets of foolscap.

"Well, there's a fine mess we're in now, Edward. Any thoughts about getting her off? After all, you've traveled this road before." Henry McMahon was ashen, obviously distraught over our situation, but still not without a trace of humor, likely unintentional, in his demeanor. He studied my face intently; it felt for a moment as though he was rummaging about in my conscious and I was simply a by-stander to his intrusion. The answer surely would not be found there! And it was almost the same question I had just put to the first lieutenant.

Suddenly, I had become the expert on ship wrecks, being the only officer aboard who had recent experience with one. But so far, mercifully, no one had offered the opinion that I was the Jonah!

"Henry, I have no idea. As I mentioned to Bogue topside, *Pandora* was lifted off the reef by the seas and then ultimately sank once the rock pinnacle was no longer blocking the hole in her hull. We do not have any seas of consequence here, and we have little idea of what's on the other side of the reef. We also have the additional concern that there are at least five and maybe more ships on the hard with us. I suspect that those ships, and keeping the others off, will be the cap'n's chief concern."

The surgeon continued to study my face. It made me a trifle uncomfortable. "I'd reckon Lawford's career is washed up with this; would you not agree?"

"Couldn't say, Henry. Of course there will be an inquiry and most likely a court-martial; always is in these situations. What they decide will determine whether he goes ashore or not. I can tell you that Cap'n Edwards, commander of *Pandora*, was found not guilty by his court-marital and, while he has yet, to my knowledge, to return to sea, he did make admiral, I am told. I know Cap'n Lawford had thought grounding and more particularly, shipwreck, was a career-ending event for a captain – he said as much to me when I first came aboard – but again, it's the court-martial board that will make that determination."

"Edward, as I am new to these things..." Earnshaw, looking up from his writing, began, only to be interrupted by the surgeon.

"I'd say we *all* are, Bill, save Edward, here, of course. This must be just..."

"That will be quite enough, Henry. I have, as a result of fate alone, been involved in a shipwreck once before and am anything but an authority on the subject. I know only what happened in *Pandora* off New Holland several years back. I am not sure there is relevance here." I was beginning to become weary of the references to my previous assignment. To make my point unmistakable, I aimed a hard look at my friend.

"As I started to say, Edward, before I was rudely interrupted," Earnshaw glanced at the surgeon. "Should we not be throwing guns and the like over the side? Pumping out water? Dumping excess weight? Seems like lightening the ship would be a good first step in getting her off the reef."

"Quite right, Bill. But I suspect Cap'n Lawford wants to see the situation in the daylight and take measured steps to determine our course of action." Truth be told, I had little idea of what Lawford was planning or why, but I was reasonably certain we would not be getting off the reef, tonight, tomorrow, or anytime thereafter.

"What are you writing down so furiously, Bill? Your Last Will and Testament? I don't think that will be necessary!" I tried to inject a little levity into the grimness that seemed to fill the room.

It did little to break the quiet concern in my shipmates, but at least Earnshaw offered a wan smile. "No, not that, Edward. It's my recollection of the events of the night and the grounding. I have no doubt, since I was the one who put her on the reef, that I shall be called upon to testify at the court-martial and don't want to forget anything important."

"A worthy endeavor, to be certain. Always best to be prepared!" I nodded at the young man's foresight. I added, "But the reality is it was not you who put her on the reef, Bill, but that bloody merchant vessel who came on board of us...twice! And as I recall, Cap'n Lawford had the deck when we actually struck."

I tried to relieve his fears, but I am not sure he quite agreed with my assessment of his situation. I did agree with him, however, that in spite of his inexperience, he had seen immediately what was needed for the ship and then for himself, at least on the surface. We would all surely be better able to see our course more clearly in the light of day. And Lawford had not become a captain through good fortune; I trusted his judgment. I finished the last swallow of my wine, stood a bit awkwardly forgetting to allow for the canted deck, and bid good night to my colleagues, heading off to find solace in my darkened cot... and perhaps load a few necessaries in my seabag for when we ultimately were forced to abandon. I knew most of the crew would be doing the same.

I wondered briefly if Henry regretted my involving him in *Convert*. Had he refused my invitation to join us, he would have been cruising in *Penelope* with Lieutenant Ware and the others looking to take French prizes to fatten his purse. Not much of a choice when compared with being stranded in a wrecked ship on a reef off Grand Caymanas Island!

My dreams were anything but restful and I found no solace in the little sleep I managed to get. I was back in the sinking *Pandora*, watching the waves wash over the deck as the bosun's mate ripped open the hatch to the temporary prison to release the mutineers we had captured in Tahiti. I was standing on deck, riveted to the Pine planks, hearing my mates shouting for me to jump but unable to move. The faces around me, both on the ship and in the churning water alongside were not my *Pandora* shipmates, but a collection of seemingly random people from my past, both distant and immediate. Jack Farnsworth swam with the first lieutenant in *Europa*, who yelled to me that the ship would be fine and not to worry. Others swam about near at hand, and standing at the main pinrail was Kendall and her sister, the barmaid, Hilary. Both were perfectly calm, not a bit wet, and smiling at the chaos around them, oblivious. In fact they seemed not at all at odds with one another. Captain Edwards, wielding the cat, his clothes sodden, strode up and down the deck, threatening any who jumped, screaming that they were cowards. Captain

Lawford was by his side. It was anything but a peaceful dream!

I awoke, my bedclothes damp with sweat, and fairly leapt from the cot, fully expecting the water to be up to my knees. When it wasn't, I took a seat in the chair, caught my breath, and took stock of my situation.

Oh, right! My ship is on a reef somewhere in the Caribbean, most likely off the island of Grand Caymanas, possibly sinking, and we were supposed to be protecting a convoy from all the dangers of sailing transAtlantic. Hmm. Didn't even make it to the Atlantic!

"Mister Ballantyne, the cap'n's compliments and would you attend him on the quarterdeck, if you please, sir." Black stood in my doorway, ever proper and always the perfect steward. To his everlasting credit, he even held a cup of coffee for me.

"I assume we have yet to sink, then, Black? You seem not to be standing in water up to your hips." I struggled to my feet, pulled on my trousers and a shirt. I thought about shoes and decided on a rugged pair of sea boots, not knowing what the day might hold.

"No sir. We ain't sunk yet, but they's every chance that will happen. And we've got a lot of company. Didn't have time to properly make a count, but I would suspect at least seven and possibly more ships with us on the reef." He offered me my hat, which I declined, and turning about, left me to find my way topside.

To say I was ill-prepared for the sight that greeted me in spite of Black's warning, would be the height of understatement. It was melancholy to a fault and made more so by the lowering sky, with clouds shredded by winds that had yet to reach us on the water – but soon would. While *Convert* had not taken much more of a list, the merchant vessel with which we had become en-snared was on her beam ends, missing her foremast, and had the water half way up her spardeck. Boats were secured alongside and it appeared as though the merchant lads had not waited for any instruction from the navy, but had begun the process of get-ting the crew and supplies ashore. Farther down the reef, masts were canted at impossible angles, decks were awash, and men and gear were floating in the water. I counted – stunned – and found nine other ships ashore; seven ship-rigged and two brigs.

With *Convert,* there were ten vessels hard aground on the reef, and, from the looks the mess, none would be getting off soon, if ever. And the sea was beginning to make up.

Convert pitched awkwardly, her stern rising with the waves as they rolled under her, lifting her somewhat – would we lift clear? – only to slam her poor hull back down on the coral like a cruel joke, grinding the wood into splinters and further opening the rent in her hull.

The wind was getting up now, blowing directly onshore and the sky becoming more and more overcast. Suddenly, the completely absurd notion flashed through my stunned mind that Popplewell would have to wait yet again to get his sight, as the sun showed not a glimmer of appearing. I almost smiled to myself at the distraction.

Well, I reckon it doesn't really matter now, does it? Unless this is a deserted bit of land, we can enquire of the residents where we have fetched up.

The seas were starting to run higher, pushing *Convert* and her stranded companions farther onto the coral with dreadful grinding, scraping, and screeching of tortured wood. Waves broke over the reef and continued, diminished, into a lagoon where a small sandy beach received the remnants. Even without using a glass, I could see a clutch of people, both men and women, milling about on the beach and standing on the bluff above it. Some of them pushed small boats into the water, I assumed to render assistance to the stranded ships.

I turned to look seaward; many of our ships were still at large, sailing off and on, but keeping their distance from an obviously dangerous lee shore. Some were hove to, apparently awaiting instruction as to what Lawford would require of them.

"Mister Ballantyne, when you have finished taking in the sights, I should appreciate your attendance here with the rest of us." Joe Bogue spoke from the quarterdeck.

I cast my gaze there and saw Lawford, Bogue (of course), Earnshaw, the two midshipmen and the master's mate, the carpenter, bosun, and Popplewell. None looked rested; all looked worried. The captain looked gaunt already. I hastened to join them, somewhat embarrassed by my captivation in the moment.

"...the masts. Too unstable with them up and their weight

is not helping our situation. Try to avoid dropping them on our neighbor, there, if you would." Lawford had just ordered the carpenter to chop down the masts! I guessed he had resigned himself to not getting the ship off the reef.

"Mister Bogue: organize the men and those who are no longer needed aboard can be ferried out to whichever of the ships that will take them. The supernumeraries and invalids as well. Have the quartermaster signal the merchants to stand in as close as they might when you are ready. I don't want to have to move our people any farther offshore than necessary in this sea, so do try to select ships that are near at hand. I suppose some can go to shore, perhaps in the boats putting out from the beach now. Perhaps the weather will moderate before nightfall."

He then turned to me. "Mister Ballantyne, please see to getting the guns overboard as well as the shot. With a bit less weight, she might float over the reef, though I have little idea yet as to the depth of water within the lagoon. Take Mister Sherwin with you.

"Popplewell, organize the ship's papers, charts, sailing instructions and the log if you please, and find a bit of oiled canvas to wrap them in."

One of the boats from the shore was about to land alongside. "Mister Earnshaw, see to greeting our visitors, if you please. And determine what assistance they might offer."

I was a bit surprised that the captain issued all these orders quite without any expression, neither in his voice nor his countenance. It was as though he were simply reading a roll call.

As Earnshaw made his way to the break in the bulwark where the boarding battens were, I noticed that there were several other native boats making their way skillfully through the mounting surf – at some peril, it appeared – to the other ships stranded on the reef. They were engaged in plucking people – sailors and passengers – from the turbulence. Some, pulled from the sea, appeared limp, clearly on the verge of succumbing to the rigors of the experience. Others, shouting and waving their arms to attract attention, seemed vigorous and able. Their shouts and screams rose above the crash of the seas and splintering wood. The native canoes saved them all, to a man...or woman.

Britannia, near to us (it gave me a strong sense of satisfaction to see that arrogant sod, Martin, had put his ship on the reef as well!) was already loading people, including a woman, it appeared, into one of the local canoes and a ship's boat. Other ships – the ones I could make out through the mist of breaking seas – were following suit.

"Mister Ballantyne, when you are done sight-seeing, perhaps you might organize the removal of the guns." Lawford seemed to be back to his original self now.

"Aye, sir. Right away!" I stopped gawking at the events surrounding us and hastened to the gun deck to find the gunner.

As it happened, our gunner had organized a gang and the necessary tackles to lift the guns from their carriages in anticipation of the order to lighten ship. I took in the well-organized crews, working in spite of the canted deck, as Gunner Thomas oversaw their efforts. When he saw me, he stepped toward the ladder.

"Ready to pitch them over the side, Lieutenant? We got about half of 'em ready to go; just got to push the buggers out the ports when you give the word." His gravelly voice rose above the other sounds in the dark of the gundeck. The horrid sound of the sea splashing into the open ports on our lower side, the gurgle of the water running along the decks, and the grunts and talk of his men as they heaved on the tackles to lift the barrels obscured some of the words, but I heard enough to understand. Without the sound a ship makes underway – the slap of lines, wind sighing in the rig, water rushing past the hull, blocks and hull creaking – the noises here sounded unnaturally loud. And the grinding of her timbers was decidedly more noticeable from down below, inside the hull.

"Aye, Gunner. Let 'em go. Reckon we won't be seein' any Frog ships here, now will we?" I had hoped a bit of irony would make our situation a little less desperate, but the inescapable fact remained – we were on a reef, shipwrecked, and facing a future unknown to any of us. And five men had already perished.

Barely had the words left my mouth when a grim-faced Thomas waved his hand and the first twelve-pounder left us with a splash louder than the breaking waves and began its journey to the bottom, either within the shallows of the lagoon, or the deeps outboard of the reef.

"I heard we're sending some of the people ashore, sir. Is that true?"

"It is, Mister Thomas. Cap'n issued orders to that effect only moments ago; any hands not needed aboard should get to the boats. We have...or at least *had*...a local boat alongside which I reckon might be taking a few of the lads ashore. As quick as ever you might get these guns overboard, you may send your men topside to the boats." As I spoke, another splash announced the departure of the second gun, consigned to the deep for all time. I could not help but compare these guns going to the deeps with the guns of *Pandora* being heaved over the side.

The seas off New Holland had been high; the wind, the cause of our devastation in *Pandora,* when it ripped a tops'l loose from its lashings, was strong – a gale – whining and screaming through the rig. Pandemonium seemed the order of the day... or evening. Here, the seas were not yet huge, though growing, and the wind was only a fresh breeze – so far. Captain Lawford seemed to have a firm grip on his ship and crew, notwithstanding the fact that his people would soon be on the beach or divided up in other vessels and his ship smashed to kindling on the reefs of Grand Caymanas Island. *Pandora* had fetched up and sunk off a low, deserted island, barely a foot above the sea, and quite devoid of life, save for large barnacle-like snails.

From the deck this morning, I had seen that the island across the lagoon from our precarious perch on the reef exhibited a bluff that appeared to be fifty or sixty feet above the beach and obviously, there were people here. But in hindsight, it did occur to me that I had seen no – or very little – vegetation. No palm trees, large bushes, or anything beyond some grasses.

And Captain Lawford, like Edwards, would be facing a court-martial, standard procedure in these situations. But perhaps like Edward Edwards of *Pandora,* the court would "honorably acquit" him. I somehow doubted that, though; Edwards had lost one ship on an uncharted reef, while Lawford was responsible for ten.

As Thomas and his men continued to drop our armament and shot over the side, I went back to the weather deck to find two more boats alongside, both occupied, and our deck at the break in the bulwark crowded with people, both uniformed and in civilian garb. To seaward, ships continued to heave to, or sail off and on, apparently awaiting instructions. One of *Convert*'s boats was struggling through breaking waves, attempting to regain the side of the ship and making heavy weather of it. Each of the three pairs of oars moved to a different rhythm, catching crabs in the seas and jerking its rower forward or back. The cox'n seemed to have little control over the progress, the men, or the direction the boat went.

Quite without warning, a wave bigger than its predecessors, picked up the stern of the boat, slew it sideways, and broke into the boat, rolling it onto its side and spilling the men into the water. The cox'n in one of the native boats saw the disaster and immediately made for the floundering men hanging onto the now overturned longboat. I watched, fascinated, as the natives plucked the shouting, soaked, and scared sailors from the water and into their vessel, and set about rowing through much calmer waters toward the shoreline, about a musket shot distant.

"Mister Ballantyne. Would you step over here for a moment, if you please." Bogue, with a local chap of indeterminate hue, but of advanced years, stood between the main and mizzen masts, both of which boasted four seamen wielding axes with great vigor, and motioned me to join him. I assumed that eliminating the weight of the masts, now at a precarious angle, would offer a bit of stability to the hulk. I clambered over a tangle of rigging to where the men stood.

"Sir? What can I do?"

"Cap'n Lawford has written a letter to the captains of the merchants out there," he pointed with his chin at the ships now half a league distant, "and he would like you to see to its delivery. This kind chap here...Mister Clarke, is it not...has offered to sail you out there in his vessel. Once the letter is delivered to Cap'n Harrison in the ship *Louisa,* read, and acceded to, Mister Clarke will return you to the shore where, hopefully, most of the rest of us will await. You may take Sherwin or Hutchins with you."

"Very well, Mister Bogue. I shall pass the word for Hutchins and collect my belongings since I surmise it will be unlikely that I will be back aboard *Convert.* Where is the letter?"

"Well, the cap'n will give it to you directly, won't he? Or perhaps I shall, should that be his choice when he is done with it." Joseph Bogue turned to the native man, Mister Clarke, and said, raising his voice to be heard above the chopping sounds, "Thank you for your kindness, sir. Mister Ballantyne will be ready straight away. You may await him at the break."

I had sent a messenger to find Master's Mate Hutchins and made my way carefully down the ladder to the gundeck and my cabin. Earnshaw had apparently already retrieved a few of his belongings and his seabag. To his everlasting credit, Black, while nowhere to be seen, had packed up some essentials for me and left my own seabag on my cot which, due to the ship's cant, listed severely to starboard. I threw in an extra pair of shoes and stockings, a pistol I thought might be handy, and one more shirt – though I did not know exactly what Black had packed for me.

My man appeared as I slung my seabag on my shoulder, not surprisingly, a concerned look on his face. "Cap'n asks that you attend him, sir. He's in his cabin." Black looked grim and more than a little haggard.

'Thank you Black. Now, get yourself up the deck and get ashore with the others. I will be going in myself after I take care of an errand for Cap'n Lawford...which is why he wants me now."

He looked at me hard for a moment, then knuckled his forehead – it occurred to me that might have been the first time in four years – and said, "Thank you, sir. I will see you ashore."

As he turned to leave, I said, "And Black. In case I might have neglected to mention it before, you have served me well and I thank you for that." He simply nodded to me and continued on his way.

The door to the cabin stood ajar, likely due to the heel the ship had taken. I knocked on the jamb and was immediately summoned in. The motion of each wave lifting the stern was very pronounced; the whole stern of the ship seemed to rise four or five feet before settling down, sometimes with a crash and other times gently. I steadied myself on the frame of the door.

"Oh, Ballantyne. Thank you for handling this errand. It is logical for you to go since you have met many of the masters and they you. Let me read to you what I am sending out to Harrison in *Louisa*. Should you think of anything I might have neglected to say, please don't hesitate to offer it." Lawford sat at his desk, one hand holding the edge of it to keep his chair from bouncing around with the gyrations of the ship. As it was, with each of the more violent leaps the stern made, the chair slid a foot or two only to be hauled back to its place by the strength of his arm.

He put on his spectacles, using both hands during a lull in the motion, and picked up a paper from a sheaf of several on his desk.

"Gentlemen, I beg to acquaint you that the officers and crew of the Convert *and the merchant vessels lately wrecked on the reefs to the Eastward of this Island are in the greatest distress, not being able from the very great surf to save any provisions or any other necessary convenience. I must therefore desire of you, either to anchor at the Hogsties, or lay off and on there ready to take the people on board as soon as it is possible to get them over, it being impracticable to embark them from this part of the island whilst the sea is so great.*

"I am, Gentlemen, your most obedient servant, John Lawford"

He looked up at me over the top of his glasses, his brow furrowed in question.

"I think that is fine, Cap'n. I am sure the captains will follow your instructions and wait for us at Hogsties." I said, but I thought otherwise.

Why would those miserable sods start to follow instructions now when they couldn't be bothered to follow them for two days sailing from Jamaica?

I waited as he folded it carefully, slowly, and watched as he melted wax and dripped it onto the edge, then pressed an ivory Royal Navy seal into the molten wax. He performed the same task with another copy of the letter, a copy which his clerk had obviously prepared before he asked my opinion. "Give one to Hutchins, Edward, so that at least one will get there."

A grim thought.

A crash from topside signaled the mizzen mast's demise, following the foremast into the sea. All that remained now was the main, and that was receiving the full attention of the carpenter's men.

The weather had not improved a jot when I reached the spar deck, stepped over the shrouds stretching across to the downed mizzen and which, for the moment, held the fallen mast tethered to us like a horse on a halter lead. It floated alongside, riding the waves more easily than the ship, but slamming into the hull each time a big wave passed under us. It was the bosun's men who now worked on the rig, cutting and hacking away at the heavily tarred shrouds, stays, and running rigging to set the mast adrift and join the foremast now floating quietly, partially submerged, in the lagoon. From the progress the carpenter's men were making, I could see the mainmast would soon follow.

I reached the break in the bulwark, found Hutchins waiting, eager to abandon his ship. Clarke's vessel, a small schooner-rigged boat equipped with oars, waited in the calm water within the lagoon, out of the reach of the waves now boiling over the reef. I watched to catch his glance and then waved to him, motioning him back to the ship.

The men handling his boat were skillful in the extreme, using the reefed fores'l on the little ship to steady her and the sweeps to propel her through the seas to our side. It was a marvelous display of seamanship, timing, and strength. Once alongside, and as the vessel rose on a wave, Hutchins and I threw our seabags, containing a very few necessaries, down to a waiting crewman, and immediately followed them into the boat. The whole operation was over in the blink of an eye and Mister Clarke quickly guided his craft over the few remaining breakers and headed out to sea.

CHAPTER FOURTEEN
8-10 February 1794
Grand Cayman Island

The beach under the bluff was crowded; men with their meager supplies gathered in small groups most likely divided by their ships and their divisions within the ships. The clusters were relatively small, but there were many of them – so many, in fact, that it appeared some were cheek by jowl with the next group. I noticed several hogsheads, some presumably, hopefully, holding water and at least one that had been floated ashore which was clearly marked "Admiralty Issue" – rum. Some of the men had organized bits of sails to create small shelters, currently occupied by many of the women passengers who looked more than a bit bedraggled, while others sat silently, forlornly on the sand, gazing out at the most melancholy sight any of us could imagine. The sun was showing signs of making an appearance; it would soon be hot and the shelters would quickly become the most sought after real estate on the beach.

The sea, tamed by the very reef that had been our undoing, lapped quietly along the beach, belying its true nature outside the coral barrier where it continued its relentless pounding, bouncing ships on the jagged coral like toys flung by a petulant child. From the ship, I had not noticed just how small the beach was. Now, approaching through the shallows in Mister Clarke's schooner, I could easily see both ends, not a musket shot between them, and narrow, with the water barely twenty paces from the bottom of the bluff.

At both extremes, the sand gave way to rough, craggy coral, sharp fossilized rock that would tear a body to shreds should one be so unfortunate as to fetch up there instead of on the sand.

I studied the groups standing and sitting on the sand as the boat scraped onto the hard, its crew leaping out to guide it safely onto the shelving shore.

In one group, I noticed a properly attired lady accompanied by a gentleman, both completely undone by the disaster, and listening earnestly to an older chap dressed in a black frock coat and round hat – perhaps the captain of one of our merchant vessels. In another group closer to the bluff, several smooth-faced boys cried their hearts out, the sobs clearly audible at the water's edge. Brothers, perhaps? My scrutiny was interrupted when Mister Clarke said, "Here we are, Lieutenant. If you would hand your gear to Jonas there and step quickly, you might get to dry land without you get too wet! You also, Mister Hutchins. Lively, now!" Hardly had he finished speaking than we were standing in the shallows. I silently thanked my foresight at choosing my sea boots when I dressed this morning!

"It appears your fellows are just there." He pointed a gnarled finger at a group wearing the Crown's uniform which I could see included Bogue and Captain Lawford. They stood well back from the water and away from the merchant sailors in the center of the small beach.

"Mister Ballantyne! Hutchins! Here! We're organizing ourselves here. Please join us." I recognized Joe's voice above the now subdued thunder of the surf and clamor of the voices on shore, calling to one another, shouting to the boats in the lagoon, or generally sending up a wailing and bothersome cry over their sorry situation.

Lawford looked at me as I stepped into their circle, raised an eyebrow in an unspoken question.

"Yes, sir. Your letter is delivered safely to Captain Harrison in *Louisa*. He read it in my presence and indicated that he would signal the others to accompany him to Hogsties and wait.

"As a matter of interest, sir, we only counted nine vessels in the offing: a schooner, three brigs, and five ships. The schooner is the one that thought we were abandoning them two days back. I did not notice which of the others had remained. The schooner was hove to practically alongside *Louisa* so I had no difficulty making her out." I knuckled my forehead since I still had no hat to doff.

"Very well, then, Ballantyne. Thank you. We'll see which of them actually will wait at the Hogsties for us." Lawford, clearly distracted by our plight, never ceased shifting his gaze around the assemblage, the lagoon where native craft – Mister Clarke's and others – plied back and forth, and the reef where our ships continued to take the punishment from the seas. His hand in unconscious habit to acknowledge my salute.

"Joe, how did you get ashore? Do we have a plan yet?" I asked the first lieutenant, recalling quite vividly how Captain Edwards, late of *Pandora,* had marshaled our resources, sent men to scavenge the wreck, and laid out the plan for our escape from the deserted island where we had landed.

"Aye, Edward. We escaped only recently in the barge. It had been the captain's intent to get through the surf line and make our way out to the ships that were hove to in the offing. He loaded me, the purser, our French prisoner, my nephew, and himself, along with a dozen or so seamen, fully intending to sail away. Soon after we pushed off from the lee side of the wreck, and, before we had even made it 'round the stern, we found ourselves caught up in the wreckage of the main and mizzen masts floating there. While sorting that out, a trio of much larger waves assaulted us and quite prevented the boat's head from coming about into the seas; she filled in a moment and only the quick action of a native boat prevented us from capsizing and being dashed to pieces on the reef. The locals plucked us out of the barge as quick as ever you might please before we could be swept back onto the reef and carried us safely into the lagoon. It was a horror that very nearly ended in disaster." He shook his head as if trying to clear the unsettling memory.

"Captain Lawford is organizing some locals, along with our sailors to see what they might scavenge from the wrecks, but I don't reckon he is holding out much hope for success in that direction. The ship was very nearly awash when we abandoned her. There are still some aboard who thought it safer in the ship than risking a small boat in these seas. They will have to be fetched off rather sooner than later." He paused and shot a glance toward the wreck, where the surf still ravaged *Convert,* clearly wondering about the condition of those who remained aboard.

He took a breath and continued. "Since he has instructed the captains out there to rendezvous at Hogsties, we have been trying to determine how best we might get ourselves there as quick as possible."

"Mister Hutchins? Do you think you might have another trip out to the fleet in you? Before they depart, I mean." Lawford set his gaze on the young master's mate.

"Aye, sir. I only would need a boat of some stripe. What is it you wish me to do, sir?"

"I want you to deliver a message to Captain Harrison. He is to send the schooner to Havana with a letter recommending the governor there to offer succor to the ships when they call and to send assistance here to the Caymanas for any of us still ashore. Additionally, should any of the ships there have room for our men, I would like to send out as many as possible rather than have them all stay here or go to Hogsties. Can you remember all that? I would write it down for you but I am quite without writing materials."

"I will have no trouble remembering that, Captain. And I will see to getting into the next canoe going to the reef." And then to reinforce his own memory or to ensure that the captain was comfortable with his messenger, Hutchins repeated, almost verbatim, the message to be delivered.

Men, both civilian and navy, were already gathering at the water's edge to secure passage out to the still waiting fleet. Several native boats and canoes as well as ships' boats continued to ply the calm waters of the lagoon, scavenging materials and provisions from the ships as best as they might. It appeared to me, seeing the results of their forays, that the pickings were poor, but the spars, cordage, and bits of wood and canvas the sailors dragged back might prove helpful to the shipwrecked crews as well as the locals.

"Edward, are not those two over there our mids? They... well, they seem upset." Earnshaw pointed out two young men sitting at the base of the bluff and engaged in what appeared to be serious conversation. I could see their shoulders heaving.

"Aye, I believe they are. And I am not surprised they are upset. Actually, I am quite astonished that more don't share their mindset. I shall go and speak to them."

So I wandered, perhaps a bit too casually, toward where the boys sat, obviously consoling each other in their shared misery. I acted as though I was surprised to see them.

"Why, good afternoon, lads. You are clearly troubled. Is there anything I can do to ease your minds? We're not in any danger now and we will get back to England, albeit not quite as quickly or as soon as you may have expected. Don't despair!"

They both looked up at me with saucer-sized eyes, one – Campbell, it was – had the tracks of tears running down his cheeks.

"Sir, Mister Ballantyne. What a disaster this is! How... when...do you think we will be saved? One of the natives told me they had not the resources to care for us, having been wiped out by a hurricane only a few months back. There seem to be few, if any provisions, coming from the men scavenging the wrecks and..." Campbell began, but ran out of words, or perhaps his fear got the best of him and he began weeping again.

"Have you fellows not heard that I have done this before? Been shipwrecked, I mean. I am sure you have. And that was in the middle of the Pacific Ocean on a deserted island and we sailed all the way to civilization in open longboats. This island is inhabited, not terribly distant from Havana or Jamaica, and ships will be around to fetch us off. Fear not. We are not in straits as desperate as you may think.

"Now, get a grip on yourselves; try to remember that you are midshipmen in His Majesty's Navy, and we must all do our best to help our situation." I finished with an admonition perhaps sterner than I had intended, but it served as a verbal slap in the face for each of them, now obviously embarrassed at their behavior.

They stood up and followed me back to the knot of navy people that included Bogue, Earnshaw, and Captain Lawford as well as, now, the carpenter, bosun, and gunner. The first lieutenant was instructing the bosun to gather what help he needed among the men – *our* men – and fashion shelter from the sail-cloth that had been scavenged and a few bits of drift wood and spars that had come ashore.

"Once the sun comes back, it is going to be uncomfortable without shade, even with the breeze here. See if it would make sense to move the people up to the bluff, there, on the high ground...perhaps ask the locals." Bogue pointed up to the denuded hump of ground above us, adding, "There appears to be a path to the top just there."

Lawford, by later in the afternoon, had sent all but about thirty of our men – he ordered the officers and mids to remain ashore at East End – out to the waiting ships with letters to the masters requesting succor for our sailors. They would sail for Havana the next day while the ones Lawford had directed to Hogsties would, hopefully, appear in that anchorage in due course to await our arrival, by what conveyance I had no idea. Native boats, I assumed, once the seas had moderated and they could navigate more safely through the reef.

There remained on the beach a vast number of seamen and passengers from the nine merchant ships which wrecked with us, people who preferred the relative safety of the shore to the passage through the surf out to their fellow merchant vessels. I guessed some three hundred or more individuals crowded onto this little strip of sand.

Scavenging operations continued apace at the site of the wrecks, some more readily available for picking over than others; several had settled by now and were mostly awash, waves crashing on them and further breaking them up. *Convert,* I was saddened to see had suffered more damage from the punishing waves and, with my glass which I – or more correctly, Master's Mate Hutchins – had carried ashore, I could make out figures on deck still struggling to clear the fallen rig and pile provisions and supplies above the breaking waves. As the reef and its prizes were about a mile distant, I could make out little detail nor determine what success, if any, they had enjoyed. I did notice a couple of men standing, waist-deep, on the reef with a makeshift raft – I think likely made from spars and hatch gratings no longer needed aboard *Convert* – but with the waves breaking around them, it was impossible to guess at their intentions. I assumed they would be making for shore directly as the day was fast waning and who could guess what further disasters might beset the wreck overnight. Perhaps the raft was being prepared for that trip. I assumed that whatever remained of *Convert* and the other ships would be further scavenged come the dawn.

The officers and our young gentlemen sat on the sand, discussing our plight, planning on how we would survive with the minimal provisions we had secured, and determining when we might engage a local boat to carry us to Hogsties, when two strikingly dignified gentlemen approached our group. Both were properly attired in shirt and trousers and wore shoes.

One of the men – the taller of the two – was the color of coffee laden with cream, but his facial features were those of a European, with a thin nose and lips. His dark eyes were wide set giving him a look of wisdom, and his dark hair was plaited into a seaman's queue. While faded, his attire was clean and intact. The other man, considerably shorter of stature, wore faded trousers and while his shirt was patched in several places, it was neatly patched and clean. He wore a beard and, on his head, a straw hat which allowed strands of straight grey hair to show below it. His skin was white, but blotchy and on his face was a scar running from his eyebrow to his jawbone, which was missing more than a few teeth. They stopped and stood, facing us, seemingly waiting for one of us to acknowledge them.

"Gentlemen. How may I serve you?" Lawford spoke to them as he raised himself, with some effort, from the sand.

"Sir, I am called Joseph Dalby and this is my friend, William Prescott. We are part of the council who manage the affairs of Grand Caymanas." The darker complected one spoke with a deep, resonant baritone.

"As you may have learned from our colleague, Mister Clarke, who I believe carried many of your people to shore in his schooner from the melancholy situation on the reef, that we here suffered dreadfully from a *hurricano* some four months back. Our crops, our animals, and many of our people were carried out to sea and lost, leaving us quite without the means for our own survival. We have only recently begun to rebuild our homes and replant our gardens." He stopped, looking from one to another of us. Then he pointed to the bluff above our heads.

"During the storm, the seas were breaking up there, on the bluff, and the house there, where many of our neighbors had taken shelter with its owner, was carried away along with seven of the people and all of the animals. Mister Clarke himself was there and can attest to the severity of the storm as he barely escaped with his life. Sadly, the owner of the house, one of our elders and a well-respected and well known citizen, perished with the others.

"We face a most disastrous situation here and have examined our consciences about it. Without the event of four months ago, our nature would have demanded we provide you with complete hospitality and nourishment." He stopped again, as if steeling himself for what would come next and looked around the crowded beach as though surveying the masses of humanity huddled there. "It is quite beyond our capability to offer you anything in the manner of help in your situation short of boats to and from your wrecks. There must be nearly four hundred of you here; consider, if you please, there are only some eight hundred citizens on the entire island, all of whom are living almost as castaways themselves. We cannot feed you nor can we shelter you. We can barely feed and shelter ourselves.

"Therefore, we, with utmost regrets and respect, ask that you remove yourselves from our island as quickly as possible, so as to burden us with your plight no longer." The man, Mister Dalby I recall was his name, breathed a long sigh, almost as though he had dared not breathe at all during his monologue.

I watched the captain to try to determine what he might say in response to the heartfelt and very logical plea. Finally, after looking about us on the beach, out to the reef where the wrecks continued to roll and bounce on the coral, and finally at us, his officers, he nodded.

"I can surely understand your concerns, Mister Darby...I'm sorry, I mean Dalby...and can fully appreciate your own plight. I am sure your citizens are indeed in straits as dire as our own. Obviously, we did not land here by our own choice...nor is it our desire to remain here any longer than it will take to remove ourselves to the ships offshore either from this beach or from Hogsties. We will not burden you with our own needs. Should any of your sailors be willing to carry some of us to Hogsties or out beyond the reef to our waiting ships, we will be most grateful. Obviously, we must wait on that until the seas calm a bit, but should you be able to organize passage for our people, we would be most appreciative and, should it not insult, I will offer payment from my government for any services you might render."

"Thank you for your understanding, sir. We will surely be able to provide boats, as best we can, to take your people off shore once, as you say, the seas abate. At this point, it is too dangerous to sail through the reef, though, as you well know, Mister Clarke has managed it several times in the past two days. He is, of course, a well-seasoned captain. I expect by tomorrow, it will be calmer." This time, it was Dalby's companion, Mister Prescott, who spoke, smiling perhaps in relief that we would not be a burden to the locals. He went on. "We would offer you shelter, but we have barely enough for our own people. We have no meat, drink, or dry clothes to offer you – a great pity, I am sure – but we have little enough ourselves. What we have not, we cannot bestow, sadly."

"We quite understand, sir. And we will manage on our own as best as we can. Do not concern yourselves with our well-being." Lawford was quite conciliatory in his acceptance of the islanders' condition. "We will continue to try to bring our people in from the wrecks and hope for the seas to diminish.

"I have instructed some of the ships to wait for us at Hogsties and should the weather prove unsuitable for your boats to sail us there, I suppose we shall be obliged to walk." He looked from one to the other of us as he said this.

For my part, thinking of what I had seen beyond the confines of the beach, I did not fancy such a walk, but I supposed I could manage it if necessary. I hoped the seas would moderate soon!

The two islanders smiled at us, offered their hands by way of saying goodbye, and made their way back up the beach, through the castaways standing and lying about on the sand. I watched them attain the path up to the bluff and followed them with my eyes as they trudged slowly to the top. Once there, they stopped and surveyed the beach end to end, the reef with its sad bounty, and the darkening sky beyond. Night was about to descend. While I could not see them with any degree of detail, I suspected they shook their heads before moving inland, away from the bluff. I certainly would have.

As the darkness became more profound, the wind eased until it stopped altogether. And with the sunset and the lack of wind, swarms of biting insects appeared – I heard someone in a nearby group of men refer to them as *mossies* – mosquitos – and so thick they actually obscured our vision! Swatting at them, while initially satisfying, proved ineffective; there was no way to kill enough to even make a dent in their population. They landed in our noses, eyes, ears, mouths if open, arms, necks, and hair. It was enough to drive a man insane. The air was filled with frustrated shouts, curses, the slap of hands on skin, and more cursing. Some of our number ran to the water's edge and flung themselves into it, holding their heads beneath the surface until the need to breathe forced them up. For my own part, it was all I could manage to try and keep them out of my eyes and mouth. They bit, drew blood, and flew away, leaving a space for their relatives to feast on me. I joined those who had found some refuge in the water, tearing off my shirt and waving it about to drive the pests away as I ran.

Shortly, some industrious soul got a fire started and, by adding damp wood to it, made thick smoke. It had the desired effect and the lee side of it where the smoke blew in the slight breeze quickly became crowded with bitten, bloody, and wet, men seeking relief from the marauding mosquitos. Within an hour, the wind again freshened and, almost like magic, the biting bugs mercifully disappeared – to our eternal gratitude.

In the aftermath of our tribulation, the sounds of the night seemed more intense, the waves still breaking on the ships and the reef, the whisper of the grasses above us on the bluff, and the restrained voices of the shipwrecked souls stranded on the beach at Gun Bay.

There were about a dozen of us – officers, midshipmen, our master's mate returned from his assignment, some warrants and Bogue's nephew, his servant. I had not seen Black, since I left the ship this morning to carry Lawford's letter to Captain Harrison in *Louisa*. Suddenly, it dawned on me that neither had I seen my friend, Henry McMahon.

"Has any of you noticed our esteemed surgeon? Is he about? I would imagine he made it off the wreck...?" I inquired of the group at large.

In the glow and shadows offered by the small fire our bosun had made for us, I saw heads shaking and shoulders shrugging. No one had seen him.

"Joe. What do you suppose happened to Henry? Did you see him come ashore? He couldn't still be on the ship, could he?" I could not imagine Henry staying out there by choice.

"I may have seen him come in from the wreck in one of the native canoes, Edward. I was a bit busy at the time, though, trying to keep our own boat from oversetting in the surf. But I have not caught a glimpse of the man since attaining dry land. Sorry."

"Hmm. I wonder what has become of him. Do you suppose he doesn't know where we Converts have gathered? Maybe he's farther down the beach with others...maybe some who might have opened that hogshead of spirits I noticed! Wouldn't put *that* past him, would I?"

It struck me that I had eaten nothing all day and was some sharp-set and more than a little thirsty. I decided to wander off and see if I might find at least a drink of water, quite doubting the likelihood of any having food to share. Perhaps I would stumble across our missing surgeon as well. I announced my intention to the group

"You must be mad, Ballantyne. No one is going to give you anything. None of us has anything to eat or drink ourselves, let alone pass out to some wandering naval officer!" Bogue was not in the best of spirits, it seemed.

As it turned out, I was indeed successful in discovering some fresh water which a group of civilians offered to me quite freely, they being in possession of at least two hogshead of it, that I could see. I gathered there were others that had been floated in from the wrecks earlier in the day. Food, however, as I suspected, was scarce; there had been several barrels of bread washed ashore, but completely ruined by seawater. Perhaps tomorrow, we might find more in the wrecks, I was told.

At the rate they are being beaten apart and settling, I would doubt that! I thought as I moved across the beach, talking with some of the groups of sailors and passengers from the wrecked merchant vessels.

"You there! Lieutenant! Aren't you the bloke what come aboard with the sailing orders and such? Few days back, it were, in Port Royal?" A voice – I could not see the person it belonged to – called quietly from knot of men gathered round a bit of fire.

I turned and studied the men, only slightly more than shadows in the darkness, the clouds obscuring the moon and stars.

"Aye, might have. What ship are you" I answered.

"*Britannia,* it is. On the reef to the south of your frigate, we were." A man stood, and stepped closer, illuminated in the glow of the fire. "Chief Mate Brian Eubank. Wasn't introduced back at Port Royal, we wasn't. Cap'n wasn't much for pleasantries!"

Now there's understatement at its finest! Sodding bastard damn near threw Sherwin and me off the ship! Wonder where he has got to.

"Aye, not so much, Mister Eubank, not so much. How have you fared...other than putting your ship ashore, I mean? Did you suffer any casualties in the disaster?"

"We did, sir. Only one...Cap'n Martin went over the side when we abandoned her, missed the boat, and fell into the sea. He couldn't swim a stroke. Sank like a bloody stone, he done!" First Mate Eubank didn't seem particularly saddened by the loss of his captain! Nor was I.

Shouldn't think ill of the dead, Edward! Poor man lost his life, likely in a dreadful way. I must offer some sympathetic platitude.

"I am sorry to hear that. Martin was a rough cove, for sure, but no one deserves that end." *Not bad,* I thought.

"He was the one put us on the hard in the first place, Lieutenant. Got us out in front – we passed you to leeward, we done – and our lookout missed the breakers until it was too late to bear off, tack, or wear. He did order the guns fired, though, to warn off the others. Guess that was a bit late, too!" The mate sounded truly apologetic for his captain's action...which was not surprising a jot, considering the results!

I wanted to grab the man and choke the life out of him. He and his captain created the disaster that we now found ourselves mired in. Bloody fools! I might have known it was them after all the trouble I had both in delivering the sailing instructions and once underway, with them attempting to pass us several times. But I refrained.

"Well, I reckon he won't be answering to the owners for his poor navigation and roguish behavior, now will he! Were you able to collect any stores or equipment before you abandoned?" I tried to study the man's face to see any reaction. It was simply too dark by half.

"Precious little; Cap'n Martin didn't think there would be time before the bloody ship went out from under us. Did get a barrel or two of bread and one of water brung up, but the barrel with the bread sprung and the bread got wet. Water we floated ashore with us. It's here. Would you like some?" Eubank acted as if he might be trying to make up for his captain's lack of earlier civility.

"Just had some, but thank you. You will likely be needing it before this travail is done.

"By the by, Mister Mate, you haven't run across a surgeon... a naval surgeon by chance?" I asked hopefully.

"Saw him before dark, Lieutenant. Seemed to be wandering

about helping folks what got 'emselves hurt, he done. Right kind chap, I'd say."

Well, at least, I know he's ashore, not stranded on the wreck or floating face-down in the sea!

"He is that to be sure. I shall toddle off myself, now, to see if I might run across him. Can't be far; I mean, this beach is only so long, right?" I stuck out my hand to shake his, but either he did not see it in the dark or chose to ignore it.

Aloft, the clouds scudded by in the blackness of the heavens showing occasional breaks where a star peeked out, the faint light quite obvious in an overcast, moonless, night. While the people on the beach had earlier talked, moaned, cried, and generally carried on about their desperate condition, they had grown tired of complaining, and found solace in the company of their mates; they quieted down sufficiently to hear that the surf out on the reef had diminished, offering only the infrequent crash and thunder of the breaking waves.

Picking my way carefully through the clusters of castaways, I suddenly found myself confronted with the unfriendly and sharp, pointed bits of coral sticking up from the sand. One step into it, and the sand gave way entirely to the razor-sharp fossilized coral. I needed no further encouragement to turn about and retrace my steps across the beach.

Once again attaining the comfort – relatively speaking – of our little camp, I sank to the sand next to Bogue on one side and Earnshaw on the other.

"What have you discovered, Edward? How are the others faring?" The flickering light of the modest fire offered a small glimpse of his raised eyebrows and concerned expression.

"The master of *Britannia* has succumbed – apparently in abandoning his ship – according to his chief mate. Interestingly, they were the first on the hard and it was they who fired the guns to warn the others. As I understand it, his was the only death in that ship; the others have either come ashore or got themselves out to the fleet offshore.

"I did learn that Henry made it ashore and is somewhere here, doing what you might expect..."

"Don't tell us! He has found a cask of wine and is enjoying it with new friends!" Earnshaw offered, injecting some much-needed humor into our situation.

"Well, he might be at that. I could not find the man, only heard instances of him visiting survivors and treating any who needed his services. I doubt he knows where the Converts are camped, so we will likely not see him until daylight." I smiled in the dark, silently thanking young Earnshaw for his well-needed and -timed wit.

"Mister Ballantyne. We have been given a cask of water, here, by some thoughtful merchant sailors. Would you enjoy a swallow? We haven't much, but we have all had some and you were absent when it turned up." Lawford's voice floated across the fire out of the darkness on the other side.

Even though I had been given a drink at the outset of my trek across the sands, I was again some thirsty and greedily drank down the cup the captain handed 'round the circle to me. It might have been a trifle salty, but it was as sweet and pleasant as the finest wines my friend Henry McMahon and I had ever shared! *Where was that man?*

Conversation died off, the men removing jackets to make pillows, laying down, hollowing out depressions in the sand to make as comfortable a bed as they might. The fire died down and the beach grew quiet. I listened to the surf for a while, realized how tired I was, and let the quiet thunder of it lull me to sleep.

I awoke with a start; the sun shone directly into my eyes, gritty with salt and filth, making them sting. And the wind was up again. It picked up the sand above the high water line and flung it, swirling, toward the bluff above us. I shielded my face and turned my back to the water; I could see that many of our fellow castaways had moved themselves up to the top of Gun Bluff, obviously in an effort to escape the pelting sand. My comrades were stirring, some up and moving about, others still supine but awake. And the almost constant thunder coming from seaward told me in no uncertain terms that the seas were raging on the reef. I pitied the poor sods who had remained in the wrecks, not just *Convert*, but several of the others as well.

"We'll be some strained getting those lads ashore in this. Looks worse than yesterday, it does." Bogue voiced what many of us – certainly yours truly – were thinking.

"That surf is going to make short work of what's left of the wrecks. Don't reckon we'll be gettin' any more salvage out there. Even what the lads managed to save is likely to be lost in those seas." The bosun squinted down his eyes, studying the reef line and its precariously perched victims.

Lawford simply stared out to sea, his sad expression an eloquent echo of our combined emotions. I suspected he was seeing, in his mind's eye, his entire career washed up on a reef and sinking right alongside his late command. Then, drawing his eyes away from the depressing scene, he picked up the cask from which he had poured some water for me last night and shook it, listening to the slosh of the liquid within. Without comment, he handed a cup to Midshipman Campbell and poured a half measure into it, signaling the boy to drink it. Words were unnecessary; Campbell was as thirsty as any of us and eagerly drank before sharing the remainder with his friend, Tom Sherwin.

The refilled cup made it 'round the group, each man taking a few small sips. We had little idea of how long we would have to make it last; drinking sparingly seemed the best course. Few of us had any misgivings about the locals offering to refill the cask; their own situation was nearly as precarious as ours. When my turn came, it occurred to me that in addition to being thirsty, I was well past sharp-set, having not eaten now for nearly two full days. My belly growled, most likely in concert with many others in the same state of privation.

"Would any of you chaps be interested in a bit of bread? A trifle salty, but it will help to fill your bellies." A familiar voice from behind us spoke the welcome words.

"Henry? Where in God's name have you been? We thought you might not have made it ashore, and then Edward, here, heard from some sailors off...*Britannia,* wasn't it?...that you were indeed on the beach." Bogue, leapt to his feet and greeted our lost surgeon effusively, his words of concern echoing all of our sentiments.

"Aye, Joe, came in yesterday in a native craft. Picked me right up at the door, so to speak, and carried me ashore in fine style! Barely got my shoes wet. Might have been before you lot got in. I saw there were some folks from the merchants who looked as if they could use some help. Then time just slipped by – I was kept busy fixing all manner of injuries from broken limbs to gouges that bled a lot and a few mental issues as well. Then it was dark and I figured if you had got yourselves ashore – some said you had – that I would have a look about in daylight. And here you are, and here I am!" He held a parcel under one arm and a medical bag under the other. In the same hand, he dragged a tarpaulin bag tied closed with a bit of twine. His jacket was gone, his shirt open at the neck, and his stock hung loosely down his none-too-clean shirt front.

"Well, there's a relief! Glad to see you, Doctor. Let me offer you a hand. What's in the parcel?" Hutchins stood and relieved McMahon of part of his burden, the bag and his medical kit, setting them near the pile of our own possessions.

"Ship's bread. As I mentioned, a bit salty and damp, but I think edible. Tastes better and better with each passing hour of not eating!" He had not lost his droll wit, I was glad to see.

Sitting on the sand with the rest of us, he unwrapped the outside covering – canvas, it appeared to be – and then spread apart the oiled paper within, displaying a pair of sizeable loaves and many biscuits – hard tack – that clearly had seen better days.

A knife appeared and Henry, with a surgeon's skill, carved off lumps to be passed about the group. While the bread was indeed a bit salty with the tang of some mold thrown in, I could imagine nothing to be tastier, even fresh from the bakery! And since we had been at sea for only a short few days, the weevils had not yet made a home in it!

While we polished off the bread – it did little to satisfy our ravenous hunger – we caught up with Henry's trials and he with ours. While none of us had been ministering to the halt, the lame, and the wounded, as the surgeon had, there was a similarity to our collective adventures both aboard *Convert* and ashore on the beach at Gun Bay.

"Do you have a plan to escape from here, Cap'n?" McMahon queried the captain. "I spoke yesterday to a very pleasant native chap who offered his services and that of his boat, but he also mentioned that with the seas running as high as they were – and it looks even worse today – that we would have to wait until the passage through the reef became navigable again."

"I am beginning to think we will have to walk to George Town, Doctor. That's the settlement at Hogsties, where I instructed to the ships to wait for us. But perhaps your new-found friend might be willing to carry a letter for me to Commodore Ford in Jamaica, should the weather moderate and his vessel be capable of such a trip." Lawford shifted his glance from the waves thrashing the reef to the surgeon.

"Oh, yes; I should think he would have little trouble managing that trip. He showed me where the entry through the reef is. Can you imagine that we missed it by only a short distance...a pistol shot, perhaps. Of course, he pointed out to me that should we have sailed through the break in the reef...even by accident, we would have quickly come to grief as the water inside is quite shallow. Less than ten feet, he said." Henry smiled, a bit ruefully, I thought.

"Aye, come to grief we would in ten feet. But I would reckon the sand of the sea bottom might be more forgiving than the coral in the reef!" Bogue had been listening to their conversation and interjected his own opinion.

"Captain Lawford?" A female voice caused every one of us to start, and turn to find the speaker.

"Yes, madam? I am he. How may I help you?" Lawford stood to greet the unexpected visitor.

"I am Missus Emilia Cooke, late of the brig *Fortune.* A somewhat ironic name, I think." The lady smiled sadly at the droll remark, and continued. "It occurred to me that since it is Sunday, in your capacity as a commanding officer in His Majesty's Navy and master of our naval escort, you might be persuaded to offer divine services for those of us who would be interested. You know, give thanks to the Almighty for our deliverance?" She smiled again at the irony of her statement, but I think we all understood her intent.

Missus Cooke, an attractively turned out lady who appeared to be in her thirties, looked remarkably well-attired and presentable considering our circumstance. Her hair was pulled back in a bun; she wore a lace-fronted shirt with a high collar and long sleeves and a long maroon skirt that showed only a slight soil and discoloration, likely, from the seawater. We could not see her feet, as the hem of her skirt dragged on the sand. Her face, noticeably pretty, offered startlingly blue eyes over a small up-turned nose. Her mouth offered full lips slightly parted, and the blush on her cheeks could have been from face paint, the sun, or discomfort at facing our situation. All together, the package held our attention. She did not mention where *Mister* Cooke might have got to. And Lawford did not ask.

"Why, yes, of course, Missus Cooke. I would be happy to lead a service for the group, offer some prayers of thanksgiving or what-have-you. Sadly, my Bible did not survive the tragedy..." Lawford paused, and twisted his head toward the scene of our devastation, then turned back to the lady. "But if there is...that is to say, should one of your number have one – a Bible, that is – that I might borrow, it would be most helpful. In any case, we can surely gather in thanksgiving." Lawford smiled – for the first time since he came ashore, I suspect – and willingly acceded to the lady's request.

It occurred to me that any one of us would have 'willingly acceded to the lady's request' regardless of what it might have been.

She smiled her thanks, turned about and made her way through the clusters of people standing about on the beach.

We all returned to our seats on the sand; not wanting to meet each other's eyes, we focused on the reef and the increasing surf pounding our ships to matchwood, each wrapped in his own thoughts. For my part, I was comparing Missus Cooke to my recollection of the lovely Kendall Smith, unable to decide which lady more suited my fancy. The constant thunder of the waves a mile distant receded into a dull resonance in the background.

The hours staggered by, Captain Lawford offered a church service most likely substantially different from any he had led in the past, as this one did not include a reading of the Articles of War at its conclusion. We sang a few hymns of praise and thanksgiving in their place. None among us seemed terribly filled with praise or thanksgiving..."lackluster" would best describe the singing. The captain also took the opportunity to explain to the group his plan to affect a rescue, why the local people were unable to help us, and mention that he would dispatch a local vessel to Jamaica to report our plight to the proper authority as soon as the seas calmed and one could sail through the opening in the reef. He also mentioned that he anticipated that several naval people would walk to the settlement of George Town at

Hogsties the following day to meet those ships of our convoy, which he hoped would be waiting for us.

And I prayed I would not be one of those 'naval people' expected to accompany him on his walk to George Town! I did not know how many of our number had looked beyond the scope of the beach as I had, but I surely did not fancy walking on the frighteningly sharp and dangerous-looking coral that seemed to go on forever. The rest of the day passed slowly. The water was passed around and sipped sparingly; the surgeon's bread now gone, we tried not to think about our empty bellies, finding that sleep was a good, if temporary escape. And of course, at dusk, as it had the night previous, the wind dropped and the *mossies* returned even thicker than the night before, driving all of us mad with frustration, anger, and unspeakable discomfort.

"Mister Ballantyne." I heard my name uttered quietly from the darkness beyond the fire – it was Captain Lawford's voice – "are you here?"

"Aye, sir. Right here." I started to rise, but he stopped me.

"I think you should accompany me to George Town on the morrow. I am hoping one of our local friends will show us the way, and, of course, we shall be obliged to walk it as I feel it unlikely that, even should the wind stay light, the seas will calm enough to allow passage through the reef.

"Lieutenant Bogue will embark on the first local vessel capable of passing through the reef and sail to Jamaica, delivering the news of our sad plight to Commodore Ford, whom I expect will promptly dispatch some relief. With a bit of good fortune – God knows, we are surely due for some! – he could sail on Tuesday and reach Port Royal by Thursday or Friday.

"Mister Earnshaw will remain here, marshaling what stores might be salvaged or wash ashore, and organizing groups to get to the ships for further scavenging when the seas calm. He will also arrange to move people out to the merchant vessels that will hopefully come back from Hogsties to collect them. The warrants and mids will assist him in that endeavor."

My heart sank! I was to make the journey over the most unimaginably, unspeakably impossible terrain. My single comfort came from the fact that the captain, a man more than fifteen years my senior, would share the difficult march with me. And perhaps, we might find a local man who can show us a better route, one where we might not have to walk over the sharp spikes of fossilized coral. One might hope, at least!

"Aye, sir. If I may inquire, Cap'n, once we get ourselves to Hogsties, what then?" I was tired, thirsty, unspeakably hungry, and dirty. Had I been otherwise, I might have refrained from questioning him.

He stared at me, his eyes reflecting the flickering light of the fire, and remained silent for several moments. I waited, realizing perhaps, that I might have overstepped the bounds of propriety.

"I would imagine we will see to organizing some of the ships to return here to collect those we can put aboard – should any of the masters have actually followed my instructions to await our arrival there – and arrange some transport to Jamaica for our own people." Lawford seemed either not to notice my blunder, or did not care.

Thinking of the uncomfortable day ahead, I bunched up my jacket, burrowed into the sand a bit, and drifted off to sleep.

CHAPTER FIFTEEN
10-13 February 1794
George Town, Grand Cayman

Execrable, appalling, horrendous, unspeakable – just a few of the words that come to mind, but do little justice to the passage we trod most of the way to George Town. Burning hot sands, jagged, sharp, rough coral, scrub vegetation filled with thorns that grabbed at one's trouser legs, and flying and crawling insects all did their best to lay us low, trip us, tear into our clothing and shoes, and prevent us from attaining our goal, the settlement of George Town at Hogsties Bay.

Mister Knowles, our local guide, chose the most passable route (he claimed) for our journey. He mentioned at the start that, with no untoward incidents, we should arrive at our destination within a day or a day-and-a-half. That thought, repeated to myself almost without pause, saw me through and kept me from giving up completely. Lawford staggered; one of *Convert's* passengers, a Captain Thomson of the Royal Artillery who had insisted on accompanying us, fell many times, only to be helped up by Mister Knowles and either the captain or me. I fell at least twice, one of which put a rent in my thigh that, initially, bled profusely and then off and on for the remainder of the journey. To say it was arduous, unpleasant, or difficult would be understatement at its finest.

Mister Knowles stepped along with a fluidity and spryness that belied his age. I guessed him to be in his sixties from his white hair and beard and the lines that radiated outward from his eyes. He was missing more teeth than he had and his voice was thin and high-pitched. Dark complected, his features, like several of his countrymen I had seen, were more European than Negroid. His body was whip-thin and lithe and he trod the path with a sure-footedness that gave me to believe that he had been this way many times before. I was grateful for his familiarity with our route; it surely saved us time and more pain.

Knowles pointed out places he presumed would be of interest to us, where the island had been cut in half by a hurricane, previous to the most recent, from Little Pedro Point all the way to North Sound. Interestingly, it was relatively high ground and had almost entirely filled back in until the storm last October, he mentioned, as we scrambled up from the coral scrub at the water's edge. We walked along the bed left by the receding water – I was unclear whether it was left by the earlier storm or the more recent one – a path more passable than any we had encountered so far. But, Mister Knowles quickly made clear, it went in the wrong direction. So back we went to the brambles and thickets.

"And this be Spots Bay. We get us back down to the beach through there." Knowles pointed at the water, clearly visible through the tangle of storm-tossed vegetation and turned to head for it. It seemed about a musket shot distant. We followed, hoping the "beach" would indeed be as described!

Oh my Lord! Spare me more of that sharp coral. My feet are done for! Never have I been so glad for the foresight of donning my seaboots when we abandoned ship! Shoes would never have survived this!

As it turned out, it was exactly that: beach composed of soft, white sand, smoothed into static ripples by the wind and water. After what we had just experienced, it was like walking on a cloud! But we had to walk along the water's edge where the sand was more firmly packed, after finding the higher beach to be so soft as to be difficult to walk on. What a contrast! The seas had calmed considerably, causing me to think that, had we only waited for just a day or so, one the native boats could have carried us through the reef and onward to Hogsties! But now, according to Mister Knowles, we were just a half-day's walk from our destination – maybe a trifle more – so there would be no point in turning back to make the trip by water.

We had camped – more or less – the night before in a patch of brown grasses above the water's edge and near a settlement of rude huts, hastily thrown together for shelter after the October storm had taken the original houses. We all collapsed where we stood, having walked the entire day over the most arduous terrain, not caring whether the ground was hard or soft, nor about the swarming mosquitos which paid their nightly visit as we stopped. Just to be off our feet was all we wanted.

Mister Knowles seemed not to have the same need as did we, saying he would see if there might be some food in the settlement he called Bodden Town. He knew some of the residents, he mentioned, and hoped they might be persuaded to share something to eat, though we could tell from his tone that he held little hope of success.

He returned after dark, walking as easily as he had at the outset of our journey, carrying a small cask under one arm and a woven basket in his hand.

"Got us a bit of water here." He handed the cask to Captain Lawford who tipped it up and drank sparingly from the bung.

Lawford passed it then to our passenger, Captain Thomson, who eagerly snatched it up and drank thirstily, spilling a quantity down his beard and on down the front of his shirt.

"Easy, there, sir. There ain't much in there, and we would all like a taste." Knowles voiced what I was thinking, and reached to take the cask from the artillery soldier.

"Very thirsty...just a moment. Another swallow, if you please." Thomson turned away from our guide and gasped as he again hoisted the little barrel aloft.

"We'll pass it around again, sir. Just let each of us have a go; only fair." Knowles again reached for the cask and this time, succeeded in taking it from Thomson's grasp. He passed it to me.

With his admonition to the army man fresh in my ears, I lifted the barrel and poured a small amount of the sweetest water I could imagine into my dust-dry mouth. I swished it around a bit, swallowed and took another small taste before handing the container to our guide and provider. He also took a small sip. It occurred to me that he might have found some relief in the settlement before he returned to our camp.

I was curious as to what the basket contained. It was neither small nor large, woven loosely from palm leaves, and had a flexible wooden handle. A bit of cloth covered whatever it held. I did not have to wait long to discover that Mister Knowles had brought us a small loaf of bread and two orange-colored fruits. Their skin was smooth so I knew that they would not be oranges, and assumed them to be some kind of melon.

He used his knife to cut some slices from the bread and handed them around, again admonishing us to eat them slowly. Of course, our ravenous artillery officer did just the opposite, stuffing his slice into his mouth all at one time.

"Might I be permitted to have another bit of water? Just a swallow to wash the bread down is all." He asked.

"Mister Knowles suggested we eat it slowly, Thomson. You chose not to. The water will come a bit later." Lawford's voice was harsh, tired, and raspy; he was exhausted.

The fruit was indeed melon, with a juicy, sweet, pulpy texture that caused each of us to offer a sigh of satisfaction as we chewed our portions. Even Thomson ate slowly, likely savoring the juice as much as the flavor!

Without passing the cask around again – it seemed unnecessary as our thirst had been slaked with the first pass and then the juice of the melons – we all fell into an exhausted sleep, to awaken as the sun lifted above the horizon the next morning. Sore muscles and stiff joints staggered us as we rose, groaning at the thought of another day of marching over this inhospitable terrain.

The morning's march had seen us to the end of the beach on what Knowles called South Sound; here we would cut inland, avoiding more of the spikey coral that ringed Southwest Point. Another settlement here looked much the same as the one at Bodden Town; rude huts built of random bits of wood, palm fronds, canvas, and cloth. People milled about, some tilling a field while others hacked at the tangled mess left from the hurricane.

That must have been some storm; they're still cleaning up after it months later and this is fairly high ground. No animals...wonder what happened to them.

No sooner had I thought of the animals than I remembered what our first visitor at Gun Bay had told us: they were all carried away by the storm! That was why there was no meat or milk to be had.

"Mister Knowles. Have there been no ships calling here from the Havana or Jamaica since the storm? I would think they might have brought you some animals to use as breeding stock."

"They come quick after the hurricane, Mister Ballantyne. Folks got goats and a few pigs, but eat 'em all right quick. Hunger does that to a body. Didn't t'ink 'bout the future, just wanted to fill they's bellies." He shot a glance at the army officer as he said that. "None of those critters got far as East End. Come in to George Town, they done, and stayed there. And got et."

As we walked through the settlement at Southwest Point, Knowles spoke to a few tired-looking people, folks, beaten by the hurricane, who had yet to regain their spirit. They simply nodded or waved a lethargic greeting to us, and resumed their toil. Few even offered a smile.

"Hogsties just a bit farther," he said, moving on through the stubble and tangle of foliage, just now greening up after their devastation from the storm.

I stole a glance at our army officer, staggering along beside me. He looked only a bit worse for the wear...until I looked at his eyes. A wild-eyed, darting look betrayed the last vestiges of his sanity. I was not sure whether the physical toll, the mental stress, the almost unbearable heat, mosquitoes, the shipwreck – or all of them – had turned his mind into what could easily become a wasteland, the final chapter of what was likely a successful career in His Majesty's Royal Artillery.

"We're almost there, Thomson. Steady on, and we'll be in George Town and heading out to one of the ships before you know it!" I tried to be encouraging...to him as well as myself!

He simply looked at me, his eyes darting around the field we were crossing. He said not a word, simply grunted an acknowledgment.

Lawford was walking in front of us, with Mister Knowles. He shot a glance over his shoulder at Thomson and me, and raised his eyebrows. "You chaps managing all right, back there? We've not far to go, now! Mister Knowles says maybe an hour or a bit longer."

"Water. Need a swallow. Just a sip to see me through. Won't take much. Mouth too dry to swallow." Thomson croaked.

The little procession halted and Mister Knowles, who had been carrying the cask with what little remained of our water, pulled the bung and handed it to the army officer. Without so much as a "by your leave" or "thank you kindly" Thomson grabbed it and tipped it up, again spilling water into his mouth, down his beard, shirt-front, and trousers.

"That'll do, sir. The others might like a swallow as well." Knowles reached to take the cask from the man. Mercifully, he surrendered it without a fuss, forestalling what could have been his undoing.

We shared out the final few swallows, secure in Knowles' assurance that we were almost there, and threw down the cask on the path.

"Let us proceed, then, gentlemen, now that we are refreshed. We've only a short stroll ahead of us now. Press on!" Lawford seemed to gain strength from the water, or possibly from the knowledge that our travail was almost done.

I tried to emulate the spring in his step and managed nicely until I tripped, not looking at where I stepped, and fell hard, opening the wound in my thigh again. It had quite nearly stopped leaking during the night, and I admit to coddling it a bit during the morning's hike. Now that it was opened up again, blood ran down my leg and into my boot. The settlement at George Town could not turn up soon enough! And I hoped with all my soul that the ships Lawford had ordered to the Hogsties would be there waiting for us.

The sun beamed down its suffocating heat; the breeze was scant. We were no longer along the coast, and the path, what there was of it, was overgrown and rough. We moved silently, too tired and hungry to even complain, each of us hoping to find George Town sooner than later, as Mister Knowles had promised. The only sounds were the occasional grunt offered if one of us tripped and the rustle of sticks and brambles as they brushed by our rubbery legs. We all remained quite within ourselves, moving simply by instinct and habit.

"Masts! There! Oh! Thank God!" Thomson saw them first and cried out, the relief in his voice obvious.

"Aye, as I said." Knowles seemed not a bit surprised as he took a look at his watch, hauled from his shirt pocket by a long chain. "Two hour and a half. Done it faster myself, and only a half day by boat, but looks like they's some of your ships yonder, Cap'n."

Indeed they were. With the end in sight, we walked with a more sprightly step, one fitting officers in the King's service. I counted eight of our merchants and several native schooners and sloops swinging easily to their anchors in the bay, boats plying to and fro along the waterfront and between the vessels. The water was dazzling in the glare of the sun, birds soared and dove into the shallows and, except for the remaining and obvious devastation from the late storm, a most normal and up-lifting vista opened before us. A grand sight, to be sure!

The settlement at George Town was larger and in better repair than those we had passed on our trek. The houses, while obviously recently repaired and rebuilt, were more stoutly constructed, more permanent looking, and more densely inhabited. The waterfront was crowded with people hauling barrows of fish, wood, palm rope, and assorted goods. A local boat, a schooner, was making its approach to the quay wall, and, as we watched, a familiar figure leaped from the vessel's rail to the shore, and, upon espying our commander, knuckled his forehead in greeting.

"Popplewell! What are you doing here? I thought you would be in Gun Bay still." Lawford was obviously not a bit dismayed to see his sailing master standing before him.

"Thought you might want a bit of help, Cap'n. Just got here now with these kind folk. Brung young Campbell with me, couple of hands as well." As if on cue, Midshipman Campbell stepped off the schooner and doffed his hat – not a regulation fore and aft midshipman's hat, but an interesting affair constructed of palm leaves - in greeting.

"Say, Cap'n, if you don't mind my sayin,' you chaps look a bit worse for the wear. Mister Clarke told me while we were sailing that there might be some turtles here to eat. These folks catch 'em, you know. Main business here in the Caymanas, I'm given to understand." Popplewell seemed, in comparison to us, rested, fed, and not a bit thirsty. He certainly didn't get much food or water in Gun Bay – must have been fed on the boat.

"We would be most grateful for a bit of food ourselves, Sailing Master. And some water, if you please. We are a trifle parched from our march from Gun Bay." Lawford was looking around, speaking distractedly, seeking refreshment apparently.

Knowles, who had slipped away once we arrived at the waterfront now reappeared, followed by two men pushing a barrow.

"Cap'n, found you somet'ing to eat. And drink. Things here not as bad as in East End. They got some food and a bit of water here. Willing to share it, they are. Please, help yourselves."

I thought Thomson would faint dead away at the sight of solid food – meat of some kind – a variety of fruits, and a small cask of water. He fell upon it without a word, grabbing up the meat (it turned out to be turtle) and stuffing it in his mouth. He grabbed for the cask, but Lawford had got it first and was drinking thirstily. I tried a bit of fruit, moist, sweet, and delicious. Popplewell and Campbell looked on, smiling, quiet.

Before too much time had passed, Lawford had organized transportation to *Louisa,* the one to which he had addressed his instructions at Gun Bay several days ago.

"Ballantyne – you and the master and Campbell see about organizing some of these other vessels to go back to Gun Bay and load as many of the survivors as they might carry. Don't worry too much about our people – I will see to them.

"I am sure that once Bogue gets back to Jamaica, the commodore will send vessels straight away to bring relief. We will go back in them."

"Cap'n Lawford?" A new voice, the accent local, called out.

"Aye, I am he."

"Sir. I am called George Turnbull. Mister William Bodden has sent me with this petition for you. If you please, sir." Turnbull extended his hand holding a folded piece of parchment.

Lawford perched his spectacles on his nose, opened the missive, and read aloud. "We the subscribers, inhabitants of the Island Grand Caymanas do certify on oath that from the distressed situation of the Island, in the article of provisions, owing to the hurricane of 19th October last, it's morally impossible for the inhabitants to support themselves and with the addition of the different ship companies wrecked on the East End of this Island on Saturday morning last, we the subscribers think it absolutely necessary for our own preservation that the different crews belonging to the wrecks already specified, must be immediately removed..." here Lawford stopped, looked up, and scowled at Mister Turnbull.

"We have already been advised of your inability to provide for our sustenance, sir, and are well aware of the privation you have experienced as a result of the hurricane. I understand that your petition makes it an official pronouncement of your council...or elders or whatever you call yourselves...but it is quite unnecessary. I have no desire to impose on your hospitality any longer than is necessary, and, in point of fact, am just now arranging for transport of our people from the wrecks to Jamaica or the Havana." Lawford quickly switched his scowl to a smile, perhaps realizing that we still might need some cooperation in the form of transport and some food for a bit longer.

The captain refolded the paper and carefully put it in his pocket. His brow furrowed as he considered a new thought.

"I expect that there will be ships of the Royal Navy soon in the offing, sir, and I further expect that they will be able to provide some relief for your own suffering. We truly appreciate your position and I hope to be able to repay your kindness by offering whatever assistance the navy might be able to provide. Should your neighbors be willing to transport any of our people to Jamaica from here or from Gun Bay, I am sure we can see to paying the captains and crews of any vessels involved."

Turnbull nodded, smiled, and said, "I will pass on your request to Mister Bodden, Cap'n. I think there might be some of our captains who have salvaged their boats or constructed new ones who would be happy to help. It is our nature." And he left.

"Cap'n, while I cannot understand why these folks here in George Town have seemingly not offered succor to their neighbors in East End and the other communities we passed through on our march, I should think we might be of help to them ourselves. It is my notion that if we are to return to Gun Bay in *Louisa* or any other, that we might try to buy some provender here and carry it down, both for our people and the locals." I had seen several indications of foodstuffs along the waterfront – mostly fish and turtles – and while water was clearly in short supply, we might be able to find a barrel or two in one of the ships to put ashore.

"Yes, Edward. But you just heard what the elders of the island have told us: 'leave, we can't be of help to you.' I suspect that would include buying foodstuffs here in George Town. They might well have only enough to feed themselves. No, I think we might have more success in seeking help from the ships – the merchantmen yonder – since they will be able to call at the Havana to replenish whatever we might need." He paused and added, "And I suspect the good folks at Gun Bay will be happy with whatever foodstuffs and water our merchant friends might be willing to provide. I shall discuss it with Captain Harrison in *Louisa*."

Lawford clambered down the quay wall into a boat we had

earlier identified as one of *Louisa*'s, and shoved off. The rest of us, Popplewell, myself, Campbell, Thomson, and a couple of sailors wandered along the waterfront, watching the boats from the merchants as they mixed with the local boats; it was a busy place, even this late in the day.

As evening approached, the wind, as it had every day we had been here, dropped off, and the local people began to disappear, some into buildings and some onto boats, which quickly put out into Hogsties Bay.

"Those damn mossies again!" Thomson, waving his arms frantically, spat as he looked about for someplace safe to weather the assault.

Knowing what we were in for, we all sought shelter; the sailing master and Campbell jumped back into Mister Clarke's schooner just as it began to pull away from the pier. Thomson and I tucked into a rude building that doubled as home and shop, where the people were surprisingly hospitable, and welcomed us as they closed the door and blinds. I don't know what the three sailors found, but I am sure they got themselves somewhere. Thomson and I were most happy to be sheltered from the onslaught after several nights in the open.

After full dark, a British long boat stroked into the quay, leaving a glowing trail in its wake and with each dip of the oars. An English voice called out my name. I hastened from our comfortable shelter – grateful that the mosquitoes had departed – to see who was calling.

"Yes, I am he: Ballantyne. How may I be of service?"

"Lieutenant: I am Johnson, third in *Louisa*. Your captain is aboard *Louisa* and has sent me to collect you, the sailing master, and a midshipman. Also mentioned an army officer. You are to return with me to the ship for supper. Cap'n Harrison has arranged accommodations for you." He looked around, obviously seeking to discover the whereabouts of the others he mentioned.

Of course, Popplewell and Campbell were still in Clarke's schooner, somewhere in the bay and well away from the shore. Thomson's curiosity had got the best of him, and he ventured forth from our temporary shelter. I nearly collided with him when I turned to fetch him.

"Very well, Mister Johnson, that is a fine offer – we accept."

I took the army captain by his arm, propelling him toward the sternsheets of the longboat. "Step aboard, Thomson, lively now. We've got supper waiting and a cot for the night. No more sleeping on the ground!"

The following day, *Louisa,* along with the ships *Alfred, LLandovery,* and *Jane,* and the brig *Mars* weighed to sail back to Gun Bay, Mister Clarke's schooner leading the way. It was good to be back at sea, and I breathed deeply of the fresh salt air once we were away from the land. Lawford stood next to me at the bulwark.

"Mister Ballantyne. I suspect Bogue has got himself to Jamaica by now and already is organizing a ship or two to come fetch us. We will load the civilians on the merchants once we arrive at Gun Bay, and the officers and perhaps twenty or thirty of our crew and I will remain to salvage what we might from *Convert.* I am hopeful the locals will assist with boats as the weather permits. Now that the seas have moderated, we should be able to get to the wrecks with little difficulty and scavenge whatever we might." Lawford was already fully restored and taking charge completely.

His plan was carried out as he intended: the civilian survivors of the disaster went aboard the merchants, ferried out through the reef in local vessels, for passage to the Havana or, in some cases, all the way back to England. Naturally, the ships had not planned on the extra mouths to feed, so a stop would be made in Cuba for sufficient stores. Captain Thomson, the members of the army 10th Regiment and their commander, Colonel Amherst, went with them, booking passage in *Louisa.*

The Royal Navy officers, midshipmen, warrants, and about thirty sailors remained encamped on the beach at Gun Bay and, assisted by local boatmen, managed to salvage a fair quantity of stores – some damaged by salt water and some intact – from the ships still perched on the reef. The weather remained remarkably calm, allowing us to work every day, collecting all manner of equipment, food stuffs, several hogsheads of fresh water, and a half dozen cannon barrels which the locals, strong and skilled swimmers, dove into the lagoon to retrieve. We stripped off as many sails as we could, and used the canvas to construct tents and shelters. We gave the excess to the grateful Caymanians.

Henry McMahon, remained with us, encouraged some local sailors to search for his wine cache, which they did and brought a great deal of it ashore to complement the hogsheads of rum we had also found. He also managed to find a good many of his medical instruments which he carefully cleaned and rewrapped in oiled canvas.

Each day, the frigate birds and gulls would swoop and dive into the still waters, filling their incessant need for sustenance. The sun shone brightly in a brilliant turquoise sky, the occasional puffy white cloud providing a bit of welcome relief as it passed in front of the sun. The local people, working side by side with us, became our friends, sharing our food and benefiting from the provender we salvaged from the wrecks. The local fishermen and turtlers sailed often, returning with more and more bounty from the sea to augment the ships' stores we English provided. In spite of the unfortunate events that conspired to put us in this position, we were a generally happy lot.

HMS *Success,* Captain Francis Roberts commanding, sailed into Hogsties in mid-March, having first hove to off Gun Bay where they fired a shot to awaken us, let us know they were here, and, I assume, to get a look at the melancholy sight still visible on the reef. We sailed in local craft to George Town to meet them after arranging with the island's elders to continue salvaging the wrecks, with the understanding that whatever they brought ashore from *Convert* would remain the property of the Royal Navy.

I am sure Captain Lawford felt conflicted when it came time to board *Success* and depart for the two-day journey to Jamaica. On one hand, he was shed of the rude accommodations and arduous manual labor we shared in Gun Bay, but on the other, he would be facing the inevitable court-martial. And Earnshaw had found the notes he had scribbled prior to abandoning – was it over a month ago? – and spent most of his time reviewing what he had written, as if his memory would not be permanently inscribed with the horror of the whole affair.

EPILOGUE
1-5 April 1794
Port Royal, Jamaica

The heat in the great cabin of HMS *Success* was oppressive. A coterie of five senior officers sat rigidly at the polished table set up across the stern, directly under the open quarter-gallery windows, a scant and warm breeze riffling the papers before them. Captain Roberts, who had retrieved us from Grand Cayman, would preside over the trial, assisted by the other four. In the forward part of the cabin, chairs had been set up for witnesses who would be called to testify and spectators; most were empty, an acknowledgment of the temperature within. Between the two areas sat Captain Lawford, Master Commandant R. Holmes, acting as judge advocate, and another officer I did not know, but whom I assumed would be acting as Lawford's advisor. There was a single empty chair facing the officers who made up the court-martial board.

The judge advocate stood, formally introduced himself, and read the letter from Commodore Ford directing the assemblage to enquire into the conduct of John Lawford, commander of His Majesty's late ship *Convert,* and such of the officers and company who were aboard at the time she wrecked, along with nine sail of merchantmen on the reefs to the eastward of Grand Cayman Island the morning of 8th February, 1794.

The members of the court were then sworn with oaths as directed by Parliament and the court martial of John Lawford began.

The captain was called to testify first; he stood, doffed his hat in salute to the Board, and then took his seat, at their invitation, in the empty chair, reserved for witnesses.

His testimony was an accurate accounting of the voyage of *Convert* from the time we sailed from Port Royal until we struck the reef. He included the names of the merchants that had accompanied us initially, then added the ones that joined at Bluefields and the four that met us off the western end of the island. I was impressed that he listed the ships without consulting a single note. He went to some lengths to describe the difficulty we had getting the ships, first just *Britannia* and then others, to follow the sailing orders and remain astern of the frigate.

"Why, Captain, did you make your approach to a potentially hazardous bit of land in the dark? Would it not have been more prudent to pass by the Caymanas in daylight, especially given that the weather was overcast and not conducive to locating your position with any degree of surety?" One of the captains sitting at the table enquired.

"Sir. It had been my intention to do just that. Sadly, one of our vessels signaled from the rear of the convoy that she was sinking – a schooner it was, bound to Ireland – and we had little choice but to go to her aid. This delayed us and, by force of necessity, the entire convoy. Mister Popplewell, our master, got a good observation and fixed our position with come confidence. That was on Friday, 7th, February. It went overcast shortly thereafter.

"After a run due west of some six hours, I altered course to the northwest. This, by my and Popplewell's reckoning, put us well to the west of Grand Cayman, some six or so leagues. Our course change was occasioned by a change of the winds to the north, and I directed the watch to bring her up a bit, sailing now north-northwest. That would have been shortly after the middle watch began." Lawford paused, took a breath, and seemed to gather himself. I knew, as did my shipmates, what would follow.

"So, Captain," a different officer of the board probed, "if I understand you correctly, your ship was ahead of the convoy and some six leagues west of Grand Cayman Island. That would seem to be a safe distance off. But apparently your position was not quite as accurate as you had thought, hmmm?"

Unfazed, Captain Lawford pressed on. "It was about halfway into the watch when the third lieutenant who had relieved the deck sent his messenger to my cabin to report that he had heard two guns fired to our leeward. Assuming it to be a signal of distress, I ordered him to run down toward the sound of the gun-fire and came on deck myself instantly.

"We soon discovered that the guns had been fired by a ship not to our leeward, but ahead of us. It was now clear that several of our charges had sailed to the fore, ignoring the instruction to maintain a position astern of the escort.

"It was at that moment that my lookout on the fore tops'l yard cried out that there were breakers ahead and close to us.

I could not tell the extent they ran in the darkness, and they seemed to be all around us. I at once made the signal for the fleet to disperse and do what was necessary for their own safety. In *Convert,* our tops'ls were already sheeted home, and she was responding nicely to her helm on a course to clear the breakers.

"Had not a ship run on board of us, we would have cleared the reef easily. However, that ship, striking us forward, pushed the bow around and forced us again toward the danger. We did manage to extricate ourselves from their headrig and reshape our course away, but the other ship, fighting for her own survival, rammed us again, this time quashing any hope of avoiding the reef. We struck shortly after that, and very soon thereafter, the ship was bilged."

Lawford stopped, clearly wondering if his words had provided the Board with a sufficiency of detail. Then he sat up straight and began again.

"Had the ships of the convoy maintained their stations and attended to the signals we showed, which I am sorry to say was not generally the case, this misfortune could have been avoided. I learned later that our position was off due to a strong northerly current which had set us to the northward of our desired course, a fact unknown to us at the time due to our inability to obtain a proper navigational fix of our position. Still, had my ship remained in the lead, as I had instructed our convoy, without any intervening vessel between her and the breakers, it is quite likely we would have observed the reef in time to warn the other vessels of its existence. At the worst, the only loss then might have been reduced to *Convert* alone. As I mentioned a moment ago, my ship was able to turn away onto a safe course, and would have succeeded, had not the merchant vessel come on board of us.

"Once we were on the shore, I discovered that the ship that had fired the guns was *already on the reef* with four or five others before her."

"Yes? And then you abandoned?" Captain Sinclair queried.

"No sir. We remained aboard, taking stock of our situation, keeping order, and preparing to abandon once it was daylight. The dawn revealed a most melancholy sight, seven ships and two brigs all on the same reef with *Convert.* There was now a heavy sea running, and the wind was blowing directly on shore.

Naturally, the remaining ships – those who did not continue on their way – were reluctant to approach a lee shore under such adverse conditions, and hence, could provide little in the way of assistance. The ships on the reef, of course, were unable to provide assistance to one another either.

"I ordered the boats over, and sent word to Cap'n Harrison in *Louisa* to wait long enough to receive some survivors then take the other ships to Hogsties, there to await further developments."

He went on for some time, detailing the facts of getting the civilian survivors out to the merchants, both immediately after the shipwreck and then later once the seas calmed. He did not dwell on our uncomfortable march to George Town, saying simply we had done it with the help of a local guide. He described sending a supernumerary Royal Navy officer with the convoy to England with a letter for the Admiralty and noted that he had sent Bogue to Jamaica. Salvage efforts got a mention and then the arrival of *Success* and Captain Roberts. Then he simply stared at the captains seated before him, waiting either for questions or to be dismissed.

With no further questions arising for Lawford, the Board called the day's testimony done and adjourned until the next morning. They announced that Lieutenant Bogue would be first to testify.

When the trial resumed, following the ritual firing of a gun and the raising of the court-martial flag, the first lieutenant offered essentially the same story as had the captain – why would he not? He was on the same ship at the same time. I reckon the board was seeking additional snippets of the story that Lawford might have left out – either accidentally or deliberately.

Once Bogue had told his story and been questioned by the board, Captain Lawford was allowed to question him. His questions all dealt with the navigational fix that Popplewell had taken and plotted the morning before the wreck and the courses steered by the ship thereafter. He also inquired about signals.

"Mister Bogue – were not signals constantly aloft directing slower ships to make more sail to keep up and the faster ones to reduce sail to maintain position? And were not shots fired to draw attention to the signals?"

Bogue answered, of course, in the affirmative, but added,

"They did little good, sir. In fact, we had the quarterdeck six pounder removed to the fo'c'slehead for that very purpose, to little avail."

"Mister Bogue. When you came on deck the morning of 8th February when all hands were called, do you recall that there was anything not done to save the ship? Was every exertion used to avoid the tragedy?"

"Yes, sir. Without a doubt."

The questioning continued, covering ground already trod in some detail in the captain's testimony. He asked about the compasses – was there any error in them? Bogue responded he knew of none. Did he agree with the master's sight reduction and resulting position on the morning of the 7th? "I had no reason not to agree."

Bogue was given the opportunity to offer any further comment to the board, but he had nothing further to add. He was dismissed and I was called to take the seat in front of the five captains.

When asked, I explained that I was not on deck during the middle watch, having only come topside just before the merchant came on board of us and we took the hard.

"During the day previous, Lieutenant Ballantyne, did you have any difficulty in keeping the vessels in convoy in their assigned positions? We have heard testimony that several had offered some vexation in that regard." One of the captains – I recall it was Captain Roberts – asked me.

"Yes, sir. From the moment we had cleared Port Royal, one ship in particular, *Britannia,* it was, seemed unwilling to remain to *Convert*'s rear. I had to remind them at least twice to avoid getting ahead of us. There were others as well, but *Britannia* was constantly working her way ahead of us."

"Were you on deck when the master fixed your position on 7th February?"

"Yes, sir, I was. Both he and our midshipmen managed to get the noon position before the weather became overcast."

"Did he happen to mention a northerly current running past the east end of Grand Cayman to you?"

"We were only marginally aware of it, sir. Popplewell knew it would not be as strong at this time of year as during the summer months. He did, as I recollect, consider the current in his course recommendation to Captain Lawford."

"In your opinion, Lieutenant, would *Convert* have cleared the reef had not the merchant vessel run on board you?"

"I believe so, sir. We had backed the tops'ls and had managed to get the ship's head around to the west when we were struck on the bow. Clearly, the merchant, in the act of extricating her own self, had not seen us; the morning was very dark and overcast. That mishap brought us back around toward the reef and we were unable to control her direction after that."

The Board having nothing further to ask, turned me over to Captain Lawford. His questions reinforced some of my earlier answers and then touched on the weather when I had the watch earlier in the night.

"How would you describe the weather when you left the deck at midnight, relieved by Mister Earnshaw?"

"It was exceeding dark, overcast with no moon. There was a moderate breeze but the seas were up, we suspected from a disturbance of some nature farther offshore. An occasional squall had blown through earlier, but at midnight it was quiet."

"Once you were ashore, did you learn from the masters of the merchants about how many vessels might have struck before *Convert* did?"

"I did, sir. The captain who first gave the alarm mentioned he had discovered three ashore before he struck and that a brig and a ship had passed close aboard him, standing out to clear the reefs. Another reported they had struck twice before finally coming to rest."

There being nothing further for me to add, I was excused and Bill Earnshaw nervously took the witness chair. He was sweating quite freely, I knew not just from the heat in the cabin. His queue was nearly dripping with moisture and the water left rivulets down his neck. He held the papers on which he had recorded his thoughts immediately following the disaster. They clearly had suffered from his clammy hands.

His testimony, both to the court and to Captain Lawford added nothing new to the information they already had. After some thirty minutes of questions and answers, he was mercifully excused. He beat a hasty retreat from the room, preferring the comfort topside to the confining heat below. And the trial closed for the day; Sailing Master Popplewell was given notice he would open the proceedings the next day.

Before he sat to testify, Popplewell handed the Board the ship's log and the chart he had used to track our progress from Port Royal. The officers at the table crowded around Captain Roberts to view the documents, some making notes of questions they would ask when given the opportunity.

Popplewell told his story – the same tale we had been hearing every day, several times – and was able, as sailing master, to offer specific positions for the convoy at various times during the curtailed voyage from Jamaica. He described the weather, courses made good, and his frustration at being unable to shoot a navigational fix after the first day. Then the questions began, and they mostly focused on the existence of a current – its strength and direction – and what knowledge he had of it.

"Have you ever been through the Gulf of Florida, Mister Popplewell. Before this, of course?"

"Yes sir. Many times."

"And what course did you typically steer from the west end of Jamaica to the Caymans?"

"West north-west, sir."

"And did you always find that that course carried you to the southward of the island of Grand Cayman?"

"Always, and sometimes, so far to the south that we never saw the island."

"What distance do you reckon the Caymanas are from the west end of Jamaica?"

"Fifty-two leagues."

"Have you ever experienced a current running between the Caymanas and Jamaica?"

"In very light breezes, we have found only a slight set to the north, but it had no effect in stronger winds."

"In the log, there are no notations of distance run during the first watch on 7th February. Why is that?"

"Sir, the distance we made was so negligible as to not merit heaving the log. Additionally, we sailed twice to the rear of the convoy and back during that time, so there was little advance of our course."

"During that time of 'little advance' of your course, did you allow for the effect of a current?"

"No sir, as I knew of none in the area."

The board worked this point to death, but Popplewell was adamant that he knew of no current. As a matter of interest, Captain Roberts, president of the board, admitted that none of them were aware of any current in that area, either. That exhausted the board's questions and Lawford took over.

His focus stayed with the current. "Have you talked with any of the merchant masters since the tragedy?"

"I have, sir. They also reported a current of which they had no knowledge. In fact, one of the captains who later returned to Jamaica, never saw Grand Cayman at all, making Little Cayman instead, an error of some fifty leagues."

Lawford then sought Popplewell's opinion on whether we would have cleared the reef had not the merchant ship run on board of us. His testimony agreed with all of his predecessors, that almost certainly the ship would have got her bow around and been able to avoid striking. He added, "Even under just her stays'ls, she would have."

"Mister Popplewell, do you think *Convert* made sufficient exertion to save herself, as well as warn the other vessels of the danger?"

"There was little more we might have done, sir, to avert our taking the hard after the merchant had fouled us. And once we had struck, you ordered a gun fired repeatedly for some thirty minutes, I recall."

Nods all around, Lawford sat down, and Popplewell was dismissed.

The day's final witness was Master's Mate Jim Hutchins. His testimony repeated much of what we had previously heard, as one would expect.

A final witness, the sailing master from HMS *Success,* was called by Captain Lawford. He asked only two questions.

"When you sailed to Cayman from Jamaica to relieve the remaining crew of *Convert,* did you notice a northerly current as you closed with the island?"

"We did, sir. A quite strong one, in fact."

"And how far off your course do you figure it set you?"

"I suppose it was close to nine or ten leagues, sir."

At that, the court martial adjourned, announcing they would reconvene the following day with a decision on the culpability of Captain Lawford and any others.

We were all nervous. McMahon, Bogue, Earnshaw, and I all saw supper ashore in one of the establishments we had frequented during our previous stay in Port Royal. Each of us found things other than the court martial to talk about, preferring to avoid any conjecture as to how it might turn out. I think we avoided it more for Earnshaw's sake – he was still nervous to the point of barely being able to eat – and since none of us had any idea what judgment the board would offer in the morning, there seemed little point in speculating.

We talked about when we might see England again. McMahon brought up the late Jack Farnsworth, wondering aloud how he might have reacted to the disaster, and Bogue reminded us of how the events had serendipitously thrown us all together.

I slept barely a wink at the boarding house where we had taken rooms – we had no ship after all – listening to drunken tars and maids reveling below me. I heard, in the morning, that the others had enjoyed the same uncomfortable night. We found a ship's boat heading out to *Success* and Bogue cadged a ride for us.

The Board was at their table, heads together and talking quietly as the room filled up. This time, every spectator chair had filled quickly, everyone eager to either glory in another's misfortune or celebrate exoneration. Naturally, all we Converts fell into the latter category.

The gun fired topside and the room at once went quiet. After the judge advocate called the court martial in session, Captain Roberts stood up.

"The board has considered every circumstance and, with maturity, weighed all the testimony surrounding the loss of His Majesty's Frigate *Convert*. We are of the opinion that the tragedy was occasioned by a strong current setting the ship very considerably to the northward of the reckoned position and have therefore adjudged that the said Captain John Lawford, Commander of his Majesty's late ship *Convert,* and such of the officers and company as were on board at the time she was wrecked together, with nine sail of merchantmen on Grand Cayman Island, 8th February last, should be acquitted."

The sigh that escaped a dozen throats was clearly audible.

AUTHOR'S NOTES

The story you have just read is clearly a work of fiction; many of the characters are creations of my imagination and some of the events that occur are likewise fictitious. At the same time, much of what you have hopefully enjoyed, actually happened and in more or less the circumstances I described.

The hurricane of October 1793 was very real and did, in fact, devastate Grand Cayman Island. And the fact that it laid waste to much of the island, its population, it crops, and its livestock, was the reason the survivors of the shipwrecks could not be accommodated by the normally very hospitable locals.

HMS *Europa,* HMS *Penelope,* HMS *Iphigenia,* and the French frigate *L'Inconstant* (HMS *Convert*) were all real ships which performed the roles ascribed to them. The conflict between the officers of the two British frigates was a creation of the author, as was the resulting duel fought at Port Royal. The Christmas party in Jamaica was used purely as a vehicle to set up the duel, provide a bit of local color, and add some interest. However, there are records of local planters entertaining naval officers at their homes with lavish parties. Interestingly, the hostility felt by Lieutenant Jonathon Jones' shipmates due to his losing his arm was misplaced; a year hence, the famous Horatio Nelson would lose his arm, then an eye, and still go on to become the lion of British naval history! Captain Rowley also questions the Navy's need for a one-armed officer.

As to the convoy and its disastrous end: fifty-eight ships sailed, escorted by a single Royal Navy frigate, HMS *Convert,* from Jamaica. While I did not list all of the ships in the convoy, those I did mention were real ships, captained by the men named in the story. Whether or not Captain Martin in *Britannia* was the difficult person depicted, I have no idea, but the ship was a constant problem for the escorting frigate and did, in fact, wind up on the reef as one of the earlier ships to do so. Royal Navy Captain John Lawford was a real person, commanding *Convert,* and was exonerated by his court-marital. In spite of his comment to Edward Ballantyne that a "shipwreck tends to besmirch one's record," his career seemed quite unaffected by it. He went on from this disaster to serve with distinction, commanding other vessels until 1811 when he was promoted to rear admiral, then vice admiral, and finally admiral. He was made a Knight Commander of the Bath in 1838, and died at age 86 four years later. At the time of this story, he was 38.

On the east end of Grand Cayman Island, on the bluff overlooking Gun Bay, there is a monument, put in place on the 200th anniversary of the disaster (1994) to commemorate a visit by Queen Elizabeth to the site. From here one might view the reef, Gun Bay, and the remains of a few other unfortunate souls who misjudged the currents. Of course, nothing remains of the ten ships which died here in 1794. Artifacts, in the form of French twelve-pounder cannon barrels, can be seen on private property just across the road from the bluff. They were likely salvaged soon after the wreck. The water inside the reef is quite shallow, about ten to fifteen feet, while outside the sheer wall of the reef, the depth drops precipitously to nearly two thousand feet!

The local people who inhabit the Cayman Islands are warm, charitable and kind; their very nature would cause them to offer succor to those less fortunate. Their make-up is varied: English and Spanish sailors who jumped ship, pirates who likewise "swallowed the anchor," and Africans, and their descendants, from Jamaica who escaped the sugar cane plantations where they had lived as slaves, made up a large measure of the population. There are to this day families named Bodden, Clarke, and others named in the story, living in Cayman. The Bodden's are probably one of the longest established families and Bodden Town still exists on the eastern end of the island. The people are as varied in skin tone as they are in heritage and the modern folks who live there say they all get along so well because "twenty percent of us are white, twenty percent of us are black, and sixty percent of us don't know what we are!" And it's quite true! Some speak with proper "almost" British accents while others speak in a patois that requires careful attention to understand. And race seems to have little bearing on much of anything. Truly, the Caymanian people are a joy to experience!

There are few "real" beaches on Cayman, save for the beautiful "Seven Mile Beach" on the western side of the island; the beaches that are there are sprinkled about between stretches of the fossilized coral, called "ironshore," and offer a welcome contrast to the often difficult coast line when one is seeking refuge from the sea!

A final note on currents: a current runs *in the direction* of its name. Hence, a northerly current runs *to* the north unlike a northerly breeze which blows *from* the north. It was the northerly current that wreaked the havoc in the Wreck of the Ten Sail.

William H. White
June 2013

ABOUT THE AUTHOR

Photo by William H. White Jr.

Mr. White is a former United States Naval officer with combat service. He is also an avid, life-long sailor. As a maritime historian, he specializes in Age of Sail events in which the United States was a key player and lectures frequently on the impact of these events on our history. White has seven historical novels and one non-fiction history to his credit, each set in the early 19th century with a focus on the young American Navy. He has also written two books based on real events in the Royal Navy in the late 18th century, one dealing with the capture of the *Bounty* mutineers and one focusing on a major shipwreck on Grand Cayman, where he lives when not in New Jersey. Additional information about the author and his books can be found on his website *www.seafiction.net*.

Follow Mr. White on twitter *@1812war*.

The War of 1812 Trilogy
by William H. White

WILLIAM H. WHITE

Volume One in the War of 1812 Trilogy

SECOND EDITION

A Press of Canvas
Volume One

Second Edition released June 2014
© William H. White 2000

William H. White's action-packed tale introduces a new character in American sea fiction: Isaac Biggs of Marblehead, Massachusetts. Sailing from Boston as captain of the fore-top in the bark *Anne*, his ship is outward bound with a cargo for the Swedish colony of St. Barts in the West Indies in the fall of 1810. When the *Anne* is stopped by a British Royal Navy frigate, Isaac and several of his shipmates are forcibly pressed into service in the *Orpheus*, actively engaged in England's long-running war with France. The young Isaac faces the harsh life of a Royal Navy seaman and a harrowing war at sea. His new life is hard, with strange rules, floggings, and new dangers. Then the United States declares war on England and Isaac finds himself in an untenable position, facing the possibility of fighting his own countrymen. A chance meeting with American privateers operating in the West Indies offers him a solution to his dilemma and a reunion with an old friend.

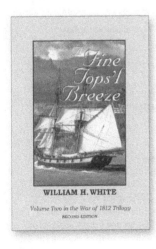

WILLIAM H. WHITE

Volume Two in the War of 1812 Trilogy

SECOND EDITION

A Fine Tops'l Breeze
Volume Two

Second Edition released July 2014
© William H. White 2001

William H. White's action-packed novel continues the adventures of the newest character in American sea fiction: Isaac Biggs of Marblehead, Massachusetts. In the second volume of the trilogy, Isaac ships as Third Mate on the Salem privateer *General Washington* in February 1813. At the same time, his friends from the British frigate *Orpheus* and the Baltimore schooner *Glory* find berths on the American warship USS *Constellation* and, eventually, they wind up on the USS *Chesapeake* in Boston just in time for her disastrous meeting with HMS *Shannon*. Throughout the spring of 1813, Isaac and the *General Washington* roam the waters between Massachusetts and Nova Scotia, taking prizes and harassing the British. When the American survivors of the *Chesapeake/Shannon* battle are confined in Melville Island Prison in Halifax, the *General Washington* and Isaac play an important role in securing their freedom.

The Evening Gun
Volume Three

Second Edition released September 2014
© William H. White 2001

WILLIAM H. WHITE

Volume Three in the War of 1812 Trilogy
SECOND EDITION

The year is 1814, the final year of the War of 1812. With the Atlantic seaboard closed by the British blockade, Isaac Biggs, Jack Clements and Jake Tate, fresh from their harrowing adventures in Canada, find berths with Joshua Barney's Gunboat Flotilla in the Chesapeake Bay. These swift and shallow-draft little vessels have become a thorn in the side of the British fleet and the British command is determined to destroy them. Barney's Flotilla is eventually chased up the Patuxent River to find temporary refuge in Benedict, Maryland, where Isaac falls in love with the daughter of a militia colonel. After several exciting forays against the British fleet, the flotilla must be scuttled and burned. Its men are called ashore to fight at the Battle of Bladensburg in an futile effort to halt the invasion of Washington, then are sent to defend Baltimore against the British siege of the harbor. Isaac, Jack and Jake witness the historic and horrifying bombardment of Fort McHenry from the outer harbor, aboard a British warship in the company of Francis Scott Key.

Written from the aspect of the fo'c'sle rather than an officer's view and through the eyes of an American, *A Press of Canvas, A Fine Tops'l Breeze* and *The Evening Gun* provide new perspectives and an exciting stories of this often neglected period in American history.

"Through Bill White's evocative prose, one smells the salt breeze and feels the pulse of life at sea during the War of 1812."

John B. Hattendorf
Ernest J. King Professor of Maritime History, U.S. Naval War College

"Sailors everywhere will rejoice in the salt spray, slanting decks and high adventure of this lively yarn of the your American republic battling for its rights at sea."

Peter Stanford, President
National Maritime Historical Society

"Read the trials and tribulations of Isaac Biggs and enjoyed them immensely. Haven't read anything like this since Forester. You write better sea stories than I do."

Clive Cussler
Author of the Dirk Pitt Series

"The War of 1812 is a forgotten war. Few Americans recall much except there were some naval engagements and we won the Battle of New Orleans. Many don't realize that Washington was burned, let alone know about the battles on the Patuxent. Bill White has brought this neglected period of our history alive with all the drama, panic, and confusion that gripped Washington, Baltimore and the Chesapeake region as a whole in 1814. The description of the attack on Baltimore and the writing of the "Star Spangled Banner" humanize an event that we don't think about when we sing our national anthem. The War of 1812 and the sacrifices that were made to preserve out liberty will be better understood after reading The Evening Gun. *An enjoyable way to learn history."*

C. Douglass Alves, Jr.
Director, Calvert Marine Museum

Second Edition Kindle and Paperback versions are now available at Amazon.com

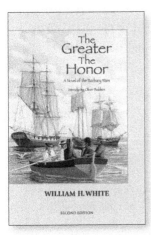

Meet Oliver Baldwin in his
first novel

The Greater The Honor
A Novel of the Barbary Wars

SECOND EDITION

by William H. White
© William H. White 2003

In William H. White's historically accurate, colorful, and carefully crafted tale, fourteen-year-old midshipman Oliver Baldwin tells the story of our fight with the corsairs of the Barbary Coast from the deck of Captain Stephen Decatur's ship as the young man, like the young nation he represents, struggles to find his way on the course to manhood. Gunboat battles, duels, and storms encourage his personal growth and challenge his maturity as he learns his role as an officer-in-training of the United States Navy. More than a "sea story," it is a coming of age story of both a young man and the fledgling navy he serves.

"This is a rollicking sea story of the American naval officers who proudly called themselves "Preble's Boys." They took their ships to a distant station to defend the new Republic. They cowed the Tripolitans and impressed the British. Finally, Stephen Decatur and the rest of Preble's Boys get their due. Their adventures and courageous acts challenge Jack Aubrey and Horatio Hornblower and they are all the more impressive because their story is true. White's skill as a novelist and his passion for historical accuracy put him on a course with Patrick O'Brian."

William Fowler, Ph.D.
Director, Massachusetts Historical Society

Reviews

"White's fourth book is his best effort to date. The novel is a 'coming of age story' about a young sailor named Oliver Baldwin who signs on as a midshipman in the US Navy during the fledgling country, The United States of America, is defending its merchants from Mediterranean pirates."

"Unique to this novel is the way that White introduces young Baldwin to the trials and tribulations of life as a sailor. The various parts and names of 18th century sailing ships can cause the novice to this period shy away from these types of stories. White does an excellent job teaching the reader as Baldwin learns and grows accustomed to life aboard a naval ship."

"I frequently found myself fully engrossed in the story, looking over Baldwin's shoulder as he works aboard the ship, makes friends with his fellow shipmates, and fights the pirates of the Mediterranean. The novel is fast paced, and the descriptions are truly magnificent. From the sea spray in your face, to the boom of the guns, to the heat of the battle, White truly puts you in the front row seat for all the action."

Second Edition Kindle and Paperback versions are now available at Amazon.com

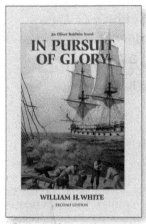

IN PURSUIT OF GLORY
An Oliver Baldwin Novel
SECOND EDITION

by William H. White
© William H. White 2008

"William White's newest seafaring novel deals with the U.S. Navy as it emerged from the Barbary Wars and enters the difficult period leading into the War of 1812. We see the action through the eyes of Midshipman Oliver Baldwin who had entered the Navy in 1803 and was serving on the ill-starred USS Chesapeake *as she put to sea from Norfolk. He is eyewitness to HMS* Leopard's *bombardment of* Chesapeake *and its aftermath in the court martial of Commodore James Barron and others in the immediate chain of command. Through his observations and those of his shipmates, we are privy to the turbulent emotions wrought by that event and the desire for revenge on the British felt generally throughout the Navy. The protagonist gains further seasoning serving with and under a variety of officers over the next few years. Under the command of Captain Stephen Decatur, Jr., in USS* United States, *Baldwin participates in the battle with HMS* Macedonian *and brings her safely back to Newport as a member of the prize crew. White cleverly recreates the language and manners of days long past while sticking closely to the basic historical facts. He weaves his fictional and historic personages seamlessly into the context of the times and vividly brings to life a time when the U.S. Navy was emerging from infancy to adolescence."*

William Dudley, PhD
Chairman Emeritus Navy Historical Center

"If you yearn to smell the salt air, hear the wind sing through the rigging, and feel the roll of the sea beneath your feet, but you don't have a ship of your own, step aboard **In Pursuit of Glory.** *If you want to duck British cannonballs and ride out storms at sea, all from the safety of your favorite armchair, set sail with William White. If you do, he'll take you on a fascinating voyage into American naval history, and you'll make port edified and entertained."*

William Martin
NY Times Best-selling Author

Second Edition Kindle and Paperback versions are now available at Amazon.com

WHEN FORTUNE FROWNS
Introducing Edward Ballantyne
SECOND EDITION

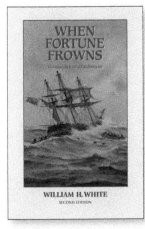

by William H. White
© William H. White 2008

Most people are aware of the story of the Mutiny on the Bounty. Few, however, know what happened to the mutineers. They did not *all* sail to Pitcairn Island; indeed only nine of them did, leaving sixteen in Tahiti by their own choice. The Royal Navy was not about to let them remain at large and sent an armed frigate, HMS *Pandora*, to the Pacific to capture them and return them to England for trial. *When Fortune Frowns* is the story of this voyage, the capture of the remaining mutineers, and the perilous and disastrous return voyage to England. Storms, tropical islands, monotony, and shipwreck all figured into the epic tale, unearthed and carefully researched by noted maritime author William H. White. A well crafted conclusion to one of the most heinous and well known stories of the Age of Sail.

William White brings to life the maritime history of HBM frigate Pandora's *quest for HMAV* Bounty *and her mutinous crew. This riveting novel is a scholarly, well-written tale with wonderful descriptions of the banality of 18th century British naval life, punctuated by brutality and occasional bravado, but always liberally flavored with the salty language of the time.*

Louis Arthur Norton, PhD
Maritime Historian and Author

When Fortune Frowns *is great historical fiction – a fascinating (and true) story, scrupulously researched and fleshed out with characters who have the ring of authenticity. William H. White has done a fine job of bringing the story of the* Pandora, *the often forgotten sequel to the mutiny on the* Bounty, *to life.*

James L. Nelson
Author of *George Washington's Secret Navy*

Second Edition Kindle and Paperback versions are now available at Amazon.com

Printed in the USA
CPSIA information can be obtained
at www.ICGtesting.com
LVHW011256161123
764133LV00010B/337